Something Shady

by
Sarah Dreher

by the same author:
Stoner McTavish - a Lesbian mystery, romance
Gray Magic - third in the Stoner McTavish series, set
    among the Hopi and Navaho in Arizona
Lesbian Stages - a selection of Sarah's plays
Captive in Time - fourth in the Stoner series, taking
    her back in time to the year 1871

Something Shady

A Stoner McTavish Mystery

by Sarah Dreher

Published by New Victoria Publishers Inc. A feminist literary and cultural organizaton, P.O. Box 27 Norwich, Vermont.

Library of Congress Card Number   86-061106
ISBN   0-934678-07-3
Fourth Printing
Printed on recycled paper.

Acknowledgements

"I would like to express my heartfelt appreciation to all the friends who helped and encouraged me along the way in writing this book, and especially to:

Nancy McAvoy and Edwina Trentham for their support, wonderful suggestions, and TACT.

Lis Brook for her constant loving enthusiasm, and for suffering through my emotional ups and downs.

Claudia and Beth of New Victoria, for taking a chance on an unknown writer.

And, last but not least, to Nutmeg and Wellington for not complaining about all the walks we didn't take."

Box 27, Norwich, Vermont 05055

To Nancy -- A loved and loving friend

CHAPTER 1

They were coming for her.

Clawed feet crunched gravel. Stopped.

The sound of sniffing. Whispers. Silence. Sniff, whisper, silence. Sniff.

Silence.

Fog coalesced in amorphous forms, turned back again to fog. Far below, the sea exploded against jagged rocks.

Listen. Listen through the sea.

Something crawled across her bare foot. She looked down. A scorpion, red as fresh blood. It tasted the air.

Don't move.

Don't breathe.

Her skin was clammy with salt and fear.

The insect inched forward, paused. Its tail trembled.

Waves of cold flowed up her spine. Her lips were numb.

I have to scream.

They'll find me if I scream.

She shuddered.

The scorpion froze.

Get it off, get it off, oh God, get it OFF!

If I don't scream, I'll go insane.

If I don't move, I'll die.

I can't move.

She closed her eyes...

... and felt its tiny feet like soft hairs brushing her skin.

Breaking, she grabbed for it. It stuck to her foot, to her fingers. She jerked it away, tearing skin, and flung the body into the fog.

The whispering came again, surrounding her, the infinitessimal hiss of rain on dry leaves. She strained to make out words.

"See, see, see, see."

This is a dream. I can wake myself up.

Wake myself up.

She closed her eyes and willed her mind toward consciousness.

Her bedroom was dark. Rain slid down the window. Beyond the glass, she could make out the flat blue light of sleeping Boston.

I'm awake. Thank God, I'm awake.

Her heartbeat slowed to normal.

Get up. Turn on a light.

She couldn't move.

1

From somewhere over her head came a child's malicious giggle.
The fog closed in tighter, caressed her face with oily tendrils.
Crackle of dried grass.
Footsteps?
Wind?
The air was still as August.
Cold.
Only the fog moved ... and something in the fog.
A wall at her back. A house, rough shingle, chipping paint.
Find the corner. Slip behind the house.
Ancient boards warm from the sun.
But there was no sun. Only the fog, the cold fog.
The wood beneath her hand began to swell.
And fall.
The house was breathing.
She pushed herself away, stared up at it. Monstrous, decaying
relic. A shutter hung by a single hinge. White pillars, cracked and
splintered. Windowpanes etched with spidery lines. The scent of
thyme rose underfoot.
A low, rhythmic thudding shook the ground. She listened for the
source. It came from the house.
Engines. Ship's engines.
Not engines, heartbeats.
The heartbeat of the house.
She backed away and tried to call out. Fog curled against her
tongue, slid toward her throat. Her feet touched gravel. Above her,
the slate shingle roof began to melt.
She took a step...
... and fell.
"Stoner, dear, you're having a nightmare."
What?
"Wake up, Stoner."
She pulled herself up and rubbed her eyes. "Aunt Hermione?"
The older woman perched on the edge of the bed, drinking tea.
Her satin peacock kimono glistened in the gray light. "I have
something important to discuss with you."
"A minute." She glanced around the room, taking inventory. Oak
bureau, desk, bookcase, floor lamp, easy chair, window seat, off-white
walls, burgundy drapes, framed photograph of the Tetons.
Everything in place.
"How would you like to go to Maine?"
"I can't go to Maine. I have to go to work." She reached for her
aunt's teacup, took a sip, and shuddered. "Maté ."
"The South American Indians have been drinking it for centuries."
"I need something stronger."

2

"There's coffee on your little table, dear."

And cold. Oh, well. She gulped it. "How long have you been sitting here?"

"A few minutes."

"Watching me *sleep*."

Her aunt stiffened. "Indeed not. Invasion of privacy is a *karmic* sin, Stoner."

"Thank God for that."

"*He*," Aunt Hermione snorted, "would have us poke and pry to our hearts' content, the old busybody."

"I'm sure you're right," Stoner muttered, and pushed back the covers. The nightmare clung to her like guilt. Cold coffee hadn't helped, maybe cold water... She stumbled toward the bathroom.

"Would you like me to pack for you, dear?"

"Pack what?"

"Whatever you say." Aunt Hermione adjusted a snowy curl. "But if you don't mind a suggestion..."

Stoner sagged against the bureau.

"Dress warmly. Maine is disgusting in March."

"Everything's disgusting in March. I can't go to Maine."

Her aunt sighed heavily. "There's a fine line between tenacity and stubbornness, Stoner. I wish you didn't cross it so often."

"March means Spring Break. Spring Break means cruises and flights to the Caribbean. Cruises and flights to the Caribbean mean work. Cancellations. Foul-ups. Lost luggage. Confusion, Aunt Hermione, massive confusion."

The older woman popped her glasses on and examined Stoner's book case. "Go to the Caribbean if you like, dear, but it won't solve our problem. Have you finished the Agatha Christie?"

She looked up sharply. "What problem? Do we have a problem?"

"I don't know how you can bring yourself to read May Sarton. She's so up-in-the-head."

"It was a gift." She clenched her fists. "Aunt Hermione, what problem?"

"A gift," Aunt Hermione said, inspecting a battered, original-edition, blue-cover Nancy Drew. "Wonderful. I can tell my friends I have a gifted niece."

In about thirty-seven seconds you're going to have a *psychotic* niece. "Aunt Hermione..."

She turned and peered over her glasses. "Claire Rasmussen."

"Who's Claire Rasmussen?"

"Nancy Rasmussen's sister. I didn't know you were planning a Caribbean trip. Is Gwen going with you?"

Stoner raked her hands through her hair wildly. "Gwen has to teach."

"During Spring Break? No wonder the Teacher's Union is up in

3

arms."

Something snapped. "I am not going to the Caribbean!" she shrieked. "Other people are going to the Caribbean. I have to get them
there."

"If those people are meant to get to the Caribbean, Stoner, they
will get to the Caribbean."

"Well, I'd like them to get there through Kesselbaum and
McTavish, not Crimson Travel." She pulled fresh underwear from
a bureau drawer.

"I've told you a thousand times," her aunt persisted, "Kesselbaum
and McTavish is destined to be successful. Not wildly successful, but
successful."

"We still have to work at it."

"I suppose you're right." Aunt Hermione settled herself on the
edge of the tub with Agatha Christie. "One must Manifest, mustn't
one?"

"Yes, and one must Manifest on time, so if you don't mind..." She
indicated the door.

"Have a nice shower, dear," said Aunt Hermione cheerfully. "When
you're in a better mood, we'll have a cozy little chat about Claire
Rasmussen."

"I don't know anybody named..."

She found herself talking to the bathroom door.

***

"Claire Rasmussen?"

Aunt Hermione poured herself another cup of maté. "She's lost.
We'll discuss it after you've eaten. You're always perfectly awful
before breakfast."

"Always?"

"Every morning, for the past sixteen years, you've been awful.
Were you awful before you left home?"

"Probably." She buttered a hunk of coffee cake. "Oh, God, I'm so
boring."

"Are you? I've always found it comforting. Do you really want to
put so much butter on that, Stoner? It's terribly rich."

"I need it to get me through the day."

"You don't eat enough." Aunt Hermione surveyed her own plate,
barely visible under three eggs, scrambled, toast with marmalade,
six slices of bacon, and a small bowl of last night's leftover coleslaw.
"Of course, I eat like a trucker."

"And never gain an ounce. How do you do it?"

"It's the work. Some days the Guides suck up energy like an Elec-
trolux. Perhaps I should go back to using a Familiar, but that seems

4

so impersonal."

"Why bother, as long as you enjoy eating?"

"That's very inspired," her aunt said brightly. "You're always so good with excuses."

"Mother claimed it was what I do best."

"My sister is a silly woman. She was a silly child, even by childhood standards. When I think of what she must have been like as a mother ... well, the mind boggles."

"Yeah," Stoner said. "It does."

Aunt Hermione surveyed the kitchen. "We need more chrome."

"I can pick some up at the drugstore after work, or do you need it right away?"

"I beg your pardon?"

"If they don't have any natural, should I get the fake kind?"

"Stoner, what in the world are you talking about?"

"Chrome, as in vitamins, minerals..."

Her aunt burst into peals of laughter. "Chrome as in napkin holders, sugar bowls. Truck-stop chrome."

"If I were going to Maine," Stoner groused, "I'd see what I could find in a flea market."

Aunt Hermione shrugged. "I wish you well. Maine's an abandoned carnival between seasons." She studied the room. "It might be fun to redo the whole kitchen in Truck Stop. We could replace the brocade love seat with barstools..."

"With torn red plastic seats." She poured another cup of coffee.

"And paint the walls pink. Our stainless steel is a matching set. We'll have to do something about that."

"Fuzzy dice instead of wicker birdcages at the windows," Stoner said, getting into the spirit of the thing.

"We need a back room. Completely dark, except for a red lamp of mysterious purpose. And girlie magazines."

"*Girlie* magazines!" She choked on her coffee. "They call them porn mags now, Aunt Hermione."

The older woman's eyes grew dreamy. "I once ate in the world's largest truck stop. Xenia, Ohio, it was. Nineteen fifty-six. On my way to a psychics' convention at Berea College. Ethel Morrissey was along on that trip. She passed into transition in '63."

"Do you still hear from her?" Stoner asked.

"Not often. She didn't care much for the material plane. Except the Xenia Truck Stop."

"Maybe, when we redecorate the kitchen, she'll drop in once in a while."

"Why, Stoner," Aunt Hermione said, "I thought you didn't believe in spirits."

"I don't, but I'm too sleepy to argue."

"Mark my words, one of these days you'll have such a revelation..."

5

"Not in March."

Aunt Hermione finished off her eggs. "If we go to Truck Stop tacky," she mused, "do you think I'll have to give up my ashtray?"

The ashtray, firmly ensconced in the center of the table like the Hub of the Universe, was old, cracked, chipped, and emblazoned with "Put your damn ashes here" in gold.

"I think," Stoner said, "it's tacky enough for anything."

"I won that ashtray," said Aunt Hermione, "in 1947, in the Penny Arcade at Old Orchard Beach."

Stoner got up and scrounged through the bread box for more coffee cake.

"Marylou will be scandalized," her aunt said. "But her mother will go wild for the place. While you're up, would you get me a little more coleslaw?"

"I really don't know how you can eat that in the morning," Stoner said, spooning it out and trying not to breathe.

"Try some. It's very refreshing."

"No, thanks." She gave up on the coffee cake, found a half-eaten cherry pie in the refrigerator, and cut herself a slice.

"Perhaps you'd rather have breakfast alone?"

"Then I'd never get to see you." She retrieved her coffee and curled up on the love seat.

Aunt Hermione sighed. "I wouldn't work nights if there were any way around it, you know. But some people don't believe psychic readings by daylight are valid. Much as I hate it, I do have to pander to the ambivalent."

"And I wouldn't work days if I could help it."

"If you worked nights, when would you see Gwen?"

Stoner frowned into her coffee. "When do I see her now?"

"Poor dear," Aunt Hermione murmured. "No wonder you're in a foul mood."

"I miss her. I understand, but I miss her."

"Well, that's the worst of it, understanding. It leaves one quite helpless."

They sat for a moment in companionable gloom.

"I do wish I were more adept at the Tarot," Aunt Hermione said at last. "Yesterday's reading was quite positive, but at my level of expertise it's hard to be sure."

"How are your lessons going?" Stoner asked, to change the subject.

"Grace D'Addario is an inspired teacher, but I don't quite have the feel of it yet. And I'm still not sure where I stand on reversals."

"Aren't there rules?"

"Like everything else in life, the occult has its gray areas."

Stoner laughed. "It's all gray areas to me." She settled back into her chair. "Now will you tell me about Claire Rasmussen?"

Aunt Hermione pulled her napkin through its silver ring. "Are

6

you sure you're quite yourself?"

"As close as I can come to it."

"Claire Rasmussen is missing."

"Yes?"

"I told her sister you might try to find her."

"Aunt Hermione," Stoner said evenly, "forgive me for being meticulous..."

"You can't help it. It's a Capricorn trait."

"... but could you begin at the beginning?"

"Claire is Nancy's sister. Nancy is a client of mine, a nurse. Am I going too fast?"

"That's fine."

"Claire, also a nurse, took a position in a private mental hospital somewhere north of Portland. Two weeks ago, Nancy received a brief, rather cryptic phone call from her, and since then there's been nothing. We've been trying to pick up impressions, but all we get is darkness."

"Ominous," Stoner said.

"Quite. To top it off, yesterday was Nancy's birthday. Claire has never missed calling on her birthday, until now."

"I see."

"Nancy's an Aries, and nothing satisfies a worried Aries but great flurries of frantic activity. I told her you might be willing to go to Castleton and have a look around."

Stoner hesitated. "Maine?"

"I know what you're thinking, dear. Those dreadful nightmares. Rocky coasts, old sea captains' houses bursting with ghosts and evil... Still and all, it may be time to confront the horror."

"You want me to confront something bursting with ghosts and evil?"

"That house has something to say to you, Stoner. I really think it won't let up until it's been said."

"I'm not sure I want to hear it."

Her aunt smiled reassuringly. "Poor Stoner. Psychic phenomena give you the willies, don't they?"

"I don't believe in them," Stoner said firmly. "They're fine for you, but not for me."

"I used to feel exactly the same way. My first experience set me to trembling so hard I registered 7.6 on the Richter scale."

Stoner laughed. "Well, that's something to look forward to."

"Now, what should I tell Nancy Rasmussen?"

"I don't know." She studied her hands. "I'd like to help, but ... if only it weren't Maine."

"How about taking someone with you?"

Stoner glanced up hopefully. "You?"

"I'd love to go, but the apprentices are serving at Grace's Esbat.

7

I'm afraid I'll have to spend the weekend cooking and attuning."

"Marylou's out. She doesn't like to travel. Cancer rising, you know."

"Marylou's missed her calling," Aunt Hermione said. "A Scorpio with Cancer rising should be running a bawdy house." She gave Stoner a sly look. "What I had in mind was Gwen."

"Now I get it. This is one of your famous manipulations."

"Manipulation!" exclaimed Aunt Hermione. "My dear, I would never fiddle with your *karma*."

"Why not? Will it make you go blind?"

"Worse than that. I might develop a fatal attraction to Jerry Falwell. The Cosmic has been known to play very nasty tricks." She toyed with her fork and cleared her throat. "Stoner, dear, while you're in Maine ... do you suppose you could ... look for a cat? Just a tiny cat," she went on quickly. "I know you're not fond of cats, but it wouldn't have to be a great hulking beast like Diablo. A cute little fluff-ball of a kitten." She glanced up. "Maybe?"

Stoner grinned. "Now we get to the truth of it."

"A sweet kitten. One with hair the color of yours, if you like, though I don't recall ever seeing a chestnut kitten."

"It's okay, Aunt Hermione. I'll try to find you a kitten." She touched her aunt's hand. "You miss Diablo, don't you?"

"I suppose I do. Animals claim bits of our souls, if we let them. And, while our souls are still connected, of course, I sometimes miss him in the material sense. He had such sensuous fur. Just the other morning, before I was fully awake, I could have sworn he was curled up against my shoulder the way he used to. Perhaps he was, in spirit." She laughed. "Your experience of Diablo was entirely different, wasn't it? You had a contentious relationship."

"That's putting it nicely."

"But a kitten could get used to you while it's still young."

What I had in mind was training. Not to claw my ankles, not to bring dead birds into the house, not to mutilate the McTavish Blue Runner Stringless Hybrid Snap Beans.

"There was sibling rivalry between you and Diablo, I suspect," her aunt said. "Perfectly natural under the circumstances."

"He treated me better than he treated the Blue Runners. "Remember the time he ate the entire season's crop and nearly put you out of business?"

"Not only me. Think of all the beanless roof gardeners in Back Bay. If you hadn't been clever enough to find some in the bottom of my knitting basket, it would have been the end of an era." She looked at Stoner fondly. "Sometimes I don't know how I'd get along without you."

"More would have turned up." In the silverware drawer, among the laundry, in the attic awaiting discovery by archaeologists in the

8

year 3000. "But there's only one of you."

"For which," Aunt Hermione said, "the world offers up hymns of Thanksgiving every Sunday morning."

"And I offer up *daily* hymns of Thanksgiving because, if there can only be one Hermione Moore in the world, she happens to be my aunt."

For the first time in her life, she saw Aunt Hermione blush. "You'd better run along," the older woman said. "If you're late for work, I don't want to be blamed for it."

Stoner pulled her raincoat from its peg by the back door. "Aunt Hermione, was Diablo your Familiar?"

"Dear me, no. He was much too violent. I've never known such a violent cat."

"I have the scars to prove it."

"I'll never forget the day he got in your underwear drawer," Aunt Hermione said happily, "and ate the crotches out of all your panties."

She clutched the doorknob. "If I can't have you, can I have Gracie Allen?"

Her aunt frowned thoughtfully. "I don't think so, dear. She isn't due to reincarnate for at least forty years."

***

Fists stuffed in her coat pockets, Stoner tramped through slush and glared at the scummy street, at the dead, glistening, black trees, at the gutters clogged with ice and sand and mauled beer cans. Overhead, the late-winter sky was the color of mildew.

Boston. The city, they said, was built on garbage. Tons of garbage dumped in a swamp. She didn't doubt it for a minute.

She searched for the light on top of the Hancock Tower, but it had been obliterated by mist. A pigeon huddled beneath a park bench, a sooty lump of misery. The windows of the drugstore on the corner were decorated with plush bunnies, plastic eggs, and unaffordable boxes of Russell Stover chocolates.

Happy Easter, she thought. Anyone who resurrects in this weather is a damn fool.

The door to the travel agency was stuck, as usual. She slammed it open with her hip and half-fell into the warm, muggy room. Marylou glanced up from her paperwork.

"Good morning. May we help you?"

"I need a ticket to hell. Make it one-way."

"You're in luck. We have two last-minute cancellations on a charter. Will you be travelling alone, or bringing the hubby?"

"Alone. " Shuddering with distaste, she draped her scarf and sodden coat over a hook in the coat closet. "Sorry I'm late."

Marylou fluttered a hand to the accompaniment of jangling silver bracelets. "Think nothing of it."

"Has anything happened?" she ran a comb through her hair, not really caring which way it fell.

"Not much. A visit from Boston's Finest warning us to be on the lookout for shoplifters. A couple of cruise reservations — I left them on your desk. And a class outing by Our Lady of Perpetual Guilt Elementary School." Marylou adjusted her skirt. "Have you ever noticed how rain brings out the nuns?"

Stoner steeled herself and glanced up at the shelf. There could be anything up there. Chopped liver, Greek salad, tabbouli. Once she had found a ten-pound wheel of overripe extra sharp Vermont cheddar cheese. Today it was deviled eggs, dozens of deviled eggs, some dotted with green specks, some with red, some she'd better not think about. "Marylou, what's with the eggs?"

"Passover. Want one?"

"It's too early in the morning for eggs." She tugged off a boot, lost her balance, fell against the wall, and stepped in a puddle of water. "I hate my life."

"Another bad night, huh?"

"Worse. Aunt Hermione wants me to go to Maine."

Marylou chose three eggs, placed them neatly on a paper napkin, and carried them to her desk. "To cavort among the moose and blueberries?"

"To look for someone. One of her clients lost a sister."

"That seems inordinately careless." She flicked a bit of egg yolk from her blouse.

"I think I'm afraid of Maine," Stoner said, picking up the egg yolk and depositing it in the wastebasket.

"Say no."

"I can't."

"Why not?"

"After all she's done for me?"

"I really don't think Aunt Hermione keeps score, Pet."

Stoner leafed through her mail. "That's not the point."

"So what are you going to do?"

"Go, I guess."

"Alone?"

"Unless you want to go with me."

Marylou screamed.

"That's what I thought."

"Take the widow."

Stoner shook her head. "Gwen won't go."

"Have you asked her?"

"No."

"Then how do you...?"

10

"I *know*, that's all. She'll be busy. She's always busy."

Marylou shrugged. "Have it your way. The cruise reservations, please?"

She went to her seat and took the first sheet from the pile. Anguilla, for God's sake. She reached for Fodor's and read through the description.

"Thirty-five square miles of arid, eel-shaped, beach-fringed land..." Arid? *Eel*-shaped? Wonderful. "Wiggles along for sixteen miles." Good God. "Whoever is at hand will welcome you and make you feel at home." Robinson Crusoe, no doubt.

Five hotels. Let's push the Cul-de-Sac on Blowing Point. There's a name to warm the soul and delight the senses.

These people, whoever they are, will *hate* Anguilla. Twelve hours after they arrive, welcomed by whoever is at hand, there will be a military coup. They'll be placed under house arrest at the charming Cul-de-Sac on Blowing Point, which will immediately run out of sushi and wine. Three days later, the President will send in the Green Berets and they'll be herded into a military transport. *It* will be high-jacked by Libyan terrorists and flown to Algiers. Algiers will refuse them permission to land. They will proceed to Johannesburg, Athens, Frankfurt, and Havana, finally touching down in the Falkland Islands while the nation is held hostage by Cable News Network. In due time they will be greeted at Andrews AFB by mobs of clean-shaven Reaganites singing "Born in the USA," interviewed (tired, disheveled, and unphotogenic) by a battalion of network reporters, and driven to the White House down streets lined with trees sporting yellow ribbons, while their luggage is sent on to Boise and never heard from again. Kasselbaum and McTavish will be held responsible for everything. We'll have to refund their money, and they'll sue us for trauma.

She tossed the book onto the desk. "Forget Anguilla. We can't afford litigation."

"Beg pardon?"

"Sorry. I didn't know you were on the phone."

Marylou waved away her apology and turned her attention to the receiver. "Gwen Owens, please."

Stoner stood up. "Marylou..."

"I," said Marylou to the phone, "am Marylou Kesselbaum. Who are you?"

"Marylou, what do you think you're doing?"

"Well, Mrs. Bainbridge, this is an emergency. I'm calling from Boston General. We've had an outbreak of hepatitis here, and we think we've traced it back to Ms. Owens."

"For God's sake, Marylou." She snatched the phone.

"Too late, Pet. They've patched you through to the teachers' lounge."

11

"I hate you."

"Me?" Gwen said on the other end of the line. "Who is this?"

"It's nothing," Stoner said. "Just one of Marylou's sick jokes."

"Well, hi, Stoner. It's good to hear your voice. What's up?"

Stoner held out the phone to Marylou. "You started this. You finish it."

"Not me," Marylou said. "I have to go to the bathroom." She scurried out the hall door.

"I'm sorry."

Gwen laughed. Her voice was like touch. "You all must be pretty bored if you're making prank calls. I haven't done that since I was seven."

"Well, actually..." She wiped her hand on her pants leg. "I did want to ask you..."

"Yes?"

"Well... Aunt Hermione ... I mean ..." She took a deep breath. "I have to go to Maine this weekend," she said in a rush. "You don't want to go, do you?"

"To Maine?"

"If you don't want to ... I mean, if you have a date or something, I'll under..."

"A *date*? Why would I have a date?"

"You had a date last weekend."

"That wasn't a date, Stoner. It was a teacher's meeting."

"You went out afterward."

"Nine teachers having beer and grinders at the Watertown Leaning Tower of Pizza may have been a date at sixteen. At thirty-one, it's a meeting."

"Oh."

"I'd love to go to Maine with you. Let's take Friday off and make it a long weekend."

Stoner swallowed hard. "Can you do that?"

"After nine years of teaching in this place, I can do anything I darn well want."

The inside of her mouth felt fuzzy. "Okay," she said shakily. "I'll call you tonight and we can make plans."

"Fine. Any time."

Stoner hesitated.

"Is something wrong?" Gwen asked.

"Uh ... Gwen, what are you wearing?"

"Tan slacks and a navy shirt. Why?"

Stoner sighed.

"Stoner McTavish, is this an obscene call?"

"Yes. No! Talk to you later."

She slammed down the phone and raced for the hall. "Marylou!" She pounded on the restroom door. "Marylou! She's going to do it!"

12

"For God's sake!" Marylou shrieked. "I thought you were a mug-
ger."

CHAPTER 2

"Do you have to read while I'm driving?"

"I'm not reading," Gwen said. "I'm looking at the map."

"It's the same thing. Honest, I'm going to be carsick."

"Okay." She folded the map. "Didn't you take dramamine?"

"If I took dramamine, I'd fall asleep and miss the scenery."

Gwen laughed. "What scenery?"

They were passing one of the score of industrial towns that form a brick necklace from Boston to Gloucester. The factories were busy. Those that weren't busy polluting were busy decaying. A small river oozed sluggishly under the highway, its surface frosted with muddy foam.

"Do you know," Stoner said, "you're part of the one-tenth of one percent of the population that can refold a road map?"

"Maybe they'll give me the Nobel Prize. Where is this Castle Point, anyway?"

"Outside of Castleton."

"Cute."

"About sixty miles from Portland, I think, as the gull flies. Look on the map."

"You just told me *not* to look at the map."

The windshield fogged over. Stoner turned on the defroster, releasing a blast of suffocating heat. She turned it off and cracked her window. The car filled with skin-crawling dampness. She closed the window, and the windshield fogged up. "I hate New England," she muttered.

"Yes, dear," Gwen said. She scrounged an old rag from beneath the seat and wiped the glass. "Better?"

"Thanks."

A Ford Bronco passed them, spraying the car with sooty mist. She flicked on the wipers. Oily streaks reduced visibility to zero. She pushed the washer button. Nothing happened. "I thought you just had this car tuned up."

"I did."

"They didn't fill the washer."

Gwen shrugged. "What do you want for $25 an hour, service?"

"Nobody takes pride in their work anymore."

"You're absolutely right."

"They shouldn't get away with it."

"Absolutely not."

14

She stabbed at the button, with no effect. "I hope you complained about it."

"How could I complain about it?" Gwen asked. "I didn't even *know* about it."

"You mean you just got in your car and drove off without checking to see if they'd filled the windshield washer?"

"That's right."

"You have to keep after people, Gwen. Otherwise, they'll walk all over you."

"I don't doubt it for a minute."

"If everyone complained, something might get done."

"Stoner," Gwen said, "there's a rest area ahead. Pull into it."

She parked the car as far as possible from a smoke-belching diesel truck and two decal-spattered campers. It put them directly in front of an overflowing trash can.

Gwen reached over, turned off the motor, removed the keys, got out, opened the trunk, extracted a bottle of windshield solvent, popped the hood, and filled the washers. "Anything else, lady?" she asked, letting the hood slam.

"I could have done that," Stoner said.

"I'm a liberated woman. Think of it as a political act." She got back in the car. "Aunt Hermione was right," she said, fastening her seat belt. "You're awful in the morning."

Stoner rested her head on the steering wheel. "I'm sorry."

"Want me to drive?"

"I'll throw up."

"Take a good look at this place. Do you think anyone would notice?"

Stoner looked around. "God, it's all so ugly."

"It won't get any better if we just sit here. Any suggestions?"

She stared out at the highway, at the endless stream of gray traffic splashing through gray water on the gray roadbed. To go back into that held all the charm of skinny-dipping in a shallow pond in an automobile junk yard. "Castleton's probably a horrible place," she said. "The restaurants, if there are any, will be closed for the season. We'll have to drive to Augusta to find a motel. The only one open will be a Howard Johnson's that smells like dirty carpets, and we'll get a room with no heat next to a reggae band from Lynn."

"Sounds like fun," Gwen said.

"We'll have to live on half-thawed hamburgers on soggy whole wheat bread and wilted coleslaw and HoJo cola, and catch salmonella."

"You don't catch salmonella, you come down with it. And they don't have HoJo cola any more. Augusta probably has great libraries, I like reggae, and all motels smell like dirty carpets."

"Do you have to be so *cheerful?*"

"What's not to be cheerful? We're on vacation."

15

Stoner shook her head. "I think we're basically incompatible."

"Only in the morning." Gwen touched her arm. "What's wrong, Stoner?"

"I want it to be nice."

"It'll be nice."

"I want it to be perfect."

Gwen reached over and ruffled her hair. "It'll be nice. And if it's perfect, what is there to live for?"

"Reruns."

"You're having nerves. It'll be what it is."

"And you're having philosophy."

"Well," Gwen said, "I'm nervous, too."

"Why?"

"Are you kidding? Our first vacation together? The situation is fraught with peril."

She had to laugh. "I hope we get along."

"We'll get along. This friendship was made in Heaven."

"Actually," Stoner said, "it was made in Wyoming."

"Rising like a phoenix from the ashes of my charred and broken marriage."

"You know, Gwen, I really wish that hadn't turned out so horribly for you."

"It was doomed from the start. I ask you, could *you* spend your life with a man whose idea of a wedding present is a pale green Renault?"

"At least," Stoner said as she started the motor, "it gets great mileage."

She pulled out into the traffic, tail-gated a van for a while, then passed and cut in front of a middle-aged, cigar-smoking successful businessman with a grimy Eldorado. Glancing in the rearview mirror, she saw with satisfaction that *his* windshield washer was empty, too.

Beyond Portland trees began to outnumber houses. The sun broke through the mist, and drops of water glistened at the tips of pine needles. Tinsel streams, swelling with early spring run-off, tossed and danced through meadows of broken weeds. Flocks of dump gulls circled hidden landfills and squawked complaints for no good reason.

Gwen sneaked a peek at the road map. "We take 1A from here."

Stoner eased into the exit ramp, paid the toll, and threaded her way through a maze of overpasses, underpasses, and rotaries designed to create havoc and bring tourists to their knees. She turned onto a road labeled 1A North — which all instinct and reason told her could only be going south.

"I used to have a good sense of direction," she said, "before I discovered Interstates."

"It only goes two ways," Gwen said. "The right way, and the wrong

16

way."

They passed through a shabby little town made up of used car lots, motorcycle dealers, and factory outlets.

"Are you sure this is right?"

"According to the signs."

"If we end up in Kittery, I'll kill myself."

"Trust me," Gwen said. "I've never gotten lost."

"You're due."

"If we end up in Kittery, we'll turn around."

"People have gone to Kittery and never been heard from again."

"I don't care as long as they have restaurants. I'm starving."

"They have restaurants," Stoner said, "but you can't get to them from the road."

A cross-wind out of the east blew up, trailing the sharp, brackish odor of low tide. The town dwindled down to an occasional weatherbeaten cottage. There was no traffic, and no sign of life.

"Do you think something's happened we don't know about?" Stoner asked.

"Like what?"

"A meltdown at Seabrook?"

"They're all having lunch," Gwen said. "Remember lunch?"

There was a tight knot of apprehension deep in her stomach. "Gwen, I'm afraid of Maine."

"Then let's go to New Hampshire. They must have restaurants in New Hampshire."

"We have to make plans."

"Plans?"

"About Shady Acres. We can't just burst in and demand to know the whereabouts of a missing nurse."

"Sounds like a fine idea to me," Gwen said. "Maybe we'll catch them at lunch."

Stoner pushed her hair back from her forehead. "Nancy said her sister mentioned something 'funny' about the place."

"Shady Acres is a mental hospital, Stoner. They're all a little 'funny'."

"We'll call first," Stoner decided. "Say we're passing through Castleton, old friends of Claire Rasmussen. Pretend we don't know anything."

"We don't know much."

"We know Nancy hasn't heard from her in two weeks. Including her birthday. We know Claire never misses Nancy's birthday."

"So maybe she forgot."

"If they say she's not here, we'll go out and look around."

"Well," Gwen said, "that makes sense."

"We have to get a feel for the place."

"Have you ever been inside a mental hospital?"

17

"No, have you?"

"No. How do we get a feel for the place when we don't know what it's supposed to feel like?"

Stoner frowned. "We'll play it by ear."

"Great," Gwen said. "That's a truly inspired, well-thought-out plan. One of the top ten military strategies of all time."

"It's better than the one I had when I went out to Wyoming looking for you."

"I wasn't *missing* from Wyoming. I was in the dining room."

"Shady Acres," Stoner said. "Do you think that has an ominous ring to it?"

"No more than Happy Valley or Sunny Dale."

"If we can't get any information, we'll have to..."

"Stoner," Gwen said sharply, "are we on some kind of religious fast, or can we stop for lunch?"

"What? Sure. There must be a place open around here."

They passed a tourist camp, two rows of identical white cottages facing one another down the length of an open field. The ocean lay flat and blue-gray in the distance. It sparked memories of childhood trips to the shore — the fine layer of sandy grit on brown linoleum, iron beds with white chenille spreads, showers with metal sides and floors of an unrecognizable material that felt a little slimey underfoot, and heavy muslin shower curtains stained along the bottom with something that looked like rust or old blood.

"It's too bad Marylou isn't here," Gwen said.

"Marylou doesn't travel."

"But she *eats*."

"It could all be a misunderstanding," Stoner said. "We could get there and find out she really did go on vacation. Maybe Nancy's only being hysterical. But she didn't strike me **as** the hysterical type, did she you?"

"I didn't meet her," Gwen said.

"Oh, right. She struck me as young but sensible and nurse-like." She thought for a moment. "Gwen, do you think I'm a good judge of character?"

"Better than me."

Stoner glanced at her. "Just because you married a man who only wanted your money, that doesn't make you a bad judge of character. Everyone makes mistakes."

"Not me. I make gigantic errors."

"Well," Stoner said, "maybe you got it out of your system. One gigantic error, and from then on it's smooth sailing."

"There were three restaurants in that town we just went through," Gwen said wistfully.

"I'm sorry. We'll stop at the next one, I promise." She pressed down harder on the accelerator. "The question is, if something *has*

18

happened to Claire, why? If it was an accident — like she fell in the ocean or something — why hush it up? She's only been at Shady Acres for two months. How many enemies can you make in two months?"

"Hundreds," Gwen said, "if you starve them."

"So maybe there's something illegal going on at Shady Acres, and maybe Claire found out about it and they had to shut her up."

Gwen threw herself at Stoner and bit her wrist.

"For God's sake, Gwen. Do you want me to wreck the car?"

"Hunger!" Gwen shouted.

Stoner pulled the car back into her lane. "So when we get to Castleton, we'd better be on the lookout for suspicious goings-on."

"I know what this is," Gwen muttered as something called "The Cockeyed Puffin," complete with booths, tables, and idle waitresses slid by. "A vision quest. We're going to go on driving, without food or sleep, until we hallucinate."

"How can you be hungry?" Stoner asked. "We just ate."

"We ate at 7:46 a.m. digital. It is now 1:30."

"Oh, gosh." She spotted a small concrete building up ahead. A Michelob sign flickered in the window like a dying firefly. Slamming on the brakes, she pulled into the parking lot and looked around. "I don't know, it's kind of grungy."

"I don't care if it's *decadent*," Gwen said. She jumped out of the car. "As long as they serve food."

Stoner watched her trot up the sidewalk and sighed.

I'm in love.

***

"Lost," Gwen said.

Stoner pointed to a dilapidated barn at the side of the road. "I recognize that. We passed it before."

"Uh-huh. We were lost then, too."

Gwen stopped the car at the foot of a rusty pole that marked a fork in the road. A bittersweet vine hid the sign at the top. "Can you make that out?"

Stoner climbed out and squinted up at it. "It says Castleton."

"Which way?"

"To the right."

"Which way did we go last time?"

"Left, I think." She got back in the car. "Want me to drive?"

Gwen gunned the motor. "Stoner, Dearest, it will be a cold day in hell before I let you drive again, especially around mealtime."

Dearest. She called me Dearest.

"I think," Gwen went on, "you must be the last surviving member

19

of the Donner party."

"What's that?"

"A group of early pioneers so obsessed with reaching the gold fields they tried to cross the Sierras in winter. They were caught in a blizzard and ended up eating each other."

"Gee," Stoner said. "You'd think they'd have been too weak for sex."

"Stoner McTavish! That is the tackiest thing I've ever heard you say."

"Stick around," Stoner said. "I can get really gross."

They sped past hibernating fields, tangles of brambles, old farmhouses shedding scales of whitewash. Decaying harrows. Barns with sprung center beams, windows reflecting the sky or turning inward on blackness.

"You'd never see anything like this down South," Gwen said. "It'd be covered with kudzu. I've known people to go away for the weekend and come back to find their houses completely obliterated."

"Not a bad idea." She looked around uneasily. "Do you think all of Castleton's like this?"

"I doubt it. This is a hoax to entrap artists."

"Then where are the artists?" She slouched down in her seat. "Gwen, I think I'm a little nervous."

"Nervous! You've been an absolute wreck all day. When you get to the throwing-up point, let me know."

"It's just... I have a funny feeling about this place."

"The people who *live* here probably have a funny feeling about it. If anybody lives here." She glanced over at Stoner. "Coming up on a nightmare?"

"Maybe."

"Nightmares can't hurt you, Stoner."

"They can if they're precognitive." The car crossed a narrow bridge and crested a hill. "Oh, boy. We've found Castleton."

The sea lay below them, dull as lead. A mackerel sky hovered over the water. The horizon was obscured by mist. To the south, the land was flat, dun-colored fields sloping down to a small, silted river. The village of Castleton huddled by the river's estuary. Four fishing boats, rust-caked derelicts, bobbed among a scattering of buoys.

At the north edge of town the land rose sharply to form a rocky, forested peninsula that confronted the ocean with cocky arrogance. A few large, crumbling houses clung to the cliffs along the road, which deteriorated into a dirt track as it reached the forest fringe. Waves crashed relentlessly at the base of the cliffs. And, out to sea, a fog bank was forming, creeping inland, groping toward the land with silver velvet fingers.

"Good God," Stoner breathed.

"Indeed," Gwen said. She looked at the map. "That must be the

20

Castle River. Castle Bluffs. Castle Point. Now all we need is the castle." She put the car in gear. "I hope you're ready for this. Shirley Jackson would have loved it."

No, I'm not ready for this. There's something wrong, very wrong with this place. And all too familiar. "I know this town," she whispered.

Gwen nodded grimly. "So do I. When I was a very young child, an ancient gypsy passing through the county fair prophesied I'd meet my fate in a setting very much like this."

"Don't joke."

"I think we'd better."

As far as she could tell, the village boasted a ramshackle grocery/liquor store complete with rusty screen and last summer's flypaper and flies, a cafe cleverly called The Clam Shack, a bar, a drugstore from the MGM back lot, a filling station with two pumps *circa* 1947, and a pink stucco four-unit motel that claimed to be the East Wind Inn. The town itself appeared to be deserted. Slowly, they drove up and down the streets looking for signs of human life.

"Do you suppose," Gwen said, "they rise from their coffins at the full moon?"

A pay phone in a plastic bubble stood by the side of the street, receiver dangling uselessly, the pages of the directory turning in the late-afternoon breeze. It was the only visible sign of modern civilization.

"What do you suppose the locals make of that?" Stoner asked.

"Probably thought it was an alien and shot it." Gwen turned the car down yet another gray street. "Know what we should do?"

"What?"

"Run like hell."

The fog began to wrap itself around the car. It poked at the windows and beaded up on the hood.

Stoner cleared her throat. "Want to look for Shady Acres, or check into the motel first?"

"After seeing the motel, I'm not sure I want to find Shady Acres."

"If we wait, the rooms might all be taken."

"By what?"

Gwen turned around and drove back to the center of town. Choosing a street at random, she pressed on for a few blocks of gray-shingled houses and listing porches. She tried another street, and another. Nothing.

"Well," she said. "what do we do now?"

"It has to be around here. We saw it, didn't we?"

"Did we?"

Puzzled, Stoner chewed her lip. We couldn't be lost again, not in a town this size. And we certainly haven't left Castleton. There's The Clam Shack, the drugstore, the village park...

21

A faded, tilted sign stuck in a snowbank caught her eye. "East Wind Inn, one block."

"Stoner," Gwen said in a squeaky voice, "that sign wasn't there ten minutes ago."

"Stop it," Stoner said. "This is creepy enough."

"Creepy doesn't begin to describe it."

The motel was set back from the road only far enough to provide space for a single row of cars, parked diagonally and carefully, a one-lane drive, and a narrow row of shriveled marigolds. A neon sign reading "E ST WI D IN " jutted out from the corner of the building. Behind picture windows, bent and scratched metal Venetian blinds resembled fences woven of gnarled twigs. The storm door to one unit stood open. Another held only a shard of glass.

Stoner hesitated. "This doesn't look very promising. Maybe we should try somewhere else."

"*What* somewhere else? If we leave Castleton, we may never find it again. It probably rises from the sea once every hundred years, like Brigadoon. If it's too awful, we can leave tomorrow."

"Well," Stoner said reluctantly, "I guess we might as well. Do you want to do the honors?"

Gwen looked toward the office door and grimaced. "Just this once, you be butch. For old times' sake."

The office was empty, the door locked. A 3x5 index card stuck in the corner of the glass promised that someone would be "back soon."

"The significant question," Gwen said when she had reported back, "is whether 'soon' is to be interpreted as before dinner, or after May."

Stoner rubbed the back of her neck. "We could kill a little time looking for Shady Acres, I guess. It must be along that road by the ocean."

"I wonder," Gwen said as she started the car, "if anyone has ever gone out that road and returned."

"Don't do this, Gwen, please." There was an odd tingling on the inside of her skin. A chill nestled between her shoulder blades.

"I'm rather enjoying it."

"I'm not."

"What's wrong?"

"I think I know what Shady Acres is going to look like."

Gwen patted her hand reassuringly. "We both know it's a Greek Revival horror. However, *The Hitchhiker's Guide to Terror and the Supernatural* says the best defense is a jocular attitude."

"Jocular," Stoner grumbled. "You're as bad as Marylou."

"And you," said Gwen, "are your usual Capricorn self."

"Okay, okay, let's go face the damn thing."

The first house on the Cliff Road turned out to be a genuine inn. Huge, sprawling, shingled, a rambling, amorphous lump of clay-like lumber, Harbor House squatted at the cliff's edge. A stone wall, whose original purpose seemed to have been to keep strollers from plunging over the precipice, had itself crumbled and fallen into the sea. Through the fog and fading twilight, the windows of the house were blank as dead men's eyes. A few sea gulls drifted over the roof, considered landing, and flew off in search of more hospitable quarters.

"Let's see if they rent rooms," Gwen suggested.

"Here?"

"I love it. Bet you anything it's haunted." She got out. " 'No one lives any nearer than the town'," she quoted ominously. " 'No one else will come any nearer than that. In the night. In the dark'."

Stoner had to laugh. "Where did you get that?"

"Shirley Jackson. *The Haunting of Hill House*." She turned and ran toward the inn.

"Freak!" Stoner called after her.

Minutes dragged by. The sky grew darker, the fog thicker. If anyone lived in Harbor House, they should be turning on the lights about now. An old family retainer, shuffling from room to room on arthritic legs, putting a flame to kerosene wicks with palsied fingers, drawing time-encrusted curtains, making his way to the servants' pantry, his knees cracking and popping with every step.

Damn it, where *is* she?

She pushed open the car door and started to get out as Gwen came around the corner of the porch.

"Nobody home."

"I thought you'd decided to move in."

"It took a while to peer in every window." She started the car.

Cliff Road steepened and narrowed quickly as they drove toward Castle Point. Some of the houses along the road were uninhabited, and uninhabitable. A porch had collapsed here, a section of roof fallen in there. One house had burned. Flame-shaped smudges of black fingered the cracked and rotting shingles. A chimney stood alone in a narrow clearing. Yards were choked with a tangle of raspberry cane and dried goldenrod. The sea bit away at the cliffs.

"Well?" Stoner asked after a while.

"Well what?"

"What about Harbor House?"

"Closed," Gwen said. "Except for a wing they use as a restaurant on weekends. I couldn't see in."

"No ghosts?"

"None visible."

"I hope it didn't spoil your good time."

"Incidentally," Gwen said, "the fleet's in. The bay is full of fishing boats."

"Also uninhabited, I presume," Stoner said, trying to enter into the spirit of the thing.

"Not by life as we know it. Don't you think it's odd we didn't hear them come in? Or see anyone?"

"The only thing that would be odd in this place would be *to* see someone. Or hear something."

At the edge of the woods the blacktop disintegrated, crumbling into a dirt road that combined all the joys of ruts and rocks. Gwen slowed the car to a crawl. The twilight was nearly tangible now. It gathered in the fog and streaked the windshield with liquid night. Dead grasses glowed in the half-light.

A chain-link fence appeared beside the road.

Stoner held herself very still, anxiety rising in her throat, feeling herself carried forward by the car toward something she didn't want to face, something she didn't want to see, something that would frighten her in ways she had never been frightened before. She wanted to tell Gwen to turn around, to go back, to get away from Castle Point and Castleton and Shady Acres and everything that was going to happen here.

The words wouldn't come.

She watched the forest slide past.

It was nearly dark when they reached the entrance. The gate was locked. A sign announced bluntly, "Shady Acres. Private. No Trespassing. Police Take Notice."

"Friendly little place," Gwen muttered. "I always wondered what that meant, 'Police Take Notice.' Are they telling them *to* take notice, or tell us they *do* take notice?" She got out and rattled the padlock on the gate. It didn't yield.

Beyond the fence, the driveway curved away into the woods.

Gwen shrugged and came back to the car. "Dismal. A depository of lost and desperate souls. I need a hot bath and a good, stiff drink."

"Let's get out of here," Stoner managed to say, "before they unleash the Dobermans."

Gwen turned the car around. "Well, what's it to be? The cozy squalor of The Clam Shack, or the fading elegance of Harbor House?"

Stoner slouched in the corner and gazed morosely at the bank of dripping hemlocks that pressed toward the road. "Harbor House."

"Harbor House it is." Gwen's face was soft in the light from the dashboard. Her hands rested lightly on the wheel. Looking at her, Stoner felt her fear begin to fade.

I want her.

Not just for now, not just for this weekend, but for the rest of my life.

***

"At least they're consistent," Gwen said as she looked around the motel room. "Est Wid In's as bad on the inside as it is on the outside."

Stoner let the dented aluminum storm door bang behind her. "I remember this place from an old movie. I think it was 'Grapes of Wrath'."

"Depression prices, too. At least they have a sense of their true worth."

The walls were a grimy, off-chewing-gum-gray-pink. Stained and faded patched green bedspreads covered the two single beds, and a throw-rug floated in solitary misery on a sea of speckled linoleum. A dingy window between the beds looked out into a wall of blackness. There was a telephone, and a cracked, yellowed plastic radio suitable for the recycling center. The sign in the office had promised "air-cooled," and it was, by a biting draft that came from nowhere in particular and everywhere in general.

Gwen tossed her suitcase onto a bed.

"We could drive to Augusta," Stoner suggested.

"Don't be silly. I've been in worse places than this." Gwen tilted her head to one side thoughtfully. "I've repressed the circumstances."

"It's clean," Stoner said hopefully.

"Not quite," Gwen called from the bathroom. "There's something growing in the tub."

She shivered in the sharp chill, and looked around for a thermostat. Over in one corner stood an ancient, blackened gas heater. Stoner knelt and glared at it.

"What are you doing?" Gwen asked.

"Trying to figure out how to light this thing without blowing us up."

There were instructions on a slip of paper glued to the base of the access door. Unfortunately, they were singed beyond recognition, and had probably been written in Japanese. She sat back on her heels.

"Waiting for inspiration?"

"Take your bath," Stoner said.

Gwen shuddered. "Not in *that* tub. I prefer to bathe alone."

"And I prefer to make a fool of myself alone, so will you do something useful?"

"Such as?"

"Make us a drink."

"With what?"

"Huh?"

"With what make us a drink?"

"In my suitcase."

She found a knob, the numbers worn off. A button, red. A small pipe with a hole. Obviously, you turn one, push the other, and hold a match to the third. But in what order, and what happens if you get it wrong?

"Premixed Manhattans?" Gwen said, holding up the bottle. "Stoner, that's disgusting."

"There's bourbon, too, for you. I figured we'd be able to find ginger ale, but I could be jumping to conclusions."

"That was very sweet of you."

"It's the least I can do. I can't believe I brought you to a place like this."

"In the first place," Gwen said, "you packed the bourbon before you saw the motel. In the second place, you'd leave right now if I asked. And last but not least, your *guilt* is driving me to drink."

Stoner grinned up at her. "Yeah, it has that effect on me, too. I think I saw an ice machine by the office door. So, scamper along. But be careful. It might be dangerous out there."

She struck a match and pushed the button. Nothing happened. All right, turn knob and try again. There was a faint hissing sound, and the match blew out.

She was muttering to herself when Gwen came back and handed her a drink. Stoner looked at the glass and frowned. "Kind of scuzzy."

"You ain't seen nothin' yet. Wait until you meet the bathtub."

She lit her last match and held her breath. After a brief sonata of bangs, rattles, hisses, and a terrifying "pop," the flame caught. "Hah," she said, and took a drink.

"How did you do it?"

"Zen." She sipped her drink, looked up at Gwen, and wanted her. "I better take a shower."

"Don't say I didn't warn you," Gwen said.

***

Whoever started the rumor about cold showers as a cure for lust, she thought as she chased the doll house sized sliver of soap around the bottom of the tub, was either a fool or a liar.

You'd better find a way to get a grip on yourself.

I could close the damper, cut off the oxygen, and watch the embers die.

Could you, now?

Any time.

So why don't you?

Because I like it. I like that little shiver in the pit of my stomach every time I look at her.

You like frustration?

"Where is it written," she asked aloud, "that every tingle of excitement must be consummated?"

"Stoner," Gwen called through the door, "is someone in there with

26

you?"

"No."

"Who are you talking to?"

"Myself."

"Want me to wash your back?"

"I do not!"

"Why not?"

"I don't have anything on!"

She heard Gwen laugh. "Honest to God, Stoner, sometimes I wonder if you're playing with a full deck."

All I need is one touch of those hands on my bare skin, and ... She finished her shower in a hurry.

Gwen lounged on the bed, an open phone book in front of her. She had changed into a pale blue shirt and charcoal sweater.

"Every time you change your clothes," Stoner said, "you look more spectacular."

"Well, you don't. You're buttoned up wrong."

Stoner glanced down.

"Come here." She held out her hand.

Stoner shuffled to the bed and sat down.

"You have to stop saying things like that to me," Gwen said as she sorted the buttons into their proper places. "You'll turn my head."

"But it's true."

"Have you taken a good look at yourself lately?"

Stoner shrugged, and felt a thrill of electricity as Gwen's hand brushed her chest.

"There," Gwen said. "You're respectable. Let's eat."

"We have to call Shady Acres first."

"I already called."

"What did they say?"

"Claire is out."

"On vacation?"

"Just out."

"Strange," Stoner said. "They told Nancy she was on vacation. Who did you talk to?"

"Some male, not very articulate. And not inclined to make small talk. Has it by any chance occurred to you," she said as she reached for her raincoat, "that Claire might be trying to avoid her sister?"

"That wasn't the impression I got from Nancy. She said the last time Claire called her, she said she was 'onto something,' and hung up fast."

"She was onto something before, wasn't she? Drugs?"

"Nancy says Claire wasn't a user."

"If I were on drugs," Gwen said, "I wouldn't tell my sister."

"You don't have a sister."

Gwen tossed her her parka. "Well, I left a message for her to call

27

me here when she got in."

"What name did you leave?"

"The only name I have, mine."

"Do you think that was wise?"

"Why not?"

"If there really *is* something funny going on, I'd rather no one knew who you are."

"That's cloak and dagger stuff, Stoner. This place is getting to you."

"I suppose." She slipped into her coat and started for the door. "Got the room key?"

"Dearest," Gwen said, "are you going out in your bare feet?"

Fog had settled in like a viscous cloud. Gwen pulled her coat tighter and shuddered. "This place gets worse by the minute. No wonder they never leave the house."

"It's probably just your average depressed late-winter fishing village," Stoner said with an attempt at bravery. "Come spring they have gigantic community house-painting parties and boogie until November."

"Right."

Street lights formed thumbprints of yellow against the darkness. The center of the town was silent. Only the drugstore was still open, spilling its light onto the glistening sidewalk. A faint blueish glow seeped from the interior of the Clam Shack. Shreds of mist caught in the branches of the trees. Somewhere out at sea, a fog horn ground out a warning.

Gwen jumped. "Just what we needed," she said, moving closer to Stoner. "We're going to wander in this fog forever like the Flying Dutchman, searching for the Harbor House."

"It's on the other side of the common, at the end of that street." The air smelled of rotting mollusks. "Follow your nose."

Naked elms rose like cracked pilsner glasses against the sky. Wooden benches gleamed wetly.

"Cut across?" Gwen asked.

Stoner tried to shake off a feeling of apprehension. "I don't know."

"What do you think? Werewolves?"

"Not enough shrubbery. Werewolves always hide in shrubbery. They stalk behind it."

"And where," Gwen asked, "did you pick up that bit of useful information?"

"Late night TV movies."

"I was afraid Aunt Hermione had begun dabbling in the Black Arts."

"She wants to keep her *karma* clean."

"Stoner, have you ever been tempted to take up witchcraft?"

"Never. Anyway, I don't have the innate talent."

28

"I think about it sometimes," Gwen said. "When everything seems hopeless." She broke away and plunged ahead across the street. "Come on. I'll bet they have a Women's Christian Temperance Union fountain."

They had a fountain, all right. Huge, ornate, and hideous. Carved waves curled about its base and met in a pillar of surf from which dolphins hung eternally in a final suicidal dive. At the top, the statue of an old woman glared out to sea.

Stoner looked up into the statue's cruel and eyeless face. "No wonder her husband never came back."

" 'Down to the sea in ships'." Gwen traced the inscription with her fingertips. " 'Donated by the heirs of Elijah Winthrop'."

"They must have had mixed feelings about him."

"This part of the country used to be crawling with Winthrops."

"How do you know?" Stoner asked, still staring at the unrelenting face.

"I teach history, as you might have heard. Castleton was the home port of wealthy ship-building families in the 1800's. Most of them were Winthrops. Their servants were probably Owenses and McTavishes."

"Let's blow up this thing and avenge their wrongs."

"Shady Acres, as we know and love it, was the home of the wealthiest Winthrops. They called it Journey's End."

"I can see why."

"The old houses along the cliff belonged to lesser cousins and in-laws. As the story goes, the Winthrops fell on hard times when their only son was killed in a gambling fight, one daughter was suspected of casting spells — which was out of style by then — and the other ran away to California with a French dancing teacher and became the 19th century version of a flower child."

"Male or female dancing teacher?"

"The books don't say. Discretion forbids. Old Elijah shut himself up in his study and pined away, reading Cicero in the original Greek."

"Latin," Stoner corrected. "Are you making this up?"

"Elijah's wife, who was rumored to be a bit fey, walked off the edge of the cliff on a foggy night much like this one. Her remains," she whispered ominously, "were never found. Meanwhile the cousins and in-laws made merry with the family fortune, and the shipyard was taken over by creditors from Boston and London, and moved down to Bath. At last report, old Elijah was still holed up in his study, hoarding his dwindling supply of whale oil and reading Cicero in the original Greek." She paused for dramatic effect. "The rest is silence."

"You're certifiable."

"Help awaits," Gwen said, "at Shady Acres."

"Or Journey's End."

" 'Journeys End in lovers meeting.' Or eating. Onward."

They could see the watery lights of Harbor House through swirling mist. A foghorn rasped a warning. A figure formed out of the darkness and lurched drunkenly past.

Stoner sidled up to the edge of the cliff and peered over. The tide was turning. Black waves exploded in phosphorescent foam against the rocks. Pebbles rattled between massive boulders as the water sucked backward into the sea.

Beneath the ocean's pounding, subtler noises emerged. Churning water in the troughs between the waves. The slap of ripples against the shore. The hiss of foam running along the tops of the breakers. The gliding whisper of water slipping across flat rocks. See, see, see.

She shivered.

"Cold?" Gwen asked.

"I need lights. The whole town's so dark."

"They probably go to bed at dusk to save on electricity. If Castleton's like every other small town, Harbor House will turn out to be the local teen-age hangout, complete with pizza, video games, and rampant pubescent sex. Want to risk it?"

"Right now I'd welcome video games and pubescent sex."

"But not pizza."

"As long as we have to be in Maine, the least we can do is get lobster."

The dining room was long, narrow, and dim. Along one wall, tables overlooked the ocean. Along the other were booths of fake-wood plastic with plastic cushions. Hurricane lamps with cork bases stood on red-and-white checked plastic tablecloths. A plastic fishnet drooped from the ceiling. Plastic buoys, plastic floats, and plastic lobsters decorated the walls.

"I think," Stoner said as she opened her plastic menu, "this place is run by unsuccessful Norwegian corn farmers from Minnesota who discovered New England Quaint on the Mass. Pike."

"Honestly, Stoner, sometimes you can be such a snob."

The waiter approached, a sandy-haired youth of unremarkable build wearing a bow tie, starched white shirt, and skin-tight black pants. He introduced himself as "Steve-your-waiter-for-the-evening."

"You girls want a drink?"

"Women," Stoner said. "I'll have a Manhattan."

He turned to Gwen. "Same for you?"

"Bourbon and ginger ale."

"Never heard of that." His nose wrinkled.

"Well, you see," Gwen said, "I'm not from around here."

"Yeah? Where you from?"

"Georgia."

"They drink that stuff down there, huh?"

"Yes. That's why they lost the war."

Leading with his pelvis, Steve-for-the-evening sauntered to the

30

bar.

Stoner looked down at her menu, expecting to be greeted by an array of cutely named hamburgers, choice of chips or coleslaw, and dieters' delites. For the first time since arriving in Castleton, she was pleasantly surprised.

"They have lobster!"

"Not quite," Gwen said, and pointed to the menu. "Lob*stah*."

"I don't care. Things are looking up."

A middle-aged man with pale skin and gun-metal hair, dressed in a baggy achromatic suit, seated himself at a window table across from them.

"Look," Stoner said. "Even the people in this town are gray."

"If you see me start to fade, get me out of here fast."

Steve-your-waiter returned with their drinks and pulled a slip of paper from his hip pocket. It looked like an old laundry list. "You girls ready to order?"

"Women," Stoner said. "I'll have the lobster, boiled."

"Baked or fried?"

"Boiled."

"Potatoes," the boy said. "It comes with potatoes, baked or fried."

"Baked."

"Sour cream, or house dressing?"

"What's the house dressing?"

He shrugged.

"Is it gray?"

"Sorta."

"Just butter, thanks. And a salad."

"No salad. Slaw."

"Is *it* gray?"

"Sorta."

"I think I'll skip the slaw."

"Comes with the meal."

Stoner sighed. "All right, I'll have the slaw. If I agree to take it, can I have coffee? Black?"

"Yeah." He engraved the order on his laundry list and turned to Gwen.

"I'll have the same."

The boy chuckled. "Girls never make up their own minds."

Stoner made a move to rise. Gwen warned her back with a glance.

"You on vacation?" Steve asked.

"Yes," Gwen said pleasantly.

"Funny time of year."

"We wanted to hit the off-season rates at the East Wind Inn," Stoner said.

Gwen kicked her. "Castleton seems like a nice town."

The boy grimaced. "I think it sucks."

31

"It does," Gwen agreed. "A little." She gave him a charming smile. "Where are all the people?"

"Screwing around."

"I see. Are there any local industries?"

"Fishing. Screwing around." He turned to go.

"We noticed what looked like a large estate," Gwen said, calling him back. "Out on the Cliff Road. Do you know who lives there?"

Steve's eyes narrowed. "What do you want to know for?"

"Just curious."

"Nobody lives there. It's a nut house."

"Exclusive?"

"Yeah," he said. "Real exclusive. You oughta see the cars some of those weirdos drive. Guess rich people have a lot of problems, huh?"

"Like anyone else, I guess," Gwen said.

"I'll tell you," he went on, "if I had the bucks some of those characters got, I wouldn't check into a joint like that. I'd split for L.A. and catch the big ones."

"You like to fish?" Stoner asked politely.

He stared at her dumbfounded.

"I think," Gwen explained, "the gentleman's talking about surfing."

"Shag me a board and a box and a 4x4 and a six-pack, and just lay on the sand soakin' up the bennies and checkin' out the chicks."

"Translation?" Stoner asked.

"He wants ," Gwen said, "to get a surfboard, radio, a 4-wheel drive vehicle, and beer. And pass his days sun-bathing and girl-watching."

"That's what I said," Steve complained.

"My friend just moved to this country," Gwen said. "Her parents were missionaries in China."

"That's cool," Steve said. He moved half a step closer to Gwen. "Whata *you* do?"

"She's a teacher," Stoner said.

Steve backed up. "Shit."

"Substitute," Gwen said quickly. "I'm trying to get out of it. As a job, it ..."

"Sucks?" Steve offered helpfully.

"Sucks. Maybe I could find work out at ... what did you say the name of that place was?"

"Shady Acres."

Gwen nodded. "Shady Acres. What do you know about the staff?"

"Nothing," Steve said abruptly, his face closing over.

"That's strange, isn't it? An isolated town like Castleton, you'd think they'd mingle with the townspeople..."

"Not as strange as coming here on vacation." He turned on his heel and crossed to take the Gray Man's order.

Stoner watched him go. "Do you think you wounded his civic

32

pride?"

"Nope," Gwen said. "I think I struck a nerve." She leaned across the table. "For future reference, when we want to get information from an adolescent, *don't* tell them I'm a teacher. Adolescents and teachers are natural enemies."

"He certainly clammed up when you asked about Shady Acres. What do you think that means?"

"Maybe something, maybe nothing. I'd have to consider on it." Stoner grinned. "Southerners talk funny."

"Yankees got no couth. Having a nice time?"

"Great." She looked down at her drink. "Gwen, do you mind terribly spending your vacation like this?"

"Like what?"

"Looking for lost nurses."

"If we weren't doing that, I'd be looking for local history. I've always wondered, what do most people do on vacations?"

"I don't know," Stoner said, "but I'm sure they don't do it in Castleton, Maine."

"Why not? It has scenery, atmosphere, and lobstah."

"Probably gray lobstah."

Gwen leaned back and sipped her drink. "Tell me, how do you know if you're a lesbian?"

"Good grief, Gwen! Not here!"

"There's nobody around, except for our little gray friend over there, and I hardly think he's interested in..."

"Everybody's interested in."

"So what are the signs, other than paranoia?"

"I really think we should talk about something else."

"Okay," Gwen said. "Let's talk about you."

Her deflector shield snapped into place. "Why?"

"Because there are a thousand things you haven't told me about yourself."

"Such as?"

"What was your dog's name?"

"Scruffy."

"What are your parents' names?"

"Walter and Dotty."

Gwen choked on her drink. "*Walter* and *Dotty*?"

"Walter and Dotty."

"Nobody's named Walter and Dotty."

"Your mother's name was Daphne. Think about *that*."

"I try not to. Walter and Dotty. Jesus." She leaned back. "When did you stop believing in Santa Claus?"

"I never believed in Santa Claus. My parents are realists."

"And you're a romantic. How did that happen?"

"I'm not a romantic."

33

Gwen smirked.

"I am *not*."

"Okay, you're not." She toyed with her silverware. "I'll bet you made good grades in school."

"Sure, it was easy. I didn't spend all my time thinking about boys." She laughed. "I spent all my time thinking about *why* I wasn't thinking about boys."

"Did that frighten you?"

"It terrified me."

"Does it still?"

"No. Gwen, are you driving at something?"

"Not me. You brought it up."

"It's awkward at times," Stoner said. "When I meet new people, mostly. I never know how they're going to react." She took a drink. "And there's the problem of when to tell them. Do you say, 'How do you do? I'm Stoner McTavish, lesbian?' Do you kind of slip it into the conversation? Or do you wait until someone makes a nasty remark about queers, and storm off in a huff?"

"As I recall, when you told me, you kind of slipped it into the conversation. Have you ever stormed off in a huff?"

"No."

"Why not?"

"It wouldn't be polite." She glanced across the room. The Gray Man was reading a newspaper.

"What was your first lover like?"

"We were in the same journalism class at B.U. Well, we weren't lovers, really. It was more like a romantic friendship. You know, long intimate talks, moonlit strolls along the Charles. After we graduated, Laurie went to Texas to law school, dropped out during the first year, and got married. Probably has six kids and low back pain by now. Texas can do terrible things to you."

"Romantic friends," Gwen said, swirling her drink around in her glass. "I like that." She looked up. "Is that what we are? Romantic friends?"

Stoner tightened her grip on her glass. "I guess so."

"Allowing, of course, for the fact that you're not a romantic."

"All right, Gwen."

Gwen reached across the table and took her hand. "I hope we'll always be friends, Stoner."

Always? I doubt it. One of these days you'll meet one of those "nice young men" your grandmother's so fond of. Six months after you marry him, he'll decide to move to Oklahoma City and you'll go along, no questions asked. I'll visit you once a year in *his* house, eating *his* food, cooked by *him* on *his* brick barbecue grill on *his* patio. After dinner we'll sit around, the three of us, making small talk in *his* living room until it's time to go to bed — you with him, and me in the

34

guest room. With luck, we'll get a couple of hours alone together in the laundromat playing with the baby. After a while, we won't know what to say to each other anymore.

She smiled tightly and stared at Gwen's hand.

"What's wrong?" Gwen asked.

"I just hope you're right."

Gwen played with her fingers. "Tell me, what's absolutely the worst thing I could do to you? The one thing that would make you hate me forever?"

"I would hate you forever," Stoner said with great seriousness, "if you asked me to wear a dress."

Gwen laughed.

"What about you?"

"I would hate you," Gwen said, "if you took me to a Marx Brothers Festival."

"Shucks, that's what I had planned for this evening."

Two plates bearing steaming lobsters floated in front of their faces. Stoner jerked her hand away from Gwen's. "Fast service."

They waited in silence as Steve-your-waiter spent half a lifetime filling the table with dishes. He surveyed his creation with a satisfied look. "Want anything else?" he asked Gwen.

"No. Thank you, Steve."

He faded into the shadows.

"Really," Gwen said, "you're so jumpy."

"Sorry. It's a reflex I picked up in King's Grant."

Gwen tore a claw from her lobster. "Where's King's Grant?"

"Rhode Island. My home town."

"Oh," Gwen said. "Sounded like a shopping mall." She moved her coleslaw downwind. "What was it like growing up there?"

Stoner shrugged and vandalized her dinner. "Not very nice."

"Have you been back?"

She shook her head. "The only person I'd want to see is Scruffy, and they had him put to sleep."

"Was he sick?"

"They did it because I wouldn't move back home."

Gwen put her fork down. "Stoner, that's the meanest thing I ever heard."

"It created some tension between us."

"I hope you never, ever give them a thing they want."

Stoner shrugged. "I'm trying." She stabbed her baked potato.

Gwen split her lobster tail, slipped the meat out, and began cutting it into tiny pieces. "When did you first suspect you were..." she dropped her voice to a stage whisper, "...a lesbian?"

"In sixth grade, when Ernie Jones kissed me on the playground and I didn't swoon with delight."

"Seriously."

35

"Seriously. You see, I was already madly in love with his mother, who drove the school bus."

"There was a woman back home in Jefferson," Gwen said. "The kids used to whisper about her being queer. For the longest time I thought they meant strange. She didn't seem strange to me, just tall. Queer doesn't mean tall, does it?"

"Not in Massachusetts."

"Back in Georgia, nice people didn't talk about things like that."

"Back in Rhode Island," Stoner said, "things like that were a constant topic of conversation."

Gwen poked at her lobster. "Living with Grandmother's a little like living in Georgia. Gracious on the outside, but..."

"She's really getting to you, isn't she?"

"You know, I honestly believe she'd rather see me married to Charles Manson than happy with a woman."

"Did she object to you coming up here with me?"

Gwen shook her head. "That would have been direct."

"Feels weird, doesn't it?" Stoner said.

"It isn't particularly fun." She strangled a lemon wedge. "I'm tempted to have it out with her, but..."

Stoner smiled. "You're too polite."

"Too scared." Gwen traced the pattern on the placemat with her fork. "She's the only family I've had since I was fourteen. When my parents were killed, she just came along and brought me to live with her. No questions asked, no hesitation."

"I know."

"She's been good to me, kinder, more loving than my parents ever were. But the past year..."

"She forgave you for marrying Bryan. Maybe she'll forgive you for being friends with me."

Gwen shook her head. "That isn't good enough. I want her to change. I've never wanted her to change before, and I don't know what to do about it."

"If I know Aunt Hermione," Stoner said, "she's taking a crack at it right now." She glared at her coleslaw. "They're probably burning incense and chanting together."

"I wouldn't care if they paint their faces with menstrual blood and dance naked in a clearing. It'd be an improvement."

"You've had a rough winter, haven't you?"

"I've seen better." She scanned the dining room and leaned forward. "Stoner, I think that man's watching us."

"I told you. Everybody's interested." She glanced over. The Gray Man's back was partly turned to her, but he seemed to be staring at Gwen.

Gwen shuddered. "He reminds me of Betty Jean's uncle Ed John that ran the O.K. Used Car lot back in Jefferson."

"Betty Jean?" Stoner said, suppressing a giggle. "Ed John? I didn't know you were the Waltons."

"Betty Jean was my friend in junior high. We used to dress up in bouffant hairdos and circle skirts and ankle bracelets, and hang around the A&W Root Beer stand in her Chevy convertible."

"At fourteen?"

"Betty Jean was sixteen. Anyway, in Jefferson you drove a car as soon as you could reach the accelerator. Betty Jean was big for her age. Or young for her size."

"What do you do with a bouffant hairdo in a Chevy convertible?"

"You spend a lot of time fixing your hair. I was the quickest back comber in the ninth grade."

"I wouldn't mind seeing that," Stoner grinned.

"Well, you never will. I put all that behind me when I became a galvanized Yankee."

"What did they call you? Or were you the only Gwen among all those Sally Jo's and Billy Bob's?"

"Eat your dinner," Gwen said, her earlobes flaming.

"Come on, tell me. I told you about Ernie Jones."

"Well... no."

"Come on."

"Gwyneth Ann," Gwen said, "and I never want you to mention it again."

Stoner hooted.

Gwen threw a lobster claw at her. "I mean it, Stoner. If you ever call me that, our friendship is over."

"Well, shucks, Gwyneth Ann, I think that's the sweetest name I ever did hear."

"Listen, Lucy B..."

Stoner froze. "Who told you that?" She realized. "Oh, shit."

Gwen smiled smugly. "Well, well. Lucy B. McTavish."

"Lucy B. *Stoner* McTavish. And you'd better forget it."

"It's a deal," Gwen said. "Aren't you going to eat your dinner?"

"I've finished." Her plate looked as if it had been attacked by terrorists. "Pick through the rubble if you want. You can have the Deadman. I don't eat it."

"The *what?*"

"Deadman. Liver."

"My mother was right. Yankees are disgusting."

The Gray Man was still watching Gwen.

"I wish he'd stop that," Stoner said.

"Probably wants your Deadman."

"He hasn't taken his eyes off of you in ten minutes."

"Maybe he's meditating and I'm in the way." She looked at him and smiled. He looked back at his newspaper. "He's watching us, all right."

37

"I don't like it."

"Neither do I."

Steve-for-the-evening materialized again, balancing a large plastic dishpan on one hip. He tossed their plates in and left.

"Well," Gwen said, "that was revolting. How about dessert?"

"Lemon meringue pie."

"It'll give you nightmares."

"I already have nightmares. Lemon meringue pie is what you eat after lobster."

"Maybe *you* do."

The boy was back. Gwen ordered coffee and pie for Stoner, and coffee for herself.

"Gwen," Stoner said, "do you think you'll get married again?"

Gwen rolled her eyes. "Has my grandmother been talking to you?"

"Your grandmother never says much to me but 'three no trump' or 'two diamonds'."

"I'm sorry," Gwen said. "Sometimes I think it's not fair of me to ask you to play bridge with her."

"I don't take her too seriously. She's probably having a mid-life crisis or something."

"At 70?"

"Maybe she's a little slow to develop. Do you?"

"Do I what?"

"Think you'll get married again?"

"The last thing I want," Gwen said firmly, "is some Lochinvar to come riding out of the West and sweep me away to his shining castle."

"I can understand you feeling like that now, but someday..."

"Someday, someday. If this world doesn't get itself together, there won't *be* a Someday."

"But if there is..."

Gwen laughed. "When I was a kid, we had a mongrel dog named Bessie. Old Bessie spent most of her time between meals lying in the sun waiting for something to happen. And, since nothing much ever happened in Jefferson, her brain got a considerable amount of exposure to ultraviolet rays. Anyway, one day she saw a chipmunk run down a hole. You could see her mind turn over and start to work in a leisurely fashion. 'Thing. Moves. Hole. Gone.' She decided to dig it out. She dug, and dug, and dug. Five years later, every time she passed that hole, she'd start right in digging again."

"Is there a point to this?"

"You," Gwen said, "sometimes bear a startling resemblance to that mongrel dog."

"And you bear a startling resemblance to the chipmunk. I'm not trying to *push* you, Gwen. I guess I just want to know how much damage Bryan did."

Steve brought dessert. Stoner tasted her coffee and made a face.

"This is terrible. Maybe I don't like coffee."

Gwen toyed with her cup. "Bryan hurt me. I'm over that. He made me doubt my own judgement. I may get over that, but so far..."

"What about love?"

"What about it?"

"Did he make you afraid to love?"

"Of course I'm afraid to love," Gwen said. "Aren't you?"

"A little."

"You'd have to be out of your mind not to be a little afraid. That doesn't mean I'm going to pack it in, are you?"

"No," Stoner said, and took a dedicated interest in the lemon meringue pie.

"You once lectured me on not letting the Bryans of this world win. Well, I took it to heart."

Let me tell you about heart, Gwen. Let me tell you about loving someone and wanting them to be happy, and knowing that what will make them happy will make *you* want to die. Let me tell you about being a lesbian in love with a straight woman. Let me tell you about *torture*.

"Stoner?"

She looked up.

"How about you?"

"Me?"

"Do you think you'll fall in love again?"

"Sure," she said brightly, feeling like a chicken surrounded by foxes. "It can happen at any minute." She scanned the room for a diversion.

Steve provided it.

"Here he comes again," she muttered.

"My," Gwen said loudly, "this is certainly an attentive restaurant."

He gestured toward the Gray Man. "Mr. Lennox wants to buy you a drink."

"Please tell the gentleman," Gwen said, "we appreciate his offer but we have to refuse."

"He *owns* this place," Steve said.

"Nevertheless."

The boy shrugged. "Suit yourself. Don't know why you'd turn down free booze."

"You would if you were a woman. Could you bring our check, please?"

Stoner watched the boy walk away. There was something peculiar about this.

"Backwoods chivalry?" Gwen speculated. "Or is business bad?"

"I have the feeling he's spying on us. The way he's been watching you..."

"Maybe he's a down-east masher."

39

"I don't think so."

"If he's spying on us, it's probably because it's the only thing to do in Castleton on Friday night."

"I'm serious. If he's connected with Shady Acres, and if there's something going on out there..."

"You think the whole town's in on the conspiracy?" Gwen asked in disbelief. "We don't even know there's a single thing wrong with Shady Acres."

"But there might be. And they know your name."

Gwen sighed. "I'm never going to live that down, am I? It'll follow me to my grave."

"I just think we should keep our guard up, that's all. You're the one who said Steve was acting strangely."

"Okay, for the rest of the trip I'll wear a bag over my head and be inconspicuous."

She watched Steve make his way back to them. His face was tight, troubled. He stood by the table and slowly, painstakingly, added up the bill.

Either he's deficient in math, or there's something on his mind. He put the check down and stood there, his mouth working.

"Is there something you want to say?" Gwen asked in her best school teacher manner.

"Yeah." He hesitated.

"If there was botulism in the coleslaw, you'd better tell us now."

"Listen," he mumbled, "you planning on staying through tomorrow night? 'Cause if you are, you oughta know we won't be open."

"Really?" Gwen said. "According to your sign..."

"It's the new moon."

"I know I'll be sorry I asked," Gwen said, "but what does the new moon have to do with anything?"

He glanced over his shoulder. "Trawling."

"An ancient tribal rite?"

"Fishin'." He turned to go.

Gwen called him back. "Can we pay you?" She held out some bills.

He took the money and counted it. "I'll get your change."

"Keep it."

He counted it again. "It's an awful lot."

"Go to Augusta," Gwen said, "and check out the chicks."

He stared at the floor, shuffling his feet. "You don't want to hang around this town," he said at last. "There's nothing to do."

"We'll give it some thought," Gwen said.

"I mean it, lady, It's a lousy place, you know what I mean?"

"I'm afraid I don't."

He grew even more uncomfortable. "People around here... well, they're kinda funny about outsiders and all ... I mean, they don't go out of their way to make you welcome."

40

"Yes," Gwen said. "We guessed that from the motel accommodations."

"Waldoboro's nice," Steve said hopefully.

"And they don't resent outsiders in Waldoboro."

"Yeah."

"We'll give it *serious* thought."

He seemed relieved. "Don't let on I told. I could lose my job, okay?"

"Okay. And, Steve, when you get to L.A., catch a big one for me."

He grinned, stuffed the money in his pocket, and scurried away.

"How much did you give him?" Stoner asked.

"Ten dollars."

"That *is* a lot."

"It was cheap to find out what we just found out." She reached for her coat. "There's something shady about Shady Acres, and it isn't the trees."

CHAPTER 3

It was the darkest night she'd ever seen. The kind of dark that swallows, not only light and shadow, but sound. It covered the town like a blanket of mold. The mist had elevated itself to drizzle. Stoner huddled in her coat and tried not to take the weather personally.

"Well," Gwen said, "when do we go?"

"Where?"

"Waldoboro."

"Do you want to go to Waldoboro?"

"Me?" Gwen said. "I don't even know what it is."

"Then why should we go there?"

"We were told to get out of town."

"Yeah," Stoner said reluctantly. "I guess we should."

"When someone tells you to get out of town, the sensible thing is to get out of town."

"Right."

"On the other hand, it kind of makes you wonder why, doesn't it?"

"Yes, it does."

They walked on for a while.

"So should we get out of town?" Gwen asked.

"I guess we'd better."

They walked a little farther.

"I've never been run out of town before," Gwen said.

"Neither have I."

"It's kind of insulting."

"Yes, it is."

Gwen kicked a pebble. "If Miss Marple were told to get out of town, would she go?"

"I doubt it."

"If Mrs. Pollifax were told to get out of town, would *she* go?"

"Probably not."

"If Cagney and Lacey..."

"That settles it," Stoner said. "We're staying."

A car rolled slowly toward them. Its headlights glowed like cat's eyes. The driver seemed to be looking their way.

The high beams flared.

"Duck!" Stoner shouted. She dragged Gwen behind a tree.

The car reached the end of the block, turned around, and came back their way.

"Is that our friend?" Gwen whispered.

"I can't tell."

She crouched low, keeping in the tree's shadow. The car turned and came past them again, then sped away into the darkness.

"I think we're in trouble," Gwen said. "Either that or the locals have a highly developed level of curiosity."

Stoner grunted.

"When we go to Shady Acres tomorrow, let me go in. They know I'm looking for Claire. I'll ask a few questions, make a little conversation, and pretend to believe what they tell me. That should put their minds at rest."

"Maybe," Stoner said.

"Meanwhile, you case the joint from the outside. But if we uncover anything — repeat, *anything* — unusual, we are going to the police. Got that? *To the police.*"

Stoner looked at the ground. "We can't go to the police."

"What?"

"Claire isn't supposed to be out of Massachusetts."

"Stoner..."

"She's on probation, for drugs."

"You told me she didn't use drugs."

"She was arrested for dealing."

"Dealing!"

"*She* didn't deal," Stoner explained. "She was hanging around with some people who were dealers, and happened to be on the scene when they were busted."

"I don't believe this," Gwen said.

"It was at a party."

"I don't care if it was in church..."

"With that on her record, this was the only job she could get."

Gwen sank onto a park bench. "Oh, Christ."

"Don't sit there, it's wet."

"Do you know what we're probably into here? Claire Rasmussen could be the leader of a ring of international dope smuggling tycoons who are using Shady Acres as a front."

"She's only 23," Stoner said. "Please get up."

"Great, she'll make the history books. Baby Rasmussen and her gang."

"She didn't know they were dealers."

"Oh, sure," Gwen said. "I hear *that* one fifteen times a day."

"Nancy believes it."

"She must be from another planet."

"We're only going to look around, Gwen."

"I know you. It won't stop there."

"We shouldn't talk out here."

"Why not?" Gwen waved her arms in frustration. "The motel's probably bugged."

43

"It's cold. It's raining."

Gwen got up. "I'm going to regret this, Stoner."

The drugstore had closed. Above the Clam Shack, a dim light flickered in a window. Smoke rose from the chimney and dissolved into the night. The air smelled of dampness and burning wood.

"Someone has a fire," Stoner said. "I wonder if they'd like company."

Gwen slipped her hand around Stoner's. "Let's go back to Wyoming this summer. You can have all the fires you want."

"Do you mean that?" she asked, stunned.

"I wouldn't say it if I didn't mean it."

"But wouldn't it bring up unhappy memories?"

"I have some happy memories, too. Don't you?"

Words can't begin to... "Sure."

"And there's the scenery. No matter what happened, you can't blame the scenery."

"You don't have to convince me," Stoner said. "I can be packed in five minutes."

The East Wind Inn appeared ahead of them. The neon sign barely glowed. Stoner felt a wave of pity for it ... and a strong urge to put it out of its misery.

"Stoner," Gwen asked, "did Aunt Hermione do a Tarot reading for this caper?"

"Yes."

"What was the outcome card?"

"The Tower."

"And what does The Tower mean?"

"Change, conflict, catastrophe. The overthrow of existing ways of life..."

"I knew it," Gwen muttered. "I just knew it."

***

"You were wrong about the shower," Stoner said. "Whatever's in there wouldn't hurt anyone."

"We probably drowned it. Do you realize we've spent a total of 45 minutes in this room and taken, collectively, three showers?"

She wrapped the cord around the blow-dryer, stowed it in the bureau drawer, and glanced in the mirror. Behind her, Gwen sat propped up in bed, reading.

Gwen caught her spying. "Now what?"

"I like you in glasses."

"Who was it that said 'Men never make passes at girls who wear glasses?' Opens up all kinds of possibilities, doesn't it?"

"Certainly does."

44

"Maybe we should go into business together. We could put out a whole line of male turn-offs."

Stoner laughed. "You're about ten years behind the times. Turning men on is in again."

"You know," Gwen said, wrapping her arms around her knees, "somewhere along the line we dropped the ball, and I didn't even notice. It's time to start the Revolution again."

"I'm ready when you are."

"First we have to make it through the night." She put her book and glasses on the bedside table. "Can you knock a little more life into that heater? It's freezing in here."

Stoner knelt and made what sense she could of it. "I think it's doing its best." A lovely idea occurred to her. "You could crawl in with me."

"I'd crowd you."

"You wouldn't." She slipped under the covers and pressed her back against the wall. "Look, plenty of room."

"Are you sure?"

She felt light-headed, reckless. "I'm sure."

"I might keep you awake."

"You won't."

"I might."

"You're keeping me awake *now*."

"Well," Gwen said, "it is awfully cold."

"And bound to get colder."

Gwen started to get up, and changed her mind. "I'd better not."

"Gwyneth," Stoner said firmly, "there's no point in both of us freezing. Get over here before I suspect you of homophobia."

Gwen grabbed her blanket and spread, tossed them on Stoner's bed, and slid in beside her. "Blackmail," she grumbled.

Stoner tucked the covers around her. "Better?"

"Heaven." But her voice was uncertain, her body tense.

"Why so tight?"

"Cold."

Stoner reached across her and flicked off the lamp. "Iowa was Iowa, Gwen. I know the rules have changed."

"Stoner..."

She kissed the top of Gwen's head. "Go to sleep."

Gwen reached for her hand, and wrapped Stoner's arm around her like a shawl. "You're really very nice, you know."

"I know," Stoner said. "It's my only fault."

She felt Gwen's breathing grow slow and regular, felt her slip away into sleep. The sea murmured in the distance. From overhead came the sound of trickling water as the rain joined with melting snow to gently wake the earth to spring.

"Change," Aunt Hermione often said, "is life's greatest mystery.

45

At every moment the past dissolves, present becomes past, and the future gathers its threads and begins to weave. Whether for good or bad, the essence of tomorrow is possibility."

Last August, I held a pillow through the night and pretended it was Gwen. Tonight I'm holding her. This summer we'll go to Wyoming. And perhaps, one day, to Anguilla to be welcomed by whoever is at hand...

***

She dreamed she had gone to visit a hospital, but she was lost, wandering through wards, searching for someone to give her directions.

Passing through a set of heavy metal doors with wired windows, she found herself in an exitless room. Cloaked figures mumbled in the corners.

She turned to retrace her steps, and saw the faces of children pressed against the glass.

They began to change as she watched, growing clawed legs...
... and hinged tails...
turning into scorpions.

She drew back, repulsed, afraid to touch the door.

And suddenly she knew that this was a place of metamorphosis, that gradually she would change...
... and when she had changed she would be crushed...
... and all the while she would be conscious.

***

The fog had burned away. The sky showed through in shreds of watery blue. Seagulls, soaring high, cut the morning air with raucous cries of ecstasy and rage.

"You were right," she said to Gwen. "Lobster and lemon meringue pie cause nightmares."

But Gwen was gone.

She stumbled to the bathroom, splashed cold water on her face, and tried to swallow her anxiety.

She hasn't gone far, her clothes are still here. Maybe she goes running in the morning. Maybe she went to look at the ocean. Maybe...

She peeked out the front window.

The car's here. She wouldn't leave without the car. She wouldn't leave me...

She looked around for a note.

If anyone came in the night, I'd have heard them. Who would come

46

in the night?

The Gray Man from the Harbor House?

Close to tears, she sank down on the bed. Damn it, I wanted us to wake up together, I really did.

The door banged open. "Good morning," Gwen said cheerfully. She slipped out of her coat and placed a white paper bag on the night-stand. "It's a beautiful day, March is bustin' out all over, God's in Her Heaven, and you're going to love the Clam Shack."

"I thought you'd left."

Gwen looked at her. "Why would I do that?"

"Where were you?"

"Trying to find you the best cup of coffee in Castleton. In view of the selection, it wasn't hard." She sat down, pulled two styrofoam cups from the bag, and peeled off the lids. "Sugar? Saccharine?"

Stoner shook her head.

"Just as I suspected. You're chem free."

"Not quite," Stoner said, sipping her coffee. "I use sugar when I'm nervous, and I drink. Do you always come on like Gangbusters in the morning?"

"Only during the school year. Teachers have to hit the ground running."

"One of the prime causes of juvenile delinquency in this country," Stoner groused, "is teacher cheerfulness."

"Grouch." Gwen poked her affectionately. "Come on, get up. It's a wonderful day to achieve."

"Go away." She pulled the covers over her head. "Come back at a decent hour."

"It *is* a decent hour."

"What decent hour?"

"Nearly nine."

Stoner fumbled for her watch. "It's only ten past eight, Gwen."

Gwen yanked the covers back. "Get *up*. There's someone I want you to meet."

"It is a known scientific fact," Stoner said patiently, "that a third of the world's population can't function before ten. Out of every three people out there driving around, one is half asleep. The other two are raving maniacs."

Gwen pulled a shirt from Stoner's suitcase and tossed it at her. "You can't assault Shady Acres on an empty stomach."

"The only thing I'm going to assault is you."

"Wow," Gwen said. "Can we start now?"

"That," said Stoner, "is not politically correct." She locked herself in the bathroom.

Gwen pounded on the door. "If you take another shower, I'll kill myself."

***

The Clam Shack occupied the bottom floor of a small, weatherbeaten house. Picture windows fronted on the street, green cafe curtains drawn against the morning sun. Inside, tables were scattered about a large, airy room. A counter with stools overlooked the grill. A blackboard on one wall announced the day's specials — meatloaf with mashed potatoes and peas, lobster rolls, cod croquettes, and chicken pot pie. Above the sink hung a titillating calendar that featured a sultry brunette in low-cut bathing suit and spike heels glancing lasciviously over her shoulder and offering Season's Greetings from the Down East Artesian Well Company.

"Isn't she magnificent?" Gwen whispered.

"If you like the type."

"Not the pin-up, dummy. *Her!*"

A wiry, dark-haired woman past middle age stood behind the counter and poured coffee.

"Sure," Stoner said sleepily. "Magnificent."

The furnishings exceeded Aunt Hermione's wildest dreams. There was chrome everywhere. Along the edges of the tables, on napkin holders, salt shakers, sugar bowls, the coffee urn, stools, chairs.

"She owns this place," Gwen said.

"That's nice."

Postcards — the old, dull-finish kind — dotted the wall behind a non-computerized, non-electric, non-digital cash register. A wooden-framed glass display case held Roi-Tan cigars, Bicycle playing cards (regular and pinochle), Tums, and cellophane-wrapped root beer barrels. Beside the front door, between signs for Pepsi Cola Hits the Spot and I'd Walk a Mile for a Camel, were Polaroid snapshots. In some, a wedding party cavorted among the restaurant's tables beneath streamers and a white paper bell. In others, the paper bell was red, cardboard cut-out letters announced "Happy New Year," and grinning couples held up plastic cups of champagne. There was a series on Outstanding Catches, limp fish dangling from lines held by burly men in grease-streaked mackinaws. An official letter from the Castleton Volunteer Fire Department thanking "Dee and Dan" for providing coffee and doughnuts on the occasion of the fire at Tatro's barn. A photostat of a check for $10.82 signed by George McGovern. And a yellowed newspaper clipping showing Archbishop Medeiros blessing the Castleton fishing fleet.

"You're right," Stoner said. "This place is..." A figure in a snapshot caught her eye. She tugged at Gwen's sleeve. "Look!"

Gwen glanced at the photo. "Good Lord," she said. "That's the most disgusting fish I ever saw."

"Look closer."

48

"What's wrong with its eyes?"

Two marble-like knobs protruded from the fish's head. They were on top, and both veered to the right of center.

"It's a flounder," Stoner explained. "The eyes drift. Gwen..."

"They certainly do. Why in the world would you want me to look at *that*?"

"Not the fish."

"There are some things, Stoner, I can live a long time without knowing."

"In the background, at the counter, reading the menu." She waited. "Well?"

"Well what?"

"Don't you recognize that woman?"

"Should I?"

"It's Claire Rasmussen."

Gwen turned to her. "How can I recognize someone I've never met?"

"Her picture. The one Nancy gave me."

"I haven't seen it."

Stoner dug it out of her wallet and showed her.

"Yep," Gwen said, "that's the lady in question all right."

"Do you realize what this means?"

"It means Claire sometimes takes her meals off campus." She shuddered. "And in very strange company."

"It *means* someone here might know her." She strode to an empty table.

Gwen followed. "Great. Let's eat."

Stoner sat down and leaned across the table. "Now if we can figure out a way to find out..."

"Try asking," Gwen said dryly.

"We have to be nonchalant about it."

"Fine, be nonchalant. I'm hungry."

The woman left the counter and approached. "Back so soon, honey?" she asked.

Gwen nodded.

"Must like the cooking."

Gwen nodded again.

"What can I get you kids?"

"One of everything," Gwen said.

"Coming up." She turned to Stoner. "What about you?"

"Just coffee and English muffins, please."

"Home fries are good today."

"Okay, I'll try them."

"I fry a mean egg."

"All right."

"Corned beef hash is on special."

49

"And some of that."

The woman turned to Gwen and winked. "Picky eater, isn't she?" Gwen looked up, smiled, and looked down.

"The question is," said the woman, "should I keep going, or quit while I'm ahead."

"What comes next?" Stoner asked.

"Pancakes."

"Quit while you're ahead."

She watched as the woman poured two cups of coffee and went to work behind the grill. Gwen sat with her hands folded in her lap like a lady.

"Is something wrong?" Stoner asked.

"No," Gwen murmured.

"Are you praying?"

"No, I'm not praying, for Heaven's sake."

She let that one go by. "She looks like the type that knows all the village gossip. This could be our first big break."

"Then you study on the situation, okay? Quietly?" Gwen curled around her coffee cup and gazed into its depths.

Something decidedly peculiar is going on here. "Gwen, have I offended you?"

"Of course not."

Two men were seated at the counter, elbow to elbow, looking cold.

"Price of lobster's shot," said one. "Three-fifty the pound down to Boston."

"Goddamn buyers," the other said. "Goin' for six ninety-nine inland. Makes me contentious."

"Went 'round over it with that Schiavone character the other day. You know, from down to Gloucester?"

The other man grunted. "Now, there's a gentleman for you."

"He's cryin' about the price of gas drivin' to market. I ain't runnin' my rig on air."

"Runnin' mine on piss."

"Hell you are," the woman said. "Runnin' it on bad temper." She refilled their cups. "You oughta clean that heap up, Virge. Looks like you got no self-respect."

"Lousy coffee, Delia," the other said.

"So's the company."

"Wife wants to know when you're comin' round."

She dropped four slices of bread into the toaster. "Yeah? Who's gonna look after this dump while I'm out makin' social calls like some la-de-da rich bitch?"

"Wish you'd come round. She's got cabin fever something fierce."

" 'Cause you keep her pregnant half the time. Oughta find something more productive to do with your nights. Folks are startin' to talk."

50

"Ain't my fault. God made me that way. Sure wish you'd come 'round."

"I got a job, Frank. You don't notice me sittin' here watching the *tee*-vee and feedin' chocolates to the poodle, do you?"

"Hire yourself a girl," the man named Virge said. "You ain't gettin' any younger."

"And you ain't gettin' any more generous with your tips."

"I'm savin' up. Day you make me a decent cup of coffee, I'm gonna march you down the aisle."

Delia barked a husky laugh. "The day you get me into a compromising position, you randy bastard, will be the day following the Second Coming."

"If you're so interested in making your fortune," Frank said to Delia, "you oughta lay in with that Shady Acres crowd."

Stoner's head snapped up.

Delia snorted.

"You cook good enough for that joint," the man said.

"Hell she does," Virge muttered. "They live high off the hog up there."

"What makes you an authority?" Frank asked.

Virge shrugged. "I get around."

Delia turned on him. "Don't mess with that bunch, Virge. They're trouble. Tell him, Frank."

"Trouble," Frank admitted.

Virge cracked his knuckles. "What do you figure they're up to?"

"Trawling," Delia grunted, and slapped an egg onto the griddle. "That's all you need to know."

"You don't trawl off that point," Virge persisted. "Current's trickier'n a New York hooker."

"Suppose you're an authority on that, too," Frank grumbled.

"New moon tonight. They'll be out."

"Not tonight," Frank said. "Fog's gonna be thick as gull shit."

Stoner nudged Gwen's ankle with the toe of her boot.

"You boys keep your noses up your own sleeves," Delia said fiercely. She ripped a page from her order pad. "You don't want to end up like Dan."

Virge slid off the stool, squinted at his bill, and tossed two dollars and a few coins on the counter. "Poor sucker. Dan was a good son-of-a-bitch." He pulled at his earlobe. "Never saw him as a guy who'd get liquored up at sea. Damn queer."

"If you believe that cock-and-bull story," Delia said, "I got some swell shore-front property on Cape Cod I'll sell you."

"Did you hear that?" Stoner whispered to Gwen.

Gwen didn't answer. She was staring at Delia, and seemed to have entered a trance.

Virge yawned and scratched his chin. "See you around, Delia. Give me a call if you ever decide to wash that damn coffee pot."

"Will not. The finer things in life are wasted on you, Virge." She turned back to the grill and pounded the hash into submission.

Frank shuffled to the door.

As he passed their table, Virge stopped and straightened his green and black mackinaw. "Morning, girls. You here on vacation?"

"Uh..." Stoner said.

"Leave my customers be, you horny alley cat," Delia yelled.

Chuckling, Virge ambled out into the sunshine.

"Sorry about that," Delia said. "Virgil thinks he's God's gift to women." She arranged their plates and adjusted a knife. "Anything else you need?"

Stoner stared at the heap of food in front of her. "Did I order all that?"

"You did."

"It looks fine," Gwen said.

Delia looked at Gwen's equally mountainous plate. "You always eat like that?"

"When you travel with Stoner," Gwen said, "you never know where your next meal's coming from."

"Watch," Stoner said. "She'll pack away half of mine."

Delia gave Gwen the once-over. "Don't look it."

"I worry a lot," Gwen said.

"Me, too." Delia plucked at the loose material of her uniform. "A month ago this fit like skin. Want some blueberry jam? Picked the berries myself, last summer. You ever hear anything so quaint?"

"I'd love it," Gwen said eagerly.

Delia sashayed into the back room.

"Did you hear what she said?" Stoner asked, digging into her fried potatoes. "She knows something about Shady Acres."

"I heard." Gwen mangled an egg.

"Maybe we can find out..."

"Find out what?"

"Something."

Gwen looked at her and smiled. "When you're excited, your eyes turn the color of emeralds." She sipped her coffee. "Do Walt and Dot both have green eyes?"

"Only my mother. Or is it my father?"

"If you can't tell the difference, no wonder they gave you a hard time."

Stoner frowned, puzzled. "How come you're so talkative all of a sudden? I was beginning to think you'd turned to stone."

Gwen seemed surprised. "Really? I thought I was..."

She broke off as Delia returned with a half-pint Mason jar and placed it on the table. "Everything okay? As they say in the finer restaurants."

"Wonderful," Stoner said. "This is the first meal I've had all week that didn't come with coleslaw."

"Slaw!" Delia's salt-and-pepper eyebrows shot up. "You want to make me puke?"

"My aunt's addicted to it."

"Would you care to join us?" Gwen asked. "As long as you're not busy. I mean, if you have things you need to do..."

"Well, I wouldn't mind taking the weight off my feet, but I chain-smoke."

"That wouldn't bother me," Gwen said. "Stoner?"

"No problem."

Delia pulled up a chair, scrounged a pack of Chesterfields from her pocket, and lit one. She inhaled and studied the glowing tip. "They say these things kill you. Hell, what doesn't?"

Up close, she appeared to be just this side of sixty. Her hair, jet black except for a sprinkling of gray at the hairline, shone with midnight blue highlights. Her face was deeply lined, her mouth full, her eyes dark and bright as polished coal. The knuckles of her hands were prominent, her arms thin, the skin around her fingernails cracked and raw. She noticed Stoner looking at them and chuckled. "Dishpan hands. Dan used to say the only thing we had in common was Greek parents and bad hands." She took a drag on her cigarette. "Well, he used to say a lot more, but it was kinda dirty."

"Dan was your husband?" Stoner asked.

"We'd have been married thirty-four years this June, if he hadn't gotten himself killed."

"Yes, I overheard the gentleman..."

Delia guffawed. "Gentleman! Wait'll I tell Virge you called him a gentleman. Won't he be the *Coq-de-la-Rue?*"

"The what?" Stoner asked.

"Cock-of-the-walk," Gwen explained. "It's an expression. It means..."

"Just what it sounds like," Delia said.

Gwen took a sip of coffee. As she put her cup down, it rattled against the saucer.

"Are you all right?" Stoner asked.

"Fine." She rearranged her toast and cleared her throat. "Nice day."

"Don't let it fool you," Delia said. "This time of year, by four o'clock you can get lost crossing the street. Where you gals from?"

"Boston," Stoner said.

"Big place."

"Yes," Gwen said brightly. "Very big." She glanced at Delia, and ducked her head.

"I get down that way a couple times a year. Always strikes me as kind of desperate, if you know what I mean."

53

"I know exactly what you mean," Gwen said. "Desperate's exactly the word I'd use."

Stoner stared at her. What *is* this?

Gwen caught her questioning look, and concentrated on lining up the ends of her knife and spoon with the edge of the table.

"Has that hash gone off, honey?" Delia asked.

"No!" Gwen ate a forkful, gave a tentative smile, and pushed her hair behind her ears.

"If you don't like it, leave it. I'm not sensitive."

"No, really, I like it. I like it very much."

Curiouser and curiouser, as Marylou would say. "If you'd rather have something else..."

"I'm *fine*."

"I thought you were hungry."

"I am. I don't have to eat like a bulldozer, do I?"

"Well," Stoner said, "you've been known to."

A murderous gleam came into Gwen's eyes. "Stoner..."

"Stoner?" Delia turned to her. "Is that a family name?"

"I was named for Lucy B. Stone."

"Well," Delia said. "How about that?" She turned back to Gwen. "What do they call you? Gloria Steinem?"

"Gwen," Gwen said. "Gwen Owens."

"Short for Gwyneth," Stoner explained.

"Pretty. Sounds like falling snow."

Gwen blushed. "It's Welsh."

The older woman draped an arm across the back of her chair and contemplated the smoke that rose from her cigarette. "Welsh. Now there's a language to tie you in knots. Looks like what's left over after a game of Scrabble." She rested her hand on Gwen's wrist. "No insult intended, honey."

Gwen stared at the hand.

Odd. Definitely odd.

"Now, I've got a name that would choke a horse. Papadopoulou. Haven't heard it in years. Folks call me Delia, or Dee, or Heyyou."

"My husband's name was Bryan Oxnard," Gwen said. "Stoner and I killed him."

Delia puffed on her cigarette. "Seems like divorce would be a lot less trouble. Catholic? Or quick-tempered?"

"It was an accident," Stoner said. "But he wasn't very nice."

"Well..." Delia nodded. "I've seen some meanness in my time. You don't strike me as the type to make a person mean."

"She isn't," Stoner said, "but he was."

"Stoner, I'm sure Mrs... Mrs... isn't interested in our problems."

"Hell," Delia said, "your problems are bound to be more interesting than mine."

"Do you have problems?" Gwen asked.

54

"Getting through the day, *that* can be a problem."

"I'm sorry."

"Not your fault, honey."

Gwen turned a deep shade of pink.

"Are you sure you're all right?" Stoner asked.

Gwen pushed her chair back. "Excuse me. I have to go to the rest room."

"Through the kitchen, to the right, and up the stairs. Don't trip on the cat." She stubbed out her half-smoked cigarette and lit another. "They say this is a good way to cut down. Seems more like a good way to go broke." She gestured at Gwen's chair. "She always that polite?"

"Not usually. I don't know what's wrong."

"Hope I don't scare her."

"I doubt it."

"Well," Delia said, "you never know. Reminds me of myself, the first time I met Dan's family. So eager to please I made everyone nervous."

Light began to dawn.

"Seems like a sweet kid."

"She's thirty-one," Stoner said.

"Honey, when you get to be my age, anyone under forty's a kid. What are you gals doing in Castleton?"

"Sightseeing."

"Here? You should have kept on to Bar Harbor. This place goes into a coma on Labor Day. Come to think of it, it's not too lively any time."

"A friend of ours, back in Boston, asked us to stop by and say hello to her sister. Maybe you know her."

Delia blew a cloud of smoke through her nose. "Probably do. I have the great misfortune to know about everybody in town."

"She's a nurse out at Shady Acres."

The woman's mouth twisted in a grimace. "Now there's a strange bunch."

"I'm beginning to get that impression."

"Darndest collection of odd-balls I ever saw outside of a travelling circus. And I don't mean the patients." She stopped herself. "You're not in the business, are you?"

"The business?"

"The 'profession,' as they say."

"I'm a travel agent."

"Dan and I went to a travel agent once, over in Augusta. Funny way to make a living."

"I guess it is," Stoner said.

"Hotels, people, trains and planes... never could figure out how they keep it all straight."

Stoner smiled. "If you knew how much dumb luck goes into it, you'd never want to go again."

"Well, I probably won't, anyway. Fun kind of went out of things when Dan died."

"I'm sorry."

"Don't mind me," Delia said. "I'm feeling pitiful today. Who's this nurse you're supposed to look up?"

"You have her picture over there. The blonde behind the flounder."

Delia got up and retrieved the snapshot. "Claire? Sure, I know her. Cut above the rest, if you know what I mean." She lit another cigarette. "You sure this is the way to kick the habit?"

"I don't know," Stoner said. "I never smoked."

"Well, don't start. It'll kill you." She studied Claire's picture. "Nice kid. Brings the patients in here from time to time. Only one that bothers to do that."

"Have you seen her recently?"

Delia pondered. "Now that you mention it, not in a couple weeks. She might have quit, wouldn't blame her."

"Her sister hasn't heard from her, either. She says that's not like her. That's why..."

"Jesus," Delia interrupted, "I hope she's not mixed up in whatever's going on out there."

Stoner turned her attention to her eggs. "What *is* going on out there?"

"Beats me," Delia said. "But something's up, and I wouldn't mind knowing what it is. I'd like to put that bunch on ice."

Gwen reappeared and slid into her seat. "I'm sorry," she said, "I tripped over the cat."

"You wouldn't be the first. Didn't kill it, did you?"

"No, I thought it was getting out of the way, but it didn't."

"You saw Aphrodite move?"

Gwen nodded.

"Say your prayers, honey. You just witnessed a miracle. Dan used to say she was only resting between incarnations. Fornications, more likely. You in the travel business, too?"

"I'm a teacher. Watertown Junior High."

"No fooling? My kid brother works in Watertown, at the Leaning Tower of Pizza."

"I know the place."

"He's the one with the gold necklace."

Gwen looked at her. "Kid brother? That man's 45 if he's a day."

Delia narrowed her eyes. "No need to be insulting."

"Oh, gosh," Gwen stammered. "I'm sorry. I..." She spotted the photograph. "How did that FISH get here?"

"It's a flounder," Stoner said. "I explained about the eyes, remember?"

"Please, Stoner, I'm eating."

"Not much," Delia said.

"Do people really go out and drag those creatures from the murky depths and take them *home*?"

Delia laughed. "They don't sit and admire 'em, honey. They eat 'em."

"I could never eat something that looked like that."

"You probably have, on more than one occasion."

"I never will again," Gwen said. "People up here must be stark, staring crazy."

"Grow them kind of rude down your way, don't they?" Delia said.

Gwen turned the color of the table cloths at the Harbor House. "I don't mean to be..."

"Forget it," Delia laughed. "I'm just trying to get your goat."

"Oh," Gwen said. "Well, that's all right."

I don't believe this, Stoner thought gleefully. Gwen Owens is falling all over herself like an adolescent with a crush on the gym teacher.

She grinned.

Gwen shot her a dirty look.

"We were discussing Shady Acres," Stoner said. "Delia thinks there's something funny going on out there."

"That's nice," Gwen muttered to her bacon.

"Not very," Delia said.

Gwen's shoulders drifted up around her ears.

Stoner cleared her throat.

"What kind of funny?" Gwen asked.

"Well, I don't exactly know," Delia said. "But if you can't find that nurse, I'd say she's been fired, or she's in trouble."

"*They* say she's on vacation," Stoner said.

"I don't figure that." Delia frowned at the tip of her cigarette. "That bunch is so tight with vacations, you'd think time was goldplated. Fellow I know was working as an aide, took two days off for his Dad's funeral, they made him make it up over Thanksgiving. If that's generous, I'm the Queen of England. And I sure ain't the Queen of England." She lit another cigarette from the stub of the last. "Really ought to give these up."

"You know someone working there?" Stoner asked.

"He quit. Took off for parts unknown. Never was much good, any..." She broke off with a startled look. "Jesus."

"Do you think he was involved in whatever it is?"

"Could have been. It never occurred to me until this minute."

"Do you know where we could find him?"

Delia shook her head. "Haven't a clue. Just up and disappeared. Jesus." She shook her head again. "But he was the type to do that, just disappear."

57

"Does the Harbor House fit in anywhere?"

"Possibly, but I can't pin it down. Still, if there's trouble in Castleton, Charlie Lennox is bound to be in on it."

"Charlie Lennox, is he kind of gray?"

"He's gray all right. Colorless Charlie we used to call him back in school. They'd be pretty hard up to be in with the likes of him. On the other hand, he has the fanciest lobster boat I ever saw for a guy who doesn't fish."

"Does he go trawling at the new moon?"

"Well, now, that's something I don't know. It'd be easy enough to find out, though. Just take a little stroll down to the wharf around midnight. He ties up right behind the restaurant."

"Assuming that there's something going on," Gwen said, "aren't you taking a chance talking so freely to strangers?"

"Maybe. But I have an instinct about folks, and right now my instinct's telling me you two couldn't make trouble if you tried. Even if you *did* kill your husband."

"Thank you," Gwen said.

"Anyhoo, I've got nothing to lose. They already took everything that mattered to me, the night they murdered Dan."

Gwen sat up. "Murdered?"

"I can't prove it," Delia said. "They claimed he fell off his boat drunk. Old Doc Evans signed the death certificate, said there was enough alcohol in Dan's blood to float the Bar Harbor-Nova Scotia ferry." She blew smoke through her nose. "Must have mixed up Dan's blood with some of his own."

"Was there an inquest?" Stoner asked.

"Sure. Everybody stuck by their story."

"What makes you think it wasn't true?"

"Dan broke every rule in the book on land. But there was one thing he'd never do, and that's drink on board the *Delia II*."

The door opened and three fishermen sauntered in, stamping slush and gravel from their boots. Delia crushed out her cigarette. "I gotta go into my Joan Blondell act." She thought for a moment. "My cousin works part-time out there, in the kitchen. I'll see if she knows anything about your nurse. Stop around here after closing."

"What time is that?" Gwen asked eagerly.

"Saturdays I stay open until nine, seeing as this is such a lively place. Come up the back way. Try not to step on the cat again. Hey!" she shouted brusquely to the men, "you boys wanta eat my cooking, leave your dirt outside."

"Hell, Dee," one of the men yelled back, "you'll just sweep it up and dump it in the chowder. You got the grittiest clam chowder north of Kennebunk."

"Can't help that. You sell me the grittiest clams."

"Do not. Sell them to Howard Johnson's."

Delia swept a glance over their table. "That comes to about five bucks. Don't tip the proprietor." She squeezed Gwen's shoulder. "Honey, if you like that jam, take it with you."

"That's very kind of you," Gwen said, blushing wildly.

"Hell, us worriers got to stick together." She slouched to the counter.

Gwen grabbed her coat and bolted.

***

"Whatever you're thinking," Gwen said, "I don't want to hear it." She stood on the sidewalk amid the slush. A cold breeze played in her hair.

"I haven't said a word."

"Your face speaks volumes."

"So does yours."

"I'm warning you, Stoner."

"You forgot the jam," she said, and handed it to her.

"How much do I owe you for breakfast?"

"Nothing. I'll put it on my expense account, under entertainment."

Gwen whirled around and started walking. "I have never," she said, "in my entire life, made such an utter fool of myself."

"It happens."

They passed the alley that separated the Clam Shack from the drugstore. It was a real alley, not the one-lane, sidewalkless streets frustrated Boston motorists hurtle down when they find themselves going the wrong way on avenues that weren't one way last week. This was a genuine small-town alley, with gravel and creeping crabgrass and backyards with garages and fences and garbage cans and the private side of everyday life.

Stoner paused to admire it and was struck with a sudden, vague uneasiness.

"Something wrong?" Gwen called.

She ran forward. The anxiety passed. "Just a chill."

"Are you catching cold?"

"There's something not right about that alley."

Gwen looked back. "Seems like an ordinary, garden-variety alley to me."

"Not to me."

"Maybe Aunt Hermione's right. Maybe you *are* psychic."

"I am *not* psychic."

"I don't know why that upsets you," Gwen said, striding forward. "There's nothing wrong with being psychic."

"I have enough trouble living my life without walking in the shadows of the future." She ran to catch up. "Slow down, will you?"

59

Gwen waited for her. "What should we do first?"

"Check out Shady Acres, I guess."

"Okay, then let's drive up the peninsula for dinner. There must be a restaurant between here and Damariscotta."

"There'd better be. Damariscotta didn't look too promising."

"I think I saw a truck stop on Route 1."

"Of course," Stoner said casually, "you might prefer the Clam Shack."

"And *why* might I prefer the Clam Shack?"

Stoner shrugged. "I thought you'd enjoy it, what with the leftover chicken pot pie and all."

"I don't like chicken pot pie."

"Cod croquettes?"

"Or cod croquettes."

"Grittiest clam chowder north of Kennebunk?"

"Stoner..."

"The kitchen help?"

"I don't want to hear another word about that," Gwen said, her voice rising. "Do you understand? Not another word."

"Sure, not another word."

"No calling me 'honey'."

"No 'honey'."

"No backdoor references to blueberry jam."

"No blueberries."

"No teasing."

Stoner grinned. "For Heaven's sake, haven't you ever had a crush before?"

"Not since I was twelve."

"Then you're about due."

"I'm a grown woman, Stoner."

"So what?"

"This is not adult behavior."

"Well, I don't know about that," Stoner said. "But it seems all right to me."

Gwen walked away. "I don't want to talk about it."

"Don't get mad at *me*," Stoner called after her. "*I* didn't do it."

"I'm not mad, I'm embarrassed."

"And I'm your friend, remember?"

Gwen waited for her on the corner. "I'm sorry," she said. "It's so disconcerting."

"Trust me." She brushed Gwen's hair out of her eyes. "I'm an authority on these things."

A scrap of paper rattled down the gutter. The wind swirled around them and bit through her coat, but inside she felt a warmth that reached out to envelop Gwen, and the gulls, and the piles of dirty snow, and all of dear, creepy Castleton.

60

"I went in her apartment," Gwen confessed.

"See anything?"

"Books and plants and candles."

"And Aphrodite."

"There were pictures, but I didn't look."

"That was very honorable."

"I didn't have time." Gwen's forehead slid into a little frown. "Do you think they really killed her husband?"

"She believes it."

"I wonder why."

"I guess we'll find out tonight. Think you can handle it?"

"Just don't let me out of your sight."

Never.

They were in front of the public library, a tiny white salt-box of a house with peeling paint and a yard rampant with dormant roses.

"I wonder," Gwen said, "if we could find out anything in there."

"Like what?"

"Just ... things." She gazed wistfully at the building.

Stoner laughed. "I believe you're addicted to libraries."

"I'm afraid I am."

"Then let's get Shady Acres out of the way and spend the afternoon in here. The Devil take Damariscotta."

"For all we know," Gwen said, "the Devil has *already* taken Damariscotta."

As they started for the car, Stoner felt a feather-tip of apprehension brush her mind.

CHAPTER 4

A fieldstone driveway curved sharply to the right, spruce and hemlock fell away, and there, on a windswept cliff, stood Journey's End.

"My God," Gwen breathed.

Slowly, Stoner opened her eyes, already knowing — by the way her fingertips tingled inside her clenched fists — what she would find. She looked at the house. Her stomach contracted into a lead knot.

"Is that it?" Gwen asked.

"That's it."

"Damn." She covered Stoner's fist with her hand. "If I had dreams about this place, I'd wake up screaming even if nothing happened."

Shady Acres, nee Journey's End, posed massive and white in a lawn of dead grasses, irridescent against a washed-out sky. A flight of stone steps rose to a porch that ran the length of the building. Tall windows flanked a heavy door with new brass hinges. On the second floor, a pair of French doors opened onto another small porch guarded by an elaborately carved balustrade. From the upstairs there was nothing to break the fall to the stone patio below. The shallow pitched roof was capped by a box-like cupola and widow's walk. At either end of the house, chimneys reached for the sky. The paint was chipped and peeling, the windows glinted silver.

Nothing moved.

"I don't like this place," Gwen said.

Stoner was too frightened to respond.

"It's ugly, Stoner. It could eat you alive. Let's throw *karma* to the winds and get the hell out of here."

"I can't," she whispered.

The house seemed to settle into a smug grin.

It wants me.

"I mean it. Forget Shady Acres. Forget Claire Rasmussen. Forget..."

"I promised Nancy..." She hunched down in the seat.

"Nobody'd hold you to that."

"If you'd seen how scared she is... Gwen, the world is full of broken promises. I won't add mine to the rest."

Gwen sighed and shook her head. "Why is it the things I love about you most are the things that drive me crazy?" She pushed open her door. "Let's do it."

The gravel parking lot faced the house. To her right were overgrown tennis courts, the remains of beach roses, a dropoff, and the sea. Invisible waves boomed on the rocky cliffs, the ocean rocked in the distance. Jutting out from the main building was a renovated carriage house. A few cars were abandoned along the drive.

Wind blew.

The house waited.

She steeled herself. All right, Shady Acres, or Journey's End, or whatever you call yourself, the die is cast, the gauntlet is flung down, we've crossed the Rubicon. I'm here.

A flare of sunlight ricochetted off an upstairs window like an obscene wink.

It knows I'm here. It knew I'd come.

"What happens now?" Gwen asked.

"If you've ever been in the mood to quote Shirley Jackson," Stoner said in a shaky attempt at humor, "this seems to be the appropriate moment."

Gwen shook her head. "What we need right now is absolute, clear-eyed practicality."

"Bearings, then." The sun was to her right. The cliff curved around and behind the house, providing vistas of the sea in two directions. "North," she said, pointing straight ahead. "East. We came from the west, so Castle Point must face south."

"Very good," Gwen said. "Now tell the class what you've learned."

"I wonder if I can get a topographic map in town."

"What for?"

"Just in case."

"Are you going to camp out?"

Stoner shrugged helplessly.

"Well, if it'll make you feel safer..."

Safer? Nothing could make her feel safer here. No talisman, no lucky charm, no medicine bag, nothing could stand between her and the Thing that waited inside.

Gwen started up the path.

"Where are you going?"

"To find Claire. Poke around. Case the joint, or whatever one does in a situation like this."

Stoner watched the house swallow her.

She slipped her hands into her back pockets and hunched her shoulders against the wind.

It's a house. Just a house. Greek Revival. Possibly Italianate. *Circa* 1790. A house like any other house. The happiest house on the block...

What do I do now?

First, get out of stage center. Then look for Claire's car.

She circled around to the west, staying close to the woods. At the north corner, a cluster of windows gave a glimpse of immense potted plants and wicker furniture. A sitting room, probably, or conservatory. It was uninhabited.

She glanced at her watch. Eleven-thirty. Maybe they were at lunch.

A closed-off breezeway at the back led to the carriage house. Here the paint was fresh, the curtains at the windows a jumble of styles and colors. Staff quarters?

She looked up. Something green coated the gutters and chimneys. It gleamed wetly. It seemed to stroke the crumbling bricks with shadowy fingers.

Moss, she told herself. Moss grows in humid climates. Seacoasts are humid climates.

A small parking lot held a few cars, but no pale blue '78 Ford with Massachusetts plates.

Maybe Claire really is on vacation.

Maybe.

The cliffs began a few yards from the back of the house. The tide was going out, waves crashing and sliding over barnacle-encrusted boulders far below. Out on the ocean, a ship cut silently through a light fog.

She hesitated at the northeast corner. The east wall should be rough with chipping paint, the ground covered with sharp gravel.

It was.

If she touched the wall, she knew it would be warm.

She didn't touch the wall.

Something pulled her to her knees in the gravel. She saw a clump of tiny gnarled twigs with brown leaves. Breaking off a piece, she rolled it between her hands and sniffed.

Thyme.

All that was missing was the scorpion.

She sat back on her heels, a wave of immobility washing over her. Now there was nothing to do but let the dream play itself out.

She closed her eyes and waited.

Something moved. Slowly, steadily.

It cracked over the ground.

Closer...

Touched her face, her eyelids.

Something cold and damp and smelling of the ocean's depths, of dark and secret places below the waves where nothing moved, where no light came, where the water was still and the silt of millenia drifted down forever, falling like black snow through eternal silence. Falling on the crushed and broken bodies of trilobites, of horsetail ferns and giant palms, of ancient reptiles and wingless birds, the wrecks of sailing ships, grinning skulls, drowned mountains, charred logs

64

from fires long burned out, shreds of ceremonial robes, the twisted metal of lost planes, lost hopes, forgotten gods, dead heroes, sluggish dreams of giant tortoises and tiny horses with teacup hooves, desperate women, spent rage, unborn children, the pollen of crushed flowers...

... the refuse of history and time before history, settling forever into darkness.

The shriek of a gull brought her back to consciousness. Wind whispered through the dried grasses. Blinking, she looked around. There was the house, the sea, Gwen's car. And Gwen, walking quickly down the path.

Stoner ran to catch up to her. "What did they say?"

"Get in," Gwen snapped. She slammed the car door, turned the key, stamped on the accelerator, and spewed gravel.

"What's the matter?"

"I hate liars."

"Did I lie?" Stoner asked.

"*Them.* 'Nurse Ramussen is away on holiday'," she chanted. "Bastards."

"Her car's gone. Maybe she is."

I saw her."

Stoner sat bolt upright. "You what?"

"Saw her." She jerked the car to the left to avoid a frost-rimmed gulley. "In the dining room."

"Did you talk to her?"

"I couldn't get beyond the front hall."

"What was she doing?"

"Nothing, absolutely nothing. You haven't seen 'doing nothing' until you see the way she was doing nothing. Whatever Claire's on, it isn't vacation."

"What do you mean?"

"I've seen that look before. If she's still dealing, I'd say she's shooting up the profits."

Stoner frowned. "Drugs. But if that's true, with her history, why would they be so secretive about it?"

"Beats me. Maybe they look after their own. Charming people." The car hit a rock and bounced.

"And why would her car be gone?"

They careened from one side of the road to the other. Stoner tightened her seat belt.

"Did you find anything?" Gwen asked.

"Exactly what I expected, down to the creeping thyme."

"Eerie."

"Yeah."

"Are you sure you've never been here before?"

"Not in *this* life." They had reached the blacktop. Gwen took the

65

first curve on screaming tires. "Which is in considerable jeopardy at the moment."

Gwen glanced at her. "What?"

The ocean appeared directly ahead. "Watch the road!" Stoner shouted. "You're driving like a maniac."

"Sorry." Gwen slowed the car to a still-unacceptable speed. "They made me angry."

"Clearly."

" 'On holiday,' he says."

"Who says?"

"The creature guarding the door. 'Isn't that Claire in the dining room?' I asked sweetly. 'That ain't no nurse, that's a patient.' 'I can see it's a patient, but it looks like Claire Rasmussen.' 'Well, it ain't,' he says. 'Rasmussen's on holiday'," Gwen snorted. " 'On holiday,' mind you. Where did he learn English, Masterpiece Theatre?"

"Please slow down, Gwen."

Gwen ignored her. "And don't tell me it wasn't Claire. I don't make mistakes." She paused. "Well, not that kind."

The car drifted onto the frozen sand edging the road. Gwen hauled it back with a vicious jolt.

"If you don't get this car under control," Stoner said, "I'm going to jump out." She put her hand on the door handle. "I mean it, Gwen."

"Here's what we're going to do," Gwen said. A wet oak leaf slapped the windshield and clung. She mashed it with two furious flicks of the wipers. "We'll go back in town and kill time until after three, then sneak onto the grounds the back way..."

"What back way?"

"Don't interrupt. We'll sneak onto the grounds and take a closer look."

"Why after three?"

"When the shifts change. If we get caught, I don't want it to be by any of the gorillas who saw me this morning."

"Very sensible."

They passed the Harbor House in all its abandoned squalor.

"Are you *sure* it was Claire you saw?"

"It wasn't the flounder. Believe me. I have a photographic memory."

Gwen's hands were strong on the wheel. They were also, Stoner recalled with a little shiver, very nice to be touched by. My *body* has a photographic memory. "What should we do until then?" she asked, mainly to keep her mind off dangerous subjects.

"Go to the library."

She smiled. "The library."

"Libraries in small towns are always run by someone's maiden aunt, who knows all the dirt back six generations."

***

But not the Oliver Winthrop Memorial Library of Castleton. The Oliver Winthrop Memorial Library of Castleton was run by a round-faced, overly cheerful young man named Al from Decatur, Illinois, with a Master's degree in library science. He had lived in Castleton for two months and knew nothing, which he was eager to share. He was also eager to share Gwen's company for the evening.

Glancing idly through the pages of an outdated History of Historic Castle Point, Stoner eavesdropped on the proceedings and felt her emotions bounce back and forth between irritation and amusement like a tennis ball at Wimbledon.

Al flirted.

Gwen pawed through the card file.

He cajoled.

She refused.

He pouted.

She rejected.

He tried charm.

She bemoaned the passing of the Dewey Decimal System.

He offered dinner and a movie.

He offered to include Stoner.

He did everything, in fact, but give up.

"Look," Gwen said at last, "do you see that woman over there?"

He glanced over and nodded.

"That," Gwen went on, "happens to be the meanest man-hating, knife-carrying, ball-busting butch in Boston. And I'm her old lady."

He stared open-mouthed.

Stoner turned three shades of red and smiled sweetly.

"She doesn't look mean," Al said with some uncertainty.

"Looks are deceiving." Gwen lowered her voice. "She's so mean she drags her Harley hog on the Mass. Pike without a crash helmet."

Stoner tried to look formidable.

"The last guy who tried to come on to me," Gwen said, "Well, you don't want to know."

Al swallowed hard.

"Let's just say he single-handedly turned Blue Cross into a non-profit organization."

"Hey," Al said, and held out his hands palms up. "It's cool. None of my business." He scurried to the return box and began wildly sorting books.

"Come on, Hulk," Gwen called to her, "let's go somewhere and get it on."

Outside, Stoner collapsed against a tree and laughed until her face hurt. "How *could* you?"

67

"The situation called for desperate measures," Gwen said.

She wiped her eyes. "You shouldn't do things like that, you know. Some men consider it an open invitation to rape."

Gwen shrugged.

"Did you mean what you said," Stoner teased, "about getting it on?"

Gwen looked away. "Maybe."

Stoner caught her breath. "Gwen?"

"I haven't forgotten Iowa."

Her heart jumped up into her throat.

"Sometimes," Gwen said, "I think I'd like to do it again."

"You do?"

Gwen nodded. In the sunlight her hair was the color of toast. "Do you ever?"

"Uh... yeah, sure..."

"But not just for the sake of doing it. I'd have to be certain."

"Certain of what?"

"That it wasn't just a fling."

"Well," Stoner said lamely, "flings can be fun."

"But not my style. Nor yours, I think. You mean too much to me to use you."

Translation: I'm not in love with you. "I appreciate that," Stoner said, forcing a light tone. "It can mess up a friendship."

"Friendships are hard to come by."

"Good friendships, that is."

"Truly great friendships."

They started walking across the common. Stuffing her hands in her pockets, Stoner found an old candy wrapper. She dropped it in the fountain. "Even mediocre friendships."

"Bad friendships."

"Rotten friendships."

"We have a good friendship," Gwen said. "Don't we?"

"One for the books."

"Except," Gwen said, missing her note of irony, "when I'm a jerk and neglect you."

"Everyone gets a little odd during Boston winters," Stoner said. "Spring is right around the corner."

A cold gust of wind hurled dust and road grit into their faces. "Not *this* corner," Gwen said grimly. "Did you get anything out of that book?"

"Not much. Your history of Journey's End, by the way, was surprisingly accurate."

"I try to be thorough."

"Except for the part about Cicero in the original Greek."

Gwen shrugged.

"At times the house was thought to be haunted," Stoner went on.

"The usual stuff — strange lights, eerie noises. Then years would go by without any manifestations. It seems to have stayed in the Winthrop family, at least through 1910, when the history was published." She squashed a glob of slush beneath her boots. "I don't know what I thought I'd find out, but I didn't."

"Maybe this afternoon will tell us something."

"You know, Gwen, Claire's not going to be playing croquet on the lawn."

"We might find a clue, though."

"And we might stumble around the woods like a couple of little kids playing Nancy Drew, and come up with nothing more than a good case of pneumonia."

"If we can hit low tide," Gwen said, "I'll bet we can get around that fence from the ocean."

Stoner stopped walking, took Gwen's shoulders in her hands, and turned her to face her. "Listen to me, Gwen, something happened to me out there this morning. I don't know what it was, but it wasn't from this world. I'm afraid, and I'm not sure what of."

Gwen looked at her, her dark eyes serious, and pressed her hand against Stoner's cheek. "I promise you, I won't let anything happen to you."

Stoner shook her head. "This isn't something you have any power over."

"Dream stuff?"

"Sort of."

Gwen rested her arms on Stoner's shoulders and thought for a moment. "Well, look, I could go by myself..."

"No," Stoner said sharply. "We'll do it together, or not at all."

"Are you being overprotective?"

"Normally cautious. Leaving aside my personal problems with the house, these people could be dangerous."

"So," Gwen said, clasping her hands behind Stoner's neck, "which is it? Do we confront this thing, or slink away like the yellow-bellied cowards we both are?"

Stoner laughed. "Some choice. Okay, we'll go, but you have to promise me you won't do anything reckless."

Are you kidding? Standing here, touching my neck, looking into my eyes? Lady, this is the most reckless act ever performed in the history of the human race. "I mean it, Gwen."

"Chauvinist."

"I don't care."

"Politically incorrect," Gwen teased.

"Not for a ball-busting butch from Boston." I want to belong to you. I want promises of forever. I want a rose-covered cottage and breakfast in bed. I want the whole damn ball game.

"Don't be afraid, Stoner. I won't let your dreams come true."

69

I know, she thought. That's just the trouble.

***

She parked the car at the side of the road where the chain-link fence made a right angle toward the sea. The sky was blue, but paling as wisps of cloud slipped in from the east. Through a stand of spruce, she could see the drop-off of the cliffs, and beyond them a solid wall of gray. Fog.

"Okay," Gwen said briskly, "let's get this organized. We sneak up to the house, staying out of sight whenever possible..."

"Staying out of sight at all times," Stoner corrected.

"... and try to get a good look into the conservatory. That should be easy. They probably have the lights on by now."

"She might not be in the conservatory."

"Of course she will. Mental patients always sit in the conservatory for an hour before dinner. It encourages socialization."

"How do you know that?"

"I've seen movies."

"Gwen, why are we doing this?"

"Well," Gwen said, "we could turn around right now. And when you see Nancy you could tell her I thought I saw her sister, but you didn't confirm it. And that Claire — if that *was* Claire — looked terrible, but you don't know why. But you *did* bring her some swell rumors about mysterious deaths and the new moon..."

"Okay, okay, I get the point."

"You keep a lookout for her car. You might have missed it this morning. And we'd better take a peek into the staff quarters. If it's too light, we'll lurk about until dark, which shouldn't be long at this time of year."

Stoner lounged against the car, amused. "You're certainly getting into this. As I recall, you were the one who wanted to drop it. Of course, that was before we met Delia..."

"They treated me like a fool," Gwen said sharply. "I get enough of that from Grandmother. And I certainly had my fill with Bryan."

"Do you think of that very often?"

"Often enough."

"Well, at least he left you this swell, gas-efficient car."

"Sometimes," Gwen said, "I want to park it on a side street and let the hoods strip it. Come on."

"I'll go first."

"Why?"

"Because I'm a chauvinist, for God's sake. Gwen, will you let me have my way *once* on this trip?"

Gwen gestured her forward. "Be my guest, pig."

Fog spilled over the cliff edge and crept through the forest. By the time they had gone five yards, Stoner's boots were soaked with droplets from damp underbrush. Water fell from pine needles overhead and trickled down her neck. She heard a scuffling sound and froze, heart pounding.

An overwintering robin scrounged on the forest floor.

"Press on, George," Gwen whispered.

"Gwen, you have to take this *seriously*."

"We're not even there yet. What do you think this is, Vietnam?"

Stoner rolled her eyes in resigned dismay and pressed on.

The woods gave way to seacoast. At the bottom of the precipice, wet sand glistened. The tide was out. A break in the cliffs formed a steep, but not impassable, slope to the water. Gravel worked its way into Stoner's boots as she stumbled down the incline.

The fence ended in six inches of water. She swung around it and shuddered as icy water poured over the tops of her shoes and soaked her pants legs, driving the sand and gravel deeper into her boots. Every step felt thoroughly disgusting. She picked her way upward, dislodging pebbles that rattled down the cliff like machine-gun fire. Pulling herself onto the grass at the edge of the woods, she paused to catch her breath.

The house gleamed eerily through the trees.

Gwen tugged at her sleeve and nodded toward the woods. Looking over, she saw an old foundation hole. At the bottom, partially hidden by dead leaves, was a blue Ford with Massachusetts plates.

"Well," Stoner whispered, "whoever did that didn't plan on Claire needing it again."

"It looks like what Betty Jean did to her Chevy convertible out at the limestone quarry, except we didn't do it on purpose."

" 'We' didn't?"

"I was along for the ride."

She had to laugh. "Gwen, sometimes I think your whole life is a series of near misses."

"I'm working on it," Gwen said.

Stoner looked around. Between the house and where they stood was a waist-high wall of black granite, fallen down in places but with an intact section high enough to hide behind. Crouching, she ran for it.

"We're in luck," Gwen said as she knelt beside her. "We can see everything."

The lights were on in the conservatory. Patients lounged in wicker chairs, some reading, some staring, nobody socializing. There was no one there who resembled Claire Rasmussen.

"I don't see her," she said in a low voice. "Do you?"

Gwen shook her head. "Maybe if we wait awhile..."

There didn't seem to be anything else to do.

Daylight was fading fast, the fog building up, the cold settling in

— and, Stoner thought with apprehension, the tide rising up the end of the chain-link fence, their one escape route. How deep was it now? Knee high? Waist high? Well, we can always swim if we have to. *I* can swim. Can Gwen swim? Great, I'm in love with this woman and I don't even know if she can swim.

The grit and dampness in her boots were driving her crazy. She wondered if anything alive had washed in there along with the seawater. Or slipped in from the underbrush. There were perfectly horrible things that clung to odd bits of twig and leaf in forests. Small, slow-moving, slimey things. Things that scurried from the beam of your flashlight. Creeping, slithering, darting things. Things that left silver trails. Things that bit and burrowed...

She shook her head and glanced over at Gwen. Mist clung to her hair and eyelashes. Her face was smooth, her lips soft. She wanted to take her in her arms and...

Pay attention. This is a potentially life-threatening situation.

If only she weren't so beautiful.

If only she weren't so nice.

If only she weren't so straight.

"Don't sit on the ground," Gwen whispered. "It's damp."

She pulled herself to her knees. "I can't get much wetter. We should have brought the Manhattans."

"Only you," Gwen said, "would want to turn this into a picnic."

"I'm going to freeze to death."

Gwen took Stoner's hands and rubbed them. "You're getting too old for this kind of thing."

Gwen's hands were warm and soft. Stoner looked at them, looked at her eyes. "Gwen, I..."

"Shhh."

A door slammed. Angry voices. Gravel crackled.

Through the twilight she made out the figure of a woman, blonde, in bare feet and a shapeless white robe, running...

... directly toward them.

Behind her came two large men in attendants' uniforms.

Oh, Christ!

Out of the corner of her eye, she saw Gwen stand and start to climb over the wall.

"Idiot!" Stoner hissed. "Get back here."

"Hi!" Gwen said loudly. "Can I help you?"

The woman stopped in her tracks.

Stoner pounded the ground with her fist. Idiot, idiot, idiot. She tried to get to her feet. Her knees gave way beneath her.

"Claire," Gwen said in a low voice, "I'm a friend of your..."

The men had reached her. "Who the hell are you?"

"I was here this morning," Gwen said. "I think I lost my wallet when I walked around the grounds."

72

Claire stood frozen between the men and Gwen.

"This ain't a public park, lady. It's private property."

"Oh, dear," Gwen said. "I assumed it would be all right. Nobody told me..."

"*I'm* telling you."

Claire made a break to her left. The man grabbed her and pinned her arms to her sides.

"She seems so distressed," Gwen said. "Perhaps I could help."

"We don't need your help." He shoved Claire at the other man. "Take her back to the house. I'll get rid of this one."

Get rid of? *Get rid of?* What does he mean, get rid of?

"If your wallet shows up," the man said to Gwen, "we'll send it to you. Now get the hell out of here."

"I'd really like to look a little more. It has all my identification, credit cards..."

"Fuck your credit cards. Move it."

Come on, Gwen, do as he says.

"You don't understand," Gwen blithered. "My entire *life* is in that wallet. If some unscrupulous person, some person of low moral character, were to find it... Well, I don't know what I'd do."

"Lady..."

"I should have listened to my husband. He's always telling me, 'Eleanor,' he says... My friends call me Nell, but he prefers Eleanor, he says it sounds so much more dignified. Don't you think it's more dignified?"

"Lady, I'm warning you."

"Anyway, Gus is always telling me, 'Eleanor, you ought to subscribe to one of those credit card services.' You know, you put your name on their list and when you lose your wallet you just call one number and they take care of everything. Isn't that remarkable? For twenty dollars, maybe less, you have to shop around... For twenty dollars a year you never have to worry about anything again."

For God's sake, Gwen, get *out* of there.

"I'm giving you five seconds," the man said.

"But knowing me," Gwen went on, "I'd forget where I put the number. I'm like that. 'Mind like a sieve,' Gus says. Goodness, he's going to be so angry. He won't say a single word to me all the way home to Illinois. Can you imagine that? All the way home to Illinois without saying a word."

"God dammit, lady..."

"Maybe I shouldn't tell him. Maybe I should just offer a reward, a handsome reward to anyone who finds it. Do you think that's a good idea, Mr... Mr..." She leaned forward to read the plastic identification tag on his breast pocket. "Mario. If you find it, Mr. Mario..."

He grabbed her arm and shoved her toward the gate. "I told you to MOVE IT!"

"Oh, I can't go out that way," Gwen said. "The gate was locked, so I came around the fence and my car's just miles and miles and *miles* from here. But don't you worry. I can go back the way I came. I'm sure you have loads of important work to do."

"I'll let you out. Hike to your car." He yanked her toward the drive.

The other man watched them slack-jawed. Claire dangled from his hands like a rag doll.

"Get the bitch back in the house!" Mario snapped.

"Bitch?" Gwen asked innocently. "Strange language for a ..."

Mario shoved her. "Shut up."

Yes, Gwen, please shut up.

Gwen ambled toward the gate, chatting voraciously. Mario dogged her heels.

The other aide dragged Claire back to the house.

Stoner waited until they were out of sight and scrambled for the shore.

Bastard. If you hurt her, I'll kill you.

She threw herself down the cliff, tearing her jeans.

Oh, Jesus, Gwen. Be all right. Please, be all right.

She plowed through water up to her knees and clawed her way up the slope. Downed branches exploded beneath her feet. She slid behind the wheel of the car and reached for the ignition.

Gwen had the keys.

God damn it!

It was almost too dark to see. In a panic, she stumbled up the road toward the gate.

Gwen materialized out of the mist and darkness, strolling along as if she were enjoying the scenery. "You look awful," she said.

Stoner stood in the road and tried to catch her breath. "Did that son-of-a-bitch hurt you?"

"No, but he certainly is rude." She looked Stoner over. "You're going to catch your death of cold."

"Don't ever, ever do a crazy thing like that again. They might have killed you."

"I doubt it. Bodies are harder to dispose of than Fords."

"This isn't funny, Gwen."

"Well, *I* think I was very clever. Another ten seconds and she'd have led them right to us. Better to be caught wandering than hiding. How did you like my cover story? I believe I'm a born psychopath."

"It was a lousy cover story. Nobody in their right mind would believe it for a minute."

"It worked, didn't it?"

"Yeah," Stoner admitted. "I guess."

"Big deal," Gwen said, starting to walk away. "My moment of triumph and all you can say is, 'I guess'."

Stoner grabbed her by the arms and shook her. "It's Wyoming

74

all over again, damn it! This isn't a game! That man could have hurt you! You wouldn't listen to me about Bryan, and you're not listening now!"

Gwen tried to pull away. "Let me go, Stoner."

"Not until you *listen*. People are dangerous, Gwen. Your father beat you, your husband tried to kill you... for God's sake, what do you *do* with that?"

"I said let me go!"

"Do you think life's a movie, with fake blood and stand-ins?"

Gwen exploded. "I'll tell you what I do with it, Stoner. I put it behind me. I tell myself, 'okay, it happened, it's over, it won't happen again.' Because if I don't do that, I'll go to bed afraid, and wake up afraid, and within six months I'll be a neurotic, house-bound woman like my grandmother. Is that what you want me to be?"

"I'm sorry," Stoner said, dropping her hands. "It's just ... if anything happened to you, I wouldn't know how to live."

"Stoner..." She reached for her.

Something in her broke. Out of control, she pulled Gwen to her roughly and kissed her hard on the mouth.

The earth turned somersaults.

I love you, I love you, I love you.

Her mind cleared. Ashamed and frightened, she drew back.

Gwen stared at the ground, her hands knotted into fists. "Leave me alone for a while, Stoner," she said softly.

"I didn't mean to do it, Gwen. Please, I'm sorry."

Gwen turned her back.

"I didn't mean to do it."

Rain began to fall.

Helpless, broken, Stoner stood for a moment, then turned and trudged slowly toward the car.

I've ruined everything.

Her arms and legs felt like lead. Her throat was tight. Her eyes burned.

I didn't mean to.

Darkness closed in hard. The rain worked its way through her jacket. She began to shiver, and didn't care.

She didn't know what to do.

Emptiness was everywhere. Around her, inside her. She rested her head against the top of the car and let the tears come.

Time slid past.

She felt Gwen touch her shoulder. "Get in the car, Stoner."

She obeyed mechanically.

Gwen started the motor and turned on the dash lights and heater. "Take off your jacket," she said, opening the zipper and peeling away the soggy wool. She fumbled in the glove compartment and handed Stoner a tissue. "It's time to talk."

Stoner wiped her eyes and blew her nose. She could feel Gwen's hand on the back of her neck. "Don't," she said, and brushed her away.

"You've been a kind and gentle friend," Gwen said, "and I haven't treated you very well." She paused. "Are you listening?"

Stoner nodded.

"Sometimes I'm not sure I know the difference between love and gratitude."

Well, I know the difference between love and pity.

"I thought I loved Bryan. Maybe I did, I don't know."

Stoner felt a rush of cold anger. I really don't need this right now.

"Love, gratitude, friendship ... they get so mixed up."

She forced herself to speak. "Can we just leave?"

"Please, I have to say this, but I want to do it right."

Save your breath. I know an exit speech when I hear one.

"I never want to do anything to hurt you."

Well, that's charming. "Look," she said gruffly, "I got carried away back there. It didn't mean anything."

Gwen stiffened. "I see."

"So let's get out of here before this road turns to mud."

Gwen didn't move.

"You do remember how to drive, don't you?"

"Yes."

"So put her in gear and scratch gravel."

"Stoner..."

Glancing up, she could see Gwen's face reflected in the windshield. In the greenish light, it looked like a death mask. "I'm not hot for your body, you know. I have other fish to fry."

Gwen looked down. "Then may I ask you something?"

"Can it wait? This car's like a sauna."

She gripped the wheel. "No, it can't wait."

"Whatever you say. You're in the driver's seat."

Gwen took a deep breath. "Do you have a lover?"

"No."

"Are you in love with anyone?"

"Yes."

"Do I know her?"

"I doubt it."

"Why aren't you lovers?"

"She's straight."

Gwen turned toward her. "Oh, Stoner, I'm so sorry."

"Those are the breaks."

"Well, I hope it works out."

"Thank you."

"I wish you'd told me."

"It didn't seem feasible."

The motor hummed, wavered, stalled. Gwen didn't move.

"You killed the car," Stoner said. She looked up. Something slid down Gwen's cheek and left a glistening trail. "Gwen, are you crying?"

"I want you to be happy, Stoner. I really do."

"Gwen?"

Another tear slipped down her cheek.

"*Gwen.*"

Gwen wiped her face on her sleeve. "I promised myself I wouldn't do this," she said. "I promised myself I'd be mature about it."

"What are you talking about?"

"I knew I couldn't expect you to wait until I'd straightened out my life. I *didn't* expect you to, but I hoped..."

"I *did* wait."

Gwen glanced at her, then away. "You loved me once," she said in a small voice, "didn't you?"

"I still love you."

"As a friend."

She took Gwen's hand. "Gwen..."

Gwen smiled feebly. "I always knew I had a lousy sense of timing."

"What are you talking about, Gwen?"

"Ever since last summer ... ever since Bryan ... I've been asking myself what I really wanted. For my life. From you. But it was all so muddled. I mean, you go along not asking, just assuming it's the way you were always told it should be. Maybe it doesn't always feel just right, but you find reasons, excuses for the doubts..."

"Please, Gwen, get to the..."

"Back there on the road, just now, when you kissed me ... all of a sudden it came together, and..." Her voice trailed off.

"*What* came together?"

"That what I've wanted, all along, was to be your lover."

"Oh, *shit*," Stoner said, and covered her face with her hands.

Gwen glanced at her. "I sound like a bad movie, don't I?"

It's not that, my friend, my love. The problem is, at this very moment, when my number has finally come up in the Great megabucks of Life, I can see ... gathering on the horizon ... the advance troops of The Terrible Giggles from Another Planet.

"Stoner, I wish you'd say something."

Come on, guys, this isn't right. It's inappropriate. Rude. Crass. Tacky.

She ground her teeth.

"Don't just sit there, Stoner. *Please.*"

Give me a break, fellas. It's Serious time.

"*Stoner.*"

"They're here," she said, and burst into laughter.

"Look," Gwen said tightly, "it's bad enough I just made a fool of

77

myself. You don't have to..."

Stoner grabbed her arm. "That isn't it," she choked. Her eyes watered. Her jaw ached.

"Well, what's so damn funny?"

"Me," she managed to say. "You. Us."

"If you don't stop this, I'm going to throw you out and leave you here to rot."

"I don't care." She buried her face in Gwen's shoulder. "I can't help it." Laughter peaked, slid over into tears. "I love you."

Gwen touched her face in a puzzled, tentative way. "Yeah, well, that's nice."

"You don't understand. I *love* you."

"All I understand," Gwen said, "is I'm sitting here with my heart broken, and your nose is running all over my shirt."

"That's the price you have to pay for being my lover."

Gwen dug a tissue out of her pocket and handed it to her. "Will you please get a grip on yourself and tell me what the hell's going on here?"

"This is truly ludicrous," Stoner said, blowing her nose. "I've spent the past seven months trying to convince myself it's all right just to be your friend, and all the time you've been trying to convince yourself it's all right to be my lover. We're talking high comedy, folks."

"Okay," Gwen sighed. "Tell me one thing. Are you in love with some other woman?"

"If you believed that," Stoner said, squeezing her tissue into a tiny ball, rolling down the window, and littering, "I have some swell shore-front property on Cape Cod to sell you."

"Then why did you...?"

"Saving face."

Gwen started the motor and drove back to town, humming softly.

***

Stoner closed the motel door, locked out the night, and stood in the middle of the room grinning like an idiot. "What do we do now?"

"Don't ask me," Gwen said as she struggled out of her rain-drenched coat. "I've never been lovers with a woman before."

"And I've never been lovers with you before."

"Aren't we supposed to fall into each other's arms with glad cries and make mad, passionate love while the heavens explode with fireworks and the orchestra plays the 1812 Overture?"

"Suits me, if that's what you want."

Gwen studied her thoughtfully. "Frankly, you look like a drowned rat. I *feel* like a drowned rat. I think repairs are in order."

78

"Showering together's supposed to be romantic," Stoner said.

"We could do that ... I guess."

She shook her head. "Too personal. Some other time. You go on and I'll make us a drink."

"Make us *two* drinks," Gwen said. "I'd walk on burning coals for you, swim a tidal wave, stop an earthquake, part the Red Sea, and battle the Moral Majority single-handed. But premixed Manhattans is pushing it." She went into the bathroom, turned on the water, and began to sing.

My lover is Gwen Owens, and she sings in the shower.

She draped Gwen's coat over a chair near the heater, braved the fog for ice, and stripped off her wet clothes.

This occasion calls for special clothing.

She rummaged through her suitcase.

Flannel. Flannel's nice to touch. Especially on a cold, damp night.

She found the Western-cut shirt with the pearl snaps, the one she'd bought in Wyoming. The one she'd worn the first day they spent together.

Jeans or corduroy? Jeans. Not the new ones. The old ones, worn soft and smooth.

She poured herself a Manhattan and sat down on the bed.

What could be better than having a drink on a cold evening while you wait for your lover, who has fawn-colored hair and deep brown eyes and sings in the shower?

How about a toast?

To all you folks out there...

To Laurie, romantic friend, living on the edge of desperation in the Texas Panhandle.

To Carol, who loved me for a while, but we weren't right for each other.

To all the lovers I didn't have and won't miss.

To the kids at King's Grant High, who got their jollies leaving notes reading 'queer' and 'pervert' in my books.

To Mrs. Jones and her school bus, wherever they are.

To all the ghosts at Shady Acres, and the staff as well.

To Mom and Dad, still waiting for their little girl to see the light.

To the remains of Bryan Oxnard, all-time loser. Reached for the moon and ended up worm-food.

And most of all, to me, Stoner McTavish, travel agent, private investigator, and lover of Gwen Owens.

"I have never," Gwen said, "seen a human being look so smug."

Stoner jumped up. "I'm sorry. I forgot to make your drink."

"Boy, this is the shortest honeymoon I've ever been on." She tightened the belt of her robe and plugged in the blow-dryer. "Haven't I seen you somewhere before?"

"You have. Jackson, Wyoming. Last summer." She tossed some

ice into a glass, added bourbon, and popped the top on the ginger ale. "How was the shower?"

"Hot. I think we're making some headway against the fungus. All this place needs is a little love and affection."

"Don't we all?"

"Listen to her," Gwen muttered good-naturedly. "We've been lovers for 52 minutes, the service is shot to hell, and she's complaining." She looked at Stoner. "Are you drunk?"

"Haven't touched it. I feel so good I may never drink again."

Gwen laughed. "What am I going to do with you?"

"Take me to Wyoming." She began gathering up her wet clothes. "Other than that, anything you want."

"I was wrong," Gwen said. "You're not like Bessie the Mongrel at all. More like the setter pup my father brought home but wouldn't keep because it was too rambunctious." She fingered the armload of clothing. "You can hang these over the shower curtain rod. If you don't have enough room, toss mine out the window. And these little dainties..." She extracted Stoner's underpants from the heap. "... can go on the hook behind the door."

"I hate you," Stoner said, turning beet red. She scurried into the bathroom.

"What about dinner?" Gwen called over the hum of the dryer.

"You have a choice. The diner in Damariscotta or THE CLAM SHACK."

"Very funny."

"Too bad the Harbor House is closed. It's such a friendly place."

"Damariscotta it is," Gwen said. She flicked off the dryer. "Oh, God, now I can't remember if it was a diner or a used furniture store."

"If you want to go to the Clam Shack, just say so. You don't have to make up excuses."

"I take it all back," Gwen yelled. "Every nice thing I ever said about you."

"Right." She came back into the room. Gwen sat on the edge of the bed combing her hair. "I think my boots have had it for the night. Will you be humiliated if I wear sneakers to Delia's?"

"I want you to wear a dress," Gwen said.

Stoner grabbed a pillow and threw it at her.

Gwen threw it back. "Does my hair look like a haystack?"

"It looks fine."

"You're sure?"

"There's a mirror of sorts in the bathroom. See for yourself."

"I can't," Gwen said. "When I look in mirrors, sometimes I look right in my eyes, and for a second I can't tell which of us is real."

"That's pretty weird, Gwen."

"I do weirder things than that. Shall we go to dinner, or what?"

"To tell you the truth," Stoner said, "what I'd really like to do is lie down and hold you for about a hundred years."

"Funny." Gwen stretched out on the bed and held out her arms. "That's exactly what I had in mind."

Stoner eased down beside her, cradling Gwen's head on her shoulder.

So this is how it is. After all the wanting and torment, it's as easy as this.

She touched Gwen's face wonderingly. From the distance came the high-pitched whine of slipping tires. "I think it's icing up. Are you warm enough?"

Gwen snuggled closer. "I'm fine."

Her body was still hot and soft from the shower. Stoner felt an answering warmth in her own.

"I love you," she said.

"I love you, too, but I have a problem."

Stoner pushed herself up on one elbow and looked at her. "What?"

"I want to seduce you, and I haven't the vaguest idea how to go about it."

"Straight women," Stoner said, and stroked the little hollow at the base of Gwen's throat. "They don't know how to do anything."

Gwen slid her hand under Stoner's shirt. "I'm liberated."

"Sure." She took Gwen's hand and moved it to her breast.

Gwen wrapped her legs around Stoner's. "I think you should know," she said in a low voice, "I've made love with men."

"Why, Gwyneth Ann," she muttered as she parted the folds of Gwen's robe, "that's the most disgusting thing I've ever heard." She shivered as Gwen ran the tips of her fingers over the small of her back. "I think *you* should know, I've made love with women."

"Vile," Gwen said, and tugged at Stoner's belt.

She pushed Gwen's robe to the sides and gazed down at her. "You are absolutely beautiful."

Gwen grasped her hungrily. "I don't want you to think I'm only in this for sex," she murmured.

Stoner laughed. "I think you are at the moment."

"Stoner?"

"Mmmm?"

"We don't really have to go to dinner, do we?"

CHAPTER 5

"We should have eaten," Gwen said as they picked their way through the darkness to Delia's back stairs. "I'll die before morning."

"I know. Sex makes you ravenous."

"Do you think she'll notice?"

"She might. Married women notice things. Dan may have left her a widow, but I doubt he left her a virgin."

"I hope she offers us tea and cookies."

Stoner squeezed her hand. "Greeks are noted for their hospitality."

"My mind feels like jello."

"It should. We made love for three hours."

Gwen stopped short. "You were *counting*?"

"Well," Stoner said, "I didn't want us to be late."

"Do you realize," Gwen said, "we've never made love anywhere but in motels? Could that be significant?"

"We've never made love anywhere but out of town. The true test will come in Boston."

"People make love in Boston all the time."

"Not with Aunt Hermione raising the spirits downstairs."

"We'll have to be careful," Gwen said, "not to open a door to the Other Side."

Stoner laughed. "Maybe it's just my mood, but that sounds like a dirty remark."

A rectangle of yellow light fell into the alley. "Look out for the stairs, kids," Delia called. "They're icy."

Gwen gripped her hand. "Do I look all right?" she whispered.

"You look gorgeous."

"Give me an *objective* opinion."

"I can't. I'm besotted by love. Nervous?"

"A little. Do you mind?"

"Heck, no," Stoner said. "Delia can't compete with a Harley hog."

"She can if she offers me a sandwich." Gwen started up the stairs, then hesitated. "You go first."

"Why?"

"I'm shy."

"Since when?"

"Since now."

"You'll be fine," Stoner said reassuringly, and bounded up the steps two at a time.

Her first glimpse of Delia's apartment surprised her. She wasn't sure what she'd expected — New England stark? Chrome Revisited? Ethnic Flamboyant? — but it certainly wasn't this. There were muted earth tones everywhere. Soft grays, gentle browns, sandstone, smokey blue. A fire burned in a beige ceramic-tiled fireplace beneath a slate mantel holding clay vases of dried grasses. On the back of an overstuffed couch facing the fire lay a hand-crocheted afghan of ivory Aran wool. The light was dim, cast by glass-chimneyed oil lamps whose bases were glazed pots decorated with swirls of pastel. Delia herself stood out in vivid contrast — black wool slacks, black hair, flashing dark eyes, nailpolish that sparkled like rubies, a thin gold chain around her neck, and matching tiny gold earrings. All of this set off by a flowing scarlet blouse of a silky material, cut so low it would be dangerous in mixed company.

"It's lovely," Stoner said.

"Thanks." Delia took her jacket and draped it across the back of an egg-shell muslin and blonde wood chair near the fire. "It reminds me of home."

"Did you come here from Greece?"

"To tell you the truth," Delia said, reaching for Gwen's coat, "I've never been there. Dan and I planned to go, but... Still, after sixty years of my parents' stories, photographs from distant cousins, to say nothing of Christmas presents of hand-picked wild herbs from the mountains, complete with pebbles and dust... Well, it feels like home."

Gwen was staring openly at Delia. "Go sit by the fire, honey," she said, patting her shoulder. "You must be half frozen."

"Miserable out there," Gwen mumbled. She lowered herself to the floor, arms around her knees, and went on staring. Her skin glowed with firelight.

"Stoner?" Delia said. "You a floor-sitter, or a chair-sitter?"

"The couch is fine." She sank into it and stretched her legs. "This is the most comfortable place I've been in days."

Delia hung Gwen's coat from a corner of the mantel. "Well, the East Wind Inn isn't famous for comfort. I'm not sure what it's famous for, you'd have to ask the Board of Health about that." She picked up a cigarette she'd left burning in an ashtray and inhaled deeply. "What can I get you? Tea, Coke, sherry, something stronger?"

"I wouldn't mind a Coke," Stoner said, "if it's no trouble."

"Coming up. Gwyneth?"

The glow on Gwen's face deepened. "Coke. Fine. Coke."

Delia crossed the room to the kitchen like a panther, all grace, sureness, and unself-conscious sensuality.

Stoner caught Gwen's eye. "Want to give her a hand?"

Gwen, apparently in shock, didn't answer.

Grinning, Stoner got up and went to lean against the door frame.

"Need any help?"

"I'm used to it."

"Then let me. Tell me what to do."

"Keep me company." Delia rummaged in a dilapidated Kelvinator with a domed top. She found what she was looking for, put two frosty, sweating sodas on the table, and began pounding the ice trays.

Stoner looked around at the rest of the room. All the appliances were old — a gas stove on high, skinny legs, with a lid that folded down to hide the burners and ceramic handles on the oven door; porcelain sink jutting from the wall without benefit of built-in cabinets; cupboards with real latches, not magnets; an antique pie safe. The table was covered with a glossy cloth, squares outlined in red and containing bright pictures of teapots and geraniums. She ran her hand across it. "This can't be real oilcloth?"

"Sure is. I got it at a garage sale. Imagine anyone parting with a precious thing like that." She popped the caps from the Cokes and poured them over ice. "Can't get anything in stores nowadays but pressed petroleum by-products." She leaned over the table and sniffed. "Smell that. There's nothing like the smell of oilcloth. Brings back the not-so-good old days."

"Aunt Hermione would love your place, especially the restaurant. She's developed a passion for chrome."

"Well, I get my fill of lustre, thank you very much."

"Her favorite possession is a cracked ceramic ashtray from Old Orchard Beach."

"Skee-Ball Alley, I'll bet. Can I interest you in a meatloaf sandwich or two?"

"It doesn't seem right, asking you to cook after hours."

"Honey, if I didn't like to cook, I wouldn't do it. There are better ways to make a living." She pulled a plate of meatloaf, a jar of mayonnaise, and a bottle of ketchup from the Kelvinator. "Hand me the bread?"

"If you could manage two for Gwen," Stoner said, "she's pretty hungry. We missed dinner."

"Good. I was afraid I had competition. Want me to heat them up? There's leftover gravy, no MSG."

"She can't hold out that long. Where's Aphrodite?"

"Down in the restaurant, getting fatter." She buttered the bread. "I heard a rumor about you kids. Al from the library claims you're an item."

"Uh..." She felt herself go red. "I guess so."

"He was hanging around over dinner, crying on my shoulder. His male ego was wounded, though why your personal habits should have anything to do with him is beyond me."

"It wasn't true," Stoner said awkwardly. "Not at the time. It is now."

Delia glanced over her shoulder. "Well, let me be the first to congratulate you. We don't get many honeymooners in Castleton. It's a cut below the Poconos, you might say."

"It's beginning to grow on me," Stoner said.

"Stay too many nights at the East Wind, and Castleton won't be the only thing that's growing on you. Does she take mayo, ketchup, or both?"

"I'm not sure." She peeked into the living room. Gwen was stretched out on her stomach in front of the fire, her head resting on her arms. "I think she's asleep. I wore her out today."

Delia raised one eyebrow. "That why you look so smug?"

"I mean...I don't mean..."

"Don't mind me," Delia said, licking a drop of ketchup from the back of her hand, "I'm just a dirty old lady."

"You're not old," Stoner said quickly.

"And I'm no lady. Guess that makes me just plain dirty." She considered the sandwich makings. "We'll give her half and half. You do your own. You strike me as the complicated type."

She put the sandwiches and Cokes on a tray, then reached into a cupboard and brought out a small clear bottle. "We might as well celebrate with this. I was saving it for our anniversary. Now it makes me morbid to look at it." She added three wine glasses. "Take it easy on that stuff, it packs a wallop."

"What is it?"

"Ouzo. You have to develop an immunity, if it doesn't kill you first."

"You're being very kind to a couple of strangers."

"Well," Delia said, and wiped her fingers on a hand-embroidered dishtowel, "we're all strangers one way or another." She laughed. "The Chinese give you fortune cookies. From Greeks you get philosophy." She filled the teakettle and lit the stove with a wooden match. "Have any luck out at Shady Acres?"

Stoner filled her in. "What do you think?"

"I think you're playing with fire." She crossed her arms and frowned thoughtfully. "Look, Stoner, it's your business, not mine, but maybe you should back off before you get in real trouble."

"You're probably right," Stoner said. "But I have too many unanswered questions."

"Curiosity can get you into some strange places."

"I suppose." She ran her fingers across the back of a chair.

"And it sounds as if you've raised their hackles."

"Gwen did. They haven't seen me."

"Your friend from the Harbor House did." She sighed. "This used to be a nice town. Dull, but nice."

"Delia, what's going on out there?"

"I'll tell you what I know while we're eating." She offered Stoner the tray. "This shouldn't be too heavy, not for a ball-busting butch from Boston."

Stoner felt the blood drain from her face. "Al didn't hold much back, did he?"

"Don't fret. He doesn't gossip, except to me. Don't know how I got so privileged. I probably remind him of his old Boy Scout den mother."

Stoner doubted that very much. An eccentric aunt, perhaps, or the Older Woman all the high school boys panted over but couldn't get to first base with. Definitely not a den mother.

"It isn't true," she said. "I'm not..."

"Good Lord, I know it isn't true. I have *eyes*, don't I?" Carrying the teapot, she strode into the living room and indicated a space on the coffee table.

Stoner lowered the tray between a stack of Greek-language newspapers and a pile of magazines that began with the current *Atlantic*, passed through *Ellery Queen's Mystery Magazine*, and ended with an old copy of *Daedalus* devoted to "The Art and Literature of the Exile."

Delia caught her staring. "Don't tell me. You're trying to figure out what a woman like me's doing with reading material like that."

"Uh..." Stoner said.

"Well, when you get to be my age, nothing'll surprise you any more. Shock, yes. Surprise, no." She placed the teapot on a tiled end table and turned her attention to Gwen. "Seems a shame to wake her, she looks so pretty there."

Pretty? In her brown corduroy jeans and Kelly green shirt, her eyelashes resting against her cheek, her hair drifting over her hands, Gwen was more than pretty. She was stunning.

"We'd better," Stoner said reluctantly. "She'll have me up all night."

"Should I ask doing what?"

"I'd rather you didn't."

Delia bent and shook Gwen gently by the shoulder. "Come on, honey, dinner's ready."

Gwen rolled over, sat up, and rubbed her face. "I'm sorry, I didn't mean to be rude." She spotted the tray. "You made sandwiches?"

Delia eased herself onto the couch. "Your *enamorata* said you might be hungry."

Gwen froze. "My what?"

"Delia knows," Stoner said. "Al spilled the beans."

"I see." Gwen glanced back and forth between them. "What did you ... think?"

"None of my business," Delia said. She poured herself a cup of tea and inspected it. "When you see what this stuff does to a tablecloth, it makes you wonder what it does to your insides."

Stoner tried to smile reassuringly at Gwen, who wasn't looking

86

her way. "She'd value your opinion," she said to Delia. "I'm her first."

"In that case..." Delia sipped her tea. "I think Stoner's a fine woman, and so are you." She took another sip. "And I'll bet you're hell on wheels in bed."

Gwen threw her hands over her face.

Stoner snorted Coke bubbles up the inside of her nose.

Delia turned to her. "As for you, I suppose you're experienced beyond your years, and have had multitudes of lovers."

"Not many. Not like Gwen. There's never been anyone like Gwen."

"Ah," Delia said wisely. She patted the seat next to her. "Gwyneth, honey, why don't you scoot over here? You'll fry so close to the fire."

Tongue-tied, Gwen moved over to lean against the couch, her shoulder almost but not quite touching Delia's knee. The older woman smoothed an unruly strand of Gwen's hair. "Going gray," she observed.

"After tonight," Gwen muttered, and reached for a sandwich, "who wouldn't?"

Delia laughed. Her laugh started in the basement, flowed up the stairs, and filled every corner of the room. "Don't mind me," she said, stroking Gwen's face with the back of her hand. "I'm an awful tease."

Stoner took a bite of her sandwich and smiled to herself. They make a nice picture. I wish I had a camera. I'm always running into nice scenery when I don't have my camera. But, if I had my camera, I'd never run into nice scenery.

"Now," Delia said, "I'll entertain you in the finest tradition of my ancestors." She lit a cigarette and glared at it. "Ought to toss the whole pack in the fire, but at today's prices..." She leaned back and closed her eyes.

"The saga of Shady Acres begins about two years ago. I should do this in rhyme, but I can't. Anyway, at that time, Shady Acres was Journey's End. Lillian Winthrop, known lovingly to the natives as Miz Lilly, lived out there alone except for occasional visits from obscure relatives and a slow-witted village girl who went out twice a week to do heavy housework. Miz Lilly passed her days puttering among her herb gardens and raising startling rubber plants in what she called the conservatory."

"We saw the conservatory," Gwen said helpfully, "and the plants."

"Don't interrupt, honey. I'm on a roll. Although advanced in years — 83, to be exact — she was sound in mind and body, attended Town Meeting once a year, and played Tchaikovsky with passable skill on an out-of-tune Baby Grand. Or it may have been Brahms. She played passably, but not always recognizably."

Delia puffed on her cigarette. "Into this idyllic picture there arrived one day, a niece — Millicent Tunes — from Jersey City, New Jersey, or some other exotic spot. Millicent, a recently-divorced clinical psychologist, had decided to devote her new-found freedom to meddling in Auntie's affairs."

She glanced over at Stoner. "Not that Miz Lilly had *affairs*, mind you, though there was talk at one time... but I won't bore you with idle sensationalism. To make a long story short, about a month after said niece's arrival, Miz Lilly began to show signs of creeping senility — forgetfulness, confusion, sudden outbursts of laughter or tears. There was a particularly alarming episode in which she climbed up on the fountain and began reciting Whitman. Millicent was concerned, or so she said to anyone who'd listen and some who didn't particularly want to, and wondered if the old lady might be better off in a Home.

"This met with immediate disapproval among the townsfolk, as Castleton has always tolerated an astonishing degree of insanity, being basically inbred and intermarried. The idea was denounced at Town Meeting, and we heard nothing more about Homes. But one morning, when the lilacs were in bloom and the birds mating up a storm in the high-bush cranberries, we were nonplussed to read in the *Augusta Express* that Miz Lilly had been declared legally incompetent, and placed under the guardianship of none other than the elegant Dr. Tunes."

Stoner grunted.

"Town opinion was about equally divided. Some thought Millicent Tunes was a saint and a martyr. The rest of us figured she was up to no damn good.

"Pretty soon strange cars began driving through town. Out-of-state license plates, foreign makes we couldn't even pronounce, much less afford. And trucks. There was work going on out at the Point, and Millicent wasn't using local labor. That caused some erosion among her admirers.

"After a while the trucks stopped coming, but not the strangers. Next thing we knew, word was out Journey's End had been made over into a fancy private mental hospital. We were skeptical at first, but when Mrs. Potts down at the Post Office announced during a session at the Cut 'n Curl that the name on Box 102 had been changed from Journey's End to Shady Acres, we figured we were in trouble."

She poured another cup of tea. "Not that we had anything against a bunch of poor, miserable souls, mind you. But Castleton's never been keen on outsiders, as you can tell from the accommodations at the East Wind. And a hospital, however small and well-meaning, attracts doctors. Doctors attract country clubs and lawyers. Next thing you know, it's Silicon Valley, Maine. Or so goes the local reasoning, which starts at ignorant and peaks somewhere near provincial.

"We had our exceptions, naturally. Bob Surner, who runs the general store and has been known to visit relatives in New York, figured it had to be good for business and laid in a supply of pate and the *New York Times*, which has gone generally uneaten and unread. And Maudie Pruitt — she took over the drugstore when her husband ran off to Millinocket with a chippie from Ellsworth — enrolled in a night course in psychopharmacology, but she didn't last out the semester. About the only real change was, the Harbor House began staying open on weekends year 'round."

"Except during the new moon," Stoner said.

"I'm coming to that." She squeezed Gwen's shoulder. "That other sandwich is for you, too, honey."

Gwen snatched it up. "I don't know why I'm so hungry."

Stoner snickered.

Gwen glared at her.

"For a while things settled down," Delia went on. "We almost forgot about Shady Acres, except when those fancy cars'd come speeding through town, kicking up dust and causing the mothers of small children fits. The kids are in the habit of spilling over into the streets, you see. Then, about a year ago, a couple of local boys — the ones with lobster boats, ambition, and not much energy — started flashing good-sized bills around town, and being mighty close-mouthed about how they came by it. And we never saw Miz Lilly again."

"Where does Dan fit in?" Stoner asked.

"He had his back up right from the start. He'd always had a special feeling for Miz Lilly. Used to set aside the best of his catch every few days and cart it up to Journey's End himself, the way his Dad did. Sometimes he'd cook it up for her, and the two of them'd sit around eating bluefish or cracking lobster shells, and talking about life and the moral decay of the modern generation and the price of shellfish down to Portland, and generally making a mess for the slow-witted village girl."

She stared off into the fire for a moment. Gwen put her hand on Delia's knee.

"Well," Delia said, linking her fingers through Gwen's, "when it started going around that her mind was slipping, Dan wasn't having any of it. 'Something's fishy, Dee,' he used to say to me, sitting in that chair and scowling at the flames. 'They're up to no good, and that's a fact.' 'They' being the elegant Millicent Tunes.

"First off, she told him not to bring his catch up to the house any more. Said Miz Lilly was on a special diet. Dan said he'd never heard of bluefish hurting anyone, senile or not. Tried to make a couple of deliveries, but she tossed him out. That stuck in his craw. And with the lobster boys talking about trawling every time the new moon came around, kind of giggling and giving each other significant looks, he got it into his head to find out what was up."

She shook a fresh cigarette from the pack, thumbed open the matchbook, and found it empty. "Would you get me a pack of matches,

Stoner? Top drawer in the desk."

Stoner unwound herself and opened the drawer. "You have a gun in here."

"Dan figured I might need it."

"Is it loaded?"

"Hell, yes. Waving an empty gun around's a good way to get yourself bumped off."

"Did he find anything?" Stoner asked, lighting Delia's cigarette.

"He did, and he didn't. The more he poked around, the more he was certain there was something illegal going on. And he had a hunch they'd spotted his boat following them on one of those new moon trips."

Stoner settled back in her chair. "Did he have any theories?"

"Well, it looked like the boys were meeting up with some larger boats out to sea. Taking something out, or bringing something in. They'd kinda drift out on the tide, no running lights, until they passed Castle Point, then rev up 'til they came parallel to the house. They'd hang off shore a while, maybe send in a dinghy — it was hard to make out in the dark, which was probably the point of it all — and then high-tail it out to what looked like a good-sized trawler."

"Did he have any idea what the cargo was?"

Gwen looked at Stoner. "Drugs."

"We think Claire might be on drugs," Stoner said. "She has a history of being involved in a minor way."

"Never looked that way to me, but it's possible. Dan didn't even come close to finding out. On his last trip, he didn't come back."

"And you suspect foul play?"

"Wouldn't you?"

"Yes," Stoner said. "I would."

"Dan thought Millicent Tunes was in it up to her elegant nose. If you've read many detective stories, you know nieces can be a nasty lot."

"I hope that hasn't occurred to Aunt Hermione. Is that as much as you know?"

"That's it."

"Have you been to the authorities?"

"After the inquest, I made a lot of noise about cover-ups. Demanded an investigation, threatened to go to the newspapers. Went a bit overboard. You go getting hysterical in a taciturn Yankee community like this and all you get for your trouble is embarrassed silence, a few remarks about 'Mediterranean temperament' — which most of them, incidentally, couldn't spell — and no action. Jared Cargill, he's a local boy, low man on our three-man force. He poked around the police files a bit, bless his heart, but if anybody knew anything, they weren't putting it in writing. State Police wouldn't touch it without a request from the Castleton force, so that was that."

Delia fooled with Gwen's hair, wrapping a strand around her finger, stroking it with her thumb. "To tell you the truth, sometimes I begin to think I'm crazy. But then I remember how Dan was about drinking on the *Delia II*, and it all starts up again. Now you show up, suspicious and thinking Claire's been drugged... Sounds like Lilly Winthrop all over again, doesn't it?"

"She could have had a breakdown," Gwen said. "They might be taking care of her."

"Without telling her family?" Stoner asked. "Does that make sense?"

"It does if they're protecting her," Gwen said.

"Sounds a little too considerate for that bunch," Delia muttered. "Anyway, they'd want to stick her family for the bills. Blue Cross doesn't cover everything."

"What about the car?" Stoner put in.

"She could have done that herself."

"And the way they treated you?"

"I was trespassing."

"Okay," Stoner said, "but explain away the boats, and Dan, and that boy warning us to get out of town."

Gwen shook her head. "I can't. But I'd like to." She looked up at Delia. "It's bad enough to lose someone you love, but to think someone deliberately *took* them..."

"I know what you mean, honey." She crumpled her empty cigarette pack and tossed it in the fire. "Stoner, if I can prevail upon you one more time, I think there's a pack of these killers in the middle drawer."

Stoner got up and looked. "I'm afraid you're out."

"Well, *damn*." She pushed herself up. "You kids hang out here and try to stay out of trouble. I won't be a minute. Want anything from the drugstore?"

Gwen jumped to her feet. "I'll go," she said eagerly.

"Don't bother, honey, I can..."

"It's no bother." Gwen grabbed her coat and ran out the door.

"Watch the steps!" Delia called after her. She shook her head. "Jesus, I hope she knows what brand I smoke. Impulsive, isn't she?"

Stoner fought back a laugh. "Sometimes."

"Sweet kid," Delia said as she closed the door. "High-strung, but sweet." She loaded the dishes on the tray. "Reminds me of my daughter. Guess we might as well do up the dishes." She filled the sink and added a stream of sky-blue detergent. "You want to wash? If I let you dry, you'll put everything away in the wrong places and make me crazy for a week."

Stoner rolled back her sleeves and plunged her hands into the water. "I didn't know you had children."

"Just the one, haven't seen her in twelve years. I'll bet she's going gray, too." She pulled at an ebony curl and let it spring back. "I started turning at thirty, but I touch up. Some day I'll let it go back to normal and scare the villagers half to death."

"Gwen likes you very much," Stoner said.

"Well, I like her, too. There's something unspoiled about her, you know what I mean?"

"Yes." Stoner passed her a plate.

"Unlike you and me. We've got some mileage on us."

"I guess so," Stoner said, not sure how she felt about that.

"Don't get me wrong, I don't mean anything unseemly. You look like you've been knocked around a little, that's all."

"So has Gwen."

Delia held up a glass and inspected it. "But you know it, and she doesn't." Satisfied, she put the glass in a cupboard. "Keep an eye on her, Stoner."

"I intend to." She added more soap to the dishwater. "People are always telling me to look after Gwen. I wonder if her grandmother will change her tune when she finds out what we've been up to."

"If she makes trouble, have her talk to me. I'll tell her what happens when you try to keep a tight rein on your kids." She handed a fork back to Stoner. "Where'd you learn to wash dishes? You left egg on that."

Stoner peered at it. "We didn't have eggs."

"Must have been me, then." She picked at the residue. "Jesus, it must be left over from last Easter."

"What happened to your daughter?" Stoner asked, dropping the fork into the sink to soak. "Or is that personal?"

"Personal? It's public knowledge. Cassie left us. She'd been going with a boy, nice kid, from one of the local farms. He was supposed to register for the draft on his eighteenth birthday. But it was 1972. You know how things were then."

Stoner nodded.

"Instead of signing up, Rob burned his draft card on the steps of the state capitol. It was only a matter of time before they came looking for him." She sighed. "Dan was kind of a flag-waver in those days, World War II vet and all. That was before Watergate took the breeze out of his bunting. Anyway, he got it fixed in his head Cassie shouldn't associate herself with the boy. They had words. Cassie was an independent thinker — we raised her that way — but Dan couldn't stop playing *paterfamilias*. When the boy went to Canada, Cassie went with him."

"Do you know where she is?"

"I got a card from her, from Toronto, a couple of months after they left. Said they were joining some other kids on a commune out in the western provinces somewhere. Might have been a ploy to put the government off their trail. I looked for her to come back after the amnesty, but she didn't. She doesn't know her father's dead."

"It must have been hard on you," Stoner said.

Delia smiled. "I don't have much patience with people who act pitiful, but I went a little pitiful over that."

"Have you tried to find her?"

"Wouldn't know where to start. She's probably changed her name to Raindove or Will-O-The-Wisp or something. I did ask the government for help, but they had more important matters. Couldn't afford a private investigator." She folded her dishtowel and hung it on a rod. "All those scared, brave kids. I wonder what happened to them all."

"I only knew one," Stoner said. "He came back and took over his father's business. The last I heard, he had a house in the Providence suburbs, a wife and three children, a VCR, a BMW, and an American Express Gold Card."

"Rob might have stayed put up there, if they got into farming," Delia said. "Farm work was in his blood."

An idea began to take shape. "What's his last name?"

"Oberlander. He's probably changed it, too. Maybe they got married. I hope so. Cassie was the marrying kind."

"You must worry about her."

"Well, I sure do miss her. But in my heart of hearts, I believe she's all right. If anything happened to her, I'd feel it. It was that way between us." She was silent for a moment. "I'd like to see her again, just to know how she turned out. I feel kind of unfinished about Cassie." She laughed. "Hell, I feel unfinished about everything. I guess when you get all the loose ends tied up, you might as well be dead."

"Cassie," Stoner said. "That's a pretty name."

"Short for Cassandra." Delia grimaced. "That's probably why she left home." She tossed Stoner a fresh towel for her hands. "I could be a grandmother by now. Isn't that a kick?" She went to the living room and peered down into the alley. "Is she *buying* cigarettes over there, or *rolling* them?"

"Want me to check?"

"Don't mind me," Delia said. "I'm a worrier." She flung herself down on the couch. "So what are you going to do about Shady Acres?"

"I don't know. Maybe I could get a job out there. See what I can find out from the inside."

"Forget that," Delia said. "The only non-professional help they hire are in the kitchen. You'd never get beyond the dining room."

"That might be something."

"My cousin, the one who works there part-time, says they never even get to see the patients. Aides do all the serving. They don't let the peons into the dining room until everyone's out. Incidentally, she hasn't seen hide nor hair of your nurse in two weeks."

93

"Maybe she'd be willing to kind of wander around..."

Delia shook her head vehemently. "Not a chance. That one's so timid she won't even jaywalk."

They sat for a moment in gloomy silence.

"If you have any bright ideas," Delia said, "count me in. If I could prove they killed Dan, I might sleep nights."

There was a scuffling noise from the alley below. A garbage can clattered to the ground.

The hairs on the back of Stoner's neck twitched. "What was that?"

"Kids, probably. Or one of Aphrodite's suitors."

She had a feeling it wasn't. She jumped up and went to the window, an alarm sounding in her brain.

She dove for the door.

The drugstore lights were out. Dark shadows filled the alley. One of the shadows was moving.

"Gwen?"

A stifled groan.

"*Gwen!*"

She plunged down the stairs, slipped, grabbed at the railing and felt splinters dig into her hand. Ignoring the pain, she stumbled to the ground and ran toward the alley entrance.

"Gwen."

A chunk of darkness moved toward her. She backed against the stairs.

Overhead, a pistol shot shattered the night. "Sons of bitches!" Delia screamed.

The darkness ran past her and disappeared. Dim light from the street silhouetted a figure hunched over.

"Oh, Jesus." She raced toward it.

"Sons of bitches!" Delia screamed again.

Gwen was on her knees, gasping for breath. Stoner knelt beside her and took her in her arms.

Delia fired another shot. The sharp retort bounced off the walls and was swallowed by fog.

She could feel the blood pounding in her temples. Gently, she raised Gwen's head and cradled her against her shoulder.

"Stoner..."

"It's all right. They're gone."

Gwen's coat was torn. An inky stream trickled from the corner of her mouth.

Oh, Christ. Oh, Christ.

A light wobbled toward them from above. "Delia!"

"Hang on." She reached the ground and ran up to them. She tossed Stoner's jacket around her.

"Get help," Stoner croaked.

"On the way." Delia touched Gwen's face. "You okay, honey?"

"No, she's not okay," Stoner snapped. "They beat her up."

Gwen clutched at her arm.

"Can you get up?" Delia asked.

Gwen shook her head.

Stoner held her tight. "What's the matter with this Goddamn town?"

Delia hurled a string of Greek epithets into the darkness.

"She's bleeding!"

Delia crouched beside them. The metallic odor of burnt gunpowder filled the air.

"We have to get her out of here!" Stoner said desperately.

"Take it easy, honey. Help's coming."

"Did you see them?"

Delia shook her head. "Too dark."

A police car turned into the alley, blue lights flashing. The door flew open and a man got out.

"What'd you do?" Delia barked. "Stop for coffee?"

The man flicked on a flashlight. "Which way?"

Stoner pointed down the alley.

The man ran off into the darkness.

"For Christ's sake," Delia bellowed, "they're half way to Augusta by now!" She fired another shot into the air.

The policeman came back, holding out his hand. "All right, Dee," he said quietly, "give me the gun."

"You *have* a gun."

"I don't want you picking off innocent bystanders."

"There *are* no innocent bystanders."

"Don't give me philosophy, Dee. Give me the gun."

Gwen took a shuddery breath. "I want to go home."

Stoner helped her to her feet.

"Okay," the man said, "what happened?"

"You can take notes in the car," Delia grumbled. "It's colder'n a snowman's prick out here."

"It's a good thing *I'm* on duty. Anybody else'd run you in for disturbing the peace. You got a wicked mouth."

Delia waved the gun. "Don't get pushy, Cargill."

He opened the door to the back seat and lifted Gwen in. Stoner slid in beside her.

"Give me the Goddamn pistol, Dee."

"Like shit I will. You probably don't know how to use it."

"And *you* don't have a license to carry one. Want me to book you on a firearms violation?"

She handed it over and climbed into the front seat. Cargill slipped behind the wheel, slammed the door, and turned up the heater. He took out a pad and pencil. "Now, let's make some sense of this."

"I thought you were a cop," Delia said. "Not a secretary."

95

The policeman ignored her. "Can you tell me what happened?" he asked Gwen.

She was bent over, curled around her stomach. "Two men. Tried to beat me up."

"Get a description?"

Gwen shook her head. "Couldn't see. Too fast."

"You know damn well who they were," Delia muttered.

"Wait your turn, Dee." He turned back to Gwen. "Want a doctor?"

"Sure," Delia said. "Let's trot her on over to Doc Evans. Maybe he can prove she slipped on the ice drunk."

Gwen reached for Stoner's hand. "No doctor," she whispered.

"Are you sure?"

"I just want to lie down." She was shaking all over.

"Where are you staying?" Cargill asked.

"The motel," Delia snapped. "Asshole."

"Look, Dee, I'm going to make allowances for you, on account of you're upset and we go back a long way. But I'd be grateful if you'd let me do my fucking job." He backed the car out of the alley. "Did they take anything?"

"No," Gwen said.

"It was *assault*, for Christ's sake, not robbery," Delia said. She squeezed Stoner's arm. "How's it going?"

"Not well." This isn't happening, she thought wildly. This can't be happening to *her*.

"Would you rather come back to my place?"

"No," Gwen said.

"Is anything broken?" Stoner asked.

"No."

"Check her pockets," Cargill said. "See if everything's there, and give me her driver's license."

"What are you gonna do?" Delia demanded. "Arrest her?"

He ignored her.

Stoner slipped her hand carefully into Gwen's pocket. Her wallet was there, and a pack of Chesterfields. She handed one to Cargill, and the other to Delia.

Delia looked down at the cigarettes in her hand, and began to cry.

"Don't," Gwen said, reaching forward painfully to touch her shoulder. "Not your fault."

"Come on, Dee," the policeman said, his voice gentle, "I need your help. Find me some identification." He handed her the wallet.

"If I hadn't sent her out for these damn things," Delia said, clutching the cigarettes, "this wouldn't have..." She rolled down the car window.

"Not your fault," Gwen said again.

Cargill grabbed Delia's wrist. "Don't toss 'em out. Ten minutes from now you'll have me crawling in the slush tryin' to find 'em."

96

"I'm quitting, Jared. Right now. I'll never smoke again."

He laughed. "I wish I had a nickel for every time I heard you say that, big Mama."

Delia sniffled. "I'm not your Mama, you mangey gum-shoe."

Jared caught Stoner's eye in the rearview mirror and winked. "I spent so much time hanging around Delia when I was a kid, folks used to say I was her illegitimate son."

"You're a bastard, all right," Delia said. "But you sure as hell aren't mine."

"Couldn't resist your cooking, big Mama. That's why I'm so mean." He glanced over at her. "Blow your nose. You sound like my four year old."

He pulled into the East Wind parking lot and stopped, wrote Gwen's name and address in his notebook, and handed back her wallet. "Think you can make it to your room?"

Stoner nodded and handed him the key. She helped Gwen from the car.

Delia turned on the bedside light. Jared lit the heater.

"Christ," Delia said, "this place looks worse every time I see it. Oughta close it down."

Gwen dropped onto the bed and rolled on her side.

Stoner stared at the floor.

Delia pulled a blanket over Gwen. "Jared, do you have to report this?"

"Why?"

"They were out at Shady Acres today, asking questions."

"Shit," Jared said. He turned to Stoner. "Anybody see you?"

"Not me, just Gwen."

"Shit."

"We have to keep this quiet," Delia said.

He rocked back and forth on his heels. His leather holster squeaked. "I'm the only pair of eyes we have over there, Dee. I can't afford to screw up."

"Who's going to tell?"

"The way you were mouthing off, the whole town knows something's up." He chewed his lip. "I gotta make that report."

Stoner had the feeling she was about to get an idea. "Do you have to mention me?" she heard herself ask.

"Guess not. You weren't really involved, were you?"

Delia looked at her through narrowed eyes. "What are you getting at?"

"I'm not sure." She forced a smile. "We'll be fine now. You don't have to stay."

"Well..." Delia said.

Jared jerked his head toward the door. "Come on, Dee. We gotta talk."

97

Hands on hips, Delia faced him down. "What about?"

"For starters, that unlicensed gun." He turned to Stoner. "I'll cruise by every half hour. If you need help, call the station. I can be here in two minutes."

"If you don't stop for coffee," Delia said.

"We have another law around here you might not have heard of, big Mama. Insubordinating a police officer." He turned on his heel and slammed out of the room.

Delia stood by the bed. "You going to be all right, honey?"

"I'll be all right."

She looked at Stoner. "How about you?"

"I think so."

"Leave us alone," Gwen said. "Please?"

"Yeah, I guess that's best. You know where to reach me. Stop by in the morning, okay?"

"Okay," Stoner said, "and thanks."

Delia leaned down and kissed Gwen's forehead. "Honey, did anyone ever tell you you have lousy luck with men?"

Then she was gone.

Alone with Gwen, Stoner steeled herself for what she had to do. First, shift the emotions into neutral.

"I thought they'd never go," Gwen said. Her mouth was stiffening, her voice thick.

Stoner sat beside her. "Is it bad?"

"It'll do." Gwen held herself very still. "Did Delia leave her gun?"

"No, why?"

"I wanted you to put a bullet through my head."

Stoner took her hand. "That's sick."

"I know. I'm going to throw up."

"I don't think that's a good idea."

"Then you'd better come up with an alternative, fast."

Ice. She grabbed the cardboard ice bucket and headed for the door. "You don't have to be brave, you know."

"Yes, I do," Gwen said. "If I start screaming, I'll never stop."

At the ice machine she pressed her head against the cement block wall. She wanted to tear the world to pieces. She wanted to kick and bite and claw until all of Castleton was a pile of broken bones and rubble. She wanted to hunt down that Thing people prayed to as God and smash its smug, impersonal face.

She pounded her fist against the wall. Damn the ugliness. Damn the cruelty. Damn the helplessness. Damn...

Don't crack. You have to help her.

Sucking her skinned knuckles, she scooped up a bucket of ice and ran back to the room.

Gwen hadn't moved.

"Try this," she said, and pressed a cube of ice between Gwen's

98

swollen lips.

Gwen rolled painfully onto her back. Her left eye was nearly shut, her lip was split. Her skin was the color of ashes.

Stoner's stomach tightened. She wrapped ice in a towel and held it to Gwen's eye. "They were from Shady Acres, weren't they?"

"I think so."

"Can you sit up?"

"Can you walk on water?"

"I'll try if you will." She looked around for Gwen's pajamas, found them draped over a chair, and brought them to her. She slipped an arm under Gwen's back. "This'll only take a minute."

"Stoner, I can't," Gwen gasped as she lifted her.

"Lean on me."

She peeled off her coat and shirt. There were finger-print bruises on her arms, ugly splotches on her back and chest and ribs. It made her ache to look at them. "God," she said, "you're a mess."

"I know."

She ran her fingers across Gwen's back. "It'd be a lot worse if you hadn't been wearing that coat."

"I'll hold the thought."

She slipped Gwen's arms through her pajama top sleeves.

Gwen drew in her breath sharply.

"Fall apart if you want."

"I can't. I'm all glass inside. Can we call it a night?"

She eased her back onto the pillow, pulled off her shoes, unbuckled her belt, and somehow managed to slide her under the covers. With a wet towel, she carefully wiped the blood and dirt from Gwen's face.

"How's your stomach?"

"Better. I really didn't want to throw up meatloaf."

"You'd have hurt Delia's feelings. She's very fond of you."

"I don't know why."

"Well," Stoner said softly, "you have a certain charm."

"Tell it to my attackers."

She looked down at the woman she loved, lying hurt and vulnerable in the ugly yellow lamplight, and felt a cold, hard anger.

They're going to pay for this, Gwen. I'm going to make them pay.

"You know what I hate most about this?" Gwen said.

"What?"

"You're taking care of me again."

CHAPTER 6

The world hadn't changed the next morning. Buildings stood where buildings had stood last night. Cars rolled down the street with mute indifference. Gulls put on their usual performance, and the fountain was ugly as ever.

It made her furious.

Even the Clam Shack looked the same. Delia wore her work dress and apron and ragged sneakers. Virge was at his appointed place, in his customary bad mood. The chrome glistened.

Delia looked up as she forced the door shut against the wind. "Everything okay?"

"As well as can be expected."

"I put up a carry-out for you." Delia slipped into a bulky hand-knit sweater and reached for a paper bag. "Mind the store a while, will you, Virge? And keep your thieving fingers out of the pastry."

"Don't get yourself exercised," the man grumbled. "Nothin' in here worth stealin'."

Out on the street, Delia pulled her sweater tighter. "That Virgil. Been sniffing around me ever since Dan died."

"Does he want to marry you?"

"*Marrying* isn't what he's after. I ought to give him the boot, but it passes the time, saying 'no.' Where's your car?"

"I parked on a side street. If no one's connected me with Gwen, I'd just as soon keep it that way."

"Are you going to stay with this thing, Stoner?"

The wind cut through her clothes. "I thought I might."

"Got any plans?"

"Nothing definite. What's in the bag?"

"Bagels, doughnuts, ginger ale, coffee. And money for those damn cigarettes."

Stoner touched her arm. "She doesn't blame you for that, Delia. Nobody does. My guess is, they were trying to scare her off."

"Nevertheless, I feel bad. Last night, every time I reached for one of those buggers, it made my stomach churn." She laughed humorlessly. "I may finally be able to quit. How is she really, Stoner?"

"Scared."

"And you?"

"Mad," Stoner said. "How about you?"

"All of the above. If I didn't have a business to run, I'd go on a rampage."

100

"I don't think this is a good time for you to quit smoking."

She decided not to tell her the worst — about waking in the first oily light of dawn to a sound like the whimpering of a puppy seeking its mother's warmth; about turning on the light to see Gwen, trembling, the realization of what had happened finally sinking in, scarcely able to recognize Stoner through her fear; about aching to hold her but having to sit helplessly by and stroke her hair, because she hurt too much to be held...

"She doesn't look too well," Stoner said.

"I wouldn't imagine."

The wind blew grit into their faces.

"Delia, do you really think those people were from Shady Acres?"

"I know it in my gut. Proving it's another matter."

Stoner thought about what she was planning to do, had spent worried, angry hours working out. It was probably crazy, certainly dangerous, and depended entirely on no one connecting her with Gwen.

"The man who watched us the other night at the Harbor House," she said. "Do you have any clear sense of where he might fit in?"

Delia bent her head into the wind. "That's one I haven't figured out. They close at the new moon. On the other hand, old Charlie Lummox isn't very bright, and wouldn't win any medals for courage. If he's working for that bunch, they're damn fools."

"He's in a position to keep track of who comes and goes in town," Stoner suggested.

"So am I. Nobody's made *me* any offers." She kicked a dented beer can into the gutter. "Still, he does have that new boat."

"Did he take it out last night, do you know?"

"Jared and I swung by there. The Harbor House was closed, but the boat was tied up to the dock. That's a puzzler."

"What about Steve, the waiter? He saw us, too."

"Steve's mind's in his pants. If he and Charlie ever had a contest to see who had the most brains, they'd both lose. As for the rest — the kitchen crew and bartender live over by Camden, don't set foot in Castleton except to moonlight, weekends."

"They must know Dan talked to you," Stoner said. "Aren't you afraid they'll try to get to you?"

Delia shrugged. "They might. I don't much care."

Stoner looked at her. "Do you mean that?"

"Sometimes. After Dan was killed, everyone said I'd get over it, just give myself time. I'm still waiting."

"Maybe you should move away from here. With all the memories..."

"Memories are what I have left. And wanting to see those bastards dangling by their short hairs." She smiled grimly. "If you want to know how Greeks feel about revenge, read Aeschylus."

"I know what you mean," Stoner said.

101

Delia rested her hand on Stoner's arm. "Look, kid, this isn't your fight. Why don't you drop it?"

Stoner rammed her hands in her jacket pockets. "It's turned personal."

"Those people play rough, as you might have noticed."

"They've messed up a lot of lives. Dan's, yours, Claire's, her sister's, maybe Lilly Winthrop's. And now Gwen. Well, that kind of thing messes up my life, too."

They walked along in silence for a while.

"I think I know what you have in mind," Delia said after a while. "And I think it stinks."

"The whole thing stinks."

"You can still walk away."

"I can't turn my back on what I know, Delia. It's a matter of honor." She grinned crookedly. "You can look that up in Aeschylus, too. Anyway, Aunt Hermione says I'm going to live to seventy-two."

"And she has second sight, I suppose."

"She's a practicing clairvoyant. She was born with a caul."

"Wonderful."

"There's just one thing," Stoner said. "I want you to be honest with me. If I stir up a hornet's nest out there, you could get stung. So if you want me to call it off..."

"I said your idea stinks," Delia said. "I didn't say to call it off."

"I don't want Gwen to know yet, not until she feels better."

"Gotcha."

The car was in sight. They quickened their pace.

"I just wish I knew if they know about me. If Charlie Lennox..."

"I think," Delia said, "I know how we might find out." They were almost to the car. "Stoner, where is she?"

Gwen was nowhere in sight.

"No!" Stoner lept forward.

"There you are," Gwen said. She pulled herself up from the back seat, where she lay like a mummy wrapped in the car blanket. "I thought you'd left me here to freeze."

Stoner yanked the door open. "Why didn't you turn on the heater?"

"Carbon monoxide." She spotted Delia behind Stoner's shoulder, and reddened. "Oh. Hi. Good morning."

"It is not. How are you doing, honey?" Delia took Gwen's chin in her hand and tilted her face upward. "I expected worse."

"It *feels* worse."

Gently, Delia touched the bruises under Gwen's eye. "You're going to have a hard time explaining this to your students."

"I'll have to wear sunglasses. They'll probably think I'm stoned."

"Sounds like a good reason to get stoned."

"They'll think I was beaten up."

Delia laughed. "Can't win, can you?"

102

"Not in the Watertown public school system." Gwen fingered her eye gingerly. "This probably violates the dress code."

There was an awkward silence, the kind of silence that happens when there's too much to say and no way to say it.

"Well," Delia said, "I gotta get back, if you can take me on an errand first." She slid into the passenger seat. "You stay in back, honey," she said to Gwen. "And keep out of sight."

"Where are we going?" Stoner asked as she started the car.

"To do a little research."

She directed them down deserted streets and onto a dirt road at the north edge of town, past fields given over to raspberry and juniper. They pulled up in front of a dilapidated farm house. Scrawny chickens flew up from the sand dooryard and settled on the hood of the car. Delia got out and shooed them off. "Stoner, you come with me. Gwen, pull that blanket over you and stay put."

She trudged up the decaying front steps and banged on the door. "Emma! It's Delia. I want to talk to you."

The house was silent.

"I know you're in there, Emma. You're too heathen to be at church, and it's too early for you to be drunk."

The door opened a crack. A middle-aged wreck of a woman peered out. Her hair was unwashed, her bathrobe held together by a series of safety pins. "Jee-sus, Delia, you want to wake the dead?"

Delia shoved the door open, knocking the woman off balance. "Where's your boy?"

The woman stared at Stoner. "What do you want him for?"

"I'm gonna offer him a college scholarship," Delia said sarcastically.

"He's sleeping."

"That's his natural state. Get him down here." She strode into the kitchen.

Stoner followed her.

"Watch where you sit," Delia said. "Emma's not exactly the Homemaker of the Year."

She dusted off a chair with a moldy dishrag and sat down. "See you got a new cat. What'd you do with the old one, eat it?"

"Run off."

"Don't blame it." She offered the woman a cigarette and lit it for her.

A scarecrow of a boy stumbled into the kitchen knuckling his eyes with one hand and scratching his matted head with the other. His chest was white and goose-pimpled above his pajama bottoms. "You call me, Ma?"

"Delia wants words with you," the woman said, and chug-a-lugged her beer.

"Make me some coffee, will ya? Fucking freezing in here." He looked up.

103

"Steve!" Stoner gasped.

His eyes widened. "Hey, what're you doing here?"

"We have some questions for you, Steverino," Delia said.

He looked around. "Where's the other one?"

"None of your business." Delia took a drag on her cigarette. "We had a little trouble at my place last night. You know anything about it?"

"Trouble?"

"Trouble."

"What kind of trouble?"

"Couple of your pals used our friend for a punching bag," Delia said.

Steve turned on Stoner. "I told you to leave, lady. I warned..."

"I'm not a lady," Stoner said. "Don't tempt me to prove it."

"What I want to know," Delia went on, "is what's your part in this?"

"I didn't do anything," he whined. "Can I see her?"

Delia stubbed out her cigarette in a cracked saucer and reached for another. Steve jumped to light it for her. "No, you can't see her. What'd you do to your hand?"

"Accident," he mumbled, hiding his scraped and scabby hand behind his back.

"Accident?" Delia said. "Kiss my foot."

"Listen, you crazy Greek," Emma squealed, "my boy's a good boy. He don't make trouble."

"Your boy's a half-assed cretin. Always was, always will be."

Emma pulled herself up to her full height and swayed a little. "You get outa my house, Delia. Talkin' about my boy that way..."

Delia ignored her. "Maybe you'd like to explain that 'accident'."

"I wouldn't hit her," Steve said earnestly. "Honest, I *like* her."

"I don't give a damn about your personal feelings. I'm asking you how you split those knuckles."

His eyes ricochetted around the room. "I busted Charlie Lennox's jaw."

There was a stunned silence.

Emma lept forward and grabbed Steve by the hair. "I told you a thousand times I don't want you fighting."

"Oh, simmer down," Delia said.

Emma opened another beer and retired to the corner to mumble to herself.

"Maybe you'd better begin at the beginning," Stoner said.

He looked at her pleadingly. "Friday night, after you guys left the restaurant, he followed you."

"Why?"

"Because you were asking questions about Shady Acres. He always told me, 'If anyone asks questions about Shady Acres, you point them out to me. I was only doing my job."

104

"Greetings from the Third Reich," Delia muttered.

"Go on," Stoner said.

"Well, when he got back, he said he was gonna call out there and tell them. He was real mad, kind of talking to himself and calling you dirty names."

"What names?" Delia asked.

"I don't want to know," Stoner said.

"Anyway, I tried to talk him out of it, but he wouldn't listen to me, so I hit him."

"Before or after he made the call?"

"Before."

"Where is he now?"

"In Augusta. At the hospital. They said his jaw's broke."

"How'd he get to Augusta?" Delia asked.

Steve hung his head. "I drove him," he mumbled.

"God damn it," Emma shrieked, "I told you not to drive my car out of town. Brand new second-hand Honda."

"I didn't hurt it, Ma."

"You better fill up the gas tank, Buster. That's all I got to say."

"Emma," Delia said, "the day you've said all you've got to say, there'll be dancing in the streets." She turned to Steve. "What's the connection between Shady Acres and the Harbor House?"

"Mr. Lennox tells them if anybody comes around asking about them." His chest was turning blue from the cold. "That's all I know."

"What about those trawling expeditions?"

His teeth were chattering. "They never let me come along."

"Ever hear any talk about what's going on out there?"

"No."

"What do you know about how Dan died?"

"Nothing."

"How long's Charlie Lennox going to be in Augusta?"

"I don't know. They said his jaw'd be wired for three, four weeks at least." He rubbed his hands over his chest and shifted from one foot to the other.

Delia grinned. "He's not going to be real happy to see you when he comes home, Mister."

Steve's face turned the color of snow. "Oh, shit."

"You lost your job!" Emma bawled. "You lost your Goddamn job!"

"I couldn't help it, Ma. I couldn't let him do nothing to her."

Stoner gripped his shoulder. His skin was like ice. "It's all right, Steve. You did the right thing."

"He lost his *job*!"

The cat left the room.

"Oh, shut up, Emma," Delia said. "The boy can work for me."

He looked at her like a hungry puppy. "You mean that, Delia?"

"Yeah, yeah. Probably do you good. Raise your standards." She looked him up and down. "Come see me later today. And make yourself presentable. You look like an empty buttermilk glass."

"You hear that, Ma? I'm gonna work for Delia."

Delia put out her cigarette and stood up. "Well, it's been real pleasant passing the time with you folks, but I have to get back to work." She handed her pack of Chesterfields to Emma. "You keep 'em. I'm trying to cut back."

As the door closed behind them, Delia muttered something that sounded a little like "Megalopolis-Constantinople-Iphegenia."

"Well," Stoner said, "we found out what we needed to know, but I'm not sure if it's worth it, sticking you with Steverino."

"It puts him where I want him. Under my nose."

Stoner laughed. "Delia, I'm beginning to think you're a soft touch."

"Yeah, a diamond in the rough. Looks like your way's clear, at least until Charlie Lummox gets his voice back."

"Looks like."

"Just for the record, I think you're an idiot."

"Thank you," Stoner said. "You're probably right."

Delia sighed. "Well, give me a lift back to town and get out of here. Keep me informed." She rummaged in her sweater pockets. "Damn, I should have kept a smoke for the ride home."

***

The traffic had grown steadily thicker. Early spring dusk robbed the countryside of color. Beside her, Gwen stirred.

"Almost home," Stoner said. "Glad?"

"I'll be glad to lie down."

"You could have gotten in back."

"Too lonely."

Stoner took her hand. "Your grandmother's going to kill me."

"Who knows what she'll do?" She played with Stoner's fingers. "I don't want you to get the wrong idea, but would you mind if we didn't tell her right away? Only for a few days, until I feel a little tougher."

"It's going to be hard to hide."

"Why, has my hair turned purple?"

"Only your eye. How will we explain that?"

"What?"

"We could say you fell out of the car rounding a curve, or got run over by a herd of stampeding cattle, but I don't think she'd buy it."

Gwen started to laugh. "I mean, not tell her about *us* right away."

"I'm in no hurry. Scared?"

"A little. Guess I'll get used to it, huh?"

"You'll get used to it." So it was starting. Damn it. Why does the world have to make such a big deal of it? It's only love.

She turned on the headlights, switched to high beams, and pulled out beside an eighteen-wheeler carrying a mysterious toxic cargo. The driver blasted his horn and shot ahead, exceeding the speed limit by at least fifteen mph.

"Be my guest," Stoner muttered. She slipped back into the right-hand lane. The truck promptly slowed to forty-five. "Now what's the point of *that*? Isn't life hard enough?"

"I'm not ashamed of us or anything," Gwen went on. "Please don't think that."

"I don't."

"I'd like Aunt Hermione and Marylou to know."

"Oh, God, Marylou. She'll pump me for details. I don't think I can bear it."

"Come on," Gwen said, "you know you love it."

Stoner sighed. "Yeah, I love it."

She wanted to pull the car to the side of the road and take Gwen in her arms and hold her until there was no more holding left in her. She wanted to take her home and put her to bed and crawl in beside her. She wanted to...

"I'd better drop you off at your place," she said. "I'll get the car to you tomorrow if it hasn't been towed."

"Stoner..."

"Or I could leave it with you and take the T."

"Stoner..."

"Unless they're on strike again."

"Stoner, stop the car."

She hit the brake and dove for the break-down lane, nearly causing a ten-car pile-up. "What's wrong? Are you sick?"

"No." Gwen put her arms around Stoner's neck and kissed her. Three carloads of homophobes sped by, horns blaring.

"I want you to know," Gwen said, "how proud I am to be your lover."

For the first time that day, Stoner looked at her. Really looked at her, past the bruises and swelling to her deep brown eyes and perfect nose and fawn hair sprinkled with gray.

This woman wants me. She wants *me*, and there are thousands of days ahead for holding. "I love you," she said, as angels sang.

"I love you, too," Gwen murmured. "I'm sorry the weekend had to end like this."

Stoner ran her fingers through Gwen's hair. "You should have been able to handle those guys. What happened to your karate training?"

"They caught me off guard." She hesitated. "Would you mind... I mean, would it be all right if I stay with you tonight?"

"*All right?*"

"I know it's silly. I just want to be with you. I can call Grandmother

107

from your place. I really can't go to work like this, so it's not as if I'd be up at the crack of dawn making noise or anything..."

"You might be more comfortable at home," Stoner said in a valiant but not-very-sincere effort to be practical.

"I'm going to be miserable, anyway. I'd rather be miserable with you than without you. May I?"

"Of course."

"And can we plan to go to Wyoming this summer?"

"Sure."

"It won't bring back unhappy memories, will it?"

"For a woman with a Master's degree," Stoner said softly, "you ask a lot of dumb questions."

***

"Well," said Aunt Hermione over breakfast, "I see your bed's been slept in."

Stoner fumbled with the jelly jar. "I should have told you, but you were out when we came in."

"Grace had a little party for the coven. It was lovely."

"That's nice," Stoner said.

"Grace thinks I'll be ready for initiation by Lammas, but I don't know. I have such a hard time keeping the herbs straight."

"To say nothing of reversals." She buttered her toast. "I'm sure you'll do fine."

"Perhaps you could make me an athalme. You're so much more mechanically minded than I am."

"I would," Stoner said, "if I knew what it was. Aunt Hermione," she went on quickly before her aunt could start on an explanation that could last for hours, "Gwen and I are lovers."

"Oh," Aunt Hermione said, clasping her hands and nearly upsetting the orange juice, "you have no idea how relieved I am. I don't think I could have borne another week of foreplay."

"Foreplay! Aunt Hermione!"

"Months of moping around the house, talking yourself in and out of moods. Gwen on-again, off-again. If that isn't foreplay, I don't know foreplay."

"Aunt Hermione," Stoner said patiently, "I don't think you understand the subtleties."

"Oh, my dear, I've never understood subtlety. Not in the least."

"She wasn't ready."

"Who's ever *ready*? Whole industries are built on not ready. You weren't ready, either."

"Yes, I was."

"You were not. I know you, Stoner. If you were ready, you'd have thrown yourself at her willy-nilly, and the Devil take the Hindmost, whatever that means."

"Maybe." She poked through the breadbox and found a stale brownie. It tasted a little like coffee grounds.

"Tell me, dear, what was the situation in Maine?"

"Not clear, but something's definitely up."

"I don't suppose," her aunt said, "you met any interesting cats."

"Sorry, no. Gwen tripped over one, but I didn't meet it."

"Well, never mind. When it's time for us to have a cat, we'll have a cat."

"Aunt Hermione, about Shady Acres..."

"Isn't that a perfectly ridiculous name? Shady Acres. It sounds like that terrible old sit-com with Eddie Albert and Zsa Zsa Gabor."

"I may have to do something... I don't want you to worry, but it could be..."

Aunt Hermione waved her fork. "Whatever you decide to do, Stoner, I'm sure will be quite sensible."

"*I'm* not sure."

"Should I do a reading for you?"

"I'd appreciate it."

Her aunt took a small Week-at-a-glance appointment book from the pocket of her smock. "I'll put you in tomorrow evening, between the blue-eyed Taurus and the Capricorn from Brockton." She frowned. "What am I thinking of? A Taurus and two Capricorns back-to-back? I'll be utterly drained, all that attention to detail."

"Could we make it tonight?"

"Of course. Gwen can help. It's so much easier to meditate with a Pisces present."

"Aunt Hermione, am I a drain?"

"Only at times, dear. Capricorns *do* have their uses."

Stoner smiled. "I'll bet you can't think of any at the moment."

"Well," her aunt said, "they're good around the house."

Gwen appeared in the doorway, still in her pajamas and wearing Stoner's bathrobe. "Who's good around the house?"

"Capricorns," Stoner said.

"I don't know about the rest of the house," Gwen said, "but they're good around the bedroom. Coffee." She scuffed to the stove.

Stoner turned her face to the wall.

"Gwen, dear," said Aunt Hermione, "I'd offer congratulations, but Stoner would probably kill me. She's very complex this morning."

"She wasn't complex last night," Gwen said. She fingered the brownie. "What's *that*?"

"A brownie," Stoner muttered.

"Looks like a dead sponge." She took her coffee to the table.

Stoner dropped the brownie into the trash.

"I think we should have a ceremony of commitment," Aunt Hermione said. "I'll summon the coven. We have a telephone tree, you know."

"We are *not*," Stoner said firmly, "ready to involve the coven."

"Not until I've had coffee," Gwen said.

Aunt Hermione perused her appointment book. "Perhaps on the next Esbat."

"That sounds like a good time," Stoner said, having not the faintest idea what an Esbat was.

"It could be a lovely celebration. Stoner, dear, would you hand me the cole..." She noticed Gwen's bruised eye. "My, Stoner, I never knew you were like *that*."

"I'm not 'like that'! She was beaten up by two men."

"Well, thank goodness. I try to be broad-minded, but I must admit I can't quite warm up to M and S."

Stoner slammed the bowl of coleslaw down on the table. "S and M."

"This is good coffee," Gwen said.

"Thank you, dear," Aunt Hermione said. "Nescafe instant run through the Melitta. Stoner wants us to boycott Nestle products, but they own half the food industry. One would have to give up eating. There's always Beatrice, of course, but they're probably just as bad, it just hasn't come to light yet. Tell me, how does it feel to be counter-culture?"

Stoner banged her head against the wall.

Aunt Hermione clucked. "Now that you're part of the family, Gwen, I hope you can break her of that dreadful habit. She's going to do serious damage someday. To herself, or to the foundation."

"After I have my coffee," Gwen said.

"I have to go to work now," Stoner said, trying to muster a little dignity.

"Run along," her aunt said. "Gwen and I have a lot to discuss."

Gwen blinked. "We do?"

"Your grandmother." She sighed plaintively. "I love Eleanor dearly, I pray for her nightly, but sometimes she's so, so..."

"Straight," Gwen said.

"Square," said Aunt Hermione. "But they're the same thing, aren't they? Interesting how the language changes. I wonder what it means." She ruminated over her coleslaw. "Yes, we definitely have to do something about Eleanor."

"I'd welcome any suggestions," Gwen said.

Stoner cleared her throat. "I'm going to work now."

"Friday night," Aunt Hermione said to Gwen, "I invited her to a very nice place down on Washington Street to see the male strippers. And she absolutely refused to go along."

"Aunt Hermione," Stoner said, "that's the *Combat Zone*."

"It's never been very combative when *I've* been there. Don't get me wrong, I don't care about male strippers, when you've seen one you've seen them all..."

"Good-bye, everyone," Stoner said loudly, "I'm off to work."

"... but you'd think she'd try it just once. My goodness, *everyone*, goes to male strippers. It's quite respectable."

"See you tonight."

"It isn't as if I'd suggested lady mud wrestlers." She looked up. "Did you say something, Stoner?"

"I'm leaving."

Aunt Hermione kissed her cheek, "Come in quietly when you get home, dear. I have a late Leo, and you know how they are."

"Don't wear Gwen out, okay? She doesn't feel too well."

"I'll put her back in bed," Aunt Hermione said, "and give her a nice healing tea."

"Don't drink *anything*," Stoner said to Gwen, "unless she looks it up first."

Gwen got to her feet shakily. "I should go home. I don't want to be a burden."

"For God's sake, Gwen." She turned to her aunt. "Make her listen to reason, will you?"

"Listen to reason, Gwen," Aunt Hermione said, attacking the coleslaw.

At the door Stoner took Gwen in her arms. She felt small and fragile. Stoner kissed her gently. "Be here when I get home, please? Don't make me think it was all a dream."

Gwen nodded. "Have a nice day at the office, dear."

***

For once, the weather wasn't behaving like a bleacher bum at Fenway park, drunk on Ego and Attracting Attention to Itself. Enough sunlight to cast shadows, too little to give them definition. No promise of spring in the air, no threat of regression to winter. Nothing hovering in the wings. An archetypcal March nothing day. The kind of weather nobody talked about. Over at Channel 5, the meteorologist must be going nuts thinking up ways to be cute without the aid of "muggies" or "thunder-boomers" or "just ducky's."

A dog of dubious parentage trotted by on important business. It struck her that, in addition to its other peculiarities, Castleton had no visible dogs. Any town without wandering mongrels was lacking an essential human dimension. Maybe the secret of Shady Acres was Body Snatchers, growing pods in the conservatory and shipping them out at the new moon.

A few doors from the travel agency, she paused to catch her breath and steel herself. She lingered over a display of half-price leftover St. Patrick's Day cards, delaying the inevitable. It was going to be

111

a raucous day.

Come on, just because you're pleased enough to burst is no reason to go shy.

But I don't know what to do with good news.

Other people jump up and down and squeal.

She pictured herself bounding up to Marylou with glad cries of, "We did it! We're lovers!" The two of them leaping hand-in-hand among the travel posters.

It made her want to crawl under the nearest car.

Which happened to be a beat-up Volkswagen with limp springs. She took a deep breath and pushed open the door.

"Well," said Marylou, "how was Maine?"

"Fine." Not looking at her, Stoner slipped into the closet.

Marylou followed and blocked the door. "Fine? What does that mean, fine?"

"Just... fine."

"Anything new?"

She pulled off her coat and tossed it on a hook. "We found Claire."

"Wonderful!"

"Well, not so wonderful, really." She brushed her hands through her hair. "We think she's being held prisoner."

"Really?"

"Something's going on up there."

"*Something's* going on everywhere."

"We met this woman, Delia? She runs a restaurant..."

"What kind of restaurant?"

"It's called The Clam Shack."

Marylou winced.

"She thinks they killed her husband."

"Who?"

"The Shady Acres people."

"Why?"

"Because he found out something."

"What?"

"We don't know."

"We," Marylou said tonelessly.

"Gwen and I."

"I figured Gwen and you. Gwen and you being the only 'we' in the immediate vicinity. Why didn't you call me last night?"

"It was late. I was tired. I wanted to wait until I saw you to fill you in." She moved toward the door. "Want to let me out of here?"

"Not until you tell me what you're feeling guilty about."

"I don't feel guilty about anything," Stoner said, feeling guilty.

"Then why won't you look at me?"

Stoner forced herself to look. "Where in the world did you get that blouse?"

"My sister sent it from Hawaii. Stoner..."

"Are those hibiscus?"

"Probably."

"Or is it hibisci?"

"How should I know?" Marylou snapped. "What's the matter with you?"

Stoner shuffled her feet and wondered what to do with her hands. "Uh... Gwen and I are ... uh ... lovers." She waited for the Roman candles to go off.

"Well," Marylou said. She stretched to reach the overhead shelf and took down a bag of cookies. "Want a Swirly-Q?"

"We're lovers," Stoner repeated. "Not as in 'we made love,' as in 'lovers'."

"I guessed as much, what with all the 'we'-ing." She offered her the bag. "Sure you don't want one? They're not as good as they were when they first came out."

Bewildered, Stoner shook her head.

"But then" Marylou muttered, "who is?"

"Marylou..."

"Less fudge. Tougher. Do they think we don't notice?"

"Marylou, aren't you glad?"

"Why should I be glad?" She strode to her desk. "I *like* fudge."

Stoner trailed after her. "About Gwen and..."

"I said congratulations, didn't it?" Marylou began rooting in her bottom drawer.

"No, you didn't."

"Well, congratulations." She slammed the drawer. "I'm delighted."

"You don't sound it."

Marylou glanced up. "I have a lot on my mind, love."

"What's wrong?"

"The building next door's going condo. I think we're next." She opened another drawer.

"If we're going condo, the landlord would have given us notice." Stoner sat on the desk. "We'll find another place."

"Will we?" She slammed that drawer. "Maybe it's time for a change, anyway. You don't want to spend the rest of your life cooped up in a marginally successful travel agency with me."

"I like being cooped up in a marginally successful travel agency with you."

"Booking moonlight cocktail cruises to Revere."

"There's nobody else in the world I want to be cooped up in a marginally successful travel agency with."

"Senior citizen tours to Plimouth Plantation."

"Marylou..."

"Whale watches."

"Mary*lou*."

113

"What?"

"What's the matter with *you*?"

"Nothing's the matter with me. I *adore* whale watches. Flukes turn me on."

"You've never been on a whale watch."

Marylou played the first bar of 'Tara's Theme' on her touch tone phone.

"I thought you'd be happy. About Gwen and ... "

"It's hardly a news flash, Pet. You've been in a state of arousal for seven months."

Hurt, Stoner retreated to her own desk. "I take it you're neither surprised nor pleased."

"Of course I'm pleased," Marylou said. "Surprised, I'm not. For Heaven's sake, Stoner, you sat on the Swirly-Q's."

She slammed her hand down on the desktop. "Damn it, I don't need this!"

Marylou started, stared, and appeared to change channels. She got to her feet and came over to her. "I'm sorry, Pet. Condo conversion drives me wild. I have visions of the end of Kesselbaum and McTavish."

Stoner almost believed her.

"You know I'm glad about the two of you. What kind of a friend would I be if I weren't glad?"

"I'd understand if you were worried. Sometimes it changes things."

Marylou threw back her head and laughed — a little too loudly. "Change *you*? If you ever changed, the planets would spin out of their orbits."

"I just wondered."

"How's Gwen, by the way?" Marylou asked, digging in the package for an unbroken cookie.

"Not too well. She was beaten up by two men."

"Outrage! That would never happen in Boston."

"It happens in Boston all the time."

Marylou waved her cookie. "Maybe in the suburbs. Should I send flowers?"

"She'll be all right. Aunt Hermione's doing something for her, God knows what."

"So she's at your house," Marylou said in a carefully casual tone. "Is that permanent?"

"Only for a day or so." She felt tired. "She didn't want to cope with her grandmother's reaction."

"Understandable, considering."

"To her being beaten up. We're keeping the other quiet for a while."

"I see."

"Only you and Aunt Hermione know."

114

"Well," said Marylou, "I feel privileged."

"Marylou..."

She perched on the edge of her desk and swung her leg. "So tell me all about it. Was it torrid?"

"Sort of."

"Details, please."

Stoner laughed. "I am *not* going to tell you the details of my sex life."

"I tell you the details of mine," Marylou pouted.

"You're different."

"No, Pet. By all available statistics, *you're* the one who's different."

Things seemed to be getting back to normal. Stoner tilted her chair against the wall. "You know I don't talk about things like that. I didn't tell you about Agatha, did I?"

"You didn't have to. I'm sure *that* was completely sordid and debauched."

Sordid, not debauched. Actually, debauched sounded kind of interesting. "Have you ever been debauched?" she asked.

Marylou pondered. "The associate professor in Civil Engineering from M.I.T. That was debauched. I *think* it was debauched. It *seemed* debauched."

"What did you do?"

"I don't really remember, to tell you the truth. We did it in a hot tub and threw my electrolytes off balance."

"That doesn't sound particularly debauched."

"With two dolphins and a harbor seal?"

Stoner hurled a pencil at her. "You made that up."

Marylou shrugged. "You asked. Do you want to go to lunch, or work?"

"Work, I guess. Is there work?"

"Party of eighteen," Marylou said, shuffling papers. "For a charter to Orlando."

"You already tried that one on me."

"This is for real." She passed Stoner a list of names and dates. Her feet hit the floor. "Our first charter! Marylou, we're a success!"

"Only if you can manage not to lose them."

***

By four o'clock she had booked the charter — which, with luck, would remain aloft for the entire trip — and was growing increasingly restless. She wondered how things were going at home. She wondered what Gwen was doing. She wondered how she was going to bring up the subject of her plan for Shady Acres.

Gwen wasn't going to like it. Marylou wasn't going to like it. Aunt

115

Hermione *might* not like it. Her therapist, Edith Kesselbaum, probably wouldn't like it. She didn't like it herself. She didn't like it even more than anyone else wasn't going to like it.

But she couldn't think of an alternative.

She tried unsuccessfully to straighten out the month's accounts. She watched the people walking by the window, but they bored her. It was a typical Monday afternoon at Kesselbaum and McTavish. Nothing was happening.

"Marylou, do you need me?"

"Always, love."

"I mean, for the rest of the day?"

"Not noticeably." Marylou looked up from the mysterious forms she was always filling in. "Going home to debauch?"

Stoner clenched her fists. "She isn't well, Marylou. I'm concerned, okay?"

"Sure, go." She dismissed her with a wave of her hand. "Nothing here I can't handle."

As she passed Marylou's desk, Stoner looked down. "Where do you get all that paperwork?"

"We live in a bureaucracy."

"How come you never let me do it?"

"Because you're incompetent." She looked up and batted her eyelashes. "About things like this."

"I guess I am. Marylou, are you sure you're all right?"

"I'm fine. Mind if I drop over later?"

"You never had to ask before."

Marylou looked back down at her paper.

"Nothing's changed, Marylou."

"Yes, it has, Pet," Marylou said, scratching out a column of figures and starting over. "Everything's changed."

***

Gwen was curled up in a corner of the kitchen loveseat, reading. She looked a little better.

"How do you feel?" Stoner asked.

"Like a million. Aunt Hermione works miracles."

"What did she do?"

"Gave me some kind of herbal something. It tasted like poison, but I haven't slept so well in months."

"Did she mention what it was?"

"Valerian, I think. She says it causes hallucinations and draws rodents. Should I worry?"

"Only if you start hallucinating rodents." Stoner slipped her hands into her back pockets. "Uh ... did she do anything else?"

"Not as far as I know."

"I was afraid she'd try to cast a spell."

"She burned some incense and mumbled a little. Is that what you mean?"

Stoner sank onto the loveseat. "I wish she wouldn't do that."

"It can't do any harm, Stoner. It's only white magic."

"Someday she's going to be tempted."

"She won't," Gwen said firmly. "She believes in *karma*."

"There's trouble down the road. I know it."

Gwen closed her book and put her glasses down. "For someone who doesn't believe in the occult, you're as superstitious as a Medieval peasant."

"Just because I don't believe in it doesn't mean I can't worry about it."

"She talked to Grandmother," Gwen said.

"How did it go?"

"She was upset, but not hysterical."

"How much did she tell her?"

"That I'd been mugged. Why didn't we think of that?" She sighed. "Aunt Hermione has the rare talent of making everything seem matter-of-fact."

"Everything *is* matter-of-fact to her."

Gwen pulled her feet up and wrapped her arms around her knees. "You're tired, aren't you?"

"It's been a long day."

It was beginning to drizzle, to the delight, no doubt, of the Channel 5 meteorologist.

"How's Marylou?"

Stoner gazed out into the twilight. "Strange."

"I'm not surprised."

"You're not?" She drew a frown-face on the misted window pane. "She's been your closest friend for more than twelve years."

"I'm not going to turn all *weird*, for God's sake."

"You know that," Gwen said. "I know that. But how can Marylou know it?"

Stoner turned away from the window. She was, frankly, tired of feeling responsible, tired of worrying, tired of problems. She'd almost welcome Shady Acres. That, at least, was clear-cut, us-against-them, the good guys versus the bad guys. Nothing murky, nothing bittersweet, no overtones or undertones. Just good, old-fashioned danger.

Except for the house.

"Did she threaten my life?" Gwen asked.

"No."

"This *isn't* going to interfere with your friendship, is it, Stoner?"

"Not on my part."

"It better not. I won't stand for it."

Stoner looked at her. "You're really are remarkable, you know."

"I am not."

"You are. Some people would be jealous of Marylou."

"That's silly."

"I love you," Stoner said.

"I heard a rumor to that effect." Gwen poured a cup of coffee and handed it to her. "By the way, Aunt Hermione also called Nancy Rasmussen."

"What did she tell her?"

"That there was something going on at Shady Acres, and Claire was caught in the middle. Incidentally, Claire doesn't have any history of mental illness — not even normally neurotic, apparently. And Nancy was pretty sure she wouldn't willingly take drugs."

Stoner sipped her coffee thoughtfully. "So that means..."

"Coercion. How long do you have to be crazy on drugs before you stay that way?"

"Probably not long."

Gwen frowned and traced the pattern of veins on the back of Stoner's hand with her fingertips. "Stoner, what are you planning to do?"

She looked away. "I haven't decided."

"Yes, you have." She waited. "Out with it."

"I guess ... " Stoner said reluctantly "... I'll check into Shady Acres as a patient."

Gwen's hand went dead. "I thought so." She was silent for a long time.

"Aren't we going to fight about it?"

"Would it make any difference?"

Stoner shook her head.

"I wish you wouldn't."

"If you can come up with another way," Stoner said, "I'll jump at it."

"You could just drop it, I guess. It's not your problem."

"After what they did to you?"

Gwen put one hand over her heart and raised the other. "I swear to hereby release you from all obligations on my behalf."

Stoner smiled. "I'm afraid that won't do it. It's a matter of honor."

"Damn," Gwen said. "I've signed on for a lifetime of irrefutable arguments." She sighed. "The world is full of nice, selfish people who don't care what happens to anyone but themselves. Why did I have to fall in love with *you*?"

"If you asked me not to do it, for your sake, I wouldn't."

"Would you ever forgive yourself?"

"I doubt it."

Gwen rested her elbows on her knees and stared at her hands.

"Well, then, there's not much I can do but get behind the damn project, is there?"

"You could threaten to leave."

"I love you," Gwen said, and kissed her. "And you couldn't get me out of your life with a Roto-Rooter."

Stoner held her. "I'm frightened, Gwen."

"*You're* frightened? I'm so frightened I may take up black magic."

From the front of the house came a banging sound like someone moving a piano.

Gwen sat up. "What's that?"

"Either a Sagittarius leaving, or Marylou's paying us a visit."

A hand crept around the corner of the swinging door. The hand held a bottle of champagne.

"That doesn't look like Sagittarius behavior to me," Gwen whispered.

"Hi," Marylou said. "Do you have a few minutes for a contrite jackass?"

"For you," Gwen said, "always."

"I thought we might raise a glass together after I apologize."

"There's nothing to apologize for," Stoner said. "I understand."

Marylou rolled her eyes. "Spare me your understanding. It takes all the fun out of guilt." She perused the cupboards. "I behaved abominably. I insulted you, I insulted Gwen, and I insulted our deep and undying friendship. I've made an appointment to be drawn and quartered immediately after dinner. Gwen, love, you look like something left by the side of the road. Don't you have any Dixie cups?"

"Thank you," Gwen said. "Dixie cups?"

"Never drink champagne from proper glasses. It cheapens the experience."

Stoner got up. "We're out of Dixie cups. Will jelly glasses do?"

"They'll have to." She handed Stoner the champagne.

"Knowing Stoner," Gwen said, "you haven't heard any of the lurid details. Let's have lunch soon."

"Now I know why I love you," Marylou said. "Can you get away tomorrow?"

"Oh, brother," Stoner said. She held up the bottle. "What am I supposed to do with this?"

"Open it, Pet. Unless you have a nuclear sub you want to christen."

"I can't open these things. They frighten me."

Marylou snatched the bottle, unpeeled the gold foil, and popped the cork. It hit the ceiling and landed in the sink.

"Stoner's planning to check in to Shady Acres," Gwen said.

"That's the most absurd idea I've ever heard." She splashed champagne into glasses. "She should be locked up."

"She's going to be."

119

"And you approve?"

"No."

"Then stop her."

"I can't," Gwen said. "It's a matter of honor."

"Honor!" Marylou waved the bottle. "Honor went out at the end of World War II."

"Marylou..." Stoner said.

"There are unbalanced people in those places, Stoner. Ask your therapist."

"I was counting on her to get me in."

"Mother will get you in, all right. She's as crazy as you are."

"I don't know what else to do, Marylou."

"Go to the cops."

"Claire's on probation."

Marylou tapped her foot.

"We're not sure enough of anything," Gwen said. "We have suspicions, some funny goings-on... Nobody knows anything. When Delia tried to get the police to help her..." She shrugged.

"From the looks of your face, they're not running a health club up there."

"But we can't prove a connection," Stoner reasoned.

"Maybe Max could call up a few old buddies from the Bureau."

"Your father's retired," Stoner said. "And if we can't go to the police with what we have, we certainly won't get a rise out of the FBI. We don't even know for sure if there's been a crime."

"If there hasn't been, there will be before you're through. You attract trouble like a magnet."

"I do?"

"Why can't you be more like Gwen?"

"Please," Gwen said. "It hurts when I laugh."

Marylou sighed. "All right, once you're inside, what's the plan?"

"I don't have a plan."

"Take a gun."

"I don't have a gun."

"Well, get one."

"In the first place," Stoner said, "I don't want a gun. I don't like guns."

"It wouldn't have to be a big one. Get one of those pretty little ladies' guns with a pearl handle."

"And in the second place, they probably search you."

"They probably do a lot worse than that."

"It's a mental hospital, Marylou. Not the Black Hole of Calcutta."

"I'm telling you," Marylou said, "those places are filled with twisted, demented, deranged, potentially violent people."

Stoner was shocked. "That's not a nice way to talk about mental patients."

"I'm not talking about patients!" Marylou shrieked. "I'm talking about the *staff*."

"Look," Gwen said, "I'm frightened enough. Can't we try to be a little optimistic about this?"

"You were eager enough," Stoner added, "to send me off to Wyoming after a murderer."

"We discussed *that* after dinner," Marylou said. "I can't be optimistic on an empty stomach."

"All right," Stoner laughed, "I get the hint. As soon as Aunt Hermione's finished with the Sagittarius, I'll run out for Chinese. What would you like?"

"Sweet and sour crow."

"Marylou," Gwen said, "It's perfectly normal for you to feel the way you do, but..."

"Normal! How disgusting!"

"Well, when you get tired of self-flagellation, there's something I need your help with."

"What's that?"

"Delia's daughter ran away to Canada. I'd like to try to find her."

Marylou rubbed her hands together. "Marvelous! Our own mystery!" She turned to Stoner. "How soon are you leaving?"

"As soon as Edith can arrange it."

"Well," Marylou said, picking up her jelly glass, "I want to propose a toast. To danger, love, and deviance."

"To friendship," Gwen said.

"To Charlie's Angels," Marylou said. She downed half her glass. "Don't count on me, though. Self-flagellation sounds lusciously kinky."

CHAPTER 7

Clutching her suitcase, Stoner hung back in the doorway and stared at the floor. Edith had warned her not to giggle. She had never felt less like giggling in her life.

Dr. Edith Kesselbaum smiled at the fat little man in the baggy business suit and steel-rimmed glasses. In his left hand he held the stringy, well-chewed stump of a cigar. With his right he fondled the chart he had been reading when they interrupted him. His fingers resembled over-fed maggots.

Edith turned to her. "Come meet Dr. Lefebre, Stoner. Dr. Lefebre is Shady Acres' clinical director. Doctor, my patient, Stoner McTavish."

She hoped he wouldn't try to shake hands. To touch that lump of stretched and swollen flesh... She shuddered and looked back at the floor.

"Hostile?" he asked, indicating Stoner with a tilt of his head.

"Withdrawn," said Edith. "One of her most troubling problems. It's my hope, in a setting like this, she can work on forming object relations. I know you'll encourage any attempt on her part to reach out."

He uttered a non-committal grunt.

"But she mustn't be pushed," Edith went on. "Let her move at her own pace. She frightens easily."

Dr. Lefebre cleared his throat with a sound like beans in a tin can. "We're professionals here, Dr. Kesselbaum. Highly trained professionals. I'm sure you'll agree we are capable of formulating an adequate treatment plan."

"Oh, absolutely," Edith gushed. "Shady Acres has quite a reputation with the Boston Psychoanalytic Society." She didn't say what kind of reputation.

He drew his own conclusions. "So you see she'll be in good hands."

Good God, not *those* hands.

Dr. Lefebre plucked a file from the "In" basket and opened it. His fingers crawled down the page. His flabby lips moved as he read silently to himself. "Seems to be in order," he said, and picked up a gold-plated Mark Cross pen. "Special precautions? Suicidal?"

"Goodness, no," Edith said. "She's Catholic."

He glanced back at the admission papers and raised an eyebrow. It looked like a shocked caterpillar. "Nothing here under religious affiliation."

"Really?" Edith snatched the papers and took an interminable

122

amount of time to locate her glasses. "My secretary drew them up. Competent secretarial help is a thing of the past, don't you think?"

The doctor nodded. "I could tell you stories..."

Edith granted him a moment of sympathetic silence.

"We don't have a priest here," he said.

"Not to worry, we'll get a dispensation. The Bishop is a personal friend. Now," she said briskly, "if we could see her room, I'll settle her in and be on my way."

Stoner was gripped by a wave of anxiety.

"The aides take care of that."

"I'd better come along," Edith said. "It'll ease the transition."

He scowled, his caterpillar eyebrows mating briefly. "It's against hospital policy."

"And a very wise policy it is, too. The last thing one wants is strangers cavorting about the halls at all hours. However, in this case..."

"If we make an exception for one, they'll all expect it."

"I understand, of course."

Don't leave me here like this! Stoner thought in a panic. "Dr. Kesselbaum..."

Edith moved closer to the desk. "To tell you the truth, Roland ... I may call you Roland, mayn't I, professional to professional? I'm having just the teeniest countertransference problem in her case. My consulting analyst recommended acting it out. I may have an insight."

"Insight," Lefebre grunted. Apparently, he didn't approve of insight.

"I know, I know, it's such a bore. But one of the risks one faces working with patients."

"I don't work with patients," the doctor said. "I make decisions."

"Well, I envy you that, I certainly do." She sighed heavily. "I had hoped for a break-through, but the rules are rules, I suppose."

"Dr. Kesselbaum," Stoner said urgently, "please don't..."

Edith patted her shoulder. "Now, Stoner, you mustn't cause trouble. I'll wait right here while you unpack. Dr. Lefebre and I can have a nice, long chat. But try not to move at your usual snail's pace. I'm sure the doctor has many, many important decisions to make."

Lefebre pressed a button on his desk. "All right, you can go up. Just make it quick."

A large, florid-faced man in white appeared in the doorway.

One of Gwen's attackers?

"Hank, show Dr. Kesselbaum and her patient to ... " He consulted a chart. "Thirty-three B." He smiled unctuously at Edith, revealing an uneven row of tobacco-stained teeth. "On the east side, facing the ocean."

"Wonderful," Edith said. "Water is very therapeutic."

"We don't do hydrotherapy."

123

"Moving water. The sight of moving water. It mesmerizes and calms, don't you know?"

He stared at her, a toad taking aim.

"According to some of the newer theories," Edith added quickly. "I'm a traditionalist myself, but one must keep an open mind. Freud himself was known to experiment."

"*We*," Lefebre announced regally, "prefer a combination of depth-oriented psychiatry and behavior modification."

"Interesting," said Edith. "One wonders, of course, at the logical inconsistency of crucial juxtapositions of essentially diverse orientations."

Stoner suppressed a smile. Edith had just called Lefebre a fool, and he was too much of a fool to know it. But she hoped she wouldn't get started on behavior modification. Edith had been known to assault it for hours, summing up her arguments with, "In a nutshell, anyone who profits from Behavior Mod deserves it."

"Excuse me," she said timidly, "I'd really like to..."

"Yes!" Edith exclaimed, coming to her senses. She nodded to Dr. Lefebre. "We've wasted enough of the doctor's valuable time."

"When you've unpacked," he explained to a spot on the wall about three feet from Stoner's left ear, "one of the other guests can show you around."

"Guests," Edith said. "How egalitarian."

His eyes made momentary, cold contact with Stoner's. "We know you'll enjoy your stay with us."

Enjoy? This is a mental hospital, for God's sake, not Camp Carefree in the Catskills.

She lowered her eyes. "Thank you." And followed Hank and Edith from the office.

They climbed a wide central staircase to the third floor. Stoner glanced around uneasily. "Check your exits," Edith had warned. Other than the front door, there seemed to be none at all.

"No locks," Edith was saying to Hank approvingly. "Very progressive."

"Don't need 'em."

"What do you do about violent patients?"

"Don't keep 'em."

"Do you have electro-shock facilities?"

He glanced over his shoulder at Stoner. "She gonna need it?"

Edith laughed. "Goodness, no."

"Good. Ties up staff time. They wander around after shock. We gotta keep after 'em in case they go over the cliff."

"Have you lost many that way?" Edith chatted on.

"One or two, but they was senile anyway."

"What are your arrangements in case of fire?"

"*Never* had a fire."

124

"I'm glad to hear it. Still, an old building like this, exposed to the wind. One worries."

Worries? *Worries?* One is frantic!

"Fire doors end of the hall," Hank growled. He glared at Stoner. "Locked, so don't get ideas about takin' social trips between floors after lights out." He turned back to Edith. "Fire escapes on the outside."

"And of course you have drills."

"Listen, Doc, you got a bunch like this to handle, you don't round 'em up unless you hafta."

"Doc," Edith murmured. "That has a friendly sound."

They had reached the top of the stairs. In a large central area stood a desk and chair, and behind them a white metal cabinet containing a collection of bottles. "Medications," Hank said. "Stay outa there." He indicated a pair of broken-down couches. "These are for staff. You wanta hang around, go down in the conservatory."

He strode through the hall and pushed open a door. "Yours."

Feeling like a lamb led to slaughter, Stoner stepped inside. The room was small, dirty white, and except for a bed, bureau, bedside table, and tiny closet, totally bare. A single window, flanked by dusty curtains, looked out to the gray sea. The sky was the color of pewter. In the distance, the fog bank was forming on the horizon. Stoner bit her lip.

"No desk," Edith said.

"This ain't a motel, Doc."

Arms folded, Hank leaned against the wall and watched them unpack. It didn't take long. Not nearly long enough. When they had finished, Edith turned to him. "If you'll leave us alone for a minute, we'll say our good-byes and I'll be on my way."

"No visitors."

"I'm hardly a visitor," Edith said.

"No visitors, Doc."

"Young man..."

He shook his head. "I got my orders."

Edith drew herself up to her full 66 ¾ inches. "This is not the Army, young man. I am a psychiatrist. If it *were* the Army, I would outrank you."

He wasn't impressed. "No visitors."

"Well," said Edith, "in that case..." She slipped a folded bill from her coat pocket. "Do you take bribes?"

"Maybe." He studied the bill, reading the fine print.

"It's not counterfeit," Edith said. "Give us five minutes. That's a dollar a minute, more than I make."

"Shrinks around here make more'n that."

"Well, you see, I don't have a yacht to feed. What's it going to be, take it or leave it? I don't bribe on a sliding scale."

125

He pocketed the money and left without speaking.

"Nazi," Edith muttered.

Stoner sat on the bed and gripped the metal frame.

"This is a terrible place, Stoner. Are you sure you want to stay?"

She nodded and tried to smile, but her mouth trembled. She turned away quickly to hide it. "I always wondered what boarding school would be like."

"If I were really your therapist..."

"You are."

"... I'd order you out of here."

"No, you wouldn't."

"Perhaps I should rethink my position on authoritarianism." Edith pulled out a compact and checked her make-up. "Lefebre's legit."

"How do you know?"

"I read his walls. M.D. from a minor southeastern medical school, state hospital residency, in West Virginia, of all places. Not the *creme-de-la-creme*, but legit." She snorted. "Framed diplomas. A sign of pomposity, or insecurity. Sometimes it's hard to tell the difference." She ran her hand over the windowsill, grimaced, and wiped it on the curtain. "His motorcar, silver Mercedes, no less, is parked ostentatiously out front. Vanity plate. RJL-MD. Roland J. Lefebre. Pearl interior, matches his suit."

"He could be an imposter," Stoner ventured.

"I doubt it. There was a golf tee on the floor of the back seat." She picked up a bed pillow between two fingers, beat it, and waved away a galaxy of dust. "This is a wretched place."

"What about Hank?"

"He may be here merely to build up enough hours to go on unemployment. Menninger's, this ain't."

"Maybe he's one of Them."

"He may well be. Illegal activities usually require muscle. Our friend seems well-endowed in that category."

"He might be one of the men who beat up Gwen."

"Unless you're certain, don't go for the throat. He could cancel you with a flick of the wrist. I suspect others do the thinking for him."

"Lefebre?"

"I doubt it. He lacks panache. From what I've seen of other places, I'd guess his role is to write prescriptions and generally give the place an air of authenticity. Which it certainly needs."

Stoner looked at her. "You mean this whole set-up might be a fake?"

"Oh, it's a hospital, all right. Accredited. I made certain of that. You don't think I'd send my favorite patient to a phoney hospital, do you? Even with a phoney illness."

"I thought therapists didn't have favorite patients," Stoner said.

"Bullshit." She crossed to the window and peeked out. "The sea

126

is truly disgusting today, isn't it?"

Stoner shoved her hand through her hair. "Edith, what should I do?"

"Act. Take action. The most important thing is to take action."

"You always told me planning was the most important thing."

"But you don't have a plan, Stoner, dear. Therefore you must act." Her eyes attacked the ceiling. "Dear God, where did they get that repulsive light fixture?" She pounced on the switch. "At least it works. We must be grateful for small favors."

"I have an idea," Stoner said. "You stay here in my place."

"Not a chance. I may be a reputedly brilliant shrink, but as a detective I'm nowhere." She chuckled. "Max would die of envy, me hobnobbing with the criminal element. He'd turn as green as a zucchini. Have you ever noticed that organically grown zucchini are unnaturally green? It must be the rotted manure." She sat beside Stoner on the bed. "Just between us, sometimes I long for the good old days. The house was bursting with secrets, agents coming and going at all hours, mysterious recording devices scattered about. Life with an FBI spouse is a reign of terror, but at least our windowsills weren't awash in seedlings and fish emulsion."

Edith tidied a corner of the bedspread. "Well, he's an improvement over my first husband. All *he* wanted to do was lie down. It's fortunate he didn't pass along any of *those* genes. But how could he? Every *inch* of him just wanted to lie down."

"Edith!" Stoner exclaimed.

Dr. Kesselbaum patted her hand. "You never have to worry about that, do you? Oh, the joys of an alternative lifestyle." She glanced at her watch. "I'd better go. King Kong could return any minute." She began to gather up her things. "Now, don't forget, you promised to jot down all your inner experiences for me. We're breaking new ground. You're the first person in the annals of psychiatry to enter a nightmare in concrete form."

"I am?"

"Well, the Jungians probably have a thousand case studies, but they're all in German. We should be good for a book, or at least an article. Possibly a stint on NOVA."

"That's nice."

"Stoner, dear, you look so *bereft*. Are you sure we're not making a mistake?"

We're making a colossal mistake. "I'll be all right," she said.

"It's against my better judgment to leave you, you know." She dug in her purse for her car keys. "Despite Hermione's assurances. Well, someone will check up on you in a few days."

A few days.

"When this is over, I'll treat you to a bash at Pizza Hut."

"I'm okay, honest."

Dr. Kesselbaum looked her up and down. "The operative word is *depressed*, Stoner. Not catatonic. Don't overact."

"I'm not acting."

"Then give me a hug."

"I can't. I might cry."

"There's nothing wrong with crying," Edith said. She pulled a handful of tissues from her purse. "I came prepared."

"I don't want to."

Edith took Stoner's face in her hands. "Remember, Stoner, you're not a patient here. Don't go native. You came to do a job, nothing more. And there are people out there who love you and are thinking of you every minute."

She felt a tightness in her chest. "Please go."

"And you promised to tell me everything about that mad, impetuous weekend with Gwen, as soon as you finish here."

"I never promised that."

"I'm your psychiatrist. You must tell me *everything*." She glanced once more around the room. "This place really is a dump."

And she was gone.

Alone, Stoner wandered to the window and stared out. The fog bank had crept closer.

You have me now, house. Let's see what you've got up your sleeve. Or chimney.

Channel 2: Docudrama. Inept detective enters mysterious mental hospital to search for missing nurse. Thin plot, unrelieved by shaky acting. One-and-a-half stars.

Or how about: *Channel 17: Thriller. Vampire house lures unsuspecting travel agent to wind-swept Maine coast for fun-and-games. No stars.*

Or: *Channel 23: Drama. Killer fog invades fishing village. Residents begin behaving strangely. Strong language, adult situa...*

"Hi, there, funny-funny-funny face," a high voice chirped.

She whirled around to see a tiny, white-haired woman in a smock rampant with yellow and orange.

"Hello," she said, as the pounding of her heart slowed to normal. "I'm Stoner McTavish."

"Stoner-Stoner," the woman sang. "Are you a nut?"

"Uh — I guess I am."

"Look out for the nutcracker." Her bright blue eyes darted about the room. "The nutcracker cracks you, and nobody backs you."

"Nutcracker?"

"Nutcracker, nutcracker, who's got the nutcracker?" the woman trilled. "Never mind, never mind, you'll find out in time. Do you have the time?"

Stoner looked down at her wrist. "Darn, I forgot my watch."

"Mrs. Grenier has a watch. Mrs. Grenier has the night watch.

128

Watch out for Mrs. Grenier."

"Who's Mrs. Grenier?"

"Who is Sylvia, what is she?" She spun in a circle. "She seems to dream, to dream, to dream. We dream and never seem."

Oh, boy, Stoner thought. Welcome to Shady Acres. "Are you here to show me around?"

"Around, a square, they took my chair."

"I'd invite you to sit down," Stoner said, "but they took mine, too."

"Down, down, down. Down in the town, there's no one around."

"That's Castleton, all right. No one around." She smiled. "Have you been here long?"

"All along, along, along with a song."

Hank appeared in the doorway. "You!" he barked. "Get back to O.T."

Stoner jumped. "Me?"

"Not you, the looney." He pushed the old woman toward the door. "Beat it, looney."

The woman curtsied deeply. "Your Eminence, your Prominence." She scurried from the room.

"Excuse me," Stoner said, "but don't you think you're being a little harsh with her?"

He glared at her. "*What*?

"She's only a helpless little old..."

"You telling me my job?"

"No, of course not," Stoner said quickly. "I'm sorry. What's wrong with her? Alzheimer's?"

"Don't ask questions. Learn that right off. Don't ask questions."

"I ... I was only trying to be friendly."

He looked as if she'd offered him a worm on a saltine. "We don't fraternize with the 'guests'." He grinned unpleasantly. "Wait here for Jerry. You can fraternize with him. After he shows you around, go to Social Service for intake." He strode to the door. "Don't make trouble, and don't ask questions."

"Yes, your Protuberance," Stoner mumbled to the empty room.

She turned back to the window and rested her arms on the sash. The fog had blurred the line between sea and sky. The world was reduced to a smudge.

Friendly little place.

She couldn't *wait* to meet this Jerry. Shady Acres' official tour guide. He probably had green teeth and pink eyes and spent his spare time carving his initials on small children.

She wondered what they were doing back home. She wondered if anyone was thinking about her, or if they were happily going about their business. Out of sight, out of mind.

I'll bet they don't even miss me. One less mouth to feed. One less Capricorn grumping through the mornings. One less incompetent messing up the monthly accounts. One less problem for everyone.

Come on, she told herself roughly, you're homesick, that's all. Homesick and frightened.

Mostly frightened.

It'll be dark soon. "No one lives any nearer than the town. No one will come any nearer than that. In the night. In the dark."

She tried to reach back through her desolation to the evening before, to touch warmth and color with her mind. But even though they had all been together — Gwen and Marylou and Aunt Hermione, and even Eleanor Burton — even though it had been funny at times, Marylou and Gwen hatching a plot to have the Watertown Junior High School Marching Band come to see her off, until Stoner was afraid they might actually do it and made them stop — even though Aunt Hermione had led them in a ritual Power chant to surround her with a field of positive energy — even though Marylou and Mrs. Burton had left early, Mrs. Burton never questioning why Gwen was staying over, even giving Stoner a little kiss on the cheek "for luck" — even though Gwen had held her sweetly through the night ... the memory was dulled, the details lost behind her own fog of ap-prehension.

"Nothing to worry about," Aunt Hermione had said. "Your aura's clear as crystal."

But she was worried.

"I'll be near the phone every minute," Delia had said this morn-ing. "Jared can cover that road in five minutes flat."

But she felt isolated, abandoned.

"I love you," Gwen had said as she kissed her good-bye. "If you need me, I'll be there if I have to smash down the gates."

But she was alone.

It's the house, the damn house. It's doing this, cutting me off from all of them. And when there's only me and It, It'll wait.

Wait for me to make the first move.

All right, I'll make the first move.

As soon as I figure out what my first move is.

Look around, of course.

Not yet. First I have to establish my credibility with Them.

What credibility?

I have to appear depressed. What would I do if I were depressed?

Stay in my room and stare at the walls.

Which is exactly what I'm doing.

Because I *am* depressed. *It's* making me depressed.

It, Them. This is crazy thinking. Before I know it, I'll be believing in a world-wide conspiracy. Armageddon. Good versus Evil. The Forces of Darkness. Twenty-four hours in this place, and I'll turn into a Conservative. Then I'll have a good reason to be depressed.

There was a soft knock at the door. Company, thank God. Human

130

contact. "Come in."

Nothing happened.

"Come *in*."

Another knock.

Annoyed, she went to the door, opened it, and found herself looking up at the tallest, palest individual she had ever seen. The boy, in his early twenties, was slim as a cornstalk, with skin the color of chalk. A lock of jet black hair fell over his forehead, making his gray eyes appear milky by contrast. His face was expressionless, his arms held stiffly at his sides. He should be striding across Harvard Yard in an oversized, second-hand Army officer's greatcoat, with a tattered copy of *Crime and Punishment* trickling from his pocket.

"I asked you to come in."

He refused to budge. "Jerry," he said.

"Stoner," she replied, and decided to get stubborn. "I invited you in. Why didn't you come?"

"You're a girl."

"Woman."

A touch of pink washed over his cheeks. "Sorry."

She really hadn't meant to embarrass him. "Well, come in now."

"Wouldn't be right."

"Are you afraid of me?"

"No."

It occurred to her that perhaps *she* should be afraid of *him*. For all she knew, he could be Jack the Ripper.

"Okay," she said, at a loss.

"It would *look* bad. People might *talk*."

Stoner smiled. "They might." He certainly didn't seem dangerous. "Are we going to stand here in the doorway?"

"I'm supposed to show you around." He spun on his heel and double-timed down the hall.

Stoner ran to catch up. At the foot of the steps, he paused.

"Dining room." He flicked his left hand toward a set of French doors leading to a room crammed with tables, chairs, and steam tables. "Lousy food."

He gestured to the right. "Offices."

"What kind of offices?"

"Staff."

He led her behind the stairs to the back of the house. "Conservatory."

It was a large room with floor-to-ceiling windows that faced west to the woods. Wicker furniture huddled in conversation nests on the parquet floor. A Baby Grand piano pouted in one corner. Against the back wall stood a fireplace with a marble mantel. It was ashless, spotless, cold, and obviously unused. Terrifying potted plants stood guard. Magazines lay neatly arranged in order of size on occasional tables. Around the corner to her right were bookcases of dark wood. The titles on the books were worn and blurred. The top shelves held an incongruous jumble of torn paperbacks and almanacs.

It had all the light-hearted charm and cozy friendliness of an operating room.

Jerry seemed to be waiting for a comment.

"It's very clean," she said.

Something resembling life flickered in his eyes. "That's *my* job. I clean."

"You do it well."

"Yeah," he said. "I'm compulsive. How about you?"

"Depressed."

"They say I'd be depressed if I weren't compulsive. What's it like?"

"Depressing," Stoner said.

"So's compulsive. Why are you depressed?"

"I'm not sure."

"No kidding?" Jerry said. "I don't know why I'm compulsive, either. They keep asking, but I don't know."

"It seems to me *they* should be able to tell *you*. They're the professionals."

He thought it over. "Gosh, you're right. I never looked at it that way."

"Well," Stoner said, "I'm no expert, but doesn't being compulsive kind of mean you have a one-track mind?"

He cocked his head. "Yeah, I sure do."

"So it isn't your fault if you don't have all the answers, is it?"

"I guess it isn't." He bounced up and down a little. "Boy, wait until I lay *that* one on my shrink."

Stoner smiled. "I'd go easy if I were you. Sometimes they don't like it when you have all the answers."

His face went blank. He looked at her sideways. "How come you know so much?"

"What?"

"They sent you to spy on me, didn't they?"

Uh-oh, pushed the wrong button. Beneath that boyish exterior there lurks a paranoid heart. "Nobody sent me, Jerry. It was only a guess."

"Prove it."

"How can I prove a thing like that?" She reached out to touch him. He snapped into rigidity. She drew back. "Please, believe me."

He considered her. "You're really depressed?"

"Very."

"Then why aren't you crying?"

"I'm too depressed to cry."

"Yeah," he said, nodding. "Yeah, that makes sense. But I'll be watching you."

"Good. Maybe I won't feel so alone."

"*You* feel alone?"

Stoner nodded.

"So do I."

"Well," Stoner said, "maybe that's why you're compulsive."

He shook his head. "You got it backward. I'm alone *because* I'm compulsive. People don't like compulsives. Compulsives aren't fun."

"Neither are depressives. Depressives don't like fun."

"Then you ought to like this place. It's no fun at all." He surveyed the room like a Forest Ranger scanning for smoke. "You can have visitors in here, when you can have visitors."

"*When* I can have..."

"No visitors for the first two weeks."

A little knot formed in her stomach. "I hadn't planned on being here two weeks."

"They all say that."

"Nobody said anything to me about visi..."

"They never tell you anything around here," Jerry said. "Until you break a rule. *Then* they tell you. And they never let you out. Never."

He walked away.

Remember, she told her rising panic, the boy is not well. Not well at all.

She followed him across the hall to the Occupational Therapy room.

Here, at least, someone had made a valiant attempt at cutting through the gloom. The room was cluttered with looms, sewing machines, and easels. Bits of material and string lay scattered on the floor. In one corner, an elderly man pounded listlessly at a round of copper. Other patients sat at long tables, meditating over mysterious objects. They glanced up furtively as she came in, and hunched protectively over their work.

A flash of orange and yellow caught her eye. In a deep corner by the windows, the old woman in the flowered smock attacked a square of poster board with an arsenal of colors. Stoner found herself drawn to the woman. She wandered over.

"Come to see the sea, Dearie?"

"I'd like to look at your painting, if I may."

"Look away, Dixieland."

She leaned against the windowsill and contemplated the picture. Bright tropical birds and multicolored flowers rampaged across the canvas in an explosion of light and movement. She hadn't expected such clarity, or such joy. Not in *this* place.

And there was something else. She puzzled over it, trying to pin down her feeling that there was an inconsistency...

She had it. The woman, in person, was as flakey as a croissant,

133

and yet she painted images that were as carefully drawn, as detailed as an Audubon print. The feathers of the birds, the veins in the leaves, every line, every highlight absolutely realistic.

"It's lovely," she said.

"Lovely is as lovely does. The dark hides the light, and light is right."

"Sure."

The woman looked at her coyly and giggled.

She was an exquisite woman, heart-breakingly beautiful. Her skin was smooth and soft as cream, her eyes sparkling and kind. Her tiny body was erect, the hands that held the brush and palette long-fingered and delicate.

"What's your name?" Stoner asked.

The woman's blue eyes seemed to pierce her mind. There was an intelligence, a consciousness, a *knowing*...

Stoner shook her head. Impossible. She's gonzo, off her rocker, around the bend, over the hill.

She was drawing something in the center of her painting. A large white flower. It obliterated two parrots and a flamingo.

Stoner recognized it. "That's a lilly, isn't..." Her heart sank. "Miz Lilly? Are you Lilly Winthrop?"

Snatching up her palette knife, Lilly scraped away every trace of the flower.

"Then this is your home, isn't it?"

"Home is where the heart is." She fisted a large brush and covered the painting with cobalt blue.

"Do you remember Delia, from the Clam Shack? And Dan?"

Lilly seemed to stiffen. "The tide comes in, the tide goes out," she chanted. She emptied the paint tube into her hand and smeared it on the front of her smock.

She had to find a way to get through to her. "Dan used to bring you fish, remember? Lobsters and bluefish."

"The sky is blue when the moon is new," Lilly sang. She reached for the black.

"Things happen when the moon is new, don't they? Is that what Dan found out?"

" 'Goblins and ghosties, and long-legged beasties, and things that go bump in the night'." Squirting the paint from the tube, Lilly rubbed it between her hands and pressed them against the ruined picture.

"What goes bump in the night?"

"Rats in the walls, and cats in the halls, and bats in the belfry." She played in the paint.

"Who are the rats, Miz Lilly?"

"They come in the night, they go in the night, in the night, in the night."

134

"*Who?*" Stoner asked desperately, "Who goes in the night?"

Lilly's hands danced and twirled across the painting, smearing, scratching, clawing.

This is not rational behavior. I'm trying to carry on a meaningful conversation with a raving psychotic.

But she might know something. Even with her mind turned to oatmeal, there might be fragments of memory, shards of information...

"*Help* me, Miz Lilly. What did Dan find out? What happened to Claire..."

Lilly whirled on her. "Get out," she whispered. "Get out before..."

"Lilly, Lilly." The voice hop-scotched toward them across the room. "*Now* what have you done?"

A young woman bounced up, red hair flying. "You must be the *new* one," she exclaimed to Stoner as if it were the most exciting thing that had happened to her in a month. "I'm your O.T., call me Becky, Lilly what a mess we have to clean you up before it dries, hope she didn't frighten you, she's completely harmless, it's just her age, look at these fingernails we'll never get them clean did you have to use black again, nice to meet you come by any time O.T.'s open all day just come on in we'll have to get better acquainted if I can do anything for you let me know."

She led Lilly, smiling vacuously, off through a swinging door in the side wall.

"Okay," Stoner said to the air. She looked around for Jerry, who had planted himself like a stone lion at the entrance to the room. There was a look of intense distaste on his face.

"I don't like her," he said as she approached.

"Lilly?"

"Becky. She thinks everything's fun."

Stoner smiled. "She is rather relentlessly cheerful."

"I don't like O.T."

"It's messy, right?"

He nodded brusquely. "I don't like Shady Acres."

"Neither do I. Did you know it used to be called Journey's End?"

"Is that supposed to make me feel better?"

"Not particularly." She followed him out into the hall. "How long have you been here, Jerry?"

"A year."

A year? In *this* place? "Then you must know your way around."

He glanced at her sharply. "I'm allowed. It's my job."

"I'm not accusing you of anything."

"I do the cleaning," he said loudly. "I have to know my way around if I'm going to clean, don't I?"

"Jerry, I don't care if you creep through the halls in the dead of night and peek through keyholes. I don't care if you bug the staff

135

offices and listen in on therapy sessions. I don't care if you filch silverware from the dining room and hold your own personal tag sales. I'm not here to watch you. I'm not spying on you. Can you process that tiny bit of information?"

"You don't have to yell," he said.

"I'm sorry." She shook her head. "Boy, are you sensitive."

"Maybe I have reason to be. Did you ever think of that?"

"All right," she said evenly. "I'll keep that in mind."

"Good. What else do you want to see?"

"Can you show me around outside?"

"We can't go outside."

She looked at him. "You mean you never get out?"

"I get out. If anyone'll take me."

"You mean family or visitors?"

His jaw tightened. "I don't have visitors."

"I'm sorry."

"I don't like visitors."

"Who takes you out, then?"

"Staff."

"I don't know, Jerry," she said. "I haven't met anyone yet who looked as if they'd go out of their way. Except Becky, and she probably can't light long enough..."

"I'm not lying," he said stiffly. "I don't lie."

"I didn't mean that."

"*She* took me out. Lots of times."

He strode away.

Stoner ran after him. "I believe you, Jerry. I'm sorry if I insulted her. I'm sure Becky's a fine..."

"Becky!" he snorted, nostrils flaring with contempt. "I wouldn't go anywhere with *her*. She's a ninny."

"Okay."

"I *told* you I didn't like her."

"Yes, you did. I forgot."

"Don't you ever listen?"

Stoner leaned against the wall. "Jerry, please. I've had a difficult day. I'm trying very hard to get along with you, but I don't seem to be able to say the right thing."

He was still angry. "I'm not so desperate I'd go out with just *anybody*."

Go out with? Is this subtly different from "be taken out by?"

She glanced down. Beside her stood a cherry table holding a deep bronze bowl filled with chrysanthemums. Idly, she reached out to pluck off a dead leaf, and discovered they were plastic. "I hope you don't have to dust these."

"I don't have to, but I do. I told you, I'm compulsive."

"So am I, a little. But I've never gotten to the point of plastic flowers."

"I like to keep things nice for..." He bit his lip.

She wanted to ask who, but was afraid of setting him off again. "You're wasted here. With your talent, you'd be a rich man on the outside."

"It's a sickness."

"Depends on your point of view. What do you want to do when you get out?"

"I don't want to get out," he said sharply.

"Please don't take offense, but I find that a little hard to believe."

"I can't leave. They might do something to..."

He's protecting someone. Someone who takes him out. Delia's words came back to her. "Nice kid. Brings the patients in here..." She decided to take the plunge. "You're talking about Claire Rasmussen, aren't you?"

He turned even more pale than his natural color. "What do you know about her?" he demanded.

"Not much, but I think..."

"Don't you think about her! Don't you *dare* think about her!"

"Jerry..."

He clenched his fists. The veins running past his temples throbbed. He brushed past her and started up the stairs. "You're supposed to go to Social Service. I hope they give you shock!"

"Damn it, Jerry," she exploded, "talking to you's like trying to pick up a raw egg."

He leaned over the bannister and glared. "I'm sorry I showed you around," he shouted. "Creep!"

Stoner watched him disappear into the shadows of the second floor.

Well, well, well, as Marylou would say. Jerry's in love with Claire.

***

By the time she had finished with Social Service — or Social Service had finished with her — she was working on a headache. Maybe it was the hour-and-a-half of endless questions (mainly relating to her financial situation, ability or lack thereof to pay for her "treatment," and job prospects once she was let loose on an unsuspecting world). Maybe it was the fact that the social worker, who had never mentioned his name, wore a sky-blue tie with pink dots against a red-and-brown striped shirt. Or maybe it was because, for all her asking, the only information she had received was the fact that dinner was at five-thirty. The Shady Acres "orientation booklet," it seemed, was currently undergoing revision — being assembled, no doubt, by non-English-speaking illegal aliens in a remote barracks in North Dakota.

She stretched out on her bed and tried to think. She had been here three hours. She had seen neither hide nor hair of Claire Rasmussen. She had met a boy, compulsive, who had access to a good bit of freedom of movement about the place, and who was about as comfortable to be with as a rabid porcupine.

And there was Lilly Winthrop, acting as crazy as a loon but painting like Andrew Wyeth. Lilly had managed to pass along some information. Well, not really information, but look at the topics she had chosen — if "chosen" was the right word — to bring up. Tides. New Moon. Someone or something going in the night. Psychotic ramblings? Or a deliberate attempt to communicate? And that final, whispered warning: "Get out."

Lilly, old gal, getting out is the best idea I've heard all day.

Restless, she got up and paced the floor.

Have to do something about this room. Early Ingmar Bergman. White, white, white. White walls. White Bureau. White bedside table. White cotton bedspread. Are we supposed to hallucinate our own colors?

Desperate, she dug her comb from a drawer and placed it on top of the bureau at a rakish angle, obsessed for ten minutes over whether or not to set out her deodorant and decided against it (too personal), tossed her pajamas over the white iron foot rail of the white iron bed.

It looked pathetic.

She *felt* pathetic.

I should have brought a picture of Gwen.

But I don't have a picture of Gwen.

How long before I forget what she looks like? The feel of her? The sound of her velvet voice?

I hate this place. It smells of disinfectant and mildew. It's ugly. It's going to eat my soul. I can't have visitors for two weeks. And I don't even have a picture of my lover.

Tears burned her eyes.

I want a picture of my lover.

Don't think about that. Think about what you've learned so far. The location of a few rooms. The view from O.T. — ocean. The view from the conservatory — dead lawn, forest, and a crumbling stone wall.

The stone wall. The one she'd crouched behind while Gwen created a diversion with the aides.

Which, she had to admit in retrospect, was pretty clever.

Except that they had found Gwen and beaten her up.

But they hadn't seen Stoner.

Or had they? What exactly could you see from the conservatory, or from the staff offices along that side of the building? If the floor was higher than ground level, and it probably was, you might be able

138

to see over the wall = enough, at least, to know that there was *someone* lurking behind it.

Gwen hadn't been attacked for trespassing. They all agreed on that. She had been attacked because she had made a phone call, had come to the house, had been caught prowling the grounds. Attacked because she had been looking for Claire Rasmussen.

They had known Gwen was at Delia's because they had been following her.

Which meant they had seen the two of them together. Had seen them leave Castle Point together. Had seen them to go the motel together. Had seen them arrive at Delia's together.

Which meant they probably knew exactly who Stoner was.

And that she had hooked up with Delia, who was no friend of Shady Acres.

She'd better take Lilly's advice and get out. Fast!

She dove for her closet, grabbed her suitcase.

Wait a minute. It was dark that night. If anyone had followed them leaving Castle Point, they would have seen their headlights. So they must have picked up the trail later, at the motel. They'd go to the motel because, when Gwen left the message for Claire, she'd left the motel number.

So start with the East Wind Inn.

There was fog that night. Lots of it. Fog as thick as whipped cream. They had stayed away from the streetlights because they were in love and holding hands. When she entered Delia's, her back was to them. When she came out, the light was behind her. She could have been anyone. And if someone had seen her behind the wall, they wouldn't have been able to identify her at that distance.

But it was *her* name on the motel register.

And they had brazenly wandered the streets of Castleton in broad daylight, too love-sick to know or care if they were being watched.

She began pulling clothes from the bureau.

Calm down! You don't even know there's anything shady about Shady Acres. Except the trees, ha ha. No one batted an eye when you checked in. Not RJL-MD. Not Hank-don't-need-'em'-don't-keep-'em. Not Social Service. And the one person who can slap a positive ID on you is taking his meals through a straw in the Augusta hospital.

If you're recognized, you can run. There are no locked doors, except to the fire escape. You don't need the fire escape, except in case of fire.

So don't start a fire.

You're losing it, McTavish.

I should have brought different clothes. Not jeans and flannel shirts and pullover sweaters. Disguise myself in a skirt, one of Marylou's fluffy blouses, victim shoes.

Right, go tottering around the halls on stiletto heels like a newborn giraffe.

And how do you disguise green eyes?

Look, Shady Acres might very well be nothing more than a good, old-fashioned Nineteenth Century Asylum.

And Aunt Hermione's Nancy Reagan.

What do you say, folks? Do I stay, or run like hell?

If I stay, I could be in Big Trouble.

If I run, we lose everything.

People are counting on you. Can you turn your back on Claire? Can you leave Delia wondering, or Gwen's attackers unpunished? We're in a battle here—for Truth, Justice and the American Way.

And They might already know who you are.

Well, she thought a little hysterically, this adds an element of suspense to the proceedings.

A buzzer sounded in the hall.

Dinner.

She ran a comb through her hair and took a deep breath.

They'd better pass out Valium in this place. I'm going to need it.

CHAPTER 88

"Food's lousy," Jerry had said, in two words raising understatement to an art form. The food was worse than lousy; it was unidentifiable. She had often wondered why you see so few dead birds, when there are so many birds in the world and they must die. Now she knew. She also knew what became of Stop and Shop's rejected lettuce, the leftover mashed potatoes from the World's Largest Truck Stop, and all the jello used in horror films.

She didn't even want to think about the coffee.

For background music, there was the low hum of 21 simultaneous monologues. She sat at a salmon-colored table with two elderly men whose minds had left for a far, far better place, and a woman with dyed platinum-blonde hair who insisted she'd be released if only she could remember the words to all the songs ever recorded by Rosemary Clooney. The younger guests were clustered near the door, under the watchful eye of a second edition Hank. Across the room, Miz Lilly divided her dinner between her mouth and the pocket of her smock. Under the circumstances, it was perfectly rational behavior.

At some unheard, unseen signal, the guests rose in a body like horned larks, shuffled past the steam tables to deposit their scraps —tomorrow's stew, no doubt— and filed out. Stoner pushed her barely touched meal into a steel dishpan full of remnants, and cringed when she saw Hank's clone glance at her leavings and make a note on his clipboard.

Social hour at Shady Acres. She watched the others sort themselves into chairs in the conservatory, and found an inconspicuous spot for herself.

Claire hadn't appeared. Not in the dining room, and not there.

She checked out the view of the wall. But it was dark, the windows had turned to mirrors, and all she saw was herself, checking out the view.

She picked up an old National Geographic and pretended to read. First order of business, find a way to get back in Jerry's good graces. He had access to Shady Acres' nooks and crannies, and, with his feelings for Claire, motivation for wanting to get to the bottom of things. It would be an Unholy Alliance, but she needed his help.

She peeked up. He sat, ramrod stiff, hands folded, on the edge of a couch by the window. She caught his eye and smiled. He looked down at the floor. She turned her attention to an article on mapping the Grand Canyon by laser.

The clock in the hall ticked, struck, ticked, and struck again.

"Excuse me."

Stoner glanced up. Jerry stood at attention, his face slightly flushed.

"Hi, Jerry."

His hands opened and closed. "Did you = uh = enjoy your dinner?"

"It was everything you said it would be, and more." She indicated a nearby chair. "Want to sit down?"

"No." Blotches of deep red appeared on his skin. "I want to apologize!" he boomed.

"For what?"

"Rudeness!"

Under normal circumstances, every head in the room would have turned their way. No one stirred.

"It isn't necessary," she said.

"I like things tidy. Rudeness is untidy."

"It's all right."

"Does that mean," he asked, his face now completely scarlet, "you accept my apology?"

She smiled reassuringly. "There's nothing to apologize for. But, in the interest of tidiness, I accept. Please sit down."

"Why?"

"You're very tall up there."

His knees and hips gave way. He plopped into a chair and tapped his foot nervously.

"Is everyone always so quiet?" she asked.

"Tranquillizers."

"You don't seem to be affected."

He glared at her. "What makes you say that?"

Stoner sighed. "Jerry, I swear on my mother's grave I'm *not* spying on you. I'm a *patient.* If I weren't a patient, would I have eaten that dinner?"

"You didn't eat it. You threw most of it away."

"So *you* were spying on *me.*"

He straightened the seams in his slacks.

"I'm not angry, Jerry. I just want you to see that curiosity works both ways."

"I'm not curious," he mumbled. "I'm suspicious."

"Well, it probably comes with being compulsive."

"Probably. I'm suspicious about everyone."

"I would be, too," she said, "if I'd been in here for a year."

Pulling a handkerchief from his pocket, he bent down and wiped a grain of dirt from the floor. "I don't swallow the tranquillizers," he said in a low voice. "Don't report me."

142

"Never. I promise."

"If they find out, they'll do bad things to me."

"What kind of things?"

"Bad things." He glanced at her. "Now you know a secret about me."

She felt as if she'd just won the Publishers' Clearing House sweepstakes. "Thank you. Why don't you swallow them?"

"They make you feel funny."

"That," Stoner said, "is the first bit of practical information I've gotten since I arrived."

He picked an imaginary speck of lint from his sweater.

"You have to practice it," he said. "Because they watch you. And you have to pretend. Walk kind of slow, and don't look at people or answer them right away."

"I see."

"It's dangerous to talk like this. They don't want us to make trouble."

"What happens if you make trouble?"

"They give you shock."

Electroshock, Behavior Mod, now tranquillizers. Edith Kesselbaum would have apoplexy.

"Why don't they want you?" Jerry asked.

"Who?"

"The people who put you here. They only put you here if they don't want you."

She reached over and touched his sleeve. "Is that what you think, Jerry? That nobody wants you?"

"I'm not talking about me," he said, moving his sleeve out of reach, "I'm asking about you."

"Nobody put me here. I put myself here."

He stared at her. "Why?"

"Because I need help."

"You came *here* for help? You must be nuts."

"Well," she said, "this is a nut house, isn't it?"

"They don't help you here," he said, watching the door. "They turn you into a Zombie. Claire says it isn't right to turn people into Zombies. Claire says this place is like The Night of the Living Dead. Claire says..." He broke off, a look of apprehension crossing his face.

"Please go on."

His lips tightened. "How come," he asked, "you know about her?"

"I know her sister. She recommended Shady Acres."

He laughed dryly. "Nobody recommends Shady Acres."

"Well, actually, she didn't. But I knew Claire worked here, so I thought it would be..."

"How'd you know I was talking about *her* this afternoon?"

She thought fast. "When you mentioned going out, it seemed like

149

something Claire would do."

He glared at the floor.

"Claire's a special friend of yours, isn't she?" she asked.

"What if she is?"

"Friends are important."

"They did things to her," he said. "And then she went away."

"What did they do?"

"I don't know."

"When did she go away?" she asked, pressing her luck. He seemed about to bolt.

"Saturday night, after she got out and they caught her."

"Are you sure?"

"That's what they told everyone. That she went away."

If that were true... My God, she thought, I'm too late.

But wouldn't he be more upset, feeling about Claire the way he does?

"Jerry," she said carefully, "is there some doubt in your mind about that?"

"I don't want to talk about this."

"Why not?"

"I might get afraid and paranoid."

"Was Claire afraid?"

He shook his head. "I told you I didn't want to talk about this."

"I only asked," she said, resting her hand on his arm, "because her sister's worried."

He jerked his arm away.

"I'm sorry. We'll talk about something else, anything you want."

"You're not like the others," he said slowly.

"Thank you for trusting me."

"I don't know if I trust you. I just wanted to talk."

"It must be lonely being the only untranquil guest in the place."

"I'm not a guest," he said. "Guests can leave. Nobody leaves here."

She wished he wouldn't keep bringing that up.

His eyes flicked toward her, then back to the door. "Do you have a boyfriend?"

"No, I don't."

"Why? Don't you like boys?"

"Not in that way."

He chewed that over. "Do you have a girlfriend?"

"Yes."

"I never met anyone like that."

"You must have led a sheltered life."

"My parents wouldn't want me to talk to someone like you."

Stoner winced. Being friends with Jerry was going to require a thick skin.

"Was I rude again?"

1444

"It's not your fault," she said. "Some people are like that. But for future reference, it might pay to be careful where you say that kind of thing."

"I've made you angry."

"No, really."

"I don't want to make you angry."

"I'm not angry."

"If you get angry, you won't talk to me anymore."

"I'm not angry, Jerry. I swear to God, I'm *not angry*."

"I don't believe you." His eyes drooped. His mouth turned downward in a pout. He looked like a puppy who, in a moment of juvenile exuberance, had just eaten the morning paper.

"Jerry, I don't blame you for what your parents are."

"Really?" He gazed at her hopefully. "You really mean that?"

Her heart melted. "Of course I mean it."

Legally, he might be old enough to vote, drive, drink, and wreak havoc on the nation's highways. But emotionally, Jerry was still a boy — an awkward, naive, and probably very frightened boy.

"I'm sorry if I criticized you," she said.

"But you *should* criticize me. Otherwise, I'll never learn to get along with people."

"You don't make it easy," she said, trying not to sound critical.

"Yeah, I know. Claire says the same thing. I'm a horse's ass."

"That's putting it a little strongly."

"My father calls me 'The Wimp,'" he said. "He's going to be President someday."

"Remind me not to vote for him."

"He says I'm a political liability."

"Remind me to tell my friends not to vote for him."

"That's why they put me in here. They live in Oklahoma, see, and this way no one can find out."

"Remind me to drop his name on the grapevine. We'll lose him the entire gay vote."

Jerry grinned. "I like that."

"Has she kept you in hospitals all your life?"

"Ever since I got kicked out of military school."

"Why did they kick you out?" She couldn't quite see him breaking the rules.

He hunched his shoulders. "I don't want to tell you."

"Well, that's all right."

"Claire says you should tell people things if you want them to be your friend."

"I suppose that's true."

"I used to run away and hide," he said, "when it was time for football practice. I was afraid of getting hurt."

"That seems reasonable."

"And the horses. They made us ride, and I was afraid to do that."

"So am I."

"But you're a girl. Girls don't have to be brave."

Stoner smiled. "You know, Jerry, you and I are going to have to have a little talk about politics."

"I hate politics," he scowled.

"Feminist politics."

"I've heard of that," he said proudly. "Like Geraldine Ferraro."

"Among other things."

"My parents didn't vote for her. They're Reaganites."

"I'm not surprised. Was there anything you liked about school?"

"Drill."

"Of course."

"And inspection. I was good at inspection. But I didn't have any friends." He cleared his throat. "Want to be my friend?"

"Very much."

He straightened his shoulders. "Will you show me how to be brave?"

"I don't know, Jerry. I'm not very brave myself."

"Is that why you're depressed?"

"I guess that's part of it."

He nodded wisely. "Yeah, it's depressing to be chickenshit."

It was beginning to drizzle. Dampness congealed and slid down the windows, smearing their reflections.

"Will you come back and see me," Jerry asked, "after they let you out?"

"I thought nobody ever got out of here."

Jerry hung his head. "I lied about that."

"Why?"

"Because I wanted to make you unhappy."

"Why?"

"Because I like you." He looked away quickly. "I'll bet you think I'm really crazy."

"Jerry," she said, "you make more sense than anyone I've met in a long time."

"You're just saying that because you're nice."

To her surprise, she felt herself blush. "Tell me, what do you do all day, other than clean?"

"It takes all day to clean properly."

"I see."

"And I see my therapist."

She leaned forward. "Dr. Tunes?"

"Tunes," he said with contempt. "Nobody in their right mind sees Tunes."

Nobody in their right mind hangs around Shady Acres, either. "You mean we have a choice?"

146

He shrugged. "Girls don't. All the girls have to see Tunes."

"The word is *women*, Jerry. Women like to be called women."

"My mother doesn't. She says it makes her feel old."

"Then she's a girl."

He rubbed his face with the palms of his hands. "Boy, it's confusing out there, isn't it?"

"Not when you get the hang of it." She toyed with her magazine. "Do you ever get a chance to wander around here?"

"*I* get to go everywhere," he said. "I have keys."

She sat up. "*Keys?*"

"Sure, so I can clean the rooms. How could I clean the rooms if I didn't have keys?"

She could hardly believe it. "You mean you have keys to every room in this place?"

"I said I did, didn't I?"

"Even the staff quarters?"

"Do you think I'm a liar or something?"

"Jerry, this is fabulous!"

He glanced at her suspiciously. "Why?"

"Well," she said, backpedalling, "if you ever want to get out, all you have to do..."

"Why would I want to get out? I don't have anywhere to go."

"But if you had a sudden urge..."

"I'm *compulsive*," he said loudly. "I don't have sudden urges."

She looked around quickly, to see if anyone had heard. But of course no one had, being in a permanent state of tranquility.

Keys. He has keys. Keys open up all kinds of possibilities.

But it wouldn't be right to use him.

My God, we may be talking Life and Death here, and you're worried about ethics?

"Uh..." she said, "having access to all the rooms, I suppose you've looked for Claire?"

"Keys are a symbol of *trust*," he said indignantly. "I wouldn't just go poking *around*." He hesitated. "Anyway, I didn't find her."

"Jerry, would you let me have a look?"

"With my keys?"

"Yes."

"What for?"

"I'm curious about Claire."

"She isn't here."

"You might have overlooked something..."

"I don't overlook things. I'm compulsive."

"I realize that, but you might have..."

He shot to his feet. His face was white, his fists clenched. "You have a lot of nerve!"

"Jerry, this is serious."

147

"You said you'd be my friend," he hissed. "And now you call me sloppy!"

"Jerry, please listen..."

She started to get up. He pushed her back into her seat and stormed from the room.

Damn!

She thought about going after him, but that might attract attention. She couldn't afford to attract attention.

Damn, damn, damn.

* * *

She stared out at the wall of liquid night and wished she'd remembered to bring a book from the conservatory shelves. It would probably be *The Bobbsey Twins at the Seashore*, but it would be better than counting her heartbeats.

She realized she'd been standing there for a long time, her mind a blank. She probed for Meaningful Thoughts, and came up with nothing more than dull, half-formed ideas.

My brain's turning to chewing gum. By this time tomorrow, the high point of my day will be changing my clothes.

It was a mistake to push it with Jerry. I should have been more laid back.

Sure, laid back. In this place, where minutes are years and hours are decades, you could die of old age being laid back.

He says Claire's gone, but he doesn't believe it. And if she *has* been gone since Saturday, why hasn't Nancy heard from her? It's been three days, time enough to get to a phone.

Of course, she probably didn't go of her own free will, not in the condition she was in.

She didn't take her car. It's passed to the Great Assembly Line in the sky.

But she could have gone. To the bottom of the Atlantic. Sometimes they wander over the cliffs.

If she'd done that, they'd have had to report it before someone came looking for her, asking questions. I mean, you don't just say, "Claire? Oh, she wandered over the cliffs three days ago, but we thought she might turn up. We didn't want to send out any false alarms."

So they'd report it. Which would bring the police, Coast Guard, skin divers, searchlights. Jerry would have noticed that.

Unless they didn't want her body found. In which case they wouldn't report it. If anyone asked, they'd claim she'd left months ago, no forwarding address.

Except that Gwen had seen her, and they knew it. They knew

148

there was a living witness that, as of Saturday, Claire Rasmussen was at Shady Acres.

Whatever was going on out here, Gwen had upped the ante. And nearly gotten herself killed in the...

Oh, Jesus, what if that beating hadn't been just a warning?

What if they'd been trying to kill her? And Delia, who was already under suspicion because of Dan, was in even deeper now.

To say nothing of yours truly.

Wait, wait, wait. Don't let the old imagination run wild again. Delia said everything had been quiet since Saturday. Jerry believes Claire is still around. So let's assume *they* assume it's all quieted down. At least let's assume they don't want to litter the countryside with corpses, which would make the police take notice. Corpses can be hard to explain in as well little a place like Castleton.

What would I do in their place? Bide my time? Try to come up with something clever? Clear out?

That's what I'd do, clear out.

But that's because I'm depressingly chickenshit.

Look at it from their point of view. You have this nurse, who has become an encumbrance. But you don't want to bump her off because there's this crazy Greek going around town shooting off her mouth that you killed her husband. So you want to keep suspicious-looking deaths to a minimum.

Okay, you drug the nurse, keep her on ice, as they say.

Then this woman shows up, asking for the nurse and poking around. Again, you want to avoid murder. So you stage a mugging, figuring she'll tuck her tail between her legs and go away. Which, it seems, she does.

So everything's back to normal, right?

Right.

So you start to relax a little. Now this depressed broad from Boston moves in. Maybe there's something familiar about her, maybe there isn't. But you don't let on you recognize her (if you do), because you don't want to tip your hand. You play it cool, keep Claire out of sight, and wait for the broad from Boston to fuck up.

Which she will undoubtedly do.

Stoner raked her hair back from her forehead. I never should have agreed to this.

Agreed? It was my idea.

Someone should have stopped me.

Like who, for instance?

Aunt Hermione is morally opposed to messing in someone else's *karma*.

Gwen and Marylou and Edith are convinced it's a matter of my honor.

Honor. Now there's a crock.

1499

And who convinced them it was a matter of honor? Guess who, sports fans.

They didn't have to *listen*, did they?

In my next life, I hope I have the sense not to choose friends who respect my wishes.

Look, you're tired and nerved up and not thinking rationally. Nobody = repeat, nobody = has made a move against you. So get a good night's sleep...

In *this* house?

Yes, in this house. And tomorrow, if the going gets rough, you can call Delia to come take you away.

After you talk to Millicent Tunes. You have to talk to Millicent Tunes, she's our number one suspect. Our only suspect. And there's not a chance in hell you won't get to talk to her, because she sees all the 'girls.'

If she calls me 'girl,' I swear I'll serve her for lunch.

If that wasn't her we had for dinner.

Hey, Gwyneth Ann, the Donner party is alive and well and living at Shady Acres, eating each...

Her door flew open with a wall-splitting bang. She jerked upright.

"*Stover McIntosh.*" The voice rumbled like a rock fall in a subterranean cave.

She turned. "Excuse me?"

Her first impression was of a pillar of white capped by a lump of rising dough.

"*Excuse you*," the voice mocked. It seemed to emanate from a scarlet-rimmed cavity in the dough.

"I didn't hear a knock," she said.

The apparition resolved itself into a woman's body. A *huge* woman's body. A huge woman's body resembling an ambulatory bureau. The top drawers were pulled out at Stoner's eye level. One was labelled, in white-on-black plastic: Gladys Grenier, RN.

"I don't knock," the bureau announced.

"I didn't know."

"You're the new one."

"Yes. Stoner McTavish. How do you do?"

"Stupid name."

"I was named for Lucy B..."

"I didn't ask." Hands on hips, the woman sized her up.

Stoner sized *her* up. Feet like cement blocks. Ankles oozing over shoe tops. Legs like peeled maple trunks mined with varicose veins. Hands reminiscent of pork roasts. Arms on which flab and muscle fought to a stalemate. Short, thick neck. A face like rice pudding, raisin eyes floating beneath pencilled eyebrows. Lipstick was caked in the corners of her mouth. Dyed black hair clung to her skull like a bathing cap. Her amorphous nose was pressed into the approximate center of her face. Her ears were tiny, pink, and lobeless.

The mouth set itself in motion. "Well?"

"Well," Stoner squeaked.

"Done staring, Princess?"

"Sorry." She dropped her glance to the floor.

"Look at me when I'm talking to you."

Look, but don't stare. Otherwise known as a double-bind, no-win situation.

She looked. Mrs. Grenier was smiling. It wasn't a friendly smile.

"Next time get your own meds. We don't have room service."

Meds? A new brand of sanitary napkin?

"I'm sorry," she said in bewilderment. "I don't know what you mean."

"Sleeping pills."

"Oh!" Stoner exclaimed, enlightened. "Meds. Pills. Thank you very much, but I don't need them."

"Everyone takes them. You're not special."

"Really, I'll be fine. I sleep like the dead."

Mrs. Grenier held out her hand. A small white pill lay embedded in the folds of flesh. "Take it."

Slowly, she reached out and extracted the pill from its matrix. She started for the door. "I have to get water."

Mrs. Grenier blocked her way. "There *was* water. At the nurses' station."

"You want me to take it like *this*?" Her mouth felt like sandpaper.

The bureau shrugged. "You made the choice, Princess."

"Look," Stoner said angrily, "I didn't know I was supposed to get it out there. Nobody told me."

A smile crawled across Gladys Grenier's face. "I warned you," she said. "Mario!"

Hank's clone appeared instantly. Apparently, he had been lurking outside.

"We have us a bad one," Mrs. Grenier chuckled.

"Look, if you'd just take a few minutes to explain the rules, I'd be more than happy..."

The nurse laughed. It was a laugh straight out of *Macbeth*, Act I, Scene 1. She nodded briskly and Mario lept forward.

She caught a flash of silver as he handed Mrs. Grenier a hypodermic. "Wait a minute." Stoner backed up. "We've gotten off on the wrong foot, that's all. The orientation manual's being revised, and..."

Mario swung her around and shoved her face-down on the bed. Pinning her wrists with one hand, he tore the button from her cuff and pushed up her sleeve.

She caught her breath as the needle plunged into her arm.

"Now," said the nurse, "you see how the land lays. Next time line up with the rest."

They let her go. She sat up and rubbed her arm, fear turning to anger. "If I get the chance, I'll see you."

"You do that, Stover." She marched from the room, trailing Mario in her wake.

Stoner tugged off her boot and hurled it at the closing door. "Stoner!" she shouted. "My name is Stoner, dammit!"

The door slammed, their footsteps faded away. Her heart pounded in the pit of her stomach. There was a buzzing in her head. She groped for her pajamas, her muscles turned to liquid. It took every ounce of strength to undress. She pulled back the covers and crawled between coarse sheets.

She had forgotten to turn out the light. She tried to get up, but couldn't. Tears sprang to her eyes.

Bullies!

Inertia oozed through her body.

A memory floated to the surface of her mind. Mario. It was Mario who had caught Gwen on the grounds!

That does it. I'm leaving here tomorrow.

Clinging to the promise, she fell asleep.

****

Someone was screaming. A slow-moving scream that began as a moan, rose to a shriek, and fell. Over and over, rising and falling.

She forced her eyes open. The light was out. Darkness lay solid and heavy a few inches from her face. The screaming had stopped. She listened for a moment. Silence.

Was that me screaming?

From the distance came the muffled sound of waves beating against the cliffs.

A tiny noise began, a whispering, like the hiss of snow on dry leaves.

It moved closer, not whispering now but scurrying, pausing, scurrying. Tiny claws scraping, tiny teeth gnawing.

Mice.

Very large mice.

Rats.

Above her head. In the attic.

Her hands were clammy.

Squirrels, she told herself firmly. Old houses are full of squirrels, making nests, raising their young, storing nuts for winter. Veritable cities of squirrels at work day and night.

Rats confine themselves to basements and sewers. I'm sure they do. I know. I read that somewhere. Rats do not scurry about the upper reaches of buildings and gnaw through ceilings to drop on unsuspecting...

Sleep and reason departed simultaneously for parts unknown.

The scratching grew louder and more insistent. How long would it take them, she wondered, to claw through the attic floor or her sanity, whichever came first?

To hell with waiting for tomorrow. I'm getting out of here now!

She struggled to sit up, and found that her muscles had a will of their own. Like Edith Kesselbaum's first husband, they just wanted to lie down.

Maybe I'm asleep. Maybe this is another of the Collected Nightmares of Sooner McTavish.

Whatever it was fell silent.

A soft tapping began.

I'm not asleep and I don't tap. Lots of things tap but rats aren't one of them.

Tree branches, for instance. Tree branches are noted for highly creative tapping.

That must be it. The tree outside is tapping on the shingles. If there is a tree outside I can't remember. But there must be or there wouldn't be all this scraping and tapping, would there?

There's something faulty about the logic.

Jesus, I'm frightened.

You never used to be a coward. You weren't a coward in Wyoming. Wyoming was a better class of people.

Look, as long as Florence Nightingale went to all the trouble to pump you full of narcotics, the least you could do is show your gratitude by sleeping.

How can I sleep with nature assaulting the house? Nature red in tooth and claw?

The tapping stopped.

The screaming began again. It sounded like someone torturing a cat.

She pulled the pillow over her head.

Either this is a nightmare or I'm in the worst hotel on the East Coast.

Or maybe I've died and gone to Hell.

Or maybe it's The House.

Well, if it is, it's the most juvenile, unimaginative, blatant...

Silence.

She waited for new horrors to start up.

But nothing started up.

Eventually she slept.

****

An ear-splitting rasp jerked her awake.

She sat up, disoriented. There was light in the room. Real light, light from the window. Beautiful, blessed daylight.

And a good morning to you, Shady Acres.

It was the rising buzzer that had wakened her. She swung her legs over the edge of the bed. Her brain was stuffed with damp moss. Her eyes felt grainy. She rubbed them hard, and watched the little red sparks chase each other across her field of vision.

I'll get up in a minute. In a minute I'll stand, walk across the floor, put my clothes on, go to the bathroom, take a shower, and trot on down to breakfast.

It was too much to do in one day.

Last night I couldn't sleep, now I can't wake up.

She let her eyelids drift shut.

Someone bounced into the room.

"She's here!" Jerry shouted.

"Huh?" Stoner said stupidly.

"Claire! She's here!"

"Tell her not to slam the door on the way out."

"She's not *here*," he said. "She's here." He hopped from one foot to the other. "I heard her last night. Didn't you hear her?"

"I didn't hear anything but the tree blowing in the wind."

He stared at her. "Are you nuts? There wasn't any wind last night."

That figures. "And I suppose there isn't any tree out... Never mind."

"She was screaming," Jerry insisted.

"That was me."

"It was *Claire*. I heard her screaming before. Before she went away."

"I thought you knew she was here."

"I knew she was alive, somewhere around here. I didn't know she was RIGHT HERE IN THE HOUSE!" He tugged at her hand. "Come on, we have to find her."

She let him pull her up. "Not now, Jerry. I don't feel very well."

"Gee," he said, peering into her face, "what's wrong with you? You have the flu or something?"

"They shot some stuff into me."

"Oh, gosh. Why'd you let them do that?"

"I didn't have a choice. Look, you're an old hand at this. Do something."

"Right. Don't go away."

Go away? At the rate her mind and body were working, she'd just about reach the door by her 53rd birthday.

If Jerry was right, if it *was* Claire last night... then it wasn't the house, she wasn't in Hell, and she hadn't taken to unauthorized screaming in the night. More importantly, it meant that Claire was 1) alive; 2) on the premises and therefore 3) findable. Now all she had to do was...

He was back, carrying a wet towel. He thrust it at her. "Here."

"Thank you." She buried her face in it. The cold shock helped a little.

"Walk around. And eat breakfast. It gets rid of that junk."

"All right."

"I should have warned you," he said. "They do that to all the new people if you make a mistake."

"It's a little hard not to make a mistake when they don't tell you what to do."

"Yeah, this place sucks."

She wandered to the window and opened it. "That's what Steve said, but he meant all of Castleton."

He looked at her sharply. "What Steve?"

"The waiter at the Harbor House."

"I thought you meant the Steve that disappeared from here last month. Big guy, sharp dresser..."

She was completely alert now. "Someone disappeared from here last month?"

"People disappear from here all the time. I guess they go home at night or something." He shrugged. "Nobody tells *us* anything."

She leaned out the window, stretching to see the roof. "Well, I'm sure patients do get released from time to time."

"Yeah, but this is different. Nobody comes for them. They just go. I go in to clean their rooms, and everything's gone. You planning to jump, or what?"

She pulled herself back inside. "Do you know what's above this room?"

"Just the attic."

"Ever been in there?"

"Sure. I clean all the rooms."

"Does anything live up there?"

He screwed up his face. "Up *there*?"

"Squirrels or rats or anything?"

"Heck, no. Do you think I'd hang around with rats?"

"Maybe you just didn't see them."

"I'd know a *turd* if I saw it, wouldn't I?" He rocked up and down on the balls of his feet. "Are you going to help me find her, or not?"

"I thought you were mad at me."

"I was just being dumb. Well, are you?"

"Of course I'm going to help you."

"Then let's *go*!"

"Jerry, wait a minute." She rubbed her face with the towel and tried to organize her thoughts. "In the first place, I can't go tearing

155

around in my pajamas..."

"Well, get *dressed*." He was hopping again.

"In the second place... Stand still, will you? You're making me seasick."

"She might be in *trouble*!"

"We know she's in trouble, which is why we have to be careful. We'll look for her, but it has to be a well-planned, systematic search. With adequate precautions."

"She might be *dying*!"

"Jerry," she said sharply, "settle down. You *must* understand about systematic and cautious. You're compulsive."

"Oh, yeah," he said. "I forgot."

"Let me get dressed. We'll have breakfast. Pretend you don't suspect anything."

"We can plan over breakfast, right?"

"*No*. We have to sit at separate tables and avoid each other as much as possible in public. We can't let anyone know what we're doing."

"Go under cover," he adds solemnly. "Right?"

"Right."

"This is going to take *forever*."

"Only if we're caught. After breakfast we'll meet somewhere and make plans."

His face fell. "We can't. You're supposed to see Looney Times right after breakfast."

"For God's sake," she said throwing down the towel. "Why didn't anyone tell me?"

"I was going to tell you, but I got excited."

"I noticed." She sighed. "I'll find you after that."

He picked up the wet towel and folded it neatly. "Listen, how come you're doing this?"

She hesitated. In his present state of arousal, he might spill the beans. On the other hand, if they were going to work together, he'd better know what they were up against. Some of it, anyway.

"I'm not really a patient. Some strange things have happened here, and I'm trying to find out who's behind it."

His mouth fell open. "You're a private eye?"

"Well, not really. I mean, sort of, at the moment."

"Far OUT!" he shouted. "This is FAR OUT!"

"Jerry, please, if you blow my cover..."

He composed his features into a mask.

"So run along and I'll see you later."

"I'll wait for you in the conservatory."

"I don't know what time I'll be through."

"That's okay. I can be anonymous for hours."

She shook her head in amusement. "Jerry, are you sure you're not undercover, too?"

"Heck, no. I don't have the guts." He disappeared into the hall, but she could hear him walking away, muttering, "Far out. Far out."

I may feel like something the dog ate off the road, but at least I have an ally.

An ally as stable as a truckload of nitroglycerine.

CHAPTER 9

At five minutes to nine by the hall clock, she sat on the hard vinyl-cushioned chair in Millicent Tunes' waiting room and tried to compose herself. She was fully awake now; breakfast had struck a mortal blow to her lethargy by being, simply, the most disgusting meal she had ever encountered. Scrambled eggs, chartreuse in color and swimming in grease. Orange juice so diluted it could pass for Boston tap water. Toast like flannel. Hot cereal dredged up from the ocean's floor. But she had eaten it, an act of bravery worthy of the Congressional Medal of Honor, because she was already in trouble with the staff and Attracting Attention.

Number One Suspect's walls were decorated with posters = a Women's Art Festival, a Virginia Woolf, a Golda Meir ("but can she type?"). Light-weight, early '70's politics. Nothing revolutionary. No vaginal art. No "Not in Our Name," No "One Nuclear bomb Can Ruin Your Whole Day." No "Woman Giving Birth to Myself." Millicent Tunes had picked up her feminist politics at a nostalgia sale.

Be fair, she reminded herself. The woman may be over fifty, and longing for the good old days of sisterhood and support groups, before it all fell apart in a frenzy of racism, classism, and hetero/homosexism.

She tried to read a copy of the American Psychological Association Division 35 Newsletter. The print was too small for human eyes and most of the articles dealt with plans for ridding the Ethical Standards Bulletin of sexist language.

I could tell them something about Ethical Standards, and it has nothing to do with sexism.

Admit it, you're nervous. Therefore cranky.

Why shouldn't I be nervous? I'm about to spend an hour (with luck, only a fifty-minute hour) with the one person whose name has been most closely linked with the Dark Side of Shady Acres. And who is, presumably, trained to see the very things people most want to hide.

She ran over Edith's instructions. Look at the floor. Don't talk too much. Be depressed.

It better be that easy.

On the wall opposite were displayed a macrame wall hanging and two standard-issue children's paintings. Suns, clouds, lollypop trees, and grotesquely grinning stick-figure people of indeterminate gender. A moribund Swedish ivy stood on the bookcase behind a happy cardboard daisy that thanked her for not smoking. The books were the pop-psych self-help variety, and promised instant health and freedom from neurosis, career-change without tears, and an immediate solution to mid-life crisis. Nothing on how to outpsych a psychologist.

She chewed her lip nervously. I should have paid more attention to technique back in those desperate days with Edith Kesselbaum.

Look, you're here to do a job. You know what you're doing. She doesn't know what you're doing. Therefore, you have the upper hand.

Who am I kidding?

The clock struck, the office door opened.

Stoner stood up, slipping her hands into her back pockets in case they decided to shake.

Millicent Tunes appeared.

She was the epitome of what is described in airline terminal paperbacks as "a willowy blonde." Tall, but not towering. Thin, in the currently fashionable yogurt-and-salad-run-three-miles-before-work way. One tapering, manicured hand rested on the doorknob. Her hair fell loosely to her shoulders. Long, straight nose. Full, slightly pouting mouth. Pristine skin. A touch of mascara, faint tan eye-shadow, muted brick lipstick. A face from a glamor magazine. Except for her eyes. Her eyes were pale brown, flecked with gold, and utterly cold.

She lifted her free hand, patted her hair into place, and said, "Stoner?" in a lilting voice.

Stoner nodded.

"I'm delighted to meet you."

"I thought you'd be older," Stoner said awkwardly.

Millicent Tunes cocked her elegant head to one side. "Will that be a problem for you?"

"Not for me. Some of my best friends are my age."

The woman smiled and revealed the largest set of teeth this side of the Kentucky Derby.

In one corner of the office stood two chairs (Danish Modern) and a coffee table. An end table holding a clip board, pen, and empty coffee mug marked the far seat as the Power Chair.

Stoner sat in it.

Millicent Tunes retrieved her clip board, smoothed her camelhair skirt, and folded herself into the opposite seat.

"Those paintings out there," Stoner said. "Did your children do them?"

"No." Millicent Tunes clicked her pen to "ready." "Tell me about yourself."

"I was born in Rhode Island, " Stoner said, avoiding her eyes.

"And now you live in Boston."

"With my aunt."

"How did that come about?"

"I took the bus."

Millicent Tunes turned her head slightly toward the window, allow-

159

ing Stoner a glimpse of her camera-ready profile. "Suppose you give me the high points. We can fill in the details later."

"There aren't many high points. I'm depressed."

"And why are you depressed?"

"If I knew that, I'd fix it."

Millicent Tunes flashed her smile. It really was quite unpleasant. "Things are more complicated than that, aren't they?"

"Yeah."

"Are you terribly unhappy?"

Her sympathy felt like slime. "I must be, or I wouldn't be here, would I?"

"Do you *feel* unhappy?"

"What?"

"Do you experience a feeling of unhappiness?"

Stoner shrugged. "I guess so."

"And how does that feel?"

"Don't you know?"

"How does it feel to *you*?"

"Shitty."

A flicker of annoyance marred Millicent Tunes's perfect composure. She buried it under another smile. "I sense you find it difficult to talk about yourself."

"A little."

"More than a little, I think. I wonder why that is."

"I guess we look at it differently," Stoner said, deliberately misunderstanding.

"I mean, I wonder why you find it difficult to talk."

"Yes, I do."

Millicent Tunes pursed her lips. "Do you have trouble talking to Dr. Kesselbaum?"

"No."

"Well, then, think of Dr. Kesselbaum and me as interchangeable."

God will strike you dead for that, Millicentness. "But you're so much younger," she said.

"That's rather superficial, Stoner." She adjusted her simple, expensive, genuine seed pearl necklace. "After all, I *am* a fully trained psychologist."

"Really?" she faked wide-eyed awe.

"Columbia," said Millicent Tunes without a trace of modesty.

"I hear they grow great marijuana there."

"Columbia University, in New York City."

"Oh. How's the marijuana there?"

The woman leaned back and tapped her pen against the arm of her chair. "Are you trying to be provocative?"

"Me?" Stoner asked, all innocence. "I don't think so."

"Nervous?"

"Kind of."

"Well." Again the soothsome smile. "I wish you'd trust me, Stoner. I'm very interested in anything you want to talk about."

"I don't know what to talk about."

"Anything you like."

"Okay." Opportunity knocking, grab it. Her mind went blank. Millicent Tunes waited expectantly.

"Do you like working here?"

"Why do you ask?"

"It's kind of in the middle of nowhere," Stoner said. "I was wondering why you'd want to shut yourself off in this Godforsaken place."

"I think," said Millicent Tunes firmly, "it would make more sense to talk about you."

"I'm running away from life. Is that what you're doing?"

"I wonder why you see Shady Acres as running away."

"If I were running away, I'd pick a place like this."

"My work is here."

"But," Stoner persisted, "I'll bet you could do a lot better somewhere else. Do you have stock in the place or something?"

"Stoner," Millicent Tunes said with a touch of annoyance, "my time —our time is valuable. We don't want to waste it, do we?"

"Gee, if you think talking about yourself is a waste of time, you don't have a very high opinion of yourself, do you?"

Millicent tossed her clipboard on the table with a bang. "Stoner..."

"I'm sorry," she said quickly. "I don't know how to start. If you could ask..."

Millicent Tunes fondled her tiny gold earrings and rearranged her expression into one of sympathetic concern. "I think I know what this is all about."

"You do?" Stoner asked warily.

"No one is going to think badly of you." Her voice was smooth and clingy, like cottage cheese that has lain forgotten for six months in the recesses of the refrigerator.

"For what?"

"Being gay."

"I'm not gay, I'm depressed."

Millicent flicked her lovely wrist. "In the sense of sexual preference."

"You mean because I'm a lesbian?"

"Yes. A..." She stumbled a bit over the word. "...lesbian."

Stoner felt no pressing need to respond.

"Do you have a primary relationship?"

"A what?"

"A lover."

"Sort of. Do you?"

She retrieved her clipboard. "Is the relationship satisfactory?"

"Not at the moment."

Millicent reached eagerly for her pen. "And why is that?"

"Because I'm here and she's there."

"What else?"

"Nothing."

"You're certain?" she seemed disappointed.

"Why not?"

"Well..." Millicent tunes cleared her throat. "...Lesbian relationships can be difficult."

"All relationships are difficult, aren't they?"

"You're being defensive, Stoner."

"Sorry."

"Sex life?" Millicent asked, taking aim at her clip board.

"Whenever possible."

"Do you *enjoy* your sex life?"

"Sure. Who doesn't?"

"Tell me about it."

She felt herself turn red. "My *sex* life?"

Millicent Tunes nodded and waited.

Stoner let her wait.

"I won't be shocked." She adjusted her hair. "Psychologists are accustomed to hearing all kinds of things."

"Pretty racy stuff, huh?" Stoner said brightly. "I'll bet you never have to buy trashy novels."

"Sex isn't trashy, Stoner. It's a natural biological function. You mustn't be ashamed."

"I'm not ashamed."

"Well, that's a very healthy attitude. Many ... lesbians feel an unconscious sense of shame."

Stoner frowned. "If it's unconscious, how do they feel it?"

"Believe me, they do."

"Not me. I figure I'm lucky. I don't have to worry about unwanted pregnancies and yeast infections."

"True," Millicent said flatly.

"How come you know so much about what lesbians feel? Unconsciously, that is."

"I told you, I'm highly..."

"Right," Stoner interrupted. "Highly trained. There are a lot of highly trained people around here, aren't there?"

"We're very proud of our staff," Millicent said. "Tell me about your lover."

Not on your life. "I thought I was supposed to talk about myself."

"That would be appropriate, wouldn't it?"

My God, the woman's cool. I'd be tempted to toss me out on my ear. But, then, I'm not highly trained.

"There's one thing," she said, perversity pushing her on.

162

Millicent leaned forward. "yes?"

"It's the other women."

"Other women? Then you're not monogamous?"

"They won't let me be. They call me at work. They show up at my house in the middle of the night. Women in filmy negligees, high-heeled shoes, denim jackets, black lace garter belts, Saran wrap. Even here, I'll look out the window some night and there they'll be, running, stumbling up the walk, rhinestones glinting in the moonlight..."

"All right," Millicent said. "That's enough."

"God knows I don't encourage them. All I want is to get married, settle down, and have five wimmin-children by parthenogenesis."

"I said," Millicentunes barked, "that's enough." Her smile cut a gash in her face. "This isn't amusing, Stoner."

"Forgive me," Stoner said contritely. "I didn't sleep last night."

"Indeed?" She made a note on her clip board. "Why was that?"

"Someone was screaming."

"Did that trouble you?"

No, nothing calms me like a soul in torment. "A little."

"You'll get accustomed to it. Some of our guests are disturbed."

"I'm not surprised, what with the rats and all."

"Rats?"

"There were rats running around in the attic."

Millicent frowned. "I'm sure we don't have rats."

"You have something."

"I see." She made another note. "Do you suffer from hallucinations?"

"No, but I have a few I enjoy."

Millicent ignored that. "What room are you in?"

"Thirty-three B."

"Ah!" She nodded. "That's directly beneath the cupola. Birds nest in the cupola."

"In March?"

"I'll have it looked into. Meanwhile, we'll give you something to help you sleep."

"They tried that," Stoner said. "It wasn't a good experience."

"Yes," Millicent said. "I heard."

"Aren't there laws against forced medication?"

This time Millicentunes' smile was genuine, and nasty. "You were given a form to sign when you arrived, weren't you?"

"Yeah, some insurance thing..."

"Included in that form was your permission to let *us* decide what treatment is in your best interest."

Stoner sat up. "You can *what?*"

"You heard me."

"Nobody told me."

169

"Nevertheless."

"Jesus Christ!"

The elegant Dr. Tunes tilted her head to one side and fixed Stoner with a gold-flecked, steely gaze.

She got to her feet. "I'm checking out."

"I don't think so. You also agreed to let us decide when you're ready to leave."

Furious, she started for the door.

Millicent caught her wrist. "If you're unhappy here, there's always the state hospital."

Stoner froze in her tracks.

"Sit down, please."

She went back to her chair.

"It changes things a bit, doesn't it?" Millicent asked.

"I guess so." She propped her elbows on her knees and rested her head helplessly in her hands.

Millicent once touched her arm. "I'm not trying to be cruel, Stoner. But we mustn't lose sight of why you're here."

Stoner tightened her jaw. I know why I'm here, lady. And, by God, when I'm ready to leave, I'll leave. Edith Kesselbaum can get me out.

Can't she?

Can't she?

"May I make a phone call?" she asked.

"I'm afraid not."

The muscles in her stomach began to shake.

Millicent moved over to sit on the coffee table and take Stoner's wrists in her hands. "I know how you feel," she said, all sweetness and light. "It's a hard adjustment at first, but when you learn to work with us rather than against us, you'll find this a very therapeutic experience."

Therapeutic? I've been in this snake pit less than 24 hours. I've been insulted by your lousy head nurse, assaulted by that cretin Mario, scrutinized, pumped full of drugs, kept awake by screaming and rats in the walls, and stuffed with pig slop served up by smiling schizophrenics. That isn't my idea of therapeutic.

"I'm here to help you, Stoner."

She forced herself to look — pathetically, she hoped — into Millicent's cold eyes. "You all make me feel like a criminal, but I haven't done anything wrong."

"Guilt is a component of severe depression."

The woman's relentless. "Dr. Tunes..."

"Millicent." She rested her hand on Stoner's knee. "Call me Millicent."

"I'd rather not."

"It helps equalize the power in the relationship."

You can have me strapped down and shoot electricity through my

164

head. You can put me in seclusion and feed me drugs until I can't stand. You can ship me off to the state hospital, all nice and legal. There ain't no equality in *this* relationship, Massa.

"Okay," she said. "Millicent."

"Good." Millicent squeezed her knee. "Now tell me what I can do for you."

"Do for me?"

"If you'll think of me as a friend, I can make your stay here a lot more pleasant and productive."

It sounded ominously like a line from an old prison movie.

"Well..." A brilliant idea flashed into her mind. "Could I go outside?"

Millicent frowned. "Whatever for?"

"Just to look around."

"Why would you want to do that?"

"It's just..." She ducked her head. "Never mind. It's silly."

"Nothing is silly."

"You'll laugh at me."

"Of course I won't, Stoner."

She shifted her feet. "I have these dreams, nightmares, about a house."

"A house?"

"Yeah." She looked up. "That's all I remember. Except, when I got there, I knew it was this house."

"How very odd. And you can't recall anything else?"

"I try. Sometimes I almost catch hold of it, but it slips away. So I thought, if I could kind of walk around a little, it might bring it back, you know?"

"I really don't..."

"Forget it," Stoner said abruptly. "It was a stupid idea."

"That isn't it."

"Maybe you don't have the authority..."

"I am in charge here," Millicent said. "Everything that happens at Shady Acres happens by *my* orders, and only mine."

Well, well.

"So may I..."

Millicent shook her head. "I don't think it would be wise."

"You tell me to trust you," Stoner said, pretending to flare up, "but you don't trust *me* to take a lousy walk around your lousy house."

"With depressed patients..."

Stoner cut her off. "Think of you as a friend." She laughed harshly. "That's the best joke I've heard all year, Millicent."

"The risk of suicide..."

"If I wanted to kill myself, do you think I'd have checked into a maximum security mental hospital?"

"What would you do?"

"Get a gun, wait for pheasant season, and mutilate every hunter I saw. If I survived that, I'd fly a planeload of explosives through the front door of the Pentagon and die happy."

"Such violence," Millicent murmured softly. Her eyes sparkled. "How does that express itself in your personal life?"

"What?"

Millicent gazed at her thoughtfully. "It would be interesting, wouldn't it, to see how that would translate itself sexually?"

"Not particularly."

"You've never been tempted to inflict pain in a sexual context?"

"Never."

"Many do. Passion enhances passion, as it were."

"That's their problem."

Millicent got up and strolled to the window. "I find it an interesting phenomenon, clinically speaking."

"Then you should meet my ex-lover."

"Was she aroused by violence?"

"Emotional violence. She may have moved on to bigger things by now."

Perching on the window sill, Millicent turned to her. "Tell me about it."

"I'd rather not."

"Did it excite you?"

"It made me want to die."

"Perhaps we should talk about that," Millicent said.

"There's nothing to talk about. It's over."

"How did this violent side of her nature show itself?"

"Look," Stoner said, "if it's exciting to you, I'd be glad to put you in touch with her."

"It doesn't *excite* me, Stoner. My interest is purely professional." She folded her arms. "I must admit, I've always been intrigued by the incidence of sado-masochism in the gay community."

"Well, I'm afraid I can't satisfy your curiosity," Stoner said, her anger real now. "Try the straight community. They call it love."

"There's no need to be defensive."

"Isn't there?"

"As a social scientist, I naturally have an interest in unusual subcultures."

"Take your unusual subculture, and shove it!"

"Aren't you overreacting a bit?"

"Am I?"

"I think you are. You're taking an intellectual discussion and perceiving it as a personal attack." She smiled. "Perhaps you're not as comfortable with your sexual orientation as you like to pretend."

"The only thing uncomfortable about my sexual orientation is your

166

curiosity about it."

"We'll see. I'm going to enjoy working with you."

Stoner glared at her. "I wouldn't want to bore you."

"I don't think you could bore anyone."

"Only my ex-lover, the sadist."

"She seems to be very much on your mind. Perhaps that should be the topic of our next session."

"It's ancient history."

"And yet you bring her up twice in the same hour."

"The conversation warranted it." She felt as if she were about to explode.

"We have to face the hard things, you know."

"Swell. But leave me out of it."

Millicent twisted a strand of blonde hair around her finger. "Resistance?"

"Whatever."

"It doesn't have to be difficult. There are techniques..."

We have ways of making you talk. "Such as?"

"Hypnosis, for one."

"Thanks, I think I'll pass."

"Certain drugs..."

"I've had enough drugs," she snapped.

Millicentunes sighed. "We want to help you, Stoner. I'd prefer to do it with your consent."

"Why bother? I signed away my rights on your phoney insurance form."

"Isn't that a little paranoid?"

"This place breeds paranoia."

"We're all professionals."

"What do you use as a training manual, *One Flew Over The Cuckoo's Nest?*"

"You're not making a very good first impression, Stoner," Millicent said, toying with her pearls. "There have been two complaints against you already."

"I didn't know you were holding a Miss Congeniality contest."

"Refusing medication, not finishing dinner."

"What do I win with three strikes, a lobotomy?"

Millicent came over and took her hands. "Stoner, Stoner, why won't you trust me?"

"You figure it out," Stoner said, and pushed her away.

Millicent raised one eyebrow. "Hostility?"

Something in her broke. "I don't like being touched by strangers!" she shouted. "I don't like being drugged. I don't like being condescended to. I don't like being locked up. I don't like being out of control."

"You're out of control now."

167

"You'd be out of control, too, if I treated you like..." Her voice broke.

"I think," Millicent said smoothly, "we need to explore your transference problems."

"Try picking up the morning paper," she choked, "and reading hate letters calling you filthy, with appropriate Biblical references. Try having obscenities shouted at you by beer-soaked adolescents in pick-up trucks. Watch the state legislature pass laws to keep you from living where you want, or working where you want. Let them tell you a state orphanage is a better environment for a child than living with you. Then come back and talk to me about transference."

"My," Millicent murmured, "so bitter."

Fists clenched, Stoner whirled on her. "Want to see *hard*? I'll show you hard."

"Would that give you pleasure?" Millicent asked with a little smile.

Stoner caught her breath, and realized she was crying. "God*damn* you!"

"That's *good*, Stoner. Get your anger out."

"Up yours!"

Tears running down her face, she gasped for air. Millicent offered her a box of tissues. She turned her back and rammed her hands into her pockets.

"I can see that this is going to be a very productive relationship." She didn't dare respond.

"If you still want to take a little stroll around the grounds, I'll tell the aides you have my permission."

"Don't do me any favors," Stoner said hoarsely.

Millicent chuckled. "You're such a brat, Stoner. Just a little scared brat." There was a friendly eagerness in her voice that made Stoner's flesh crawl. "You trusted me with your feelings. The least I can do is trust you..."

She started to protest, and stopped herself. She'd already lost her self-respect. The least she could do was salvage a few hours of freedom. "Thank you," she said, the words tasting like moth larvae in her mouth.

Millicent touched her shoulder. "This seems like a good place to stop for now. We'll take it up again tomorrow."

Wiping her eyes on her sleeve, she stumbled through the door. Lilly sat in the waiting room perched on the edge of a chair.

Wonderful. A witness.

She tore across the hall and up the stairs to her room.

I won't let her do this to me again. I won't. I won't.

"I want to go home," she said aloud.

"Can I help?"

She turned.

Lilly stood in the doorway.

"I'm sorry you heard that, Lilly," she said. "I'm not usually so.... so....."

Lilly smiled.

"Would you like to come in?"

The elderly woman sat on the bed and folded her hands in her lap.

"I don't know what's wrong with me," Stoner said. "I don't know what made me think I could...."

She hesitated. But what could be safer than talking to Lilly? The woman was in her own private world, and she desperately needed to talk to someone.

"I shouldn't have lost my temper," she said. "But, damn it, she made me so angry. I know she's your niece, Lilly, but Millicent Tunes is a 24-carat bitch."

Lilly patted her hand. "Well, she certainly didn't get it from my side of the family."

Stoner stared at her. "Lilly?"

"It could be her own unpleasant nature, of course, but then her father was a no-account s.o.b. at heart."

She couldn't believe her ears. "I thought you were...."

"Crazy?" Lilly laughed. "I'm as sane as you, dear. Probably more so, if you're doing what I think you're doing."

Stoner shook her head to clear it. "You're... but everyone thinks...."

"Exactly what I want them to think," Lilly said, her eyes sparkling. "I've missed my calling. I should have gone on the stage."

"This is very confusing," Stoner said.

"It is, isn't it? I'm a bit bewildered myself. What in the *world* are you doing here?"

"Looking for Claire Rasmussen."

Lilly tapped her fingertips together. "Poor Claire. I'm afraid she bit off more than she could chew. She found out something, you see."

"Do you know what she found out?" Stoner asked, sitting beside her.

"I haven't the slightest idea. They hide it very well. And I've felt it was better that I not show too much curiosity. They can turn very nasty."

"Yes, I believe you."

"My dear, as they used to say, 'you ain't seen nothing yet.'" She sighed. "And if I did manage to sniff out their secret, what could I do? Go to the authorities? In the eyes of the law I'm mentally incompetent."

"But you're not."

"I was. Shortly after Millicent came here, I went completely off my rocker. I suspect she put something in my food. Probably LSD or some such. I had some truly startling visions, let me tell you. As for what I actually did, I'm afraid that's all a blank. Though I do recall reciting poetry from the inn of the town fountain. I hope it wasn't bawdy."

"I heard it was Whitman," Stoner said, still in shock.

"Well, that's not too bad."

"Excuse me, Lilly ... I mean, Miz Lilly..."

"Lilly will do. I'm quite used to it."

"What I don't understand is, how did you let her get away with it? I mean, if you're not very fond of her..."

"Oh, I'm not," Lilly said. "Not fond at all. Never was."

"Then why did you let her in in the first place?"

Lilly smiled. "When you're getting on in years, relatives who haven't given you the time of day in the past begin to flock around. They expect you to die any minute, you see, and they want to be in on the inheritance. Well, I told Millicent in no uncertain terms that there was nothing here for her. That was my great mistake. It forced her hand."

"But you're not drugged now."

"During one of my rare moments of lucidity = I had a few, even then = it occurred to me that, if I didn't make her think I'd gone completely 'round the bend, I'd be taking LSD for the rest of my natural life. And I certainly didn't want that. Goodness, I've had revelations about the Cosmic that would curl your hair."

"Once your mind was clear," Stoner said, "couldn't you have run away?"

"At my age?" she laughed. "My dear, I may have all my mental faculties intact, but my days of leaping over hill and dale like a jackrabbit are long gone." She fingered her smock. "Dan is dead, isn't he?"

"I'm afraid he is."

"Poor boy," Lilly said, shaking her head sadly. "I imagine Delia is taking it hard."

"Well, she keeps going, but I know she hurts."

"I do wish there were something I could do. Maybe I can, if you can get to the bottom of things."

Stoner kneaded her face. "I'm afraid I'm not doing very well with it."

"Nevertheless, here you are. The answer to my prayers, and just as I was about to give up hope. Isn't life amazing?"

There were footsteps in the hall, coming their way.

"Oh, dear," Lilly said. She got up. "They watch me like a hawk. We'd better not meet like this again."

"Lilly," Stoner said, "you're a fantastic woman."

"Thank you, dear. But please do what you have to do in a hurry. I don't think I can hold on much longer."

She scurried from the room.

"*There* you are," Becky said from the hall. "Wandering again. You're supposed to be in O.T. now, remember?"

170

"O.T., O.T., O.T.," Lilly sang.

The footsteps receded.

Stoner gazed at the empty doorway. Two years, and I couldn't even make it through a day.

Enough self-pity. I came to do a job, and by God I'm going to do it!

She went to the bathroom, washed the puffiness from her eyes, and ran downstairs to meet Jerry.

***

He was pacing the conservatory, taking random swipes at the tabletops with his dust cloth. Magazines lay in unruly piles. One sofa cushion was askew. Not exactly a pig sty, but anyone knowing Jerry would raise a questioning eyebrow.

He saw her coming and bounced up to her. "Can we go get her now?"

"We have to talk first," she said firmly.

"Yeah, okay."

"Not here in plain sight."

He dragged her into the shadows of a corner. "We can't just mess around," he said urgently. "They're *doing* things to her."

"What things? And who's doing them and why?"

His face fell. "I don't know."

"All right, that's why we have to be careful. We don't know what we're up against." She took a deep breath. "I'm going to take you into my confidence. But you have to promise you won't reveal a word of what I tell you."

"I promise," he said quickly.

"I mean this, Jerry. If anyone finds out, or even guesses what we're doing, our lives could be in danger. Claire's life could be in danger. Do you understand?"

"Sure. I'm not stupid."

"Nobody must know what we're up to. Not even your therapist."

"I never tell him anything. He's a dumb cluck."

"If anyone suspects, they might try to intimidate you, to make you tell."

He laughed. It had the rusty sound of an unused hinge. "Did you ever go to military school?"

"No."

"Then you don't know what intimidation really is."

Stoner smiled. "You're right. I apologize."

He shrugged self-consciously.

"Okay, here's what I know. Nancy Rasmussen, Claire's sister..."

"Claire talks about her a lot," Jerry said.

"Nancy's worried about her. So last weekend my friend and I..."

171

"Your girlfriend?"

"Yes, my girlfriend. We came up here to see her. They claimed she was away on vacation."

"She wasn't. She was right here."

"My friend saw her. Later, we sneaked back onto the grounds. We found her car in the woods, in an old cellar hole."

His eyes got big.

"They caught my friend, but they didn't see me. That night, two men tried to beat her up."

"Two *men* beat up on a *girl*?"

"On a *woman*. We think they did it to scare us off. That was Saturday, the night you say Claire disappeared."

"Gosh," he said. "Then they know who you are."

"It was dark. I don't think they recognized me."

"*I'd* recognize you."

"I'm counting on them not being as perceptive as you."

He squared his shoulders and nodded solemnly.

"There's more," Stoner said. "Delia, who owns the Clam Shack..."

"I've been there. It's a nice, clean place."

"I'll tell her you said so. Coming from an expert, she'll take it as quite a compliment."

He fidgeted. "Get to the point, okay?"

"Delia's husband drowned about a year ago. She thinks he was murdered because of something he found out."

"About *this* place?"

"She believes there was a cover-up. That's why she can't go to the police. We don't know who might be in on it."

"What did he find out?"

"He never got a chance to tell."

Jerry chewed that over. "Far out," he said.

"Now, it's possible Claire found out something, too, and that's why they're 'doing things' to her."

"Why didn't they kill her?"

"I don't know. Afraid of too many unexplained deaths, maybe. And she was on parole. They might know that, and be afraid the police will start poking around if she disappears."

"So they make her crazy instead."

"It's occurred to me," Stoner said. "But what good would that do?"

"Simple," Jerry said. "If she's crazy, and she talks, no one will believe her."

"Jerry, that's brilliant!"

"Well," he said diffidently, "I've had some experience along those lines."

"And since this is a mental hospital, they could claim they kept her here to cure her."

"Shitheads." He glanced at her. "Pardon me."

172

"If the Department of Corrections came asking questions, they'd say they didn't know she was on parole, turn her over, and that would be that."

"Okay," Jerry said. "Let's go find her."

"Not so fast. We have to find out what *she* found out."

"Why?"

"Suppose we find her. Do you think they're going to open the gates and send us off with a picnic basket and best wishes for a happy life? More likely we'd end up like Claire. And if we escape without evidence, we're just three escaped mental patients. To get the police to even listen to us, we have to find out the truth and be able to prove it."

"That's going to take *forever*."

"Not if we plan it right."

"What do you figure? Another day?"

Stoner clenched her fists. "Jerry, please. We have to think this out."

"Okay, think."

"You say you've searched the building?"

"I told you that."

"Including the cupola?"

He frowned. "Nobody goes up in the cupola."

"Do you *know* that?"

"If anyone was up there, they'd have me clean it, wouldn't they?"

"Not necessarily. I think that's where Claire was last night."

"It isn't *heated*."

"I'm sorry."

His face turned crimson. "Nobody'd be that mean."

"Jerry, anyone who's capable of murder would be that mean. Do you have a key?"

"Not to up there."

"Well, they'll probably move her, if they haven't already. How about the cellar?"

"There's only a root cellar. Nobody cleans root cellars. Why would they move her?"

"Because I told Millicent Tunes I heard screaming..."

"Why did you do that?" he yelled. "For crying out loud!"

She grabbed him by the shoulders. "It was a mistake. I didn't think. Keep your voice down."

"They'll kill her!" Jerry rasped.

"I doubt it. If they suspect someone might notice, they'll be more careful. And *we* have to be careful."

"Careful?! You call what you did careful?"

"Jerry!" she said sharply, "if you want to help me with this, you have to control yourself. I have dangerous work to do. I can't take the time to argue with you every step of the way. So make up your

173

mind. Either settle down and do what I tell you, or I'll walk out of here and forget the whole thing."

He hung his head. "I'm sorry. I'm just so scared for her."

"It's all right to be scared. I'm concerned, too. But I've done this kind of thing before." Hell, in a world full of treachery, what's one little lie? "I know what I'm doing. I have contacts...'" She lowered her voice. "In the FBI."

He gazed at her, awestruck. "Far out," he breathed.

"So," she said roughly, "which is it? Do we do it my way, or do I do it alone?"

He pulled himself to attention. "What's the drill, Chief?"

She frowned sternly at him. "Make me a map of this house. Every room, and who or what's in it. Try to find a book on the history of the place. It's old enough, there might be one. Look for any clue to secret passageways or hidden alcoves."

"What good's a book going to do?"

"*Don't ask questions.*"

"Sorry, Chief."

"Good detective work requires a lot of research. It isn't glamorous, and it isn't exciting, but it is necessary."

"Right."

"I want you to think about all the patients who've disappeared from here in unusual ways. Try to remember anything you can about them, no matter how unimportant it seems."

Jerry beamed. "That's how they always solve mysteries, isn't it? Something that looks unimportant at the time...'"

"This isn't a novel. Don't get your hopes up. But it can't hurt. I'm going out to search the grounds. After lunch, I'd like you to take me to Claire's room."

"You're supposed to be in O.T. after lunch."

"I'll handle it. You be ready, and meet me by the door to the staff quarters. Got that?"

"Got it."

"Remember, behave normally."

"I'm not normal."

"Whatever's normal for you." She gestured at the room. "And clean up this mess. Anybody with a grain of sense would know your mind's somewhere else."

He made a dive for the nearest pile of magazines. She caught his arm. "One more thing." Tearing a corner off a newspaper, she plucked a pencil from his pocket and wrote down Delia's phone number. "Memorize this, and destroy it. If anything happens to me, call this number and say, 'Stoner's in trouble.' Nothing more. Do you understand?"

His eyes were like saucers. "Is that a code?"

"Sort of."

174

"Gosh!"

"And remember, Jerry. If you do anything to tip them off, we're all dead."

***

A chilling mist probed the seams of her clothes. She shivered, pulled her jacket tighter, and breathed the salty air of freedom. Millicentunes had been true to her fashion-plate word. The aide had let her go with only a disapproving glance.

She poked at a pebble with her toe. Strange, that sudden change of mind. For all their talk about obeying rules, not making trouble ... just when it seemed she had cooked her goose in one outburst of temper, she got her way.

Had she made such a spectacle of herself that Millicent felt sorry for her? That was a chilling thought.

Or maybe the woman just likes being shouted at. It fits in with her "professional interests."

More likely it was a display of power. Millicent giveth, and Millicent taketh away. Blessed be the name of Millicent.

Anyway, don't look a gift horse in the mouth. It might have Millicent's teeth.

She whistled a little under her breath. If she's willing to let me look around, she can't be very suspicious of me.

Unless this is a trap.

She stopped whistling.

Sometimes they wander over the cliff.

She strolled casually along the path to the parking lot, and whirled suddenly to look up at the house.

No one was watching her. No one was following.

Still, eternal vigilence is the best defense.

She cut across the brittle lawn to the cliff's edge. The sea was the place to start, where Dan had seen whatever he had seen. Glancing back periodically, she ambled to the south, then turned and started back. The ocean lay a hundred feet below at the bottom of a perpendicular granite wall. Through the gathering mist, she could make out a frosting of barnacles, but no mussels. The tide was somewhere between high and low. As far as she could tell, there was no way up or down that glistening wall.

The water was calm today, rocking lazily beneath a sky turned slate. Mist coalesced, dispersed, coalesced like phantoms toying with substance. A gentle surf hid the greedy undertow.

She pushed on.

Then she saw it, a section of rock, cracked by frost and eroded by time, fallen away from the land. Boulders lay tumbled at the bottom like a tower of blocks pushed over by a bored child. The rocks were slippery as oil. Moving carefully, crawling from boulder to boulder, she made her way steadily downward. A natural staircase.

At the edge of the water she stopped, panting a little with cold and exertion. So far, so good. It would be possible — not easy, but possible — to move cargo up the cliff from here. But even a rowboat would have to tie up somewhere. She looked around for a mooring.

A tidepool, black with cold, lay at her feet. Droplets from a breaking wave shattered its glassy surface. She studied the puddle, then gazed out to sea. Choosing a wave, she followed it to shore. It crashed against the rocks. Spray exploded skyward, and rained down into the pool. She followed another, then another. On the eighth try, the surface of the tidepool lay unbroken. The tide was going out.

She backed up against the cliff, out of reach of the wind, hardly feeling the cold, and watched the receding sea edge. She wondered if Jerry had memorized the phone number yet, and pictured him in an agony of indecision — wanting to follow orders and destroy the slip of paper (by eating it, no doubt), but needing to check it one more time to be sure he had it right.

What if he *had* eaten it, but didn't have it right?

What if they needed help, he had time for one quick call, dialed, said "Stoner's in trouble," hung up, and had the wrong number?

Her best friend, Panic, stopped by for a visit.

He won't get it wrong. Jerry would never make a mistake. Jerry's compulsive. You can always count on a compulsive to get things right.

Dear God, don't let him be cured before we need that number.

Blue mussels appeared, plastered to the sides of half-submerged boulders at her feet.

Mussels don't live in air.

Low tide.

In the instant of stillness before a wave swept over the rocks, something caught her eye. She scrambled toward it. A large, rusty iron ring embedded in the rock. Mooring, check.

She turned and surveyed the cliff rim. Anyone docking here at low tide would be invisible from the house. But the way she had come down would take them directly beneath the east windows. There had to be another way.

She started climbing up, scanning the cliff, waiting for the chimneys of Journey's End to appear on the horizon.

Part way up she stopped. Another series of step-like rocks drifted to the right. She clambered up them. In a few minutes the path levelled off, following a ledge to the northern tip of the peninsula. The house was still invisible. But sooner or later they would have to risk being seen.

Not necessarily. The house was over a hundred years old. And in those days before central heating, houses were often built windowless on the north, to block the coldest of winter's winds. Unless it had been renovated...

She hurried up the last few rocky steps and pulled herself onto the dead grass at the top of the cliff.

The house turned a blank face northward.

"Well," she said aloud, "now I know." A ship could hover off shore, hidden by moonless darkness. At low tide, they would transfer the contraband to a dinghy, row in, and stash the loot in the root cellar.

But they'd have to work fast. In the short time she'd rested, the sea had returned to cover the mooring.

And they'd have to be strong. She hadn't exactly been pumping iron, but she wasn't out of shape, either, and the climb had winded her. Even without a load of Colombian Gold on her back.

But maybe, with enough able bodies... After all, ants could haul hundreds of times their weight, working together. Ants and ancient Egyptian slaves, and Mayflower Moving and Storage men. Hey, buddy, wanta buy some grass, just came over on the Mayflower?

She got to her feet and shot the house a triumphant glance. How does it feel to lose a round?

Journey's End appeared to withdraw into itself to plot revenge.

She trotted around the back of the house, safe now from watchful eyes. Mounds of grainy snow lay on the ground, here where the sun never quite reached. It probably wouldn't melt until August. On the Fourth of July you could come out here and make snowballs.

Not that I plan on being here on the Fourth of July.

I don't even plan on being here on the first of April.

One week ago, I didn't plan on being here at all.

One week ago, the last thing I expected to be was a patient in a mental hospital. Even a terrific mental hospital like Shady Acres.

She stopped and watched her breath puff in the cold.

I am not a patient here. I have to remember that. I may have a room, and a therapist, and be drugged nightly, but I am *not* a patient.

I am a detective. A private investigator. A spy. A tracer of lost persons. Like Cagney and Lacey. Charlie's Angels. Scarecrow and Mrs. King.

Stoner and Jerry. Hoo, boy.

Root cellar. Just where it was supposed to be. A flight of stone steps set into the ground. At the bottom a whitewashed door. She raised the latch and pushed. It swung wide without a sound.

No rust on *these* hinges, no sir.

Slowly her eyes adjusted to the twilight of the underground room. It was empty. The walls were made of stone and crumbling mortar. A small window, caked with dirt, let in a pale, sickly glow. With the light from the doorway, she could barely see.

The pressed dirt floor was littered with footprints. No roots in the root cellar, but plenty of traffic.

177

She studied the walls for signs of another exit. Nothing. The room was completely cut off from the rest of the house. No hidden trap-door in the ceiling. Spiders had caroused there for millenia. And, if someone decided to come along and lock that door, no way out.

Better leave it open.

No, someone might notice.

But if they lock me in...

Oh, for God's sake, make up your mind!

She closed the door, which left her in almost total darkness.

She opened it.

Dropping to her knees, she searched the floor. No tell-tale flakes of white powder. No nerdles of gray-green leaf. These people were tidy, she had to grant them that.

She sat and leaned against the wall. Here was an odd thing; somewhere, amid the footprints, there should be other marks — of boxes or at least sacks. Surely they'd put it down, wouldn't they? Unless they passed it on immediately, in which case why bother to rendezvous here?

And what were they passing on, anyway?

She took another hard look at the footprints. They were all remarkably similar. Two, three people at the most had made those marks. And they had done a great deal of walking in a very small space.

Pacing? Waiting for something? A signal from the ship?

In a cold, damp, enclosed room with no lights, no moon, and no way to look seaward?

Not likely.

She searched the floor again. Nothing, not even a discarded cigarette butt.

So what does that tell you? That this is a holding tank for health freaks?

If I really do have psychic powers, as Aunt Hermione claims, I should be able to attune to the atmosphere and pick up a message.

She folded her legs and arms in what she hoped was a properly meditative fashion, closed her eyes, emptied her mind, and waited for something to occur to her.

What occurred were two commercial jingles, the theme from a TV sitcom, last month's net income at the travel agency, a reminder to make a dentist appointment, and the last verse of "Send In The Clowns."

Okay, that's it for the cellar. Let's see what Claire's room brings to light.

CHAPTER 10

The two old men who shared her table hung like vultures over their plates, mouths permanently gaping, and spooned in the stew. Some of it fell back out. Some dribbled a little, puddling up in the clefts of their chins to be caught in the next spoonful. The remainder disappeared, sucked down their throats by some mysterious mechanism which didn't seem to involve swallowing.

If this is what Behavior Mod does for you, she thought, they'd better switch to Dream Analysis.

Her other lunchmate, whom she now recognized as Ione from 37B, had given up — or completed — Rosemary Clooney, and was on to Early Childhood Memories. Hoping to be distracted from the vultures, Stoner turned toward her and gave her full attention.

"Our milk was delivered in glass bottles," Ione said. "Round glass bottles with discs of cardboard in the top. You had to pry them up with a paper tab, and sometimes it tore. The milk and cream always separated — it wasn't homogenized, you see, and there wasn't anything added, it was just milk. In the winter it might freeze, and the cream would rise in an ivory pillar, right out of the bottle. You had to watch for cats when that happened. They'd go from house to house, all up and down the alley, following the milkman. Sometimes there was a yellow cellophane cap over the top, fastened with a black paper band. They don't wrap things in cellophane any more. It's all plastic and cardboard. It's safer, you see, and it all looks the same."

She glanced at Stoner. "It's hard to care about things when they all look the same."

"Yes," Stoner said, "it is."

"When you bought something at the five and dime, even if it was only Cutex nail polish or Evening in Paris perfume, you took your time because even though they were all alike, they weren't all the same. You could see how the different bottles felt, and how they sounded when you tapped them against each other. So when you finally made up your mind, and paid for it and took it home, it was really *yours*, because you'd picked it out from all the things that were alike but not the same."

"You're right. I never thought of it that way."

Ione smiled. She had a nice smile, that smoothed out the strain wrinkles around her mouth. "You're too young. You missed all that. I'm sorry you missed it."

"So am I," Stoner said.

"Our five and dime smelled like caramel corn. There were seats near the front door, across from the paper fans and greeting cards, where you could sit and wait for the rain to stop or your taxi to come. A couple of old ladies used to sit there all day long. They wore black sturdy shoes with laces, and carried black handbags. They never talked to each other, just sat there staring into space or maybe at the pictures of waterfalls and mountain lakes on the paper fans across the way. I'll bet they don't do that now. I'll bet if they did that now, someone would come and tell them to move along."

"Probably."

"There were three dairies in town. Seven thousand people and three dairies. In the spring the milk and butter would taste of wild garlic. It was the first sign of spring, even before the bluebottles bloomed." She frowned. "I don't remember if the milkman came every day. I wish I could remember. Everything would be all right if I could remember if the milkman came every day."

"Tell me more," Stoner said, genuinely intrigued.

"We had a screened-in porch over the garage. The garage was attached to the house, part of the house, really. The living room and the garage shared a wall. Every time my father drove the car into the garage, he'd tap the wall with the front bumper. I used to think some day that wall would just crack and collapse, and the whole house would fall on us, but it didn't. There were cots on the sleeping porch, and in the summer when the nights were hot — sometimes it was so hot you thought you could hear the trees perspiring in the night, drip, drip. I suppose that was only humidity condensing on the leaves, or insects feeding. Last year, when the gypsy moths invaded, you could hear that drip, drip all night long. I'd wake up and think I was home, listening to the trees perspire. But my husband said it was the gypsy moths chewing, or defecating — that's what he called it, defecating. I wish he hadn't told me. I don't think people should tell you everything, do you?"

"No," Stoner said, "I don't."

"They should ask first. They should say, 'I happen to know what that sound is. Should I tell you, or would it ruin it?' That would be more polite."

"Definitely."

"I used to sleep out on the sleeping porch. The sheets felt damp and a little gritty. I liked that. It made me feel as if I were camping. Summer thunderstorms smell like dust and electricity. They say everything looks too big when you're small. I don't remember that. I remember everything being the right size. I had to stand on a chair to reach the glasses in the kitchen cupboards, but they didn't seem too big. You just had to stand on a chair."

She realized she liked this woman. She wondered what she was like outside Shady Acres, and pictured her having her hair done

180

every Thursday and reading movie magazines under the dryer. "How long have you been here?" she asked.

"Since January. My husband put me here because I wouldn't take down the Christmas tree. He doesn't like Christmas trees. He says they drop their needles all over and you're still finding them in June, down in the carpet. I liked that, finding Christmas in June, down in the carpet. He got one of those big plastic bags you put around the base of the tree and stick the trunk through, and when you're ready to throw it out you just pull it up and tie it and carry it away."

Ione stared into her coffee cup. "I hated that. I kept looking at the poor tree, standing there so brave and pretty with its little bright lights, and that constant reminder that it was going to be thrown away, thinking no one really wanted it."

A tear slipped down the side of her nose. "I loved that tree. I didn't care about dried-up needles and fire hazards. I wanted to keep it there for months and months, and then put it out in the yard for birds and rabbits to hide in. He said I was crazy. He said he'd have me locked up if I didn't throw it away. He stood there and watched while I took off all the glass balls and the tinsel and the little bright lights. And all the time I was crying and saying, 'I'm sorry, tree. I love you, tree.' Then he pulled the plastic bag up around it and threw it in the gutter for the garbage men to take away. And he had me locked up anyway."

She looked at Stoner, tears dripping from her chin onto the table. "Do you think the tree knew I loved it?"

"I'm sure it did." She felt like crying herself.

"Do you know what I wish? I wish I'd pulled the plastic bag up over *him* and tied it shut and thrown it in the gutter for the garbage men to take away."

"When you get out," Stoner said, "give me a call. I'll help."

"I thought I could get well if I could get someone to understand about the tree. But they don't understand."

"No, they're not that kind of people."

"They want me to be normal. But how can you be normal when the milkman doesn't come any more, and the garbage men take the tree away?"

"I don't know," Stoner said. "I really don't know." She touched Ione's arm. "I'm sorry about the tree, and the milkman."

Ione patted her hand. "You'd better not let on, or they won't let you out either."

"I hope *they* don't squeal," Stoner said, indicating the two old men.

"They never talk. I think they're mechanical toys, like they used to have in penny arcades, and every now and then someone drops in a quarter and makes them move."

Stoner laughed. "You know, I think you're right."

Ione ate a few forkfuls of her lunch.

181

"How can you do that?" Stoner asked.

"Do what?"

"Eat that stuff as if it were real food."

"Don't think about it."

"What *is* it?"

"Lunch."

"What kind of lunch?"

"I happen to know," Ione said, her eyes crinkling. "Should I tell you, or will it ruin it for you?"

"On second thought, you'd better not." She stabbed at a bit of something translucent and forced herself to eat it. Fortunately, it was tasteless.

"May I tell you a secret?" Ione asked.

"Sure."

"You won't repeat it?"

"Absolutely not. I'm not on very good terms with the staff."

"Well... " Ione dropped her voice. "Sometimes I think this isn't a hospital at all."

Stoner looked at her. "What makes you say that?"

"I don't know much about hospitals, but don't you think they ought to treat us better?"

"Definitely."

"Would a real hospital lock someone up because of a Christmas tree?"

"They might," Stoner said. "It's a crazy world. Was that all you did?"

Ione hesitated. "Actually... I poured Mr. Clean in his personal computer."

"They shouldn't lock you up for that. They should give you a medal."

"And I poured honey on his hairbrush, and sprayed all his neckties with Clorox."

Stoner choked. "What else?"

"Well ... this is really bad. You'll probably hate me."

"Never."

She leaned over and whispered in Stoner's ear. "I went out in the yard and gathered up all the dog-doo I could find and stuffed it down in the toes of his shoes. Isn't that awful?"

"Terrible!" Stoner said. She laughed until her eyes watered. "That's absolutely the worst thing I ever heard."

Ione giggled. "I enjoyed it, too. Every minute."

"Ione, you're probably the healthiest person in here."

The woman glanced up over Stoner's head, and turned pale.

"What's the matter?"

She focused her attention on her lunch.

Stoner turned and found herself staring at Gladys Grenier's midriff

182

bulge. She raised her eyes to her face. It didn't look pleased.

"Mrs. Grenier!" she said with forced enthusiasm. "What a pleasant surprise!"

The nurse slammed a paper cup down on the table. "Dr. Tunes said you're to have this."

It contained a single yellow pill.

"What is ..." She stopped herself. "Thank you."

Mrs. Grenier folded her arms and waited.

"I'm supposed to take it, huh?"

"No," said Gladys sarcastically, "it's for your hope chest."

Stoner looked at the pill.

She looked at Gladys Grenier.

She decided which was the lesser of two evils. "Cheers," she said, and swallowed it.

The nurse stared at her.

She held up her hands. "All gone."

"Cheekin' it?"

"It never crossed my mind."

"Drink some of that coffee."

She obeyed at great personal risk.

Mrs. Grenier turned on her heel and strode off.

"If they want you to be normal," Stoner said to Ione, "they should set a better example. Do you know what that stuff was?"

"Probably thorazine."

"What does it do?"

"Not much, except make you funny in the head."

"You know," Stoner said, "I can't seem to warm up to that woman."

Ione glanced toward the door. "She doesn't like you."

"How can you tell?"

"She doesn't like anyone."

The other patients were shuffling to their feet.

"One o'clock," Ione said, and sighed. "A third of the way through another day in Paradise."

"I thought Grenier didn't come on duty until three."

"She's always on duty. This place is her life."

"Some life," Stoner said.

"Some life," Ione said.

"I'd feel sorry for her, but it isn't in me."

"Well, don't cross her. Claire Rasmussen crossed her, and God knows what they did to her."

Stoner's heart skipped a beat. "How did she cross her?"

"They had a fight, something about the files." She loaded her dishes on her tray. "You could hear it all over the place. Claire yelling about unprofessional, Grenier yelling she should stay out of the files. Next thing anyone knew, Claire was nutty as a fruitcake. Finished with your lunch?"

Stoner nodded. "Did anyone explain it to you?"

"I asked Millicent Tunes. She said Claire had been stealing from the drug cabinet and overdosed on something." She added Stoner's dishes to her own, dividing the leftovers between their two plates. "That didn't exactly fit in with what I'd heard, but you don't ask Millicent Tunes too many questions. She just turns them around on you. 'I wonder why you're so interested.' You know."

"I know."

"Maybe she did take the drugs. This place drives you to acts of desperation."

They were the last ones left in the dining room. Stoner got up."Well, try not to get desperate."

"Not me," Ione said. "I want to get out of here. I will, too, if I can remember if the milkman came every day."

***

She had to get out of O.T. and meet Jerry before she got too funny in the head. She was already having trouble concentrating. Thoughts would arrive, hang around for a few seconds, then slip away. She tried Becky's coffee. It tasted like the water poured off a can of chunk light tuna.

Searching for inspiration, she looked around. The same man sat where he had yesterday, glassy-eyed, banging away at the same round of copper. The same nebulous patients huddled over their same occult crafts.

At Shady Acres, time was frozen.

"What would you like to try?" Becky asked.

"I don't care. Something messy."

"Pottery's messy. It was my favorite in school."

"Maybe..."

"Water everywhere, oozy clay. Once I was throwing a pot, isn't that a funny thing to call it, throwing a pot, and it slipped off the wheel. I guess I pumped too hard. We found bits of clay for weeks afterward. Even if you're careful there are spatters, of course we don't have a wheel here, or clay, only water. Is there something messy you could do with water?"

"That's okay," Stoner said. "I'll think of..."

"Writing paper!" Becky bubbled. "Make your own writing paper. You tear up old newspapers, see, and boil them down and spread it all out,and if you want to add color, you can make a *real* mess."

"Sounds complicated."

"Oh, it *is*. Complicated and messy and ecological. Are you interested in ecology? But Jerry throws the papers out every day. I'll bring you some from home."

"You don't have to bother."

" I feel guilty, anyway, about all the papers I waste. My boyfriend and I get the *New York Times* every Sunday, but we end up not reading it. It's so intimidating, and I always think the typographical errors are real words, because after all it's the *New York Times*..."

"Maybe I could paint?" Stoner suggested.

"You could, I guess. Lilly's used up the black and cobalt blue, but I'll ask her to share the rest. Well, not *ask* her, you don't ask Lilly things, she won't answer, did you know she's Dr. Tunes' aunt?"

"No," Stoner said. "I didn't."

"I think it's just grand the way Dr. Tunes takes care of her. I mean, it must be hard on her, seeing that poor old woman waste away day after day. She could put her in a nursing home, but she doesn't want to make her leave her house. Isn't that the sweetest thing?"

"Adorable. The woman's obviously a saint."

"Well," Becky said. "I wouldn't call her a *saint*, really, but she's awfully nice to poor old Lilly."

Right. She's screwing poor old Lilly to the wall in just the sweetest way. "Let me ask her," she said. "I don't want her to think I'm angry about yesterday."

She walked away before Becky could think of another way to be helpful.

Lilly pretended not to notice her.

"How's it going?" Stoner asked in a low voice.

"Going, going, going. Lots of goings on around here."

"I need an excuse to get away for a while."

Lilly hummed and worked on her painting.

"I want to look at Claire's room, but I'm afraid if I just leave they'll be suspicious."

Palette in hand, Lilly turned to her, scooped up a handful of paint, and slathered it down the front of Stoner's shirt.

"Jesus," Stoner said, "don't get carried away."

"Oh, Lilly," Becky cried, springing to the rescue, "you've done it again." She dabbed ineffectually at Stoner's shirt with a bit of shredded Kleenex. "I don't know why she's taken such a dislike to you, I really don't, she's usually meek as a lamb."

"It's okay."

"You'd better take that shirt off and wash it right away. Acrylics, you know. Once they harden there's not a thing you can do."

"Right," Stoner said, and headed for her room.

***

She tossed the shirt into the back of her closet, put on another, and crept down the stairs.

185

Jerry lurked in the shadows.

"We have to work fast. Is it safe?"

He looked insulted. "Would I get you into anything that wasn't safe?"

She decided against entering that potentially-endless discussion. "What about the staff?"

"All out. Working or in town. There's never anyone around when I clean. I think I make them nervous." He unlocked the door with an air of immense self-importance and led her down the short hall that ran behind the conservatory.

The staff bedrooms were laid out along the south side of a hall that looked like a motel. Mr. Inside/Mr. Outside carpet, smoke alarms, sprinklers, and emergency lights. The north wall was blank.

The first door bore a simple nameplate: Grenier. Tempted by curiosity, she reached for the knob.

"Come on," Jerry hissed.

"Can't we take a peek? I'd love to know how she lives."

Jerry shook his head sternly. "She's a pig."

"But..."

"Maybe you're in charge of this caper," Jerry said, "but this is *my* territory."

She pouted and followed him down the hall.

Claire's room was on the end. He turned the key in the lock and stepped aside.

"You first," Stoner said.

He entered the room as if he were entering a cathedral. "Close the door," he said. "Someone might come."

She looked around. The furnishings were delicate, old-fashioned, and feminine. Ruffled curtains framed the window. Watercolors in pastel tones hung on the walls. A patchwork quilt lay neatly on the bed. The harsh outlines of an institutional straight-backed chair were broken by a cushion covered in the same patchwork design.

"She made those herself," Jerry said proudly.

"Nice."

"I'll take the closet."

"Don't overlook anything, however unimportant it..."

"You've said it a million times," Jerry said. "Do you think I don't listen?"

The desk top was empty except for a blotter, pencilholder, and a calendar open to February. She slid out the single wide drawer. A box of stationery, a few stamps and paper clips, and a stack of letters held together by a rubber band. She flipped through them. They were all from Nancy, the only connection Claire had retained from her previous life. The dates on the postmarks ended in mid-February. Someone had been intercepting Claire's mail. It seemed to suggest they had been watching her for some time before her

186

"overdose." Or they had removed any with incriminating questions.

Which told her nothing, wasn't surprising, and made her nervous.

She turned to the bureau. On a hand-crocheted doily stood a triptych of photographs. The picture on the left was of Nancy, taken on her graduation from nursing school. She wore a starched white dress, blue cape and cap, and carried a single red rose. Next was a blurred family group — Nancy, an older couple, and Claire herself, confident, sunny, smiling as if the world were hers for the asking. The last frame held an earnest young man in Marine uniform, the innocence of childhood still clinging to his cheeks.

"That was her fiance," Jerry explained over her shoulder. "He was killed in Lebanon."

A small terrarium lay in the center of the bureau. It was a tiny forest scene made up of reindeer moss, British soldier lichens, partridge berry, Princess pine, a chunk of driftwood and a small ceramic doe. Stoner touched it. "This is lovely. Did she make it?"

"I did."

Moved, she reached over and caught his hand. She could feel him stiffen. "We'll find her, Jerry," she said. "I promise."

He leaned over to study the terrarium. "Aw, gee, it's all busted."

Someone had removed the Saran wrap top and replaced it carelessly. The little plants were dying.

"I guess she didn't like it," he said, his voice breaking. "She tried to fix it."

"Maybe not. I'm always taking the tops off things like that, to see how they work."

"She could have asked," he muttered, and went back to the closet.

Stoner decided to check the bathroom. All of Claire's toilet articles were there. If she hadn't known the 'vacation' story was a lie, she'd know it now. Claire might have gone off and forgotten her toothbrush, but not all of it. And certainly not her bar of hypoallergenic soap. No one with sensitive skin would take a chance on finding that in a local neighborhood pharmacy. She filed that bit of information away to be used as evidence later.

"She's still here," Jerry said from the other room.

Stoner poked her head around the door. "What?"

"Her blue sweater's gone. It was here yesterday."

She put two and two together. "So that's how you knew. You check the closet every day, don't you?"

He turned the color of a stop light. "Yeah, I do, so what?"

"Don't be embarrassed. That's extremely useful."

"It is?"

"Absolutely. It's the first *real* proof we have that she's alive."

"But we heard her."

"We *think* that was Claire," she corrected him. "It wouldn't stand up in a court of law."

"Would this?"

Probably not, but she didn't want to discourage him. "No doubt about it. This is absolute proof that, as of today, Claire is alive and in the vicinity of Shady Acres."

"Gosh," Jerry said.

"It proves my friend *did* see her. It proves Nancy *did* get that phone call..."

"What phone call?"

"Claire called Nancy a while ago. That's what made Nancy suspicious. She sounded odd."

"How long ago?"

Stoner tried to remember exactly. "I'm not sure. About two weeks."

"Right before she started acting funny," he said thoughtfully.

"And about the time she and Mrs. Grenier had a fight. Jerry, did you hear that fight?"

"Sure, everybody heard it."

"Do you know what it was about?"

He shook his head. "They were in Lefebre's office with the door shut. How'd you know about it?"

"Gossip." She went back to searching the room. "I think there's a connection between that fight and Claire's ...unusual behavior."

"It's okay to say crazy," Jerry said as he rummaged deeper into the closet. "Being crazy's nothing to be ashamed of."

Stoner lifted the desk blotter. There was nothing under it. "You know, you might be the last true liberal left in the country."

"Don't let my father find out. He hates liberals."

"That," said Stoner, "is the least surprising thing I've heard in my entire life." She knelt to peer under the bed. "What's the underwear situation?"

"How should I know?" he squeaked indignantly. "I don't go around pawing through girls' underwear, for Pete's sake."

"Well, if you did, you'd know whether they launder it and put it back. Which would tell us if they want to be sure the police know she was here right up to the time..."

"*What* time?"

She shoved her hand through her hair. "Okay, it's my theory Claire found out things they didn't want her to find out."

"Why don't you paint that on a billboard, so you wouldn't have to keep repeating it?"

"So far, they think the 'crazy' scheme is working. But, if they find out someone's on to them..."

"Like us."

"Like us. Well, they might decide to arrange an 'accident.' And to make it look like an accident, they'd have to prove she was here up to the time of the accident."

188

"Well, that's great." His face was florid. "That's great. You really know how to make a guy feel *great!*"

"Oh, God." She realized what she'd done. "I'm sorry. It's all speculation. We don't have the slightest clue anyone is even thinking of killing Claire. For all we know, they feel perfectly safe. Anyway, it's not our problem."

"*What do you mean it's not our problem?*"

"I *mean*, if they suspect someone's onto them, what to do about Claire is *their* problem, not ours."

"Great." He beat his leg with his fist. "Greatgreatgreat."

"*Jerry.*" She tried to gather her thoughts. "Look, I'm just trying to reason like a criminal."

"You call yourself a detective and you don't even know how to reason like a criminal? Where'd you get your license, out of a Cracker Jack box?"

"I don't have a license. I don't need a license. I'm perfectly capable of thinking like a criminal, but they've got me on some kind of drug and..."

"What drug?"

"Ione says probably thorazine."

"Ione!" he exploded. "You brought *her* into this?"

Stoner bristled."No, I didn't. But if I did, what's wrong with that?"

"Nothing," he shouted. "Let's get *everyone* involved. Let's make an announcement over the P.A. system!"

"Keep yelling. That'll do it."

"Who else did you tell?"

"Lilly, sort of."

He stormed around the room. "She's as crazy as a *loon*, for crying out loud!"

"No crazier than you."

"You're making a mess of this whole thing."

She'd had it. "Want to take over?" she demanded, throwing up her hands. "*You* call the shots. *You* make the decisions. Go on, tell me what to do next. You're in charge."

"I don't think you're a private eye at all."

"You're right, I'm not. But I'm all you have." She folded her arms stubbornly. "I'm waiting. Tell me what to do."

"You don't know how to do *anything*," he snapped. "Old history books. Maps. Look around her room. What is this obsession with *detail?*"

"Okay, Sir Galahad," she snapped back. "Climb on your white charger and storm the fortress. Bring the whole damn thing down on our heads."

He clenched his fists and stuck out his chin. "You think like a *girl!*"

"You *act* like a *boy!*"

He glared at her.

She glared at him.

His face twitched. A series of rapid, high-pitched sounds escaped his throat.

Oh, dear Lord, he's cracking up. "Jerry, don't..."

"This is really *funny*," he gasped. He giggled.

A bubble of laughter burst from her. Then another. And another. She sat down on the bed, holding her stomach.

Still giggling, he sat beside her. "Really *funny*."

She threw an arm around his shoulders and laughed until her jaw ached.

"You know what we sound like?" Jerry asked, slipping his arm around her waist. "My parents."

"I figured your mother for the mousey, down-trodden type."

"She is, when she's sober. When she's loaded she peels the paint off the walls." He rolled his eyes. "I don't mind missing *that*."

"My mother did the yelling in our house."

"Must be hereditary," he said.

She punched him in the side.

He punched her back. "So what do we do now?"

She pulled a handkerchief from his sweater pocket and wiped her eyes. "I haven't the vaguest idea."

"Back to the books, huh?"

"Let's try the files. If we can find out what Claire knows, it might give us a clue." She thought for a moment. "That patient who disappeared. Steve. Do you know his last name?"

"I've heard it. I'd probably recognize it."

"Can you get into Lefebre's office?"

He stood up. "Piece of cake. I'll go in and clean. That always runs him out."

"Didn't you already clean in there today?"

"So what?" He shrugged. "I'm compulsive. It'll make him think I'm deteriorating."

***

We were lucky, she thought as she settled down in the O.T. room with drawing paper and magic marker. If anyone had heard us, we'd be on our way to electroshock.

Still, it might be a good idea to play perfect patient for the rest of the day.

Which wouldn't be hard. Too little sleep. Too many emotional ups and downs. And, speaking of downs, Millicentunes' yellow miracle pill. It was all beginning to add up to a gigantic case of the blahs.

She drew a series of brick-shaped boxes, filled them in with horizontal lines, and blackened the spaces between the lines. Through the open door she could hear the snarl of Jerry's vacuum, broken by occasional unidentifiable bumps and bangs. She was just begining to wonder if Jerry was systematically bludgeoning the good Roland J. Lefebre to death when the Doctor of the Year himself waddled into the room. Huffing and puffing with annoyance, he poured himself a cup of Becky's poisoned coffee and sat down to read the *Wall Street Journal.*

"That's really *good!*" Becky chirped. "What is it?"

"The Great Wall of China." She rotated the page. "I can't seem to get the perspective right."

"You will," Becky encouraged. "Keep at it."

"What happens to these things after we're finished with them?"

"It's yours to keep. Of course, Dr. Tunes will want to take a look at it first."

"Of course." She added a few knives, guns, ropes, and pools of blood to give the lady a thrill.

"I like that," Becky said. "It has a certain ... quality."

Stoner laughed. "If you ever get tired of O.T., you can open a Tact School."

"I might, but there doesn't seem to be much demand for it these days."

"Tell me the truth. What do you really think of this?"

"Well," Becky said reluctantly, "it's sort of grim. But Dr. Tunes will like it."

"You've noticed that about her, have you?"

"It's none of my business, of course, but sometimes I wonder if she's not a little ... weird."

"It's worth thinking about," Stoner said.

"I probably shouldn't have said that, her being your therapist."

"Don't worry. There's no love lost between us at the moment."

"Sometimes," Becky said, "I wonder why she's in this line of work. She doesn't seem to enjoy it."

Stoner concentrated on her drawing. "Maybe it pays well."

"It must. Have you seen her jewelry? And her clothes? I've been here more than a year, and I swear she's never worn the same out-fit twice."

"Maybe she's independently wealthy," Stoner suggested.

"If I were that wealthy, I wouldn't work. I'd ..."

"Open an exclusive dress shop?"

Becky giggled. "We shouldn't gossip like this."

"True," Stoner said. "But I don't know any other way to gossip."

"I think I'd better circulate," Becky said, "before I start enjoying myself and lose my morals completely. Let me know if you need help."

"Thanks," Stoner teased, "but I can lose my morals all by myself."

Becky shot her a look of mock disapproval and wandered off.

Stoner erased her from her list of suspects.

The afternoon passed, as they say, uneventfully. Jerry dropped by to tell RJL-MD his office was ready. The psychiatrist grunted ungratefully and waddled out. Jerry followed, not indicating by thought, word, or deed what he had found.

She managed to steal a few moments alone with Lilly, to share with her what they had uncovered in Claire's room. They agreed it wasn't much.

Mrs. Grenier made the rounds twice, and took notes on her clip board.

Hank made the rounds once, and took notes on his clip board.

Shortly after three, Mario made the rounds, and took notes on his clip board.

Supper was Welsh rarebit, presumably, and another Millicent Tunes special.

Ione speculated on the possibility that the milkman had come every other day, but bogged down on whether it was Monday, Wednesday, and Friday, or Tuesday, Thursday, and Saturday. The mail, she recalled, used to be delivered twice daily on weekdays. She couldn't remember when it had changed.

Stoner contemplated a world in which people who threw away Christmas trees were the ones who were locked up, and decided she'd pick that planet for her next incarnation.

The whole hospital seemed subdued. Possibly because of the weather, which was drizzly and turning to ice.

The thorazine went about its appointed task of putting her out of touch with reality and onto another plane. She had the feeling she was standing slightly to her own left. She wondered if this was what was meant by "being beside yourself."

By the time supper was over, she was ready to fall asleep. But first she had to check in with Jerry.

She slouched into the conservatory and found him reading an Old Farmer's Almanac. "Anything?" she asked.

"Plenty. Steve's file's gone." He held out a hand to ward off her next question. "No, I didn't overlook it. If it had been there, I would have found it." He grinned crookedly. "There was some hot stuff in yours, though."

Anxiety penetrated her fog. "What stuff?"

"They think you're queer. Can you imagine that?"

"Very funny."

"And they don't buy your depression story. They have you down as an antisocial personality."

"What does that mean?"

"You lie, cheat, and bear watching."

"Then I'd better be more careful. I guess you'll have to be my leg man."

"Shucks," Jerry said, "my Dad wanted me to be a Tit man."

"Any sign they tried to take Claire out today?"

192

"Nope. And from the looks of the weather, they won't be doing it tonight. I didn't know you were Catholic."

"I'm not," Stoner said. "We put that down so they wouldn't think I'm suicidal."

"Who's 'we'?"

"Dr. Kesselbaum. She's my therapist on the outside."

"Did she put you up to this?"

"She helped."

"Holy cow," Jerry said. "What's the world coming to?"

"Listen, do you think they suspect we were up to anything today?"

"Doubt it. Seems to be business as usual around here." He studied her. "You look beat."

"It's the drugs."

"Better start cheeking them."

"I don't know how."

"Slip them under your tongue and spit them out later."

"Sounds complicated."

"Better than being out of it. Practice with buttons or aspirin. Am I going to have to worry about you?"

"I'll be all right as soon as I get some sleep."

"I hope so," Jerry said. "You're the brains in this outfit."

Stoner smiled. "You're in a good mood tonight."

"Yeah. You know, this is the first time in my life I ever got away with anything."

"We're not out of the woods yet."

"We're not even *in* the woods yet." He tapped the almanac with one finger. "Interesting reading in here. You should take a look at it."

Stoner yawned. "Don't be subtle. My mind isn't working."

"You know how you figured they were bringing stuff in at low tide? Well, guess when the tide's lowest."

"Full moon," she said.

"*And* new moon. Low tide and no light. How's that for evidence?"

"Solid. Anything else?"

"What do you want, miracles?"

"Sleep."

He frowned with concern. "Be cool, Chief. You look like the Night of the Living Dead already."

"I'll be all right. I think." She turned to go.

"Hey, Stoner?"

She turned back. "Yes?"

"I have to apologize again."

"What for?"

"This afternoon. Touching you like that."

"That was okay, Jerry. I touched you, too.

"I don't want you to think I'm forward or anything."

"Don't worry. I know you're backward."

193

"I hope you're not offended."

"I'm not offended, Jerry. People touch. My girlfriend touched me five seconds after I met her."

"Yeah, and look what *that* led to."

She shook her head. "You know, I think I liked you better when you were anxiety-ridden."

He laughed. "Sleep tight, Chief. I have everything under control here."

Mrs. Grenier met her on the stairs. "Where do you think *you're* going?"

"To my room, if that's all right. I'm exhausted."

Mrs. Grenier looked her over. "If you're not going to socialize like everyone else, get in your pajamas."

"All right."

"And don't get any ideas about taking a walk."

In this weather? "It never occurred to me."

"You might be Millicent Tunes' little pet," Mrs. Grenier said, "but after four o'clock *I* tell you what to do, understand?"

Stoner nodded meekly. "Mrs. Grenier, I have the feeling you don't like me."

"Don't take it personal. Everyone knows queers are scum."

"That's exactly the kind of attitude I'd expect from a fine, upstanding woman like yourself."

Gladys Grenier grinned. "Watch it, Stover. There's nothin' I'd like better 'n to toss you in seclusion."

"Heaven forbid! I wouldn't last a day without your smiling face."

"I see we understand each other," Mrs. Grenier said, and clomped on down the stairs.

Stoner watched her go. Millicentunes' pet? Now there was a thought to warm the heart.

I wonder what privileges and obligations that entails.

"Oh, Gladys," she muttered aloud, "you make me tired."

She slipped into her night clothes and stretched out on the bed, feeling useless. Plan for tomorrow. Mind's too fluid. Tomorrow and tomorrow and tomorrow... Tomorrow's another day. Tomorrow, tomorrow, I love you, tomorrow...

Tomorrow is a word which, with repetition, loses all meaning.

Yesterday I promised myself I'd leave today.

Now I can't remember why.

Damn the drugs.

Can't fall asleep and miss med time.

Med time, bed time, bean time, mean time. But in the meantime, meantime, all they gave me is the in-between time...

I'm turning into Dory Previn. Jesus was an androgyne, with my Daddy in the attic...

What was Jesus doing in the attic with my Daddy? Screaming in

194

a car in a twenty-mile zone?

Dory Previn, where are you now? The woman's movement's in trouble, and we need your sense of order.

Beware of young girls who come to the door, wistful and pale, of twenty and four...

Like Claire Rasmussen. If only Claire Rasmussen would come to the door, delivering daisies with delicate hands...

CONCENTRATE!

What did Glad-ass Grenier say? "After four o'clock..." After four o'clock, Shady Acres is Tunes-free. Can we use that to our advantage?

Maybe, if I could get my neural impulses to jump their synapses. Tote that barge, hold that line, jump that synapse. Go, team, go!

Her imagination produced random images: a willow tree, flickers of lighting, faces of people she'd never seen, words in languages she'd never heard. Residues of past lives? Seepings from the Collective Unconscious?

There was a town she'd visited often in dreams, but had never seen in waking life. A seaport town, at the mouth of a river. Along the beach stood a rambling hotel, lights sparkling through the night. She stood on a hill, next to a house whose lower floor was cut from the side of an embankment. Rooms and apartments above, a tavern below. The tavern was bright, the walls of polished pine. Over the door was a sign decorated with folk drawings of birds and flowers. The tavern's name was written in Portugese. There were people inside, laughing, singing, drinking. The door stood open. She stepped forward to enter, and tripped.

She jerked awake. Her room was cold, the lights harsh and unfriendly. From the hall she could hear low, mumbling voices, shuffling footsteps.

Line-up time.

She pulled herself to her feet. Her joints felt stiff.

The Angel of Shady Acres presided over the medication table. "Well, Stover," she boomed, "no room service tonight?"

Ione dawdled by the stairs, watching her out of the corner of her eye.

She took the cup the nurse held out. "Thank you."

There were two pills. One white, one blue. What...?

Don't ask.

She turned away and started back to her room.

"No, you don't." Mrs. Grenier's voice shook the foundations.

Stoner gestured toward the bathroom. "I thought I'd..."

"Take them here."

Shrugging, she slipped the pills under her tongue and drank a sip of water. "Okay?"

Hands on hips, Gladys Grenier loomed over her. Stoner looked up innocently and smiled in a shaky kind of way. The pills dissolved with

195

a decidedly nasty taste.

"More water?" Mrs. Grenier asked.

She shook her head. There was bitter grit all over the inside of her mouth.

The nurse smiled wetly. "Think you're pretty smart, don't you, Stover?"

"Stoner."

"Well, *Stover*, I've handled a lot tougher cookies than you."

"With great facility, no doubt, given your superior training and experience."

Mrs. Grenier's eyes narrowed to slits. "Don't play games with me."

You have it all wrong, Mrs. G. We're not playing a game at all. "Try not to take it personally," she said pleasantly. "Good night, Mrs. Grenier."

Ione met her by her door. "Are you all right?"

"Sure."

"I know she's infuriating," Ione said, "but you really shouldn't bait her."

"I can't help it."

"Seriously, Stoner. She can do terrible things to you."

"This place is like prison."

"You don't have to adjust, just pretend to."

"I'm trying."

Ione shook her by the arm. "Try harder." She smiled. "As they say in the old movies, keep your powder dry."

***

She stood by the window and stared out at the night. The clouds were breaking up. Moonlight glistened on an ice-covered world. Smooth, slippery ice. Hands-and-knees ice. The kind of ice that closes runways at Logan Airport and has the pigeons falling on their faces all over the Boston Common. Jerry was right. No one was going anywhere tonight.

She tasted the bitterness in her mouth and felt rage erupt like a geyser. Glad-ass Grenier. If Millicent Tunes is into sadism, she has a perfect subject under her own roof.

Every pore in the woman's body oozes meanness. She should be dead, or staked naked in the Castleton common, exposed to all the world as the vile creature she is.

There are hundreds, thousands of people out there who are out of work. And that woman has a job.

Which shows you what kind of a world we're living in.

Come, now. She obviously has problems. Major problems of a serious psychological nature. So try a little charity. Not Aquarian charity, with its unselective compassion for All Humankind. Christian charity — the kind that leaves the recipient forever bound by debts of gratitude. The kind that dispenses snippets of tolerance out of an unshakeable certainty of its own superiority.

Mrs. Grenier, may the Righteous Right take an interest in your case.

If hate does bad things to your *karma*, I've had it.

The cold was tightening. She looked at the bed, with its one pathetically thin blanket and worn cotton spread.

I should get more blankets.

From Glad-ass?

Just an idea.

Piling all her spare clothes on top of the bed, she crawled in and prepared to spend a miserable night.

But she hadn't counted on the wonders of Modern Medicine. She had no sooner closed her eyes when the magic pills delivered their knock-out punch.

In her dream she lay on her bed in her parents' house in Rhode Island. It was summer, a still, dead night, the air so heavy even the bats refused to fly. Darkness pressed against her and weighed her down. Somewhere a bird gave a faint, pitiful chirp and fell silent, the vacuum-silence of three o'clock.

Something was in her room. She heard it breathing. Panting. Sniffing. Searching for her. It drew nearer to her bed. Stopped. Waited. She held her breath and prayed for it to go away. Quiet, but she could feel it there. Suddenly it sneezed, and she knew what it was. The mongrel dog she had left behind when she ran away from home. "Scruffy!" she cried, and put out her hand to stroke his soft, silky coat.

And touched instead a slimey thing, jelly-like and alive. It had no skin.

Her scream woke her. She sat up, trying desperately to penetrate the cocoon of darkness.

A blade of light slid into the room as someone opened the door and slipped inside.

"Stoner."

'Ione?"

"I heard you screaming," Ione said.

She rubbed her face. "Sorry, it was a nightmare."

Ione pushed some clothes aside and sat beside her. "It's freezing in here."

"They probably turn off the heat on March first."

Leaning forward, Ione felt the radiator under the window. She snatched her hand away. "It's red hot."

Oh, boy. Supernatural cold. Stoner hugged herself. "This place must be drafty as a barn."

197

"I don't feel a draft."

"Let's not think about it. It might be one of those things we don't want to know the answer to."

Ione laughed. "This is a strange place, isn't it?"

"It certainly is."

"Want me to get in with you?"

As a matter of fact, yes. "You don't have to."

"I remember what it was like to be new here,"Ione said, sliding beneath the so-called covers. "Lonely and frightening."

"Sort of."

Ione slipped an arm around her."This is fun. Kind of like a slumber party."

"I've never been to a slumber party." Already she was feeling warm and sleepy.

"Why not?"

"Lesbians didn't get invited to slumber parties when I was a kid."

"Well," said Ione, "isn't that a silly thing?"

As she was sliding down into sleep, a thought drifted by: Journey's End has made its first move.

She snapped awake.

Beside her, Ione stirred. "Are you all right?"

"Yes. I'm sorry I woke you."

"Did something frighten you?"

"No, it was just one of those things." She reached for Ione's hand. "You smell like Evening in Paris."

"How would you know?" Ione murmured sleepily. "Bet you never smelled it."

"Well, you smell nice."

"Wore it for so many years, it probably changed my body chemistry. Least I don't smell like caramel corn."

"Did you work in the five and dime, or only go there a lot?"

"Worked there. Notions. Needles, thread, hooks and eyes, garters, buttons." She squeezed Stoner's hand. "Go to sleep, Stoner. Cold spots can't hurt you."

"I'm not afraid."

" 'Course you're not. Should I tell you a bedtime story?"

"As long as it's not a ghost story."

"Once upon a time..."

She fell asleep to the murmur of Ione's voice.

***

Ione was gone in the morning. A shaft of sunlight — actual sunlight — forced itself through the grimey window pane. There was blue sky, only a few innocuous clouds. The ocean, gray-green, pounded

198

the shore. Gulls exulted. Ice melted.

Stoner threw open her window and leaned out. The air was sharp and cold. She breathed deeply, trying to expel the effect of the drugs. Her lips felt thick. The inside of her head was packed with wax. What she needed was a good, brisk five-mile walk along the shore, the crackle of dried grass underfoot, the tang of salt and balsam.

What she was going to get was breakfast and another session with Millicentunes.

She put down her tray and slid into her usual seat. "Thanks for last night," she said. "It helped."

Ione smiled. "The first few days are the worst."

"You took a big chance."

"I don't get many opportunities to live dangerously."

An aide delivered her thorazine from a tray of white plastic cups. He watched her swallow it, and moved on.

"How come you don't have to take this?" she asked Ione.

"I did at first. Everyone does at first."

Stoner kneaded her eyes with her knuckles. "I feel half-formed."

"It hits you pretty hard. Maybe you should ask Dr. Tunes to reduce your dosage."

"We don't get along very well."

Ione touched her hand. "Play along with her. It'll be easier on you in the long run."

"I wish I could."

"I mean it, Stoner. One way or another, they always win."

She looked around the room. "Does anyone ever get out of here?"

"Of course they do."

"Have you ever actually seen anyone released? With your own eyes?"

Ione laughed. "You have the jitters." She wiped a faint lipstick smudge from her coffee cup with her thumb. "I stopped wearing lipstick when I first came in here. Now I remember why."

"Are they helping you?" Stoner asked.

"Dr. Tunes says I'm making progress."

"Do you think you are?"

"It doesn't matter what I think, does it, in terms of getting out?"

Stoner bit into a slab of soggy toast and washed it down with Mystery Juice. "Don't you call her Millicent?"

"She wants me to, but I can't bring myself to do it. It's such an ugly name." She frowned. "I shouldn't criticize. It's not her fault, what her parents called her."

"Lots of people I know have changed their names," Stoner said. "To things like Solstice Fire and Moonwoman."

"Really? Are you part Indian?"

She poisoned herself with a bite of scrambled egg. "It has to do with freeing yourself of the Patriarchy."

199

Ione looked at her blankly.

"They don't keep their fathers' last names, because they're male names, see, and male names are patriarchal. It's like, if you keep your father's name, or your husband's name, that implies a kind of ownership, and..." She bogged down in the complexities.

"That's very interesting," Ione said. "I knew a girl named Roseann Tinklepaugh. She lived out at the edge of town, across from the Orange and Black Diner. They kept a bear in a cage, at the diner. Right in the parking lot. I don't know why. It was next door to the canning factory, on a curve at the bottom of the hill.We called it Dead Man's Curve because of the accidents. They had at least two accidents a year, usually on New Year's Eve. They'd stop at the diner, you see, on their way home from the Ten Mile House. That was a road house, a gin mill. You couldn't see the cars coming over the hill, and they'd pull out of the parking lot right into the traffic and through the Tinklepaughs' front window. They straightened out that curve in 1951. They took the bear away, too, but I don't remember when that was. I was 17 in 1951. I think the bear was gone before that. I guess it died. I would have, being kept in a cage in a diner parking lot."

"Ione, you know more sad stories than anyone I ever met."

"My husband says it's because I look at things that way. But I didn't make it up. The bear was really there. That can't be my fault, can it?" She tapped the table with one fingernail. "Maybe I'll change my name when I get out of here. But he wouldn't like that."

"I thought we were going to bag him and leave him for the garbage man."

"I could change my name after that. Maybe to Personal Computer."

"You're getting the idea," Stoner said.

"But I can't get out until I remember when the milkman came."

"What's with the milkman? Did you have something going with him?"

"I have to get it all right, everything in the right order."

"All of it?"

Ione nodded. "All you have is the past, you see. If you lose that, you lose everything."

"What about the future?"

"If you think this world has a future," Ione said, "you're the craziest one in here."

"Thanks. That makes my day." She choked down another bite of cold egg. "Ione, do you have any idea why Mrs. Grenier was so angry about Claire seeing the files?"

Ione sipped her coffee and thought it over. "I guess she didn't have the authority."

"Claire's a registered nurse. How much authority would she need?"

"Don't ask me," Ione said, piling her dishes on her tray and pushing

200

back her chair. "People in the mental health business get a little nuts on some subjects."

CHAPTER 11

Stoner shoved her hair into a semblance of neatness and made faces at Millicent Tunes' Swedish ivy.

If Grenier's right, if I really am Tunes' "pet," I should be able to work it to my advantage, right?

Wrong. We're talking about manipulation, which is not something I do well. In fact, the only thing I do well — truly well, at genius level — is get myself into situations in which I don't know what I'm doing. Such as the current one.

We're no closer to solving this thing than we were two days ago. Claire is still missing. We don't know why she's missing, except that it has something to do with the files, which are also missing. We've made an absolutely brilliant connection between the new moon, low tides, and ships hovering offshore — which connection I could have made without ever leaving home. I'm pretty sure something is being brought in up the cliff, but I don't know what. Illegal aliens? Defectors from Communist countries?

Oh, great, let's blow the lid off an underground railroad from Russia.

Or maybe they're taking something *out*. Plutonium for Libya? Designer jeans for Poland? Defectors from Capitalist countries?

Defectors from Capitalist countries?

Possible. Very possible.

What kind of defectors? Folk singers? Exchange students? CIA agents bound for the jungles of Nicaragua? Secular humanists?

My God, what if Millicent Tunes is working for the Government? What if Shady Acres is a front for a secret government agency selling peace activists into slavery in England?

Cute, McTavish.

Well, what *are* they up to?

Who would want to get out of the country under cover of darkness, sneaking away like a thief in the...

Criminals!

Of course. It was right in front of me the whole time. Now all we need is proof.

Which puts us back on square one.

"You're very pensive this morning," said Millicent Tunes, presenting herself in lime green. Her Ode to Spring, no doubt. Not her best color.

"Hi."

"Lovely day, isn't it? One can almost feel the sap rising."

Stoner, who had begun to rise, dropped back into her seat. "It's very nice, yes."

"I have a surprise for you."

"You do?"

"Today we're going to hunt rats."

"We are?"

"If I show you there are no rats, you won't be obsessed with them."

I don't want to look for rats. I want to look for EVIDENCE. "That's nice," she said.

Millicentunes frowned disapprovingly at her lack of enthusiasm. "Of course, if there are things you'd rather talk about..."

"I'd love to look for rats," Stoner said quickly. "You see, with the drugs and all... I'm a little off-center. But I do honestly think it's a great idea. I can't think of a thing I'd rather do than look for rats." Oh, shut up, she told herself.

Millicent looked at her oddly.

"My head isn't very clear," Stoner said. "The drugs?"

"An excursion's exactly what you need, then." She tossed a lime green sweater across her shoulders and strode toward the hall.

"Uh," Stoner said, lurching after her, "Dr. Tunes, do you think maybe you could cut my dosage? I feel funny."

"Millicent. You agreed to call me Millicent."

"It doesn't seem right."

Millicentunes smiled condescendingly. "Authority problems."

"Naturally. I'm American."

"You'll find out in time," Millicent said, "that I may be in charge here, but underneath I'm just human."

I have some serious doubts about that, but I'm not about to argue authority problems with the authorities.

They climbed the stairs to the third floor and passed behind the nurses' station.

"That's where the keep the drugs," Stoner said. "The ones I think I'm getting too much of."

Millicent opened a narrow door. "This isn't really an attic." A blast of cold air fell out. "More like a crawl space. But you can see it's perfectly clean."

It ran the length of the house, with space enough to stand only beneath the peak of the roof.

"Look around all you like." Millicent flicked on a single light. A naked bulb. The ubiquitous naked bulb, symbolizing squalor and lost hopes in all movies, plays, and TV dramas.

Stoner pretended to search the room, knowing there was nothing to find. The floor was clean enough to perform surgery on. "I guess I imagined it," she said. "Probably because I'm taking too many drugs."

"Now the cupola." Millicent pulled down a trap door in the ceiling. A flight of narrow steps descended to the floor. "Be careful on the stairs. They're steep."

Stoner hung back. If I go up there and she closes that trap door...

"You're not afraid, are you?" Millicent asked. The idea seemed to amuse her.

"I'm not quite steady on my feet, that's all. You know, the drugs?"

Millicent's smile rivalled the White Cliffs of Dover. "Don't worry. I'll be right behind you."

Heavy irony.

She took a deep breath and scrambled up the steps, turning quickly at the top.

Millicent was right behind her.

She looks like a lime popsicle, Stoner thought.

"Isn't this cozy?" Millicent asked.

It was a small room, about seven feet square. The floor was worn and dusty. Glass windows looked out on all sides. The widow's walk encircled the cupola.

"How did they get out there?" Stoner asked, pretending to be fascinated.

"There used to be a door. It's been boarded over for decades. The Winthrop ladies would wait up here for the men to come home from the sea. They'd hang a lantern from that hook at night to welcome them."

The lantern hook was attached with new, Twentieth Century nails. On a dark night, the light would be visible far out on the ocean.

"Interesting."

"Isn't it?"

Stoner touched the window panes. On the outside was a heavy wire mesh. She looked at Millicent Tunes questioningly.

"That screening was put up long ago. To keep the birds out." She pointed out a rough hole in the pine board wall. "As you can see, it didn't work. They peck their way in."

For long-ago screening, it was suspiciously rust free.

Millicent came to stand beside her. Her arm brushed Stoner's. "Charming view, isn't it?"

"Yes."

"I like to imagine the old days, when they sat up here on summer evenings to watch the stars and catch the breeze off the water."

Sometimes they wander over the cliffs. Do they ever wander off the widow's walk?

She looked up at the rafters, then down at the floor. Nesting birds make a mess. Bits of mud, twigs, droppings. There wasn't even a stray feather.

"It must be lonely for you here," Millicent said in a low voice.

"A little." No rust on the wire, no litter on the floor.

204

"Cut off from your lover this way, it must be a worry."

Stoner looked at her. "It must?"

"You never know what might be going on. Is she attractive?"

"Very." She studied the hole in the broken boards. The wood was splintered outward. Nothing had tried to get in, but something had definitely tried to get out.

"Do you like attractive women?"

"If their hearts are pure." The lantern hook was twisted, as if someone had pried it loose and used it as a wedge.

"Have you been lovers long?"

"Not very."

"Oh, dear," Millicentunes sighed.

"Oh, dear?"

"New love is thrilling, but until the relationship is firm, anything can happen. Don't you agree?"

"I haven't given it much thought. The drugs make it hard to think."

"Was she in a relationship when you met her?"

"Sort of. She was married."

"Oh, *dear*," Millicent repeated with greater emphasis.

"It was a crummy marriage."

"Has it occurred to you, Stoner, that she could be involved with you on the rebound?"

Stoner looked at her. "I really doubt it."

"Well, of course you'd know better than I, wouldn't you?" She patted Stoner's shoulder, and left her hand there.

"Yes. I would."

"You don't have to convince *me*." Millicent squeezed her shoulder. "I don't even know the woman."

Is something going on here?

"On the other hand," Millicent continued, moving her hand to the base of Stoner's neck, "if you have deep-seated doubts you'd like to talk about..."

She slipped away and pretended to be intrigued by the view from the north window. "I don't have any doubts."

"Of course you don't," Millicent purred. "Dear Stoner, so trusting."

She nearly laughed. "That's me."

Tunes propped one lime green hip against the shallow window sill. "How would you like to give her a call, just to relieve your mind?"

Now, there is one wonderful idea. To hear her voice... "Great."

"Of course, you really aren't permitted to make phone calls."

Stoner faced her. "I thought you were in charge."

"I am, but there are certain rules we can't break. For the sake of the morale of the other guests, you know."

Yeah, I noticed morale was at an all-time high around here.

"Well," Stoner said, turning back to the window, "it was a nice thought, anyway."

Millicent crossed the room. "On the other hand, if you were to come to my house tomorrow evening..." She touched Stoner's back. "... you could call from there."

"Your house?" Stoner asked warily.

"I have a cottage just off the grounds. It overlooks the ocean. The view at night is an enchantment."

She couldn't think of a thing to say.

"We could have a fondue, and a little fire in the fireplace. I have an excellent collection of classical music. Do you like classical music?"

"Sort of." Millicent was fondling her hair.

"I live alone. We wouldn't be disturbed."

Who wouldn't be disturbed? *I* would be disturbed. I'm already disturbed.

"It's a date, then?" Millicent asked.

What do I do if she makes a pass at me? Kick her in the... "Well, I appreciate the offer and all, but you must have better things to do."

"No." Her voice was husky. "I don't."

"Like reading medical journals or something?"

"There's more to life than medical journals."

"Writing up case histories?"

"You must think I'm terribly stuffy, Stoner."

"Not at all," she said quickly. "Only, well, you're my therapist."

"And a woman." She ran her hand down Stoner's spine. "Come, now, surely you'd like to get away from here for a night?"

A night? A *night*? By all known standards, supper and music are an *evening*, not a *night* "Well..."

Maybe I can deteriorate between now and then. Start raving. Hallucinate. Tear my clothes.

Channel 5: Sexually frustrated psychotherapist lures innocent travel agent to isolated beach house for fun and games. Strong language, adult situations.

"I'm waiting," Millicent murmured.

"I'd better not. Gwen might get the wrong..."

The hand against her back went dead. "Gwen? Is that your lover's name?"

Christ and all his disciples! "*Glen!*" she said loudly. "Short for Glendora. A nickname. Kind of a joke between us..."

"Really?" Millicent asked flatly.

Get yourself *out* of this, McTavish. "Hey, what the heck? Sure, I'll come. She doesn't have to know, does she? I mean, this is between us, right? Patient and therapist, right?"

Millicent looked at her for a long time.

"Did I say something wrong?" Stoner asked. Oh, shit.

"Patient and therapist," Millicent said.

"Yeah. You know, me patient, you therapist?"

A tiny smile curled at the corner of Millicent's mouth. It was worse

206

than the full-tooth treatment. "Then it's all settled. I'll pick you up by the front door at five." She looked hard into Stoner's eyes. "You won't be sorry."

Sorry? I'm already sorry. Consumed with remorse. In Jerry's words, chickenshit. "Should I ... should I bring anything?"

"I have everything we need," Millicent said.

I'll bet you do. Rubber hoses, cattle prods, bamboo under the fingernails, sodium pentathol... "Good," she squeaked.

Millicent turned and glided down the narrow stairs. Stoner followed like a dog trotting after its master.

"You see?" Millicent said at the entrance to her waiting room. "No rats."

Stoner forced herself not to comment. "Yeah, well, thanks for showing me."

Millicent ran her fingers lightly down Stoner's arm. "Would you mind terribly if we cut short our session today?"

"Not at all." She tried not to appear eager.

"I have things I must do. You know how it is."

"Yeah, fine."

"And we'll have all the time in the world tomorrow night."

"Sure."

"You're very understanding, Stoner."

She shrugged. "I try."

Millicentunes paused in her doorway to deliver her curtain line. "I think we'll reduce your medication. You seem to be adjusting quite nicely."

The door closed behind her.

Good God, what have I done?

***

She didn't know how long she'd been sitting there, in shock, watching the ice melt. She could have been asleep. For all the serious thinking and plotting and planning and analyzing and scrutinizing and detecting she'd done, she could have been dead. The patients were whooping it up in the O.T. room. Jerry was pushing a mop. Hank was off somewhere making notes on his clip board. God was in His Heaven, and nothing was right with the world.

A sliver of ice detached itself from the conservatory roof and shattered on the pavement below.

Claire. Where the hell is Claire?

I know she was in the cupola, but she isn't there now. She hasn't left the building, Jerry would have seen. There's no way to the root cellar from inside.

So where *is* she?

What if they killed her? What if I forced their hand? What if...
She slumped deeper into the chair.

I never should have gotten involved in this. All I've done is screw up. Travel vouchers and charters to Disney world, that's what I'm good for.

Self-recrimination is a luxury you can't afford.

"Gwen might not understand." Why didn't you hand Tunes a signed confession in three languages, explained for the slow?

Maybe she won't put two and two together.

Oh, sure.

She might not. She might have other things on her mind. Things like fondue and firelight.

Then what did that long look mean?

Who knows what long looks mean? People give each other long looks all the time. Sometimes they're just spacing out. Sometimes they're plotting revenge.

Well, tomorrow night will certainly be entertaining. At best, I'll spend the evening warding off groping hands and playing dumb. At worst, I'll spill the beans and wander over the cliff.

Hey, look on the bright side. Nothing's changed. This is still your basic life-threatening situation.

And you'll probably be watched.

On the other hand, you might be able to fix it.

She forced herself to her feet and went to Millicent's office.

The Sweetheart of Sigma Chi was on the phone, her back to the door. Stoner tapped on the wall.

Millicent swung around. Her face lit up. "Call you back," she said. "Someone needs to talk to me." She hung up.

"I didn't mean to bother you..." Stoner said.

"It's no bother. Come in, come in. I was just straightening out a mix-up with the laundry. They sent us the wrong order. Now, what would we do with fifty pounds of diapers, pray tell? Is there something on your mind?"

She shuffled over to the desk and stood there, shifting from one foot to the other. "About this morning, when I said that about my lover, you know, Glen?"

Millicent nodded expectantly.

"Well, I hope I didn't put you off or anything. I mean, you looked kind of funny."

Millicent laughed. "Oh, my dear, I'm so sorry. It was the name Gwen. I had a very, very dear friend back in graduate school by that name. And when you said it, well, it just brought back a flood of memories."

She felt herself relax. "I was afraid I'd said something wrong."

"Actually, to be perfectly honest..." Millicent toyed with an earing. "I was a little hurt."

"Hurt?"

"The way you kept insisting on pointing out our *professional* relationship. You see, I was hoping we could put that behind us for one evening." She raised one lovely hand. "I know, I know, it seems a little *outre*, as it were. But you already have a therapist back in Boston and, well, frankly..." She paused and sighed heavily. "You see the kind of patients we have here. It isn't often we have someone as attractive as you among us. And this is such a lonely business."

Stoner looked down at the floor. "Thank you. I... uh... find you very attractive, too."

"I'm *so* glad. I do want us to be friends, don't you?"

"Yes, very much."

"But if you think, for one minute even, that this would interfere with my being able to help you, please do say so."

"I will, but it won't."

"Grand. Until tomorrow night, then?"

Stoner forced herself to smile. "Tomorrow night. I'm really looking forward to it."

"And I," said Millicent, "am counting the minutes."

Back in the hall, Stoner grinned to herself.

I got away with it. Maybe I really *am* an antisocial personality.

And maybe we both did a swell bit of play-acting.

Think positive thoughts, as Aunt Hermione would say.

But stick to that deadline. You may be able to pull that off for five minutes. A whole evening is something else again.

She found Jerry on his knees in the back hall, scrubbing away at a two-hundred-year-old stain. "What's that?" she asked. "Blood?"

"I don't know. It's been driving me nuts for months."

She leaned against the wall and watched. No wonder he was in love with Claire. Judging by her room, they had neatness in common.

Something nudged at her mind. Something about Claire's room. She chased it around...

... and caught it.

"Jerry, would you say Claire's careful about her personal habits?"

He scowled and squeezed the soapy water from his sponge. "Of course. You think she has B.O. or something?"

"Does she always keep her room neat?"

"You saw it."

"And sentimental? Is she sentimental?"

"Sure." He glanced up, brushing the hair out of his eyes with the back of his hand. "What are you getting at?"

"Doesn't it strike you as odd that she'd spoil that terrarium?"

"I guess so."

"I need to see her room again."

She studied the glass bowl and shriveled plants. "How long would it take this to dry out?"

"I don't know," he said from the deep in the closet. "Once they're dead, they're dead. Oh, shit!"

"What's the matter?"

"Her coat's gone. They've killed her."

"If they were planning to kill her," she said, peering down into the terrarium, "they wouldn't worry about her catching cold."

"They would if they wanted to make it look like an accident."

"Jerry, last Saturday she came flying out the door dressed in nothing more than her nightie. I don't think they'd feel the need to dress her up."

"Then they took her away."

"Not last night, they didn't. And you've been watching."

"I can't be everywhere at once, can I? And you're half in outer space all the time." He stood beside her and clenched his fists. "Where *is* she?"

"The root cellar, maybe."

He made a dive for the door. She caught his sleeve. "There's something we have to do here first."

"That place is *freezing*."

"And it doesn't have a lock. I don't think that's our answer."

"I'm gonna look, anyway."

"In a minute." She picked up the terrarium. "Do you mind if I take this apart?"

He shrugged unhappily. "Go ahead, it's already ruined."

She removed the plastic wrap and set it aside. Jerry looked as if she were cutting out his heart. "Would you rather do it?"

"I don't care." His voice dripped misery.

Carefully, she poked her fingers into the caked soil, and prayed there was nothing living in there. A Princess pine toppled. Jerry winced.

Under the driftwood she found what she'd been looking for. A slip of paper, folded to the size of a postage stamp. She held it out. "I think this is for you."

"For me?" He seemed reluctant to touch it.

"Read it."

His hands trembled. "It's just a bunch of names and dates."

"Do you recognize any of them?"

"Yeah, there's Steve. *Steve Braestrup*. I should have remembered that. It sounds like bra strap."

"Any others?"

"Dave Amato. Karl Eichorn. I never knew he spelled it with a K."

Her heart leapt. "We have it!"

"We do?"

"I'll bet every one of the men on that list was a patient here, and those are the dates they left."

"I don't get it."

"*And* I'll bet you won't find their files."

"I didn't find Steve's," he said. "Want me to look for the rest?"

She thought for a moment. "You could, but I don't think you'll find them. Jerry, if you had something you wanted to hide, and someone found it, would you put it back in the same place? Even if that someone wasn't a threat to you any more?"

"I dunno. I'd never be dumb enough to leave it lying around in the first place."

"If you *were* dumb enough?"

"How should I know how I'd think if I were dumber than I am, for crying out loud? Will you get to the point?"

"Well," she said. "I know what I'd do. I'd put it somewhere safer."

"Like in the bank?"

"Like somewhere locked. Have you noticed a filing cabinet or a drawer that's always locked?"

"I don't go prying around here," he said indignantly, blushing lightly. He looked away and concentrated on fixing the terrarium.

"If you did, if you were the sort of person who was naturally curious, and maybe a little bored, and you wanted to make absolutely certain there wasn't a speck of dust anywhere — like on the edge of a drawer or something — you might try opening a few, mightn't you?"

"I might," he muttered.

"Well?"

"Millicent Tunes' desk, lower left-hand side." He glanced up. "But I can't look in there. She keeps the key with her."

"Then we'll have to break in."

"We can't do that. It's illegal. Even the cops can't do that."

Stoner smiled. "But we're not cops."

"Okay, we'll do it." He started for the door.

"Later, Jerry. At night, when nobody's there."

He started to twitch. "Why do you keep procrastinating? Why can't we do something *now*?"

"We *are* doing something now. We're gathering evidence. Next, we'll check the dates on those slips of paper against the almanac. I'll bet we'll find there was a new moon on every one of those nights."

He cocked his head on one side. "So what?"

"Now we know what Claire found out. They've been using this place to smuggle people..."

"Kidnappers!" he shouted.

"Maybe. I don't really think..." She looked down at the list of names. "While they were here, did any of these men behave strangely?"

"Everyone here behaves strangely."

211

"As if they were being kept against their will?"

He dug around in his memory. "They kinda kept to themselves. Steve and Dave were real restless, and Karl griped about the food. But they didn't try to get away or anything, and they didn't act drugged out."

Stoner wandered to the window. "They must have been going underground."

"In *this* joint?"

"Until they could get out of the country." An aide was walking toward the parked cars. She drew back and watched as he glanced around, slipped into the passenger seat of a battered Mustang, and lit a cigarette. "I'll bet they have contacts in every state. Psychotherapists. When the heat's on, a person can go to this therapist they know about, and they refer them to Shady Acres." From the way the aide held his cigarette, between his thumb and forefinger, she guessed it was marijuana. "Once they're here, they wait around for the new moon, hide in the root cellar until low tide, and escape to a waiting ship. They might even have a string of hospitals like this all up and down the East Coast. Maybe even the West Coast."

"Like McDonald's," Jerry said.

"Sort of."

"But *I'm* not a crook."

"That's the beauty of it. Most of the patients are real. So the crooks just blend in."

"Gee, it must be great to have an imagination like yours."

Stoner looked at him. "Is that an insult?"

"Heck, no. I wish *I* thought like a crook."

"Yesterday you said I didn't think like a crook."

"So I was wrong," Jerry said. "I mean, who expects a girl to be devious?"

Stoner laughed. "Most people."

"Well, how am I supposed to know what most people think? I don't even *understand* most people."

"Neither do I." She took the paper from him. "When we run this list through the computer, I'll bet we'll find every one of them is wanted by the FBI."

"How can we do that?"

"I told you, I have contacts."

"I figured you were lying." His eyes lit up. "This is really big stuff, huh?"

"The biggest. You're about to become a National Hero."

"Me?"

"Claire knew they'd guessed she'd uncovered their secret. She knew they'd try to shut her up. So she hid the list in the terrarium and left the cover askew, counting on you to notice and find it."

"Far out." He puffed out his chest. "I told you she was smart."

Naturally, he insisted on checking the root cellar. She let him go alone, with dire warnings that the very existence of the Free World depended on his not giving them away. Even if he found Claire, she told him, he was to do nothing until he'd reported back.

For now, she'd better make herself visible to the staff. She'd already been out of sight too long.

She went back to the conservatory and settled down with the list and the almanac. The dates ran back to last April. The almanac began in November. She'd have to compute back eight months.

If she could figure out the system.

It's one thing to think like a crook. Thinking like an accountant is a little more difficult.

She had just about made it to July when she heard a familiar voice from the hall.

"I have to see Stoner McTavish."

Her head shot up.

Marylou stood in front of the receptionist's desk.

"Visiting hours are from one to three," the receptionist said.

"This is business."

"What kind of business?"

"I'm Dr. Edith Kesselbaum's secretary."

The receptionist turned back to her copy of *People Magazine.* "Means nothing to me."

"Dr. Edith Kesselbaum is Stoner McTavish's psychiatrist on the outside."

"Well, she ain't her psychiatrist in here."

"She wants me to get these signed," Marylou persisted, pulling a sheaf of official-looking papers from a battered attache case.

The receptionist barely glanced up. "What are they?"

"Insurance forms."

The woman gave a world-weary, long-suffering sigh and got up. "Okay, I'll take 'em in."

Marylou backed casually out of reach. "I have to do it. 'Do it yourself,' Kesselbaum says. Christ, shrinks give me a pain. Rake in the bucks like they were popcorn, and get apoplexy if one lousy insurance payment's late."

"Know what you mean," the receptionist grumbled.

"Kesselbaum's a bitch." Marylou settled herself cozily on the edge of the desk and took out a pack of cigarettes. "Smoke?"

The woman stared longingly. "Can't. I'm on duty."

"Go ahead. If anyone comes in, I'll take it and you start raising hell."

"Thanks." She lit up and inhaled greedily. "Shit, that tastes good."

"I'd quit the crummy job in a minute," Marylou went on. "But I need the money. Want to finish business school, upgrade myself, know what I mean?" She swung her leg. "She pays crap, wants your soul for it. Make one mistake, you get the axe."

"They're all like that."

"You'd think they'd be embarrassed. Hell, I know how much that office takes in per week." She leaned forward confidentially. "Kesselbaum drives a white Lincoln convertible, and pumps her own gas."

"Cheap," the receptionist said, blowing smoke through her nose.

Marylou nudged her. "You got it. Cheap. But the way I figure, if I can hang with this job, I got nowhere to go but up."

"That's what you think. Wait'll you been around."

"First thing I'm doing when I cut loose from Kesselbaum, I'm joining 9 to 5."

"What's that?"

Marylou feigned shock. "You never heard of 9 to 5? It's a union."

The receptionist frowned. "We don't think much of unions up this way."

"That's because you're oppressed," Marylou said, poking her with her finger. "Next time I'm in the neighborhood, I'll drop you off some literature. No pressure. Just look it over. Let me know what you think."

Come on, Marylou, stop organizing the workers and get in here.

Marylou glanced at her watch. "Shit, I gotta go. Don't want her to think I'm fucking around on her time. Where's McTavish?"

"Conservatory. Supposed to be in O.T., but she never does what she's supposed to do. Contrary."

"You don't know the half of it," Marylou said. "I type up Kesselbaum's notes, you know?" She rolled her eyes. "There's stuff in her file you wouldn't believe."

"Yeah?" the woman said.

"The kind of things she's into..." Marylou shook her head. "Can't even bring myself to say it."

The receptionist swiveled around and stared at her.

Stoner pretended to be engrossed in the almanac.

"Listen," Marylou said, "if she ever writes her autobiography, run, don't walk, to your nearest bookstore." She pulled a tin Band-Aid box from her purse and dumped the contents. "Ditch the butt in here when you're through."

"Thanks again."

" 'S nothing." She jumped down from the desk. "Us working girls have to stick together."

She marched into the conservatory and planted herself in front of Stoner's chair. "Well, if it isn't Stoner McTavish, unkempt."

"What?"

"You look as if you dressed for a fire drill." She patted Stoner's hair into place. "Tuck in your shirt, for heaven's sake. You have com-

214

pany."

"It's the drugs," Stoner explained as she rammed her shirt tail into her belt.

"So now you're on drugs? Really, we leave you unattended for 48 hours and you go completely to pieces."

"I try not to swallow them, but I'm not very good at it."

Marylou surveyed her critically. "Should I bring you some uppers?"

"I feel rotten enough. Marylou, what are you doing here?"

"Checking up." She plopped into an arm chair. "Tell me everything."

"How's Gwen?"

"Wretched. She languishes about the agency for hours on end picking at her cuticles. I don't know what we ever saw in her."

Stoner found herself grinning. "She misses me?"

"We all miss you, Pet. Life without you is dreary, dreary, dreary." She leaned forward. "What have you found out?"

"Claire disappeared last Saturday. Before that she'd been strange, withdrawn, maybe hallucinating."

"Do you suspect foul play?"

"I always suspect foul play, remember? But we think she's still on the grounds. We have to look around more. Some patients have left suddenly, and there's a list of names we found in Claire's room." She dug it out of her pocket and handed it over. "My guess is they're fugitives from the law, being smuggled out from here."

"That's the American way," Marylou mused. "Ship our problems to Third World countries. Want Max to run this through the computer?"

"Does he have access?"

"Old FBI agents never retire, they just take up organic gardening." She glanced at the list. "Have you committed this to memory?"

"As well as I can. I don't really trust my memory these days."

Marylou drummed her fingers on the arm of the chair. "You don't look well, Stoner, not well at all. Poor color. Hesitant speech..."

"Really? I wasn't aware of it."

"Withdrawn, strange. Are you hallucinating?"

"If I am," Stoner said with a thin smile, "I'm hallucinating you."

"Sure you don't want uppers?"

"Positive. Marylou, please don't tell anyone you saw me like this."

"I have to, Pet. Otherwise I'd have no credibility in the future.Is there anything you need, other than a haircut?"

She shook her head. "We may be able to wrap this up soon. We'd better..."

" 'We-ing' again. That doesn't bode well."

"Jerry and I," she explained.

"Jerry!" Marylou eyed her sharply. "Stoner, just because you're stuck out here, cut off from everything you know and everyone you love, is no reason to cheat on Gwen."

"Jerry's a boy."

"So much the worse. It's an old story, you know. Two women having a perfectly lovely time, when along comes some muscle-bound stud spouting poetry and feigning sensitivity. And before you know it, it's all shot to hell."

"Wherever did you get an idea like that?"

"I've started reading. It was your suggestion."

"Only because TV makes you crazy. *What* do you read?"

"Whatver I can grab off the shelf at the Public Library. I have a card, you know."

"Well, take something from my bookcase."

"Oh, my God!" Marylou squealed, her eyes turning big and round. "Don't tell me Nancy Drew's like *that!*"

"Only if you read between the lines."

"All right, but it seems a little juvenile."

"You don't have to read the Nancy Drews," Stoner said with a sigh. "I keep them around because they remind me of my childhood."

"Which was unspeakable." She glanced at her sideways. "I have to tell you, Stoner. I consider what you're doing very tacky."

"I beg your pardon?"

"You and Gwen have been together less than a week, and you go running off to the boonies to get involved with God-knows-who-or-what..."

So Marylou had found her place in all of this: having come to grips with The Relationship, she was going to make by-God-sure everyone behaved properly. "It gets tackier. I have a date tomorrow night."

"You *what?*"

"Have a date, with a woman."

"What woman?"

"Millicent Tunes. My therapist."

"That's unethical!" Marylou sputtered.

"Unethical for her, not for me." She grew serious. "To tell you the truth, I don't like it. I think she's coming on to me."

"Of *course* she's coming on to you. The woman obviously has no scruples. What's her part in this scam?"

"She's in it all the way."

"Does she suspect you?"

"I think so. I may have given myself away."

"I've told you a million times," Marylou said, "don't give it away, sell it." She frowned. "Look, Stoner, in all sincerity I think you should get out of here."

"I haven't accomplished anything."

"So what? People fail every day. Some fail their whole lives, and you don't hear *them* complaining. Edith's first husband made a career

216

of failure."

"I heard."

"So pack it in."

"I can't do it, Marylou. I'd never be able to look in the mirror."

Marylou sighed. "I suppose not. How's the food?"

"You don't want to know."

Jerry strolled by the window and caught her eye. He shook his head. Catching sight of Marylou, he hunched his shoulders and scurried off.

"Who was that?"

"Jerry."

"He's an infant. You're trusting your life to an infant?"

"He's a good kid, and he knows his way around."

"Humph," Marylou humphed.

"He's in love with Claire."

"Well..."

"You'd better go," Stoner said. "I'm trying not to attract attention."

"I suppose so." Marylou shrugged into her coat. "By the way, we have a lead on Cassie Papa... Delia's daughter."

Stoner perked up. "Really? How?"

"It's too complicated. Sign the damn insurance forms so I can bust out of this puke-hole."

"Are you going back to Boston?" she asked, picking up the pen.

"I thought I would. Why?"

"Because..." She glanced up at the marble-mantelled fireplace and suddenly knew ... something.

"Because..."

Because I want to come with you. I want to get away from here. I'm afraid. Something terrible is going to happen here, and I don't think I can stand it.

The fireplace opening was black and cold and pulled at her. The book cases shifted slightly.

"Stoner?"

Don't you feel that, Marylou? That gripping, pulling? Don't you see the house moving? My God, am I the only one who *feels* it?

"Earth to Stoner."

There was movement at the edge of her vision. A bird. No, the shadow of a bird. The *idea* of a bird.

"Look, Pet," Marylou said, "I don't like the way you look. Do you really think you're in any shape to..."

Of course she doesn't see it. This is *my* nightmare, not hers. My very own monogrammed, personalized nightmare. Lucky me. How many people have their very own personalized...

"I mean it, Stoner. I think you should get out of here."

She looked up. "Sorry. Spaced out. I think I'm allergic to

thorazine."

The idea of a bird settled on the mantel and began cleaning its feathers.

"Are you sure you know what you're doing?"

Stoner forced a laugh. "Sure, I'm sure. It beats cruise reservations."

"Well..." Marylou stood for a moment, awkward and indecisive.

Stoner smiled and handed her the pen and insurance forms. "Tell Edith, if she decides to rip off the insurance company, I get half."

"*I* get a third, for my trouble." She gripped Stoner's hand. "Come through this in one piece, that's all I ask."

She turned quickly and sashayed from the room, coattails flying.

Stoner watched her go, forcing herself not to look at the bird. Because, of course, it wasn't there.

Depression settled over her like a cloud.

***

"Missed you in O.T.," Ione said as she sat down to lunch.

"I had things to do."

"Things like gallivanting around with Millicent Tunes?"

Stoner buttered a slice of harmless-looking bread. "She thought if I saw the attic I'd forget the rats."

"And did you?"

"I never believed in them in the first place."

Ione laughed. "You have to stop taking those drugs. You're not making any sense at all."

She picked at a shred of limp carrot embedded in a mound of decomposing lemon jello. "I can't get the hang of this 'cheeking' business."

"Takes practice," Ione said. "Of course, they watch you closer than most."

Stoner put her fork down.

"They've pegged you as a trouble-maker," Ione went on. "You won't be able to take a deep breath without someone coming down on you."

They suspect. They *know*. They're only biding their time, waiting for me to make a mistake.

But maybe, as Edith Kesselbaum often pointed out, she wasn't as transparent as she thought. "A common error among introverts," she would explain. "Your inner life being so real to you, you naturally assume everyone else knows what you're thinking."

And Shady Acres isn't overly endowed with staff. Other than the kitchen help (unseen but certainly heard), the receptionist (permanently glued to her swivel chair and non-union), Lefebre, Tunes, Social Service, Becky, and Jerry's therapist (who might be a figment

218

of his imagination), the place is apparently run by Hank, Mario, two nameless and unremarkable young male aides, and the redoubtable Gladys Grenier. Who is worth her weight in rhinestones, what with her superior training and intellect.

"What do you have to do," she asked Ione, "to be labelled a trouble-maker?"

"Offend Gladys Grenier."

"Well," she said. "I've certainly done that."

She tried the soup. It tasted like sugar and acorns. "God, what's *this* stuff?"

"Peanut butter soup."

"That's the most disgusting thing I've ever heard of."

Ione smiled in sympathy. "Take my advice, shove it in and don't think about it."

Hank loomed in the doorway with his tray of little white cups.

"Here we go again" Stoner muttered.

Ione reached for the ketchup. "When I get his attention, ditch the pill."

He was making his way around the room.

"What are these things supposed to do for us, anyway?" Stoner asked, watching him.

"Make us upstanding and manageable citizens. Don't you feel upstanding and manageable?"

"I feel sullen and moody."

"I'm sorry to hear that," Ione said. "You're the best thing that's happened to me since I got here."

He was at the table next to theirs, plunking down his little white cups of manageability.

"Thank you. You're very kind to say it."

"I said it because it's true, not so you'd nominate me for Mental Patient of the Year."

He came to roost beside her.

Stoner smiled.

Hank didn't smile.

She held out her hand.

He dumped the pill in it and waited.

"Hank, honey," Ione said in a syrupy, un-Ione-ish voice, "can you get the top off the ketchup for me? I'm weak as a cat today."

He hesitated, torn between duty and flattery. Flattery won. He turned to Ione and concentrated on the bottle.

Stoner slipped the pill down the front of her shirt and finished off her water.

Hank grunted, muttered, and cursed. Giving up, he slammed the bottle down on the table. "Do without," he growled, and stalked away.

"Thanks again," Stoner said. "Lucky that cap was stuck."

"It wasn't. I just screwed it good. My husband says it's what I

219

do best."

"Capping bottles?"

"Screwing."

Stoner laughed. "I'll bet you're a riot of a mother. Do you have many kids?"

"Not a one. I screw and screw, but it doesn't take."

"That's too bad."

"Just as well," Ione said. "I'd probably screw that up, too."

"You're going to a lot of trouble for me."

"Well, you need looking after."

"I do?"

"You're kind of pitiful."

"I am?"

"Like you don't know what to make of this place."

Stoner made hard little balls of chunks of bread. "It's not quite what I expected."

"That's a fact," Ione said somberly.

"I appreciate your kindness. It's in short supply around here."

"That's another fact."

"But I don't want to get you in trouble."

"Being in here's trouble."

"I know, but ... well, with the staff feeling about me the way they do..."

Ione grinned. "You surely do keep them riled up."

"It might be safer for you to stay away from me."

"Want me to butt out?"

"That's not it..."

"Seems to me you *need* a friend, Stoner."

"It could be dangerous."

"You carrying a contageous disease?"

"Look, you've stuck your neck out for me enough," Stoner said. "Don't do it again, all right?"

"You're cranky. Have a bologna sandwich."

"I don't..."

"It'll take your mind off your problems. Believe me, next to these sandwiches, everything else is small potatoes."

"Ione..."

"Too bad you weren't around during the early Fifties," Ione reminisced. "That was the *nadir* of American cooking. Everything we ate was pre-cooked, pre-canned, pre-frozen, and pre-posterous."

"Ione, listen to me."

"You don't eat enough to keep a bird alive."

"*Ione.*"

"You know, I've never liked that name, it's so gray and mousey. Stoner. Now, there's a good name. Straight forward, has character. Where'd you get a name like that?"

220

"I was named for Lucy B. Stone. Ione..."

"My first grade school teacher's name was Miss Olmstead. She lived with her blind mother. Third grade was Miss Kellogg. She boarded with the doctor's widow and Miss O'Donnell. Miss O'Donnell was sixth grade. Mr.Fox was fifth — no, fourth. I missed eighty days of school that year. Six weeks for measles. There were complications. I had to stay in a dark room, because sometimes measles ruined your eyes. You lay around and listened to the radio. They had good programs, not all music and sports and preaching like now. 'Stella Dallas,' 'Lorenzo Jones and his wife, Belle,' 'Our Gal Sunday'." She laughed. " 'Can a girl from a little mining town in Colorado find happiness as the wife of a wealthy and titled Englishman?' The answer's 'no,' in case you hadn't guessed. In the morning we had 'The Breakfast Club.' They broadcast from a hotel in Chicago, and in the middle of the program everyone would get up and march around the Breakfast Table. Guess they thought it would be good for digestion."

Stoner gave up. Anyway, there was no way she could explain to Ione why she should stay away from her. Not without revealing her plans. And that knowledge could be dangerous in the long run. "Maybe we should introduce marching around the breakfast table here," she said.

"Those two..." Ione tilted her head toward the two old men. "... would fall plumb off their perches."

"You know," Stoner said, "it's amazing how much you remember."

"It comes over you at middle age. You start to notice how fast everything changes. Makes you want to hang onto what was simple."

"On the way up here I saw some tourist cabins that brought back memories."

"Well, don't get too caught up in it. Proust smelled a cookie and ended up with seven volumes of literature." Ione glanced at her. "Do you mind my running on like this? There aren't many people to talk to here."

"I've noticed." She launched an assault on the jello.

"I see you've hooked up with Jerry. Sweet kid. He's compulsive, you know."

"I know."

"Too bad he's not female. He'd make my husband a great wife."

"You ought to ditch that guy," Stoner said. "He sounds like nothing but trouble for you."

"Oh, I'm too timid to go without. And you can't get a job at fifty, even if you're trained to do something, which I'm not. Can't even go back to the notions counter. They don't have notions any more. Or clerks. Just kids at cash registers by the door. The big hardware chains are the worst. Guys that don't know beans about hardware. If they can't find what you're looking for, they tell you it doesn't exist."

"The thing that frustrates me," Stoner said, "is nails and screws. Every time I have to replace a screw, it's a size I don't have. What this country needs is a good, all-purpose screw."

Ione smiled. "Babe, you might not have noticed, but that bunch in Washington has been giving this country a good screw for the last six years."

Stoner dropped her spoon in the mayonnaise.

"Look me up when you get out," Ione went on. "My husband says I'm an all-purpose screw."

"You know what that makes him, don't you?"

"What?"

"An all-purpose screwdriver."

Ione slapped her shoulder and hooted. "I swear, you're a breath of spring."

"Never. Spring has forsaken Shady Acres."

"Well, it's a strange place, all right. I still can't get over how cold your room was last night."

Stoner toyed with her sandwich and wished Ione hadn't brought that up.

"And that's not the only funny thing," Ione said. "When I was sneaking into your room, I could have sworn there was someone on the stairway behind the fire doors. Only a shadow, but it sure looked like a man. Or a woman."

Stoner felt her pulse quicken. "What do you mean?"

"Well, I'm probably mistaken. The light was dim. But there shouldn't have been any light at all. Nobody goes there. The doors are locked. Do you think I imagined it?"

"I doubt it." She tried to control her excitement. "Is that all you saw?"

"That's all. It was probably just my fancy. I'd been sound asleep, and you started screaming your head off. Well, it was right startling."

"I'm sorry about that," Stoner said. "I have nightmares."

"Lordy, don't we all? Dr. Tunes says I have to start accepting my life, instead of always wanting something."

"She would."

"But even Robert E. Lee was always wanting something. He said that once, 'I'm always wanting something.' If it was all right for Robert E. Lee, it ought to be all right for me."

"What do you want, Ione?"

"I used to want to be a country singer. With a white fringed skirt and shiny white boots and my name spelled out in sequins on my guitar. But I wouldn't call myself Ione. I'd call myself Patsy or Lureen or Suellen. Roseann Tinklepaugh played the flute. She was double-jointed. Her thumbs bent backward. So did her elbows. Maybe her knees did too. Maybe if you shot her up in the air, you wouldn't be quite sure which way she'd landed."

She saw something beyond the fire doors. It might have been Claire, but what would she be doing out there?

"What's beyond the fire doors?" she heard herself ask.

"Nothing. Just the stairs."

"Are you sure?"

"Well, I've never been there. I gave it some thought when I first got here. I was feeling kind of bored and desperate, I guess. But those doors are locked, and I'm too old to go climbing out on the fire escape."

Stoner looked at her. "Could you get out on the fire escape?"

"Sure. It's right beside my window. You can almost touch it if you lean out. But it's coated with ice most of the time, and, anyway, I'd probably get caught, and I'm not all that fond of thorazine."

"But there was someone on the stairs last night."

"I can't be sure. Why so interested?"

"Well," Stoner said reluctantly, "there might be something going on. I really can't talk about it until I'm sure..."

"A scandal? Wouldn't that be fun?"

"Not particularly. Look, Ione, can you forget about this conversation?"

"Probably not. But I won't mention it."

"Especially not to Millicent Tunes."

"All right."

"If she were to suspect ... Well, it's just better not to talk about it."

"I won't."

The old men creaked to their feet and shuffled away toward the garbage cans.

"I hope," Stoner said. "Tweedle-Dum and Tweedle-Dee don't talk."

"If they do, no one's ever heard them."

Stoner punctured the jello salad, with little apparent impact. "You see, I think I'm onto something here, but it wouldn't be fair to you if I said too much."

"I understand," Ione said.

"So you shouldn't ask questions."

"No questions."

"It's nothing personal."

"I won't take it personally."

Stoner felt strangely let down. She spread her daub of transparent mayonnaise around the rim of her plate. "Aren't you curious?"

"Sure, but you told me not to ask questions."

"You see," she said insistently, "things aren't what they seem around here."

"I see."

Her let down feeling deepened into hurt. "Darn it, Ione, I could be in danger. Don't you care?"

Ione looked at her. "If I didn't care, I wouldn't have crept down the hall last night to comfort you, would I?"

Embarrassed, Stoner glanced away.

"But," Ione went on, "you told me not to ask questions."

"You didn't have to do what I said."

"Do you want me to ask questions?"

She knew she was blushing. "I do and I don't."

"Well, when you make up your mind one way or another..."

"I'm not really here as a patient," she said. "I'm under cover."

Ione laughed. "Sure. That's what they all say."

"I'm serious. I'm working for Claire's sister. She thinks the people here have done something to Claire, and I want to find out what and why."

"No kidding?"

"I can't tell you more than that. A lot of people are involved, but I'm not sure who."

"Son of a gun," Ione said. "I knew there was something fishy about this place." She took Stoner's hand and gave it a little shake. "Look, Babe, I don't mean to tell you your business, or to criticize, but I don't think you should talk about this so freely."

"I'm not talk..."

"You practically begged me to pry it out of you."

"Did I? I guess I did. Oh, God, my judgment's slipping."

"I don't know why I did that. It isn't like me."

"Then you'd better be careful not to take any more of their drugs. It strikes you funny."

"I didn't take any this time."

"Thorazine isn't aspirin. It has a half-life of about two days."

They were the last ones in the dining room. Hank watched them impatiently.

"I think we'd better go," Ione said. "But not together. Give me a five-count lead."

Stoner watched her walk away. Two days? And tomorrow night it's fondue and firelight with Millicent Tunes.

If I know old Millicent, it won't be just firelight and fondue, it'll be drinks before, wine with ... and before I know it I'll be spilling my guts.

She tried to shrug it off. What the heck? I always do my best work with a deadline.

***

"Did you make the map?" she asked, pretending to study the bookshelves.

"Look in *Jamaica Inn*," Jerry mumbled out of the side of his mouth.

She took the book down and extracted the map. Or maps. There were three of them, one for each floor, with an insert of the cellar and notations of compass points and scale. Each room was intricately drawn, neatly labelled by occupant and/or function, and showed the location of each piece of furniture. If Jerry's conscience had allowed him to search through closets and drawers, he undoubtedly would have listed their contents as well.

Now that's what I call grounded. Solid. Precise. Of the earth. They had a calming effect.

"These are beautiful," she said. "How did you do it so fast?"

"Fast? It took me last night and all afternoon. I had to check some of those rooms two and three times."

"Why did you have to check them?"

"To see if I got it *right*, for Pete's sake."

She looked toward the solarium windows. The light was sharply angled, and smeared by fog. "What time is it?"

"4:03."

She had lost more hours. Sitting in her room, staring at nothing, immobilized.

I have to get out of here before I turn to stone.

She gathered up the scattered threads of sanity and turned her attention to the maps. "What about the staff quarters?"

"They're on page one, where they should be. Do you think I'd put them on the *roof?*"

She looked them over, paying special attention to Gladys Grenier's room. But it was only a floor plan, no different from the others except that, beneath the woman's name, Jerry had written "slob."

Stoner tapped it with her finger. "Editorializing?"

"I couldn't help it. She makes me so *mad*."

"You know, Jerry, when we finally solve this thing, it'll be the biggest disappointment of my life if she isn't involved."

"Fat chance."

She looked back at the map. "No empty rooms?"

"Just Claire's."

"What about the fire stairs?"

"Can't you read?" He bounced up and down on the balls of his feet. "It says, 'Uncharted Territory'."

"I wish you had a key to those doors."

"Well, I don't. Are we going to get on with this, or what?"

"Give me a minute to think."

"You always want time to *think*. Do you have mud in your head or something?"

She tightened her grip on her temper. "I'm sorry, Jerry. I don't feel well."

"*Again?*"

"I'm afraid so."

"Gee," he said, "is it that time of month or something?"

"I'm drugged, remember?"

He peered at her. "Yeah, you look kind of stupid."

225

"Thank you."

"Hey," he grinned, "it's a great cover."

"It would be, if it were only a cover." She folded the maps. "I need to show these to Lilly before..."

His hands twitched. "Why *Lilly*, for crying out loud?"

"Because she knows the house. She can tell me if there are rooms you aren't aware of."

"You mean I spent all that time making these so you could find out if there's something *missing*? Why didn't you have her do it?"

"Because," she snapped, "I knew it would keep you from going off half-cocked. Any other questions?"

He seemed about to have a fit. "I could have been looking for *her*."

"*And* alerting everyone within a ten-mile radius." She took a deep breath. "Jerry, I understand how you feel..."

"You don't understand how I feel," he pouted. "Nobody understands how I feel."

"If it were Gwen we were looking for, I'd be berserk. And I wouldn't use good judgment. When you're in love..."

"Who said I was in love?"

"Nobody had to say it, Jerry. It's obvious."

He turned the color of a flamingo. "Well, so what?"

"So I think it's very nice."

"It isn't nice," he said miserably. "Everyone'll laugh at me."

She touched his arm. "I dare them to try."

"Well..." He shuffled his feet. "Well... well, when are we going to get her out of here?"

"Soon."

"When's 'soon?' Next Christmas?"

"*Soon*." She shook her head. "Jerry, this is hard enough..."

"You haven't done a thing all day," he groused, "except sit around talking to some *girl*."

"That *girl* was my FBI contact."

"Oh," he said sheepishly. "Girls do all kinds of things these days, don't they?"

"You're getting the picture."

"Is she your girlfriend?"

"No, Marylou's peculiar, but she isn't queer."

"Can I meet your girlfriend?"

"I hope so. Did you notice anything happening today?"

"Just you loafing around like a sick dog."

Stoner shoved the maps into her hip pocket. "Jerry, you are the rudest individual I've ever had for a partner."

His eyes lit up. "I'm your *partner*?"

"Unfortunately."

"Far *out*! What do you want me to do next?"

"If you could look for those files..."

226

He tossed his head. "You're obsessed with files. It isn't healthy."

"I told you, we need hard evidence."

"I'll bet there aren't any files."

"There have to be," she explained for what seemed like the thousandth time. "If the police came here looking for Claire, and someone mentioned those names, they'd have to produce files."

"Not if the guys left."

"Real hospitals keep files for years, in case the patients come back."

"They don't have much faith in their cures, do they?"

"If we don't find the files, our only chance of proving anything is to catch them in the act. And that could be months from now."

"Yeah, I guess you're right."

"So," Stoner said, "what do you say we sneak into Dr. Tunes' office after she leaves tonight?"

He hung his head and stared at the floor.

"What's wrong now?"

"I have to turn in the keys at three. I didn't want to tell you because I wanted you to think I was a big shot."

She squeezed his hand. "It's all right. I still think you're a big shot."

"Naw, I'm just a big shit."

Her heart went out to him. "You're brave, and you're loyal. That makes you a big shot in my eyes."

"It makes me sound like a German Shepherd," he said with a little smile.

"And I'll bet you kept one eye on the doors all day, to see if anyone tried to sneak Claire out."

"Yeah, I did. They didn't."

"Get much cleaning done?"

"The halls are perfect. The rooms..." He grinned and shrugged.

"I knew I could count on you."

"Are we going to stand around forever?" He was starting to twitch again.

She could feel herself reaching a decision. "Jerry, the drugs they're giving me make me do strange things. I lose track of time. I talk too much..."

"Who to?"

"Just Ione, and she's safe. But I'm supposed to spend tomorrow evening with Millicent Tunes..."

"You're not going to talk to *her*, are you?"

"I didn't *plan* to talk to Ione. I couldn't help myself."

Jerry pondered the floor. "I'll bet they're giving you more than thorazine."

"Do you think so?"

"Unless you're accustomed to blabbing..."

"No, I'm not."

"Hey, look, Chief, I don't want to scare you, but..."

227

"Go ahead, scare me."

"... has it occurred to you you might be being set up?"

Stoner nodded grimly. "It's entered my mind." She looked at him. "Whatever we're going to do, I guess it's time to do it. If you want to back out now..."

"*Me*?"

"... I won't hold it against you."

"You've got to be *kidding*."

"All right, for better or worse, we're in it together."

He squared his shoulders. "When's it coming down?"

Stoner drew in her breath and committed them. "Tonight."

CHAPTER 12

She looked around the O.T. room. Becky was nowhere in sight. Lilly stood in her usual place behind her easel.

"I hope you don't want me to dirty your shirt again," Lilly said under her breath. "It's a terrible waste of paint."

She shoved the maps into Lilly's hands. "Just look at these and tell me if Jerry's left anything out."

"He's very thorough," Lilly remarked. "It's a fine quality in a young person. Of course, when he reaches my age, it'll be interpreted as a sign of derangement." She looked at the pages from all angles. "Quite complete."

A ripple of disappointment went through her. "There's nothing missing?"

"Not that I can ... wait." Lilly's forehead puckered in a puzzled frown. "There used to be a little room ... a storage room, right about ..." She pointed to the third floor Uncharted Territory. "... there."

"Beyond the fire doors?"

"And under the eaves, on the attic level. I played there as a child, but I haven't thought of it in years. We used to call it the Tower."

Of course, the Tower. Aunt Hermione's Tarot reading. "I should have known. That's where they're keeping Claire."

"Oh, I hope not. It's very small and quite uncomfortable. An adult could barely stand. And it isn't heated."

"She has a coat. Is there a door to the fire escape?"

Lilly took a pencil from the pocket of her smock and filled in the map as she spoke. "It opens into a connecting hall, here. Then the stairs begin ... what they call the fire stairs. They were only the back stairs to us. Coming in from the fire escape, the Tower room would be just a few feet in, on your left."

"The fire escape door, is it locked?"

"Probably. But, as I recall, the lock was rusted out. It's at that southeast corner, and takes quite a beating from the sea winds. They might have fixed it."

"I'll take my chances."

"Better take a screwdriver instead. Stoner, what are you planning to do?"

"Climb up the fire escape and get her."

She shook her head. "It's coated with ice, and the drop to the pavement..."

"I don't know any other way, Lilly. Do you?"

229

"No," Lilly said. She fumbled with the hem of her smock. "But I don't think it's a good idea. Not a good idea at all."

***

She had to pretend to eat, even though her stomach was a rock of anxiety, and her hands shook, and little black dots swam and darted in front of her eyes.

"You shouldn't have taken that pill," Ione said.

"I couldn't help it. I practiced with buttons for an hour. I still looked like a cow chewing its cud."

"I'd have dropped a dish or something, to get Hank's attention." Stoner smiled. "I don't think that would work twice, do you?"

"Well, drink lots of coffee."

"How do we know it's coffee?"

"It started out as coffee. What else would it be?" She eyed Stoner critically. "What's going on inside that head of yours?"

"What? Nothing, why?"

"You're wiggling like a room full of thirteen-year-olds. You're working yourself up to do something, aren't you?"

Stoner tried to settle down. "Yes."

"But I'm not supposed to ask what."

"Right."

"You're sure I'm not supposed to ask?"

"Positive. I'll explain later."

Ione gathered up her dishes. "Well, all right, as long as you promise not to feel rejected."

"I promise."

"Whatever it is, you don't look happy about it."

"I'm not."

"Should I worry?"

"Probably."

"When should I stop worrying?"

"You'll know."

Ione sighed. "Another sleepless night. I feel it in my bones."

She left.

The vultures left.

Everyone left, Lilly dawdling behind long enough to catch her eye and shake her head in dismay.

Even Hank left.

Alone, she stared at the table and force-fed herself coffee.

Plan it out.

Through Ione's window to the fire escape. Up the fire escape and unscrew the lock on the door. Don't forget the screwdriver.

I hope Becky hasn't inventoried the tools in O.T.

230

What if the lock's a deadbolt?

Pry off the hinges.

If that hasn't made enough noise to wake the dead, look for the Tower. Get Claire, same M.O. Down to the second floor, where Jerry will be waiting by the fire doors. Through the hall to the main staircase. Tricky, our best chance of being seen. Hope the aides are asleep, or playing poker, or watching TV, anything but what they're supposed to be doing. Break into Tunes' office. Break into her desk. Get the files, if there are files. Call Delia. And run like hell.

She shoved her hand through her hair and choked down more coffee.

It isn't going to work. What if I slip on the fire escape? What if Claire cries out? What if someone spots Jerry? What if opening the fire doors sets off an alarm? What if, what if, what if...?

Don't think about that. If we go late, and quiet, and fast, it can work. And if we're caught, scream. Scream to bring the house down. Create confusion, chaos. Maybe we can still make it.

But most of all, keep the terror at bay.

A chill went through her. What about the house? The house will try to keep me. The house wants me.

Nonsense. Houses are inanimate, incapable of feeling or volition. Houses are piles of brick and wood and mortar. Nails, screws, paint, angle irons, hinges, putty ...

And cold spots.

There is no such thing as a cold spot. There's a logical explanation. I refuse to believe in invisible forces.

Such as gravity?

She choked down more coffee.

"You gonna sit there all night?" The voice was familiar, the accent wasn't. "I gotta get home."

She looked up. "Gwen!"

"Keep it down," Gwen said under her breath. She slammed a plastic basin of gray water down on the table and began wringing out a vile-looking sponge.

"What are you doing here?"

"Keeping an eye on you. I heard infidelity was in the air." She raised her voice. "Okay to work around you?"

"This is insane, Gwen."

"Don't look at me," Gwen muttered. "Pick at your food. Someone might come in."

Stoner dropped her eyes to her plate.

"After Marylou called, I got Edith Kesselbaum to give me a ride. It was the worst experience of my life. That woman's a demon behind the wheel."

"Is something wrong with your car?"

"Marylou has it."

231

"*Marylou*? Gwen..."

"After she talked to you, she decided to stay in Castleton. Said something was up." She laughed her velvet laugh. "I wonder how she's enjoying the Est Wid In."

"Gwen, Marylou doesn't..."

"Max sent you a message," Gwen interrupted, scrubbing furiously at a non-existent spot on the table. "The men on your list are all wanted by the FBI."

"What for?"

"Crimes against humanity."

"Mafia?"

"Some. Some neo-Nazis, some self-employed."

"Is Edith Kesselbaum still around?"

"What *is* this shit?" Gwen said loudly. She picked at the imaginary spot.

"Is Edith..."

"She's at Dee's. Waitressing." She shook her head. "I'd rather be here than *there*. Talk about a madhouse."

So the troops were assembling. It was a comfort to know help was available. But she and Jerry had to do their part first. If they failed, all the help in the world would be too late.

She risked a peek at Gwen. Even in the soiled and wrinkled apron, she was gorgeous. "Nobody would ever believe you're the kitchen crew."

"I'm filling in for Dee's cousin, who was called away by an unexpected death in the family."

Stoner glanced around. "I might have given you away, Gwen. Stay out of sight."

"Eat."

She forced herself to chew a crumb of cardboard piecrust. "They know your name, Gwen."

"They will if you keep saying it. I go by Eleanor Oxnard here."

"This is crazy."

Gwen shrugged.

"It's dangerous. We're not Charlie's Angels."

"Stuff it, Sabrina." She rinsed the sponge and went to work on a chair seat.

"I don't want you here."

"They won't recognize me. My life is circumscribed by the kitchen and this charming room."

"Promise me you won't take any chances."

Gwen retrieved a paper napkin from the floor and shoved it into the pocket of her apron. "Jeez," she said, "you people are sloppy."

"Promise me."

"No."

"You don't know what you're doing."

"You do?"

"That's different."

"There's a name for people like you, Dearest," Gwen whispered. "Patriarchal."

"I'm sorry." Dearest. I'd forgotten about Dearest.

"We have a lead on Cassie," Gwen said. "Marylou's been calling the post offices in every small town in Saskatchewan."

"The post offices?"

"Marylou thinks they're all run by middle-aged spinsters who know everyone in a fifty mile radius." She started on the backs of the chairs. "Actually, they're probably run by earnest young men named Al who have master's degrees in business administration."

"That's going to cost a fortune."

"Only you would worry about that."

"I've seen the accounts."

"She's charging it to the FBI. Says if they'd done their job right in the first place, we wouldn't have to do it for them. What's it like in here?"

"Awful."

"What do you think of Millicent Tunes?"

"Let's just say," Stoner said, "at Shady Acres, the cream doesn't rise to the top."

"So why are you dating her?"

"I'm not dating her."

"According to Marylou..."

"Don't tell me you believe that."

Gwen splashed dirty water in her general direction. "Bears looking into."

Stoner laughed. "You should talk. When did Delia become Dee?"

"Don't be an idiot."

"She's attractive, exotic, older woman, no rough edges."

"I like rough edges," Gwen said. "Especially yours. Come to think of it, some of your smooth edges aren't too bad, either."

She felt the color rise to her face. "For Heaven's sake..."

"Do you think I'd lose this job if I ripped off your clothes and ravished you right here?"

"You certainly would."

"Then I'd better not. We need the money." She attacked another chair.

Stoner watched her. "I've never been so glad to see anyone in my life."

"Bet you say that to all the girls. Making any progress?"

"I'm pretty sure I know where Claire is. But I have to find the files on those missing patients."

"What for?"

"Evidence. Anything I tell the police is hearsay, circumstantial,

233

something like that."

"You have about two dozen witnesses."

Stoner nodded. "All mental patients. What would their testimony be worth, against a psychiatrist and a Ph.D. from Columbia?"

"Still, that many people can't have the same delusion, can they?"

"How do you think Reagan got re-elected?"

Gwen straightened and arched her back. "Look, lady, if it's all the same to you, I gotta get out of here. My old man'll shit a brick if dinner's late."

"Wherever Bryan is," Stoner said, "I'm sure he's not shitting bricks." She started to load her tray. "You look ridiculous in that apron, Dearest."

"Good. You won't try to turn me into a *hausfrau*."

Stoner grinned. "You can be butch the first and third weeks of every month."

"Incidentally, you don't look so damn pretty yourself. What are they doing to you?"

"Drugs."

"Are you all right?"

"Fine." She *did* feel fine, like herself again. "You're magic, Gwen."

"Anything you need?"

"A Manhattan. And two weeks alone with you, preferably in a warm climate." She got to her feet. "Listen, I'm going to make my move tonight. Stay close to the phone, will you?"

"What move?"

"The less you know about it, the better."

"Stoner..."

"I have to keep my wits about me. If I think you might try to do something, I'll worry. I may have to change plans at any minute. If I don't show up, and you come charging in like the U.S. Cavalry, it'll blow everything to bits."

"I can't just sit around Delia's leafing through old magazines, Stoner."

"Stay by the phone. When I get Claire, I'll call you, and you come with the car. If you don't hear from me, you'll know I've decided to wait." She glanced at her guiltily. "I'm sorry. I wouldn't do this to you if there were any other way."

"Well," Gwen said reluctantly, "all right." She edged closer. "I know it's corny, but ... please be careful."

"I'll be fine."

"Remember," Gwen said, and brushed her hand. It sent shock waves through her. "I love you."

"When I get out of here, I'm going to make love to you like you've never been made love to before."

"Do it now."

"Can't." She headed for the garbage bins. "Never mix business with pleasure."

Gwen followed her. "Come on, do it now."

"It would take all night."

"Stoner," Gwen said, grabbing her elbow, "in all seriousness, please don't let anything happen to you. I couldn't bear it."

"Nothing'll happen. Please, get out of here. I mean it."

"All right," Gwen sighed. "It's lousy work, anyway."

"And don't worry," Stoner said softly. "With you in my life, nothing bad could possibly happen to me."

***

But of course it could.

She glanced at the hall clock. Six-thirty. Four and a half hours to Ground Zero. By eleven, the patients would be asleep, and the aides hanging out in the staff lounge watching X-rated movies on a VCR.

What to do in the meantime? Sit in the conservatory and try to appear calm? Pace the floor of her claustrophobic room? She opted for pacing and claustrophobia.

Jerry lurked near the conservatory door. An aide was playing checkers with Ione. Lilly rocked, slapping her bare feet flat on the parquet floor, and hummed to herself.

Stoner hung in the doorway, looked around, pretended to be indecisive.

Jerry eased closer.

"Eleven," she said in a low voice. "Second floor fire doors."

"Right, Chief. What did Lilly say?"

"There's a room you didn't know about, at the top of the fire stairs."

"Flyin' high," he breathed.

"After I get Claire, we'll meet you, break into Tunes' desk, and be on our way."

"No sweat."

"I wish I had your confidence."

He grinned. "I have a good feeling about this, Chief."

"Why?"

"Because, win, lose, or draw, it's the last night I'll ever spend at Shady Acres."

"If they don't catch us."

"They might catch us," Jerry said, "but they'll never take me alive."

"Fine talk," Stoner said with a smile, "coming from a chickenshit Wimp."

His grin threatened to light up the room and give them away.

"I'm going upstairs," she said. "If you don't hear otherwise...'"

"It's 'go' for eleven."

"Dress warmly."

"Got it."

She felt a surge of affection for him. "I don't care what your father says. You've got the Right Stuff."

He flashed her a thumbs-up.

She crossed the room and told the aide she was going to lie down. The aide grunted. Ione sneaked her a worried look. She left the conservatory and trudged up the stairs.

Nothing to do now but wait.

As Jerry said, it was her last night in Shady Acres. But it was going to be a long one.

She changed into pajamas. Later, she'd pull her clothes on over them, in case she had to do a quick change back.

Sure, if they catch you, just whip off the outer layer and claim you were sleepwalking. Through locked doors. Cute.

Maybe I'm going at this the wrong way. Maybe there's a more rational approach.

Maybe we should all sit down and discuss it calmly.

"You see, Millicent, I only want to retrieve Claire Rasmussen and have you locked up for the rest of your unnatural life. So, if you'll cooperate, I'll promise not to dangle from your ice-encrusted fire escape thirty feet above the ground."

Thirty feet. How many bones can you break falling thirty feet onto a flagstone patio? How many bones are there in the human body? If I fall, they'll have to pick me up in a dustpan. If they pick me up at all.

I haven't climbed anything higher than a stepladder since I was ten. I broke my arm that time.

I should have gone on that Outward Bound weekend with the Cambridge Women's Center. Then I wouldn't be in this mess, because Agatha would have accused me of sleeping with every woman on the trip, and killed me.

Hey, as they used to say in the war movies, nothin' gonna happen to me, Joe. I got everything to live for.

And the jerk who said it was usually a goner before they even hit the beach.

Poor bastard, he had everything to live for.

You're a coward, McTavish.

Did I ever say I wasn't?

Have a little faith. God looks after fools and Irishmen.

I'm not a man, I'm not Irish, and if there is a God, He's not going to be kindly disposed toward me after the things I've said about Him lately.

Every time a sparrow falls, He knows it.

He watches it fall.

She heard a soft ticking and turned to the window. Pellets of sleet pattered on the pane.

A cold chill materialized at the base of her spine and oozed its way upward to her hairline.

Stop scaring yourself. You're in it, and there's only one way out.

She crossed to the closet. Warm clothes, not too bulky. Have to be able to move freely. Jeans, flannel shirt, sweater. Jacket? Too constricting. Sneakers, not boots. Boots are cumbersome. Screwdriver filched from O.T. All set.

Now, we wait.

The other patients began filtering up the stairs. Hank and Nameless conferred briefly in the hall. Water ran, toilets flushed, doors closed. Footsteps plodded toward the nurses' station.

Thorazine time.

She lined up, received her little yellow pill. Both aides watched her closely, double-teaming. She swallowed it.

Let's hope it does something for anxiety.

She sat on the edge of her bed and counted the stitches in her sweater.

Roll call.

The senior staff is through for the day. Roland J. Lefebre is probably putting through a call to his stock broker or meeting with his investment club. Good old Millicent Tunes is polishing her fondue dish, browsing through her excellent collection of classical music, and spiking the chablis with sodium pentothal. Becky is curled up with her boyfriend and last Sunday's *Times*. Social Service is laying out a psychedelic tie to go with his plaid shirt. The receptionist is researching the local 9 to 5 chapter. And the kitchen crew has gone home to whip up franks and beans for their husbands, who are shitting bricks.

At the moment we have on the premises and visible, Hank and one other aide. Hank? Hank was here at lunch. He should have left at three, when the shifts change. Where's Mario? And Gladys Grenier? Maybe it's their day off. Maybe they've gone up to Bar Harbor to eat gourmet ice cream and dance the night away.

And Claire is in the Tower, hallucinating her brains out.

Ione tapped on the door, stuck her head in, and took in the clothes lying on the bed. "Going somewhere?"

"Yeah."

"Not wise."

"I want to check out the fire escape. May I use your window?"

"Now?"

"Later."

"Sure, but you don't have to dress for that."

"This time tomorrow you'll understand everything, okay?"

Ione frowned. "All right, but I want you to know I feel very left out."

"Count your blessings."

"You're treating me exactly the way my husband would."

"Ione," she said, "I'm not going to let you guilt-trip me."

"It was worth a try."

"Look, I might need you later. Can you stay awake?"

"I wouldn't fall asleep for the world. I might miss something." She retreated.

Stoner went back to counting the stitches in her sweater.

Down in the entrance hall, the clock bonged.

One hour to go.

She turned out her light and listened to the darkness, but all she could hear was the stumbling thud of her own heartbeat. It was unpleasant, the steady pounding of fear. Think of something else.

She thought of Gwen, and wanted her — not with that odd, silent blend of passion and tenderness with which she'd lulled herself to sleep these many months. Wanted her completely, to look at her, to touch her, to complain with her about the weather, to laugh and make her laugh, to hold her and be held by her, to shop with her in Filene's Basement, to cry against her, to ride the T with her, to stroke her hair, to tell her stories, to listen to the rain with her, to argue and make up, to give her gifts for no reason, to spend time apart for the joy of reunion, to be afraid with her, to nag and be nagged, to brave the streets of King's Grant for the first time in sixteen years, to misunderstand and be misunderstood, to travel with her and buy her the tacky souvenirs she liked, to collect bright stones, to love her.

Gwen was life. Gwen was real.

Gwen was waiting.

Her fingers found the stitches in her sweater and went on counting in the dark.

***

By the time the clock struck eleven, she was dressed and wide awake, and nervous as a beagle on the opening day of hunting season.

She cracked her door and listened. Silence.

She peered down the hall toward the nurses' station. The fluorescent desk lamp cast a gun-metal glow. The chair was empty.

Okay, Aunt Hermione, send positive energy starting .. now.

Back in Boston, Aunt Hermione looked up from her reading, shuddered, looked at her watch, and crossed the room to light a candle.

How do I know that?

Don't think about it. It's time to go.

She hesitated.

238

I said GO!

Look, this is bad enough. Don't make it worse by shouting at yourself.

Go, damn it.

She slipped through the door and eased it shut behind her. Pressing against the wall, she took a step toward Ione's room and heard a sickening squeak.

Rubber soles. Linoleum.

Pulling off her shoes, she slid to Ione's door and lurched inside.

"Goodness!" Ione said. She was sitting up, fully dressed. "Are you trying to scare me to death?"

"Shhh. Open the window?"

It rattled like an empty freight train. Ione leaned out, looked down, looked up, turned, and planted herself, arms folded stubbornly.

"You're not going out *my* window," she whispered, "until you tell me what this is all about."

Oh, why not. "Shady Acres is a front," she said as she tied her shoes, "for a smuggling ring. I guess you could call it a smuggling ring. They smuggle fugitives out of the country."

"I'll be darned." Ione began to laugh. "Wait until that know-it-all husband of mine finds out he's been taken for a ride. He won't be able to get it up for a month."

"Now will you let me out?"

"Running away?"

"I have to spring Claire Rasmussen. Somehow she found out what they were doing. I think they have her stashed away on the floor above us."

"I see." Ione moved aside.

Stoner leaned out the window and glared at the fire escape. Too far away to reach like this, but if she put some push behind it...

"Hold it," Ione said. She went to her handbag and took out a pair of leather gloves. "These will help you hang on." She removed a disposable penlight from her keyring. "And you'd better take this."

"Thanks." She tried the light, slipped on the gloves. "If they catch me, don't admit you know anything."

"That's just about what I do know."

She scrambled onto the window sill and crouched, measuring the distance. A gust of wind blew sleet into her face. "Rotten night for this," she muttered. She swallowed and forced herself not to look down.

"Not yet," Ione said, ripping the top sheet from her bed and tearing it into wide strips. "I saw this in an old movie once." She knotted the strips together and tied one end around Stoner's waist and the other through the radiator pipe. "Will it reach?"

"It'll reach, but will it hold?"

"Maybe. Enough to slow you down some."

"How will you explain about the sheet?"

"One way or another," Ione said, "the dog-doo's going to hit the air conditioning tonight. Torn sheets will be the least of our problems."

"I'm sorry," Stoner said. "I didn't mean to get you involved."

"I'm involved. Let's just get it over with, Wonder Woman."

Tentatively, she put her foot on the outside window ledge. It was wet, but not too slippery. But wood is warmer than metal. The fire escape would be another matter. Pulling her other leg out, inching forward, she stretched. This time her fingertips touched metal. But not enough to hold. She'd have to jump for it.

Last chance to back out.

No.

She flung herself away from the ledge.

And hit the metal railing with a bone-bruising thud. For a horrible moment there was nothing beneath her, nothing holding her but one hand.

The weight of her body dragged her down, wrenching her shoulder.

Her fingers began to slide.

I've bought it.

Her foot touched something that held.

Gasping, she wrapped her other arm around the railing and looked down. The flagstones glowed, beckoning. The muscles of her arms burned and trembled.

A wave of sleepiness flowed over her.

Let go. Fall. You would fall forever, softly, gently, nothing to fear...

"STONER!"

It was Aunt Hermione's voice, from somewhere deep inside.

Thank God, she's attuning.

With a monumental effort, she pulled herself onto the steps and rested.

The first hurdle behind her, she felt her adrenalin subside. The muscle-softening, mind-numbing effect of the thorazine rushed in to fill the gap. She turned her face to the sleet and let the icy water wash away her drowsiness.

Keep moving.

She untied the sheet from around her waist and watched as Ione hauled it back inside.

That's that. From now on, this trip is strictly one way.

The fire escape door was locked, but the lock was rusted. A few fumbling twists of the screwdriver ripped it loose with a minimum of noise. Flicking on her flashlight, she looked around the narrow hall. There, on her left, was a door, still labelled "Black Tower" in a faded, childish crayon-scrawl.

She tried the knob. The door held. Locked.

A sound. Scurrying, patting, like tiny fingers racing around the door frame.

She drew back. Listened.

The sound resolved itself into sleet beating on the shingles overhead.

Maybe.

Kneeling, holding the light between her teeth, she began to unscrew the doorknob. It came off in her hand. She set it aside. A small metal bar appeared in the hole where the knob had been. She pushed it to the left, there was a tiny "click," and the door swung open.

She got to her feet and stepped inside, letting her light play across the grimy floor.

Nothing.

She turned the light to the corners, chasing back the shadows.

There was ... A pile of rags? She couldn't make it out.

The light flickered, threatened to die. She shook it.

The pile of rags took shape, moved...

"Claire?"

The woman looked up. Her face was expressionless and white as marble. Her eyes were blank, circled with darkness. Her hair hung in lifeless strings.

Stoner turned the flashlight on herself. "I'm a friend of Nancy's, Claire. I'm here to..."

Claire huddled deeper into the corner. Stoner took a step backward and lowered herself slowly to her knees. "I won't hurt you. I want to help. Please, trust me."

Claire's eyes darted about the room and came to rest on Stoner's face. "Nancy?" she whispered.

"Nancy sent me."

She reached out a hand. Claire didn't draw away.

"I've come to take you home."

Tentatively, Claire's hand moved toward hers.

"That's right. Trust..."

The room grew suddenly darker. Claire's eyes flicked to something beyond Stoner's shoulder.

She turned.

Searing light sent arrows through her brain, blinding her.

"Well, Stover."

Her vision cleared.

Gladys Grenier. And Mario.

She sprang to her feet, putting herself between Claire and the others.

They stared at each other.

Mrs. Grenier's mouth twisted into an ugly smile. "How do you like our little prisoner?"

241

Anger exploded in her. "You people are disgusting!"

"Sticks and stones," said Gladys Grenier placidly. "Get her, Mario."

He lunged forward, whirling her around and pinning her arms behind her back, squeezing both her wrists in one meaty hand.

"Tie her," Mrs. Grenier barked.

"What with?"

"Her shoelaces, dummy."

Still holding her wrists, he bent down and clawed at her shoe. She kicked out at him. "Bitch!" he growled, and slammed his fist into her side.

It knocked the breath from her. Mrs. Grenier grabbed her shoulders and shoved her against the wall. Splinters punctured her face.

Fighting would get her nowhere. She decided to try the War Resister maneuver, and went limp.

"No, you don't," Gladys Grenier said, hauling her upright by her hair.

The laces cut into her wrists. "Cretin," she said.

Mrs. Grenier turned her and slapped her face, bringing tears to her eyes. "Don't talk like that about my boy."

She looked up. "*Your* boy?"

"Takes after me, don't he?"

"He has all your charm, Glad-ass."

The nurse hit her again. "Watch your mouth."

Mario pushed her toward the door. Out of the corner of her eye, she saw Claire's hand reach out, grabbing for his ankle. He kicked her away.

Stoner stumbled and lost a shoe.

In the hall Mrs. Grenier took over, digging her fingers into Stoner's arms while Mario replaced the doorknob.

"You're in trouble, McIntosh," Gladys said, her breath hot and rancid.

She didn't dignify the remark with a response.

Mario finished his work and sidled up to her. "Want this back?" He held the screwdriver less than an inch from her face, the blade pointed toward her eye.

Mrs. Grenier beamed with maternal pride.

"No."

Gladys gave her a shake. "No, what?"

This wasn't the proper time for the John Wayne macho bit. "No, sir," she said meekly.

Mario grinned.

Between them, they pushed, shoved, and dragged her down the hall. She lost her other sneaker.

The fire doors banged. She had to shout, to alert Jerry. There wasn't time to think of something creative.

"HELP!"

Mrs. Grenier kicked her shin.

They threw her into her room and followed. Mario closed the door. The seriousness of her situation began to penetrate her anger.

"Tie her to the bed," Mrs. Grenier ordered.

He forced her to her knees and unfastened the laces. She tried to strike out. Mrs. Grenier grabbed her by the chin and slammed her head against the iron railing. She held up a ham-sized fist. "Don't tempt me," she hissed.

Stoner decided not to tempt her.

Mario tied her wrists to opposite bedposts and stood back to admire his handiwork. "Now what?" he asked.

"Watch her." Mrs. Grenier left the room.

Mario lounged against the wall and lit a cigarette.

"Excuse me," Stoner said. "I don't think we're allowed to smoke in here."

He flipped the flaming match in her direction. It fell to the floor and died.

"Well, don't blame me if you get in trouble with the fire marshall."

Minutes slipped by.

Aunt Hermione, help me.

In her mind's eye, she saw her aunt get up and go to the phone.

Footsteps in the hall. One set heavy and thundering, another light and quick.

Oh, shit.

Millicent Tunes stepped into the room, smiling like a pipe organ. She wore black. Black velour pants and matching pullover shirt. Black boots of a soft, satiny material. Her hair tied back in a black scarf.

"I see you dressed for the occasion," Stoner said.

Millicent's smile faded. "I don't think you're in a position to be sarcastic."

"Right. Inappropriate affect. Mario, make a note for my file."

Mario lowered his eyelids to half-mast.

"Get me a chair," Millicent ordered. She snapped her fingers impatiently. "Now!"

His lips tightened. He pushed himself away from the wall and slouched out of the room.

"And make it snappy!"

"Better be careful," Stoner said. "Ole Rambo can turn pretty mean."

"Yes," Millicent purred. "I can see that." She touched a finger to Stoner's face.

Stoner jerked her head to the side.

"Did he hurt you? I'm so sorry."

"Don't credit him with that. The glory goes to Miss America, there." She smiled at Gladys Grenier.

243

"It must have been just awful," Millicent said softly, stroking her face.

"If you want to turn on, I can give you the details."

Millicent Tunes shook her head. "Stoner, Stoner, whatever are we going to do with you?"

Good question. She decided not to ask it.

"I've done everything in my power to win your trust, and look how you betray me."

"Eat shit and die," Stoner said.

Millicent turned to Gladys Grenier. "Gladys, see what you can do to make her behave, please."

The nurse slapped her hard. Little red lightning streaks of pain shot through her head.

"Did that excite you?" Stoner asked, blinking back tears.

Millicent gazed at her thoughtfully. "I believe it did. Did it you?"

"You should give her a try. Of course, she has kind of a limited repertoire."

"Want me to hit her again?" Mrs. Grenier asked.

"Later, perhaps. First we'll have a little chat."

Mario returned with the chair. Millicent placed it just out of reach of Stoner's feet. She sat down and crossed her elegant legs.

"I don't think these sessions are helping," Stoner said. "Maybe I should switch to another therapist."

Her face was on fire. She listened to the sleet rattling against the window, and yearned for the cold feel of it against her skin.

"Are you in a great deal of pain?" Millicent asked.

"I'll live."

Millicentunes laughed.

"You set me up, didn't you?"

"Me?" Tunes' eyes were innocently wide. "You set yourself up. You really shouldn't have told me about Gwen." She swung her elegant foot. "In all fairness..."

"By all means," Stoner said, "be fair."

"I wouldn't have guessed a thing until you brought her up. But it was too much of a coincidence. First she comes here asking questions about Claire, making a nuisance of herself, upsetting hospital routine. And a few days later you show up, mention the very same name..."

"I know the scenario," Stoner said. "But it's not an unusual name."

"Unusual enough. And the way you tried to cover up..." She gave a tinkling laugh. "That was quite amateurish. I remembered that the boys mentioned seeing someone else that night. Well, all it took was a little visit to the East Wind to check the guest register, and *voila*." She adjusted her gold bracelet. "I must admit, I'm very annoyed with Mario for not recognizing you."

"It was dark," Mario muttered. "That crazy Greek was shooting

244

at us..."

"Shut up," Millicent snapped. "We'll discuss it later."

The muscles of Mrs. Grenier's face tightened beneath their rolls of flesh.

"Don't talk that way to her boy," Stoner said.

Millicent ignored the remark. "When you were so reluctant to come to my little house... Well, anyone could put two and two together."

The phone in the downstairs hall began to ring.

"Want me to get that?" Gladys asked.

"Let it go."

It's Aunt Hermione. If no one answers, she'll .. she'll ... what *will* she do?

"I knew," Millicent went on smoothly, "all we had to do was wait under the fire stairs until you came looking for Claire. You were bound to show up sooner or later."

"I gave up my day off," Gladys Grenier said. "That's time-and-a-half."

Millicent sighed. "Oh, Gladys, don't be tiresome."

Call Delia, Stoner thought. Aunt Hermione, call *Delia*.

The phone went on ringing.

"If you had it all figured out," Stoner said, stalling for time, "why did you let me get this far?"

"I could have acted at any point," Millicent said, "but I decided to let you think you'd gotten away with it. This is so much more fun, isn't it?"

"Yeah, it's a real carnival."

"Naturally, we'll have to do something about your little friend. But that won't be too hard. Accidents happen all the time in Boston." She licked her lips. "Would you like to tell me who else is involved?"

"I work alone," Stoner said.

Millicent smiled, tilting her head to one side. "I really don't believe that, Stoner. But I'll let Gladys handle the details. It wouldn't be right, a woman in my position."

"Dirty work's beneath you, huh?"

"Let's just say violence is more suited to Gladys' nature."

Stoner glanced at Mrs. Grenier, who was staring at the back of Millicent's head. She seemed offended.

"You've made quite a bit of trouble for me, Stoner," Millicent went on. "But I'm sure it can be straightened out in time. You're really very naughty, you know."

"I had a reprehensible childhood," Stoner said.

"And I'd so hoped we could be friends."

Stoner laughed. "That'll be the day."

"It's too bad, really."

The phone stopped ringing.

245

"So," Stoner said, "what happens now?"

"I'll leave that to Gladys, too." She got up.

"Don't you want to stay and watch?"

"Mrs. Grenier will give me a full report. She knows my requirements." She came over to stroke Stoner's face. "I'm afraid this is goodbye. Such a shame. We could have had a lovely time."

She turned to go.

"Hey, Millicent," Stoner said, "did anyone ever tell you you look lousy in black?"

In the hall, the sound of Millicent Tunes' laugh echoed and died.

Stoner looked at Gladys Grenier. "How can you work for a woman like that? Don't you have any pride?"

Mario stepped toward her. "Want me to sock her, Ma? I could rough her up, like I did the Owens bitch."

"Listen, you little creep," Stoner snapped, "the last guy who messed with her ended up at the bottom of a ravine. It took three pack mules and half the Forest Service to get him out. He was *dog meat*, Mario."

"Tunes is going to have your ass," Gladys said to Mario. "You should have recognized her."

"Honest, Ma, it was *dark*."

"It really was," Stoner said. "I didn't recognize him, either."

"Shut your face," Mrs. Grenier bellowed.

"You're absolutely right. Your family business is none of my affair."

Come on, Aunt Hermione, call *Delia.*

The phone began to ring again.

Oh, God, she thinks she had the wrong number.

Delia. Call *Delia.*

"She could have handed you her calling card," Gladys said to Mario, "and you'd have still been too dumb to recognize her."

"I'm sorry," Stoner said, "I ran out of calling cards, but I have some on order. They'll be along any day now."

She tried to see what Aunt Hermione was doing, but it was all a blank.

"So what do you want me to do?" Mario asked petulantly.

Her muscles were tightening, hurting. "I could use a back-rub," she said.

Mrs. Grenier snatched her by the hair. "I told you to bug out."

"But that's what nurses do, isn't it? Give back-rubs?"

"Ma, what are we gonna do?"

"Look," Stoner said, "if you want to take orders from Millicent Tunes, it's your life. But it seems like a waste of your talents."

Fury consumed Gladys Grenier's face. "Don't push me, McIntosh."

"*Ma...*"

"Mrs. Grenier, I have nothing but the utmost respect for you and all members of your profession. Long hours, inadequate pay, unpleasant working conditions. You could do much better than this."

"*Ma*." He tugged at Gladys' sleeve. "Tell me what to *do*."

Call Delia, Gwen, Marylou, *anyone*. Please, Aunt Hermione.

Mrs. Grenier let her go and took a step back. "We're getting out of here."

"Huh?" Mario said.

"Let Tunes find someone else to boss around. The rate she's going, the whole thing's coming down on her head."

Mario nodded toward Stoner. "What about her?"

"Don't mind me," Stoner said. "I'm happy where I am. You two just beam on up."

"You don't want me to rough her up?" Mario asked plaintively.

"Get rid of her."

He seemed to turn a little pale. "What?"

"You heard me."

"You don't want me to rough her up?" He was almost pleading. "I thought we were supposed to get names..."

"Are you deaf?" Gladys shouted, "or just stupid?"

"Neither," Stoner said. "He just wants to rough me up."

"Ma..."

Gladys Grenier's face turned blotchy. "God damn it, Sonny, do what I told you." She slammed out of the room.

"Fuck your fist, Ma," Mario muttered. "I got principles."

"Difficult, isn't she?" Stoner asked.

"Fuckin' bitch."

"Mario, you're a true judge of character."

He scowled. "I'm thinking."

"Sorry."

She heard the thunder of Gladys Grenier's dainty feet returning. The door flew open. Gladys shoved a filled hypodermic syringe into Mario's hand. "Stick her with this. All of it. I'll bring the car around front." She slammed out again.

"With all this noise and slamming and banging and shouting," Stoner said, "nobody's going to get a wink of sleep tonight."

He stared at the hypo.

She stared at the hypo.

This is really quite warm and cozy, the two of us, alone in the world except for each other, staring at...

"Want to make a deal?" she asked.

"Huh?"

"Ten big ones. All for you, Mario. We'll keep it between us."

"No deals."

"Rats. It always works in the gangster movies."

I'll say one thing for thorazine. It mellows you out. I mean, I'm in serious trouble here. Time to panic, right?

It's kind of interesting.

"I think I'm stoned," she said.

"For Christ's sake, lady, I'm trying to think."

She cocked her head to one side. "Something troubling you, Mario?"

"None of your business."

"My friends say I'm a pretty good listener."

His jaw worked. He frowned. He turned the hypo over and over in his hands. "I never offed a broad before," he said.

A male chauvinist hit-man.

"Why start now?" she asked reasonably.

His face cleared. He nodded, the way people do when they've reached a difficult decision.

He looked at her.

Now, folks, this is the moment for serious screaming.

She tried, and ended up with a rusty squeak.

"I don't like this," Mario said.

"You should try it from my vantage-point."

He took a step toward her.

She pressed back against the bed. "You're a good kid, Mario. Don't spoil your record."

He hesitated.

"Look, she's your mother, and I truly do admire your devotion, but don't you think it's time you started making your own choices? I mean, she won't always be here to guide you, and..."

"You'll talk," he said.

"Never. I promise. I've never broken a promise in my life."

He contemplated the floorboards. The seconds slipped by.

"Think about your future," Stoner said. "Aiding and abetting wanted criminals, that's nothing. Assault? With a good lawyer, maybe three to five. But murder's something else. Murder puts a nasty stain on your soul. You don't want a stain on your ..."

"Who says?" he said angrily. "I can kill as good as the next guy."

"Sorry, I didn't mean to insult you."

"I offed the Greek, didn't I?"

"If you say so."

His eyes narrowed. "You been talking to that asshole Hank?"

"Well," Stoner said, "he did imply he was the one..."

"Don't listen to him."

"Oh, I won't, I'll never believe another word he says."

"A broad..." Mario chewed his lip. "A broad — shit, a broad could be someone's mother or sister or something."

"I know," Stoner said, nodding vigorously. "My three children ... I don't know what they'd do without me."

"You don't have any kids. You're not married."

"My *brother*. My brother would start drinking again. He has a problem with liquor."

"I don't give a fuck about your brother."

Jesus, this man is complicated. "What about my mother? My poor widowed mother. Think what this would do to her."

He looked at her. He looked at the syringe. He looked at her again.

"You said you had principles," she persisted. "Do you know how rare that is? In all the world, there probably aren't more than ten men with principles. You're a *God*, Mario. Better than the Pope, even. Do the world a favor. Be a God."

"But Ma..."

"Think how proud she'd be, having a God for a son."

I called for help. Hours ago. Why doesn't somebody come?

Because this is a mental hospital, and in mental hospitals people call for help all the time.

Ione knows she can't take this on alone. Jerry knows he can't do it alone. And neither of them knows about the other.

Mario shook his head from side to side, slowly, like a dying Bison. "I'll do it."

"You won't get away with it."

"Ma'll know what to do."

"Your mother," Stoner said desperately, "couldn't think her way out of a paper bag."

His face flamed. "Shut up about my mother."

"I'm sorry. I'm sure she's a fine woman, who just happens to find herself in difficult circumstances."

He took a step toward her. "My Ma can fix anything."

I won't beg. He's not going to make me beg. "Please," she begged.

He stood over her.

She cringed.

In a sudden, jerking motion, he yanked up her shirt and plunged the needle into her stomach.

Molten lead seared her nerves and radiated outward through her body.

She screamed.

He pulled the needle out, threw it in the wastebasket, and ran from the room. His footsteps disappeared into silence.

The phone began ringing again.

I'm going to die.

Aunt Hermione said I wouldn't die. Aunt Hermione wouldn't lie to me.

Her heart raced. The room swayed. All feeling was gone from her legs. Her hands were numb.

Why did Aunt Hermione lie to me?

Tears slid from her eyes and burned channels down her face.

I'll never see them again. All the people I love.

It isn't right to die without seeing the people you love.

I want Gwen.

249

But Gwen was miles away, sitting by the fire in Delia's living room. Gwen didn't know what was happening.

And if Aunt Hermione knew, there was nothing she could do.

The phone went on ringing, and ringing, and ringing.

"Answer the Goddamn phone," she shrieked.

My last words. Thirty-two years of living, and how do I sum it up? What message of truth and beauty do I leave for the next generation? "Answer the Goddamn phone."

She began to laugh, laughing and crying at the same time. Then she was only crying, sobbing. I don't want to die.

Her stomach hurt, her head pounded. A cloud of lethargy surrounded her, sucking her downward.

"Goodness," Ione said, "you look like a crucifix."

She dragged her head up. "Ione..."

"Sorry I didn't come sooner." Ione began untying the knots that held her wrists. "Had to be sure the coast was clear."

"Hold my hand, Ione. I'm dying."

Ione felt the artery at the base of her neck. "Nonsense. Your heart's pounding like a jack-hammer."

Her hands were free. Ione rubbed her wrists. "Come on, get up."

She tried to stand. "I can't. I'm dying."

"Your legs are asleep." She pulled her up. "Walk around."

"I'm *dying*," she insisted, and walked.

Pins and needles stabbed her legs and feet. Hope flickered.

"What did they give you?" Ione asked.

"I don't know."

"Well, you'd better keep moving, just in case."

Her mind snapped into gear. "Get Jerry. Keys, we need keys. Claire's up there. Tell him it's Plan B."

"Don't go away," Ione said.

"Hurry!"

Alone, she dug her boots from the closet and dragged them on. Her hands felt thick and awkward. Her head was spinning. Maybe Mario had lost his nerve. But he had injected her with something, and when that something took over... For the love of God, Ione, don't stop to watch "Divorce Court."

Keep walking.

Gladys and Mario are gone. But Hank's still here, and Millicent Tunes, and Lefebre, and God knows who else. We're not out of this yet.

She paced the room. Don't fall asleep.

She spotted the wastebasket, and picked it up. Mario's syringe lay on the bottom, half full.

So he had compromised. He'd given her enough to put her out of commission. And if it killed her ... he had left that to chance.

Mario had decided to be half a God.

250

Thinking made her sleepy.

Don't muse. Bemuse. Amuse.

Dory Previn Time.

She forced her attention outward, scanning the walls for a break in the whiteness, something she could focus on.

A small patch of dusty green caught her eye. A fungus of some kind. She touched it. Powdery, like mildew. She wiped her hand on her shirt. It seemed to be growing, spreading.

She leaned closer. It moved. Up and down. In and out. Rhythmically.

Breathing.

Horrified, she stared at it. And heard a hissing sound. Broken. Hiss, hiss, break. Hiss, hiss, hiss, hiss, break. Hissssssss.

The fungus was whispering.

It was growing. Faster. It was the size of a hand, a towel, a throw rug. And still spreading.

She turned to run and slammed into Jerry.

"Keys," he said, and tossed them to her.

"It's *whispering*, Jerry. The damn fungus is whispering!"

"Don't be a jerk. Fungus doesn't whisper."

She clutched at his sleeve. "Look, there, on the wall!"

"Are we going to discuss the interior *decorating*, for crying out loud?"

She made herself look at the keys. "Where did you get them?"

"We mugged the aide," Ione said proudly from the doorway. "Jerry picked a fight, and I slipped up behind him and beaned him with a lamp. We were magnificent!"

"What about Hank?"

"He was in the bathroom. Jerry locked the door. He's making a terrible noise. I wish you'd been there."

"Come on!" Jerry screeched. "For Pete's sake, girls!"

"Okay," Stoner said. "You two break into Tunes' office and find those files. Can you pick a lock on a desk drawer?"

"Obviously," Ione said, "you've never been married."

"We need a diversion."

"Lilly," Jerry said. He dove for the door, dragging Ione after him.

"When you get the stuff, clear out. Keep running. And make that phone call!"

Deep in the ground below the house, a hollow thumping began. A slow, steady pounding that vibrated through the floor. Like a ship's engine.

It grew louder.

The heart of the house was beginning to beat.

Fire doors. She stared in dismay at the mass of keys in her hand. Find it. Find it.

She fumbled endlessly. Minutes ticked away.

251

The pounding grew louder.

The lock turned with a rasp of metal on metal.

She glanced up and saw her face reflected in the heavy wired windows. On the other side of the glass, centipedes crawled slowly, congregating toward the image of her face. Their eyes glowed red.

She drew back.

Don't think about it.

Gathering her strength, she yanked the door open and plunged through.

The stairs and hall were black with scorpions.

She started to cry.

I can't go through with it.

The pounding filled the stairwell, filled the halls, filled her head. The air vibrated with it, beating against her ears like fists.

She closed her eyes and eased forward. Insect bodies cracked beneath her feet. Live insects scuttled across her shoes, clawed at her ankles, crawled up her legs.

He throat was thick with revulsion.

Her head ached from the pounding.

Hallucinations, she told herself.

She put her foot on the first step and pulled herself up.

The house pulled against her.

Let me go, you bastard.

The steps groaned. The bannister cracked.

Hallucinations.

She reached out to the wall to steady herself, and felt her hand sink deep into something warm and slimey. It sucked at her fingers.

She yanked it free.

And went on climbing, straining against the house.

She tried to run down the hall. Everything was in slow motion, like a bad dream, like running under water.

The room. The door.

No screwdriver.

Key, damn it. There has to be a key.

She tried one. It didn't work. And another.

Think it through.

Ione's tiny flashlight lay on the floor.

Beside a blood-stained sneaker.

Hallucination.

She snatched the light, flicked it on.

She could barely make out the name on the lock.

Yale.

Well, boola-boola to you, she thought wildly.

She flipped through the keys, narrowing her choices to four.

The third one worked.

She found the light switch.

Claire huddled in her corner, her face blank as death.

"Claire!" she shouted. "We're getting out."

Claire didn't move.

"Look, I know things aren't going well for you right now..."

A movement at the narrow window caught her eye. A gray slab, like a gigantic fish scale, falling through the night.

Another. And another.

Shingles. The house was shedding its roof.

Hallucination.

"To tell you the truth, I'm not in real great shape myself, but this is an emergency.So if you could put your problems behind you for a little while..."

A chunk of rusted gutter clanged to the patio below.

"...when this is over we'll get together and compare horror stories."

Claire looked at her. Her eyes focused. She reached up, touched Stoner's hair.

Her fingers came away dripping blood.

Hallucination.

"Blood," Claire said.

But *whose* hallucination?

She grabbed Claire by the shoulders and hurled her to her feet. "Goddamn it, *move!*"

Dragging the woman behind her, she raced down the fire stairs. They shattered beneath her feet.

Keep going.

The walls were melting. Water stains revolved slowly, oozing dampness. The odor of thyme filled her nose and choked her.

You're not going to stop us.

Her lungs burned to bursting. She tightened her grip on Claire's hand. "We can make it," she said. She didn't believe it.

The second floor hallway was filled with fog. Yellow fog. Acrid, sweet, like rotting fat.

She pushed through it.

One more flight.

The house began to hum.

She lost her footing on the stairs and grabbed for the railing. It was red hot.

"Jesus!" She tore her hand away.

The humming grew to a moan. To a roar.

A crack appeared in the floor at the base of the stairs. Chunks of planking fell away.

Oh, no, you don't. By God, you don't.

Bits of plaster dropped around her. Spiderweb lines shot through the walls. Glass shattered.

Journey's End was tearing itself apart.

Hallucination, she told herself ferociously, and jumped. A strip of splintered floorboard ripped her leg.

"Blood," Claire said.

Stoner began to giggle.

Her head was filled with bubbles. Dancing bubbles, making her lighter than air.

"You're diseased!" she shouted to the house, while her feet hovered above the ground. "Vile, detestable, scabrous, rotten!"

A sudden fall of air hurled her to the floor.

She pulled herself to her knees, balanced on the brink of the widening gulf, and reached back for Claire's hand.

Claire stretched toward her.

Stoner yanked her across.

The floor heaved.

Her joints were on fire, her muscles turned to jelly.

The front door stood open. She crawled toward it. It receded, spiraling into the distance.

We're not going to make it.

"Chief!" Jerry shouted from beyond the door.

Hallucination.

"Move it, Chief. They're coming!"

Footsteps pounded in the hall above, racing toward the stairs.

The open door was a tiny rectangle of darkness far away.

She sank to the ground.

Jerry grabbed her roughly. "Don't you quit on me now, damn you!"

This is no hallucination. He's real. He's...

Upstairs a woman shrieked. The footsteps stopped, paused, ran the other way. Another shriek, then another, a dozen voices shrieking. The sound of a struggle, angry shouting, a high-pitched laugh.

She looked up at Jerry. "What's that?"

"Lilly, creating a diversion." He threw an arm around Claire and hurled her out into the night. "Come *on*, Stoner."

"Can't make it."

He pulled her to her feet. She wavered.

"MOVE IT!"

"*I can't.*"

The footsteps were coming their way again.

Jerry glanced toward the stairs. "All right," he said, "stay here. *Girl.*"

She felt her anger begin to rise.

"You're weak," he said contemptuously. "Chickenshit. Fuck-up. All you're good for is making babies."

"Pig!"

"Sugar and spice and everything nice," he chanted.

She lunged for him. "I'll kill you."

"Have to catch me first." He ran from the house.

"Stupid asshole pig!" Furious, she scrambled after him.

254

He danced just beyond her reach. "Catch me. Come on, sweetcakes. Let's see those buns wiggle."

She lunged again.

"Hey, hey, hey," Jerry called. "Look at the tits on that one. Sure would like to grab a handful of those tits."

"Macho punk!" she screamed, and began to run.

"Not my fault," Jerry called. "I've spent half my life in institutions."

There was gravel beneath her feet. Pellets of sleet scoured her face.

Jerry broke for the gates. She raced after him.

Behind her, the house howled with rage.

Jerry glanced over his shoulder. "You okay, Chief?"

"Okay," she shouted. "Split up!"

She dove into the woods. Ahead, she could see Ione standing by the fence waving a white handkerchief, calm as the Lady of the Manor welcoming weekend guests.

Stoner began to laugh. "Cheap trick, Jerry," she panted.

She could hear his voice over the clatter of feet on gravel. "Tell it to the Marines, sweetheart."

Pulling together the last of her energy, she plunged foward. Something grabbed her foot. There was a sickening, popping noise, like a string of Chinese firecrackers. Pain exploded up her leg and set off sparks in her brain. The ground rushed up at her.

Her foot was caught in an exposed tree root, her ankle bent at an unworldly angle. She looked back. Two men appeared in the doorway, hesitated, and ran toward her.

She struggled against burning pain. The tree root held.

"Keep going!" she shouted to Jerry.

"Gate's locked!"

"Climb it!"

He threw himself against the chain links and fell back.

The men kept coming.

Overhead, the sky began to swirl.

At least we tried, she told herself. At least we didn't make it easy.

She closed her eyes to wait.

An ear-splitting crash shattered the night, a sound of tearing metal.

She looked up. The men were retreating. Light flooded the driveway. A car was wedged in one side of the gate. The other side was torn away.

Someone ran to her, knelt beside her, eased her foot free of the root. She gritted her teeth against the pain.

More lights.

Shouts.

People running.

Sirens.

A gunshot.

A white convertible slid to a halt on the drive. The door opened, and Nancy got out. She reached for Claire, pushed her inside.

Jerry swung himself through the car window.

We made it, Stoner thought.

There were strong arms around her, a soft face against her face. "What do you know?" Gwen said. "The police took notice."

She let herself sink into unconsciousness.

CHAPTER 13

There was color everywhere. Blue, red, yellow, green. Smudges of colored light against a white background. As she watched, it seemed to move slightly...

Hallucination.

From somewhere below came a familiar clatter and clank. A sound of running water. Dishes being washed. Everyday noises. Normal, mundane, friendly noises.

This is no hallucination.

She turned her head slightly, wincing at the pull of stiffness in her neck muscles. She was in an unfamiliar room, a room brilliant with reds, browns, amber. In the curtains, on the bureau, lying across the bed. A stained-glass shade pull hung at the window, swaying gently in the breeze. Puzzled, she pushed herself upright and felt a throbbing pain in her ankle. She fell back.

"Easy," Gwen said. She uncoiled herself from the armchair and came to sit on the bed.

Stoner blinked. "Am I sane?" She asked fearfully.

"At the moment, yes. In general, no."

"Where am I?"

Gwen's velvet laugh caressed her. "Really, Stoner, how corny can you get? Delia's. How do you feel?"

"As if I'm coming down from a bad trip."

"It was a bad trip, all right." She rested her hand along the side of Stoner's face. "I'm glad it's over."

"Is it?"

"Yes."

She moved her foot and gasped. "I think I broke something."

"It's only a wicked sprain. Edith left you some painkillers. Want one?"

"I've had enough drugs for a lifetime."

"You know what that means, don't you?" Gwen asked. She made a face. "Aunt Hermione's herbal teas."

She fumbled for Gwen's hand. "Is everyone all right?"

"Everyone but R.J. Lefebre, Hank, and your loving shrink. They're in jail."

"The Greniers?"

"Gone with the wind."

"What happened to..."

Gwen squeezed her hand. "Everything's fine. You'll get all the details later. Right now I just want to look at you."

She reached up and touched Gwen's hair. "More gray?"

"If you don't like it, tough. It's your fault."

"I like it," Stoner said. "I like it very much."

"Is there anything you need?"

Her mouth felt dry. "Water. I'll get it." She started to get up. Every muscle and joint in her body assaulted her. "My God, I feel as if I've been blitzed by the entire L.A. Rams defensive line."

"What's wrong with the New England Patriots?" Gwen said, pushing her back and going to the bureau for the water.

"Have you looked at their record lately?" She reached out for the glass and drew back as her shoulder screamed.

Gwen handed it to her. "You're in pretty bad shape, aren't you?"

"Gladys and Mario bounced me around a bit. I'll be okay."

"I know. There's no permanent damage. Edith let me check you out for breaks."

"I'm sorry I missed it," Stoner said.

"Marylou's furious. She wanted to watch."

"One of these days Marylou's going to go too far."

"I guess I should help you work out some of the knots," Gwen said. "On the other hand..."

"What?"

Gwen looked at her thoughtfully. "Would you say your mobility is restricted?"

"To about three inches in any direction. Why?"

"You can't move?"

"Not without intense pain."

A wicked gleam came into Gwen's eyes. She started unbuttoning her shirt.

"Gwen," Stoner said apprehensively, "what are you doing?"

"I finally have you right where I want you." Her shirt fell to the floor.

"Gwen..."

She slipped off her shoes.

"This isn't fair, Gwen."

Gwen smiled a little smile and slid out of her jeans.

"Not politically correct."

She took off her wrist watch.

"I'll tell. It'll be all over the Cambridge Women's Center in twenty-four hours."

She pulled back the covers and started to get in.

"They'll never let you teach a Coming Out workshop."

"I'll say I didn't Come Out," Gwen said, reaching for Stoner's pajamas. "I'll say I Crossed Over."

"They won't let you teach that, either."

She slid her hand up Stoner's side and touched her breast. "All

258

you have to do is get up."

"I *can't* get up." Every cell in her body jumped to its feet and applauded. She didn't want to get up. "I'll scream."

"Scream."

She didn't scream.

"Now, my ball-busting butch from Boston, *I'm* going to make love to *you* like you've never been made love to before."

***

"Well," Stoner said, "you certainly learned some interesting things being straight."

Gwen punched her lightly. "I'll have you know, everything you've experienced in the last hour I made up myself."

"Then you have a heck of an imagination. To say nothing of technique. No wonder you look so self-satisfied."

"You look rather self-satisfied yourself."

Stoner folded her arms behind her head and watched the colored lights waltz across the ceiling. Shady Acres and its horrors seemed a hundred miles and centuries behind her. "I love you, Gwyneth Ann."

"I thought I told you never to call me that."

"I like it."

"So do I, when you say it." She propped herself up on one elbow. "How are your knots?"

"I'm completely knot-free. I wonder if they know about this in locker rooms."

"I'm sure they do."

She reached out and touched Gwen's face. "Will you tell me what you did that night?"

"What night?"

"The night I left Journey's End."

Gwen kissed the palm of Stoner's hand. "My God, you're persistent. You remind me of..."

"Someone or something you knew back in Jefferson, Georgia. It's important, Gwen. I need to know ... all of it."

"Okay," Gwen said. "After I left you, I came back here, and Marylou and Edith and Delia and I sat around making plans. Except we couldn't make plans, because we didn't know what you were doing. And that, Dearest, is because you refused to tell me."

"All right, all right." She snuggled against Gwen. "I made a mistake. I'm a jerk. I was born a jerk, and I'll die a jerk. I can't help it, it's my nature."

"Well," Gwen said, "now that we've established that... About eleven-thirty, Aunt Hermione called. She'd had a premonition that

259

something had gone wrong."

"It certainly had."

"She'd phoned Shady Acres, but no one answered."

"I heard the phone," Stoner said, "but I was a little tied up at the time."

"We knew we were supposed to wait for your call, but we didn't know what to do. I mean, imagine the dilemma. If you were sneaking around, trying to get out without attracting attention, it wouldn't do for us to go charging in. On the other hand, if Aunt Hermione was right — and she usually is — you probably needed us to make like a SWAT team. Meanwhile, Aunt Hermione was going to keep calling, to divert them from whatever you might be doing."

"I wasn't doing anything except dying, and listening to the phone ring."

"Anyway, we decided we'd better move. Then Delia couldn't find her keys. As it turned out, Aphrodite had hidden them in the garage, where she keeps the skeletons of birds and mice. And we wanted to take as many cars as possible, to make as much noise as we could."

"You made plenty of noise."

"So we got Steve to hot-wire Delia's car, and she called Jared. *He* called the state police, saying there'd been a break-out at Shady Acres and the patients were running loose, looting and pillaging. That way he could by-pass the Castleton force."

"Edith went to Lefebre's house — she said she should nab him herself, as a professional courtesy, psychiatrist to psychiatrist. On the way, she dropped Marylou at Millicent Tunes' place, complete with Delia's gun and a fake FBI ID. Later, we found her sitting in Tunes' living room, eating fondue and drinking chablis and listening to classical music. Tunes was locked in a closet, and not very happy about it all.

"As soon as they'd left, Jerry's call came, and Delia and I took off. You know the rest."

"Except for one thing," Stoner said. "Who broke down the gate?"

Gwen grinned. "Three guesses."

"*You?*"

"Me."

"I'd never suspect you of violence."

"You never suspected I was in love with you, either. Really, Stoner, you have a lot to learn about me."

And I'm going to love every minute of it. "Did you happen to notice anything .. strange ... about the house?"

"In all that confusion? I had other things on my mind. How's your ankle, by the way?"

"On fire."

"I'm sorry," Gwen said. "I got carried away."

Stoner held her tighter. "It was worth every minute of it."

260

Something that felt like a laundry bag full of sand plopped on the bed. "What is *that*?"

Gwen looked up. "Just Aphrodite."

"My God, that's the fattest cat I ever saw.

"She's pregnant."

Pregnant? It gave her an idea.

"I have to talk to Delia." She eased out of bed.

"Stoner, dear, you're naked."

"Oh." Balancing on one foot, she retrieved her pajamas and pulled them on. Delia's red satin dressing gown languished on the back of the chair. She hopped over to it.

"Use the crutches," Gwen said. "That's what they're for."

She shoved them under her arms and hobbled to the bureau. Raking her hands through her hair, she glanced at herself in the mirror. "Good grief, I look like a butch whore."

Gwen was on her knees, burrowing under the covers. "I've lost a sock."

"Don't bother. I'll be right back."

"We have a busy day ahead," Gwen said. "I'd prefer to face it with my socks on."

"Well, all right, but you're going to look pretty silly with nothing on but your socks."

Gwen hurled a pillow at her.

She banged awkwardly down the stairs, bouncing off the walls. Delia was at the grill.

"Delia!" Stoner shouted.

"Good God!" A spatula flew. Delia picked it up and tossed it in the dishpan. "You're certainly back from the dead."

"Is Aphrodite really pregnant?"

"You've been unconscious for two days, and all you want to know is if Aphrodite's pregnant? Alexander Haig could have seized control of the government in a military coup, and you want to know if the cat's pregnant?"

"Is she?"

"She doesn't *always* look like a hairy Goodyear blimp," Delia grumbled, scrounging a clean spatula from the utensil drawer and flipping a pancake.

"Do you have homes for all the kittens?"

"I don't even know how many she's going to have. From the looks of her, a couple of dozen at least."

"Could I take one for Aunt Hermione?"

"That can be arranged."

"Do you think any of them will be black?"

"Probably." She slid the pancakes onto a plate and added bacon. "One of the toms was."

"*One* of the toms?"

"Gang bang." She carried the plate to a customer and refilled her coffee cup. "Hungry?"

"Starving. I feel as if I haven't eaten in days."

"You haven't, not much. Slept like a bear, though."

She could remember sleeping, drinking, being helped to the bathroom. The rest was blank. "Is this Sunday?"

"Monday." Delia chuckled. "You should have seen this place yesterday. Half the town, the ones who talked against me after Dan's death, stopped in for coffee. It's the closest they can come to an apology. Incidentally, now that you're up and about, you'll have to vacate the bedroom. Cassie's coming home tomorrow."

"Oh, Delia, that's wonderful."

"Sure is. Course, I'm jumping out of my skin with nerves. Afraid she won't like me after all this time."

"I can't imagine anyone not liking you."

Delia scrounged in her pocket for a cigarette. "Well, thanks. I'm a grandmother now, guess I'll have to quit smoking. Wouldn't be dignified." She glanced at Stoner. "They're all legal, unlike Aphrodite's progeny."

"She married the boy?"

"Yep. I wish I'd been there. I've never seen a hippie wedding. Has three kids. One's starting Junior High next year. How the hell do you talk to a kid in Junior High?"

Stoner lit a match for her. "Gwen says you don't talk to them. All they do is twitch." She hesitated. "Listen, about Dan ... it was Mario Grenier who killed him."

Delia's eyes filled. "Guess that closes that chapter."

"I'm sorry."

"Don't be." A tentative smile played at the corners of her mouth. "I knew the old fool wouldn't drink on the *Delia II*. Mario. He's the one that got away, isn't he?"

"I'm afraid so."

"He'd better watch his step. I have a half-Greek grandson now, and Greeks are big on revenge. I'll bet there are guys being bumped off back in the homeland right this minute, in the name of Agamemnon. You two want breakfast in bed, or what?"

"*Delia*."

Delia winked. "I wasn't born yesterday, you know."

"I think," Stoner said, "we can manage our own breakfast."

"Well, if you need anything, give a yell." She squeezed Stoner's shoulder. "Sure glad to see you among the living, kid. Even if you *do* put me in mind of a drag queen in that kimona-wrapper."

"Delia, have you been out to the house since that night?"

"Yep. First thing Lilly wanted when the dust had settled was half a dozen lobsters and a few pounds of bluefish."

"What kind of shape was it in?"

"Needs paint, but it always did. What are you getting at?"

She shifted her weight from her crutches to her good foot. "That night, when I was getting out, I thought it was falling apart."

"Journey's End? That place'll stand for another two hundred years."

"You didn't notice any cracks in the walls? Or shingles missing from the roof?"

"Nope."

Stoner heaved a sigh of relief. So it was all a hallucination after all.

Delia was looking at her with a puzzled expression. "What made you think that?"

"I guess it was the drugs. I saw things."

"Couldn't have been the drugs. Edith took a blood sample to the lab at Augusta, just to be on the safe side. Other than thorazine and a veterinary tranquillizer, you were clean."

"A veterinary tranquillizer?"

"That's what Mario stuck you with." She stubbed out her cigarette. "We found the syringe in that frozen food locker you were using as a room. It might've killed you, but it wouldn't make you see things."

The floor gave a lurch.

Frozen food locker?

"Hey, Dee," a lobsterman shouted, "can we get a little coffee around this dump?"

"Hold your water!" she shouted back.

"Jesus, thought maybe you were goin' out of business or something."

"You don't like the service, go stink up the Harbor House." She patted Stoner's arm. "Don't worry about that place. It always was damn peculiar. Guess it had it in for you."

Stoner caught her sleeve. "Delia, do you believe in haunted houses?"

"Honey, I believe in everything." She started to leave, then turned back. "Almost forgot. Jerry dropped off a letter for you." She handed Stoner an envelope. "Said it was his final report."

She tore it open.

> "Chief—
> Tunes, Lefebre, Hank, and the Castleton police chief are in the pokey. More arrests to follow.
>
> You were right about the files. They were full of information — names, dates, contacts. Lefebre sang like a canary when confronted by the evidence. Seems they were playing both ends against the middle, blackmailing the guys they helped escape. They won't even be

safe in jail. Greed is a terrible thing.

Your girlfriend totalled her car on the gates. Seemed very pleased about it. She's weird, but some looker!

Claire's gonna be okay, according to Dr. K. As soon as she gets her head together she'll come back and be a companion for Lilly. Delia offered me Dan's boat. Think I'll take up fishing.

The house is back to normal. I thought it was a goner that night — floor torn up, roof falling down and all. How do you figure that? Lilly says it's haunted. She ought to know, I guess.

That's about it. Stop out and see us when you get tired of lying around. On second thought, we better meet in town. I don't think Journey's End likes you.

Jerry."

***

She had one last dream of Journey's End. The house was itself again, white, solid, riding like a schooner at the sea's edge. Thyme grew between the flagstones. The brass hinges glistened. It was summer, a lazy day of blue-green ocean and azure sky. The conservatory doors stood open, and through them drifted the soft bright notes of a piano concerto.

The scene changed. She was standing in an unfamiliar landscape. Sun-baked grasslands stretched to the horizon, broken by sharp canyons. To the north, a high mesa, its sides composed of layers of mauve and gray and pale yellow. A crumbling adobe town rested on the mesa's crest. The air was hot and dry.

Her feet were planted between deep wagon ruts that led off into an endless desert of shimmering white sand. Her fingers curled around a small gnarled stick. Strange words surrounded her.

She squinted against the sun and saw, emerging from the wavering distance ...

... something walking toward her.

THE END

In addition to writing Stoner McTavish novels, Sarah Dreher spends her time writing and producing plays. She is also a practicing clinical psychologist. She lives in Amherst, Massachusetts with her life partner, two dogs and associated wildlife.

Other Books from New Victoria

Other Mysteries by Sarah Dreher

A Captive In Time—Stoner is inexplicably transported to a small town in Colorado Territory, time 1871. When—if ever, will she find a phone to call home? ($9.95)ISBN 0-934678-22-7

Stoner McTavish—First Stoner mystery—Dream lover Gwen in danger in the Grand Tetons *"Sensitive, funny and unabashedly sweet. Stoner McTavish is worth the read."* ($7.95) ISBN 0-934678-06-5

Gray Magic—Stoner and Gwen head to Arizona, but a peaceful vacation turns frightening when Stoner becomes a combatant in the struggle between the Hopi Spirits of good and evil. ($8.95) ISBN-0-934678-11-1

Mystery

She Died Twice —Lauren—The remains of a child are unearthed and Emma must relive the weeks before Natalie's death as she searches for the murderer. ISBN 0-9-34678-34-0 ($8.95)

Woman with Red Hair—Brunel—The mystery of her mother's death takes Magalie and her lover into the French countryside, her only clue the memory of a woman with red hair.($8.95) ISBN 0-934678-30-8

Death by the Riverside—Redmann—Detective Mickey Knight finds herself slugging through thugs and slogging through swamps to expose a dangerous drug ring. ISBN 0-934678-27-8 ($8.95)

Romance/Adventure

Falling Through the Cracks— Rogers—California dreamin' was becoming a reality of soup-kitchens and unemployment lines in the early '70s. ($8.95) ISBN 0-934678-29-4

Touch of Music— Clarke—Roxanna and Becky are part of a lesbian household. Conflict plagues their relationship until Roxanna's daughter is hospitalized, and they find that their differences are not so important. ($8.95) ISBN 0-934678-31-6

Kite Maker— Van Auken—A tough dyke who's never had a girlfriend drives up to a women's bar in a spiffy new Cadillac convertible…and drives off with Sal on a wild adventure in search of a long lost friend. ($8.95) ISBN 0-9346768-32-4

Cody Angel—Whitfield—Dana looks for self-esteem and love through emotional entanglements—with her boss, with Frankie, a bike dyke, and Jerri, who enjoys sex as power. ($8.95) ISBN 0-934678-28-6

Humor

Coming Out— More Fun'n Games, puzzles, humor, advice for Lesbians—Dean, Wells and Curran ($8.95) ISBN 0-934678-33-2

Short Fiction/Plays

Lesbian Stages—"Sarah Dreher's plays are good yarns firmly centered in a Lesbian perspective with specific, complex, often contradictory (just like real people) characters." — *Kate McDermott* ($ 9.95) ISBN 0-934678-15-4

Secrets—Newman—The surfaces and secrets, the joys and sensuality and the conflicts of lesbian relationships are brought to life in these stories. ISBN 0-934678-24-3 ($8.95)

Available from your favorite bookstore, or order directly from

New Victoria Publishers, PO Box 27   Norwich, Vt. 05055